Gypsy Waves

A Stanford Romance

E. Scott Spencer

ISBN: 978-0-9785587-2-3

Published by Horsington Press,
Martindale, Texas

Also by E. Scott Spencer:

Seniors Have It Tough

Haunted Steel Adventures

For further information , please visit

www.escottspencer.com

AUTHOR'S NOTE: This book, its characters and actions, are fictitious: locations and names, if real, are used fictitiously. Layout: InDesign, type Adobe Garramond Pro, Lithos Pro. Printed by Lightning Source.

Chapter 1
William's Presentation

In Room 382, a darkened lecture hall at Stanford University, William Stowell, the Math Department's most promising student topologist, furiously tried to replace the bulb in an ancient 3M overhead projector while speaking to his audience. He struggled at the front of the room while people fidgeted in the late September heat and yawned with boredom. William wanted to convince the Dean of the Math Department to grant him funds for an unconventional research trip to Egypt. The students in the audience had come to see his unusual presentation, but the math was so obscure that most had lost interest. On a good day William's task would have been difficult, but today the old equipment made it impossible. Finally he threw a dead light bulb in the trash and continued without visuals. He could see that some students were playing games on their laptops. William continued nervously, but his frustration with the projector caused the pitch of his young voice to rise.

"If you could only see this multi-dimensional scatter plot, you'd understand how closely the major pyramid dimensions match a linear combination of the integers in the square of the sun," he said in his tense British accent. "The numbers are so close that we must send an expedition to Egypt, with modern equipment, to get better data. Once we have accurate measurements the correlation will be perfect. It'll reveal the tremendous mathematical sophistication of the people who built the Great Pyramid eons ago." Several students slipped out the door. Others snickered in disbelief as William clenched his teeth in frustration.

"And if I could have gotten this bloody projector to cooperate, you would have seen that the sides of the pyramid are slightly concave. No one has ever measured the exact radius of concavity but we could do it now. Modern laser surveying equipment is perfect, and the cost would be trivial, compared to the insight we would gain."

A girl in the front row, Zarlie Istvan, gently raised her voice and interrupted, "Excuse me, what's a radius of concavity?" William had seen, but not talked with, Zarlie several times before.

As she spoke, William overheard the guy next to her, Tony

DiMarco, growl, "Don't waste our time you fucking dimwit." He was sitting next to her in the front row, and nearby students must have heard his foul remark too.

William, startled to hear such crude language, sensed tension between Tony and Zarlie. He instinctively started to answer her question carefully and politely, perhaps to show that he was on her side. Tony glared and mumbled angrily as William focused on Zarlie. "The sides of the pyramid are curved inward slightly, they're not flat, and if we were to draw a circle, perpendicular to the surface, a circle that fit exactly, the radius of the circle would be a measure of the depth of the curvature of the side of the pyramid, that's the radius of concavity."

Zarlie smiled slightly and nodded, then wrote furiously in her notebook.

Tony, with an unfriendly smirk, spoke before William could resume his pitch. "Listen smartass, you could also measure the stainless steel pyramid on top of the Chrysler Building in Manhattan and obtain a weird set of numbers, but it wouldn't mean shit except to Van Allen who designed it in twenty-nine."

"Those numbers would be perfectly rational in the context of structural engineering," William replied cautiously.

"Bullshit, the Art Deco design of the Chrysler Building is an artist's vision. Check out the hood-ornament eagles on the sixty-first floor and the murals in the Lobby. The design has no relation to math or sacred engineering." Tony spoke with a crude New York accent, and his over-fed face appeared violent because an ugly scar cut across his lips. "I'll lay you eleven to one that your pyramid builders just liked the aesthetics of their structure and the dimensions have no secret meanings at all."

From the back of the nearly empty lecture hall, Professor Skilling's stentorian voice interrupted before William could reply. "I'm sure that all of us know the shape of the pyramid so there's no need for you to worry about the slide. Perhaps you would like to share your conclusion with us now as your time is up."

Through an open window, the ancient campanile bells in their modern glass tower on Lassen Mall could be heard striking the Westminster Chimes, followed by five hour chords.

William, exasperated and only partially through his presentation, lost his composure and shouted back, "The conclusion is obvious. The Great Pyramid was built by a brilliant race tens of thousands of years ago and they left their knowledge in its dimensions and measurements. There's no writing inside because they left their secrets for a future generation, you and me, to read and decode. Egyptologists don't know math, but we do. We've got to go there, get accurate data, and analyze it. This will be the discovery of the century."

"I think we've heard enough conjecture William, now if . . ."

William interrupted Skilling, raising his voice, "How can you ignore the fact that the proportions exactly match the diameter and mass of the earth, the distance from the earth to the sun, the size of the moon and its distance from earth, and what about the perfect alignment on the cardinal directions. Today they're just slightly off, because the plate it's sitting on has moved due to tectonic forces over the past twenty thousand years."

"William, your time is up!"

"But we're right on the threshold of a monumental discovery. We've got the tools, and with satellites we can see how accurately everything fits. There must be zillions of secrets encoded in the math that describes all those weird passages and angles inside, we just need a little money and the answers will be ours."

The department head, Professor Schmidt, had walked to the front of the room, clicking on the lights as he passed the switch. "That's enough William."

"But dammit, we're almost there, how can you be so blind to the truth?"

As the lights came on, they revealed the almost empty lecture hall, with William alone at the front, standing before whiteboards covered with mathematical symbols. It was clear that William did not belong in this milieu. Everyone else sported a calculated cool look in shorts or khaki pants, short sleeve shirts and track shoes, but he looked unkempt in his old wrinkled tweed jacket, stained tie and shaggy hair. William was six feet tall, blond and blue-eyed with the broad shoulders of a swimmer, but his sloppy impoverished appearance, steel-framed glasses, and British accent conspired to hide his attractive body. In Hollywood, he might have been cast as a young blond hunk, but William lived in the world of math, not movies.

As William gathered his materials, Professor Skilling ignored him and walked out with Tony. William knew he hadn't convinced anyone if his own advisor left without congratulating him on the presentation. Professor Schmidt walked to William's side and smiled condescendingly.

"I appreciate your enthusiasm, but there is no way the School of Mathematics can support a foreign expedition to measure a pile of rocks. The little discretionary funding we have comes from government and industrial sponsors, and they are looking for useful results, not something like this."

William turned to Schmidt, "But how do you know that

my results won't be fantastic?   Geez, by your criteria, you wouldn't have financed Edison, Einstein, or Columbus."

"Last year we funded Christopher Snow and Vijay Pande, who with the help of thirty thousand free networked personal computers, successfully simulated part of the complex folding process that a protein molecule undergoes to achieve its unique, three-dimensional shape. That's an example of what research at Stanford is about, plenty of bang for the buck."

"Whatever happened to the motto of this university, 'Die Luft Der Freiheit Weht', Let the Winds of Freedom Blow?" William demanded.

"William, the winds of freedom are blowing, but they don't cost anything.   You're asking for funding for what most mathematicians would consider a crackpot idea.   None of us object to you studying anything you want, on your own time, and with your own resources.   That is the practical meaning of the school motto." With that, Schmidt left the room.

William noticed that Zarlie was still in her seat and was glancing at him strangely, while quietly writing copious notes. Zarlie wasn't a math student, and he wondered what she was doing in the audience. Maybe Tony was her boyfriend as they had entered together, or at least that was William's impression before Tony's rude remarks. Tony, an advanced math student, was the essence of mathematics applied to practical problems.   He was usually in the gambling casinos of Reno and Las Vegas, carefully studying the ways in which the games operated.   The expensive but casual clothes covering his bloated body and his fancy car contributed to the rumor that he had won thousands, maybe millions, as a result of his gambling studies and clever analyses.   He had no interest in writing technical papers or in giving lectures.   Whatever he developed, he kept to himself.   Tony belonged to an Italian family from Secaucus New Jersey with values based on fear, money, and muscle.

In sharp contrast, William had grown up in an aristocratic but poor academic family near Oxford University.   In his family, publishing important, even obscure, papers and books, for the advancement of human knowledge, was the supreme accomplishment.

As William started to erase the whiteboards,   two geeks harassed him at the front of the room.   One was a magenta-haired girl with the mathematical symbol **pi** tattooed on her forehead and the other was a short guy with thick glasses.   William argued, "I just know that there is a secret to this structure.   The dimensions form a set of numbers that must have a much deeper meaning, and I'm sure the encoding relates to magic squares."

The girl retorted, "Hey, I can't argue with your determination and the effort you're putting into the solution of the G.P. as a math puzzle, but maybe, just maybe, you're sweating over a worthless cause. Maybe there's no puzzle and your numbers are nothing more than spurious correlations."

William wondered at the contrast between the girl's attractive and minimally-clothed body and her bizarrely decorated face and hair, then answered with confidence. "All the normal areas of math are over-studied. Hell, look at our grad school. Those nerds are just pecking away at old theories and playing with computers. Even though the pyramid's very old, it is filled with huge opportunities now that we have decent measuring equipment. Nobody today thought that studying the mathematics of the Great Pyramid is worth doing. It's virgin territory."

"Hey, speaking of virgins, how about taking me to the math-around-the-clock party? With your screwy ideas and my good looks the union of our sets would be perfect."

William blushed at the invitation, but before he could reply the other geek sneered, "How are you going to prove that mathematically-sophisticated people, and not the archeologically-correct ancient Egyptians, actually existed and built the thing?"

"Why don't you ask Burt Rutan, the famous aeronautical engineer? He's stated publicly, in print, that the Great Pyramid was built by aliens before the last ice age. Maybe he's found proof."

The geeks left, joking between themselves as William continued to erase the boards. There was a tinkling laugh from the front row as Zarlie, packing her notebook, prepared to leave. William turned to her, "Do you have everything you need? I can wait to erase this."

William had noticed Zarlie's unusual appearance before, but he had little time for girls and he was still wondering about her interaction with Tony: no girl he had ever met would have tolerated Tony's crude remark without a nasty reply. He thought that she appeared to be Italian, with long dark hair and sensuous eyes, but her accent was middle-European, lacking the soft charm of Italy. He noticed that she wore uncommonly bright clothes and moved with a fluid grace, like a dancer and that her face was angular and narrow, but not unpleasant, sort of like Audrey Hepburn's.

"Oh, I wasn't paying attention to the math, just making notes about something else, something that came to me while we were sitting in the dark waiting for the projector."

"Well, thanks for coming: I hope you enjoyed it."

"I love hearing about ancient mysteries. I hope you get your expedition started soon."

William finished erasing, picked up his pile of notes, and

pounded the projector with his fist. The spare light came on, and he laughed out loud, then switched it off.

They left the lecture hall at the same time and to his surprise, Zarlie asked, "Which way are you going?"

"Bookstore. A math book I ordered just came in."

"Same direction, but I'm going to a bio seminar in the basement of Dinkelspiel."

Stanford campus, Inner Quad, outside William's classroom

William couldn't believe that she wanted to walk with him, a shy math geek with zero girl-skills: what a nice end to such a disastrous lecture. Although she had seemed quiet and peaceful in the lecture hall, she now walked fast, and with a purpose, taking every diagonal and cutting every corner on the most efficient path to her destination. William hustled to keep up.

Suddenly out of the corner of her vision Zarlie saw a black cat running in the distance. On its present course, it would cross in front of them in a few seconds. Zarlie hesitated briefly, arguing internally with herself, then mumbled a few words. The cat froze, changed direction abruptly and ran away.

"Did you say something," William asked.

"No, just muttering to myself, trying to remember stuff for seminar." She gave no hint of the struggle she was fighting inside.

As they approached the weird fountain sculpture known among students as Mem-Claw, William turned for the bookstore, "Maybe I'll see you around quad?"

"Sure William, see you around."

He would have liked to talk more with Zarlie, but didn't know what else to say, so he retreated into math, the subject that engulfed all his waking hours. In a few moments he had his new book and hurried across campus in the late afternoon haze: his only thoughts were on mathematics. His head buzzed with numbers and the relationships among them. This was his whole life as he started his senior year. Ever since childhood he had been fascinated by math, studying anything he could find, both in traditional areas as well as in obscure fields like the pyramids, ancient cathedral floor plans, numerological interpretations of old texts, writings of the Masons and Rosicrucians, Von Daniken's books about ancient astronauts, and anything else that held even a hint of an unsolved mathematical mystery. By normal standards he was a very bright mathematician, having won many contests and a huge IBM scholarship that covered all his school expenses. But by his own standards he was a failure. William knew that Fermat, LaPlace, Euler, DaVinci, and most famous mathematicians had made outstanding breakthroughs in their teens and early twenties. He was acutely aware of his age, twenty, and the fact that he had not made any comparable discoveries. In January he would be twenty-one and, at the current rate, unpublished and unknown.

At this time of day, the other students were thinking of dinner, homework, dating, sports, and television. William was thinking that he had only a little over six hours until midnight, when another day of his life would have passed without a major discovery. He vividly remembered a warning he had seen scrawled on a bathroom wall, *"Today was the first day of the rest of your life, and you blew it."*

Chapter 2
Zarlie

Zarlie rushed into a basement conference room used for seminars and small classes and plopped down into a soft red chair. (Stanford's school colors are red and white and it is amazing around the campus to see how many ordinary items reflect this color scheme.) This was an casual setting, a place where advanced students could talk openly with their professor, not a formal classroom.

Zarlie still could not get over her lack of self-control with the black cat and sincerely hoped that the cat had not suffered. Inside, she struggled with three ideas. One: no modern scientist, especially a biochemist, could possibly believe that a black cat crossing one's path would bring bad luck: predestination, the power of a cat over one's fate? Ridiculous! Two: she knew that she could mumble ancient Hungarian phrases which often seemed to cause things to happen, such as the cat changing direction: this was impossible to believe rationally but it worked more often than pure chance would allow and she had been doing it since childhood when she had learned the secret words from an old lady. Three: she had sworn to herself that she would never again use whatever mysterious powers she might possess to interfere with the life of another creature, at least not until she understood the situation scientifically and could use her talents for good rather than evil. But in spite of her resolutions and misgivings, she had just, almost instinctively, shot a petty curse into an innocent cat, when any normal student would have just kept walking, or even enjoyed seeing a happy cat running across the grass after a squirrel. Zarlie knew that none of this made sense. She was, at least according to her scholarship paperwork, a brilliant biology student with a great academic record, a budding scientist of the first rank, not a wacko spiritualist who escaped from a screwy upbringing in rural Hungary.

Zarlie's quest to understand her strange capabilities from a scientific viewpoint colored all her thoughts: she knew she was different from other people, but she saw that as an advantage not a handicap, and her odd background, abilities, and beliefs provided many subjects to investigate. Her goal, and the reason she was in school, was to discover the scientific basis for unusual human and animal strengths and senses. She wanted to be the first modern scientist to bridge the gap between science and the spiritual world.

The seminar began normally, but soon Zarlie raised an issue she had been studying on her own, even though they were supposed to be discussing a dissection the class had just completed. "Let's talk for a few minutes about Ridley turtles and their thousands-of-miles migration from the Cayman Islands across the oceans, and what we might find inside them if we cut one up in the lab. The textbook zoologists just offer vague mumbo-jumbo about how sea turtles navigate, but recent studies show these turtles must be sensing the vertical component of the earth's magnetic field, even though it's incredibly weak. We know they don't use the horizontal component, the one that spins compass needles. They use the vertical field, the one that causes compass needles to dip slightly. The vertical magnetic field has just been mapped by satellites and it matches the turtle migration paths perfectly. How can turtles do this? Where's the sensitive magnetic sensor in the turtle" You can never find it in a dissection or on a microscope slide. My theory is that they sense the weak geomagnetic fields by feeling perturbations in electromagnetic fields they generate in their brains. They generate their own magnetic fields inside their bodies by making electrons flow around their nervous system, then sense the very slight variations in their internal fields caused by the earth's magnetism."

"That's ridiculous Zarlie. In the first place, the earth's vertical magnetic fields are so weak that no biologic creatures could possibly sense them, and then to suggest such an unproven sensory mechanism is absurd. It has no basis in science," the professor argued, as he tried to steer the discussion back to the lab work.

"So what's your explanation? How could the turtles go thousands of miles across the sea, and they have been tagged and their travels verified, so it's real, they do it every year and come right back to the correct spot, even under cloud cover and in darkness and in storms?"

Another student joined the argument, "Hey, and if we humans want to measure these fields, what do we do? We generate an electromagnetic field in a coil of wire inside a box then electronically observe the perturbations caused by the earth's magnetic field, just like Zarlie's turtles do biologically. You can apply electromagnetic field theory and do the math: it's a valid and very sensitive way to measure magnetic fields, but you need some serious electronics. Petroleum geologists do this stuff all the time when they're searching for oil."

"There's no scientific proof of this happening in animals. Such a sensory mechanism in living creatures has never been observed and properly documented in any species. Turtles aren't made from transistors and coils of wire. Now let's get back to yesterday's dissection and talk about science instead of speculation."

"Careful professor, remember what Velikofsky said in 1949

to the Princeton graduating class when he admonished them to ask new questions and seek new answers because this is how knowledge advances and old ideas are replaced. Don't bet everything on the official explanations for they can be out of date in a heart beat," a third student added in broken Chinese-English.

"Velikofsky was an idiot, as science over the past fifty years has clearly shown: look at his silly ideas. For example, petroleum did not rain on the earth from a passing comet, and Venus was always a planet, not a comet captured by the sun within the time frame of recorded human history. Now if you don't want to talk about my course's subject matter, then go home, I'm too busy to deal with this crap."

The professor grabbed his notes and stormed from the room, leaving the surprised class behind.

"I bet we're in for a wicked mid-term" one of the students observed as they slowly departed.

This was not the first time that Zarlie had interjected strange ideas into scientific discussions and the abrupt ending to the seminar didn't bother her: it would give her an extra half hour in the lab for her own research. She headed across campus toward the med school and the new genetics labs. As she walked quickly, she ate an apple and a peanut-butter sandwich from her backpack for dinner-on-the-run. Zarlie rarely ate normal meals with other people: she just didn't have time.

Zarlie had been bent over a microscope for hours when her TA (Teaching Assistant, a graduate student who helps professors in return for tuition money) entered. "Zarlie, what are you doing here at this hour? Still cutting up strange creatures and peering at their guts?"

"I've already done my class work, this is my own project, and don't worry, it isn't costing the U a dime."

"Are you hoping to publish something, or make a big discovery? I could help you know, it isn't as though you're some kind of expert already."

"Thanks, but you wouldn't be interested, so leave me alone OK?"

"Hey I was just trying to help, and by the way, I noticed that you didn't enter your cell phone on the registration paperwork: what's your number?"

"I don't have a phone, and I don't anticipate any reason that you or the prof would need to call: send me an email if you've got a message."

"You're kidding. How do your friends stay in touch? We just wanted the number in case there was a change in class schedule or assignments, or something."

"I don't have time for chatter. Just send me an email: I check it twice a day. Now, if you don't mind, you've wasted ten minutes of my time and the stain on the specimen I was viewing just faded out, so damn it, I've got to start over. Shit, just go away!"

"Geeze, I'm sorry, I was hoping you might like to take a break and go for some coffee and relax a little: I'm not an idiot you know, I might be able to aid you if you would open up and ask for help, just once in awhile."

"Look, I'm really busy and I don't have time for sitting around doing nothing. It's not about you, I'm just not interested in guys and polite conversation. I want to get on with my work and finish with this specimen, so I'm sorry if this seems rude because I don't mean it that way, I don't have time for goofing off. OK?"

"Sure, but when you do need help, you could ask, maybe you could learn to work more efficiently: you're not the first person to study cells you know. There're lots of tricks and techniques that you may not have discovered."

"Fine, thanks, I'll ask for help when I need it, so good night." The TA left and Zarlie went back to work on her specimen. Zarlie figured that the TA's real interest was in her body and in the faint possibility that she was on to something that might be important and which could boost his career by associating with her. In either case, a waste of her time. Zarlie knew that he had no idea of how hard she had worked to get to this country, to this university, to this lab, for a chance to study in one of the world's pre-eminent biochemistry environments. If he had only known about her struggles, about starvation, about the killings, he might not have approached her so casually. He had no idea of the fights she had survived, of the years she had spent plotting, scheming, and ruthlessly moving toward her goal. He would have been shocked to hear how she had used her body to escape from Hungary during the Communist years, and what she had done to her sleeze-o benefactor, before leaving his mangled body in a Swiss hotel as she flew to a new life in America. For the really poor, obeying the law was not a viable option.

Chapter 3
A Minor Breakthrough
Rewarded

William worked feverishly into the night in his small, messy, one-room garage apartment behind the home of Professor Einaudi, a geologist who lived on Lowell Way. For William, this living arrangement was ideal. He could study continuously without interruption, bicycle to the math department in five minutes, and meals from his microwave and one-burner hotplate were fast and without extraneous conversation. In terms of drive, work ethic, and intelligence he was far older than his years, but if you were to ask almost any girl who chanced to meet him she would have laughed at his naiveté and social inexperience. Tonight he continued his pyramid studies, trying to manipulate the numbers contained in magic squares into something meaningful. William had long been fascinated by the properties of 'Magic' squares, which are grids of numbers with interesting mathematical features. Some of the squares have been known to initiates as far back as the dawn of recorded history. One of the most basic examples, the three-square, can be written with rows:

$$[\ 4 \ 9 \ 2 \ ],$$
$$[\ 3 \ 5 \ 7 \ ],$$
$$[\ 8 \ 1 \ 6 \ ].$$

Each row, column, and diagonal adds to fifteen, and each of the integers from '1' to '9' is used only once. William loved the symmetry and elegance of sophisticated numerical designs like this.

Just before midnight, William smiled with surprise and satisfaction, then waved his arms and leapt into the air with a shout of joy. He had just invented a way to automatically convert the numbers inside a large magic square into pictures. He was working with the twelve-by-twelve Zodiac Square, which has twelve rows of twelve numbers each. He speculated that somehow the numbers in

14

each of the twelve rows could be manipulated to generate the twelve signs of the zodiac. It seemed logical that the first row would generate Aries, since the zodiacal year starts with Aries, the Vernal Equinox, March 21 in twentieth century calendars, and that successive rows would generate the other symbols in their natural order: Aries, Taurus, Gemini, Cancer, Leo, Virgo, Libra, Scorpius, Sagittarius, Capricornus, Aquarius, Pisces.

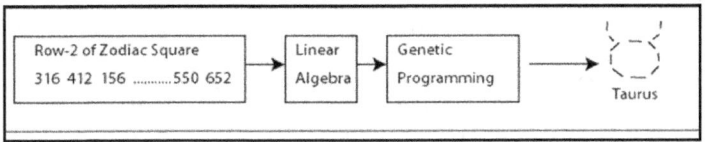

William's method for generating zodiac drawings

William used his knowledge of advanced mathematics to write a computer program to express his ideas. He started with linear algebra to manipulate the twelve numbers in each row, then used genetic programming to discover algorithms that would convert the resultant numbers into graphics commands that would enable a computer to draw pictures on a monitor. In Genetic Programming, developed by Stanford's Professor Koza, a computer wrote its own software using Darwinian cross-breeding, survival of the fittest, and mutation to slowly work toward an answer. The hard part of this approach is to steer the computer in the right direction by giving it clear criteria for success, so that it discards bad solutions instead of letting them breed. William developed and ran the software on his old personal computer.

William checked his watch, one minute before midnight. Today had not been in vain. He had made a small, but original, contribution to the world of mathematics and it was only September. There was still time to do something more important by his twenty-first birthday. He smiled as he carefully wrote the details of his discovery in his notebook.

William usually slept six or seven hours, then returned to work. As he threw his clothes over a chair and fell into bed at one in the morning, he was content for the first time in weeks. Although the pyramid lecture had been a flop, it had jogged his brain into making a minor, but very clever, breakthrough. As he recalled the lecture, he remembered Zarlie, and wondered about her as he fell asleep.

As soon as he awoke, he called Professor Schmidt. "May I see you this morning? I've made a small discovery and it would mean a lot to have your signature in my notebook as a witness."

"Have you discovered the meaning of the pyramids?"

"No, but I do have something original, and you'll have a big laugh, because it's even further out than pyramid work. I've made a breakthrough in astrology!"

"My goodness, well meet me in my office at ten."

"Don't worry, this won't need financial support, but I'm going to apply for a software patent."

William whistled to himself, dressed carefully, shaved, treated himself to a big breakfast at Tressider Union, then walked around the old Quad to mathematics corner. He loved the pavements with their diagonal square patterns amidst the symmetrical colonnades and tried to fit them both into a mathematical series as he walked. He was careful not to step on the lines between the squares, because he remembered the childhood poem about Christopher Robin, ". . .you must never step on the lines in the squares or the masses of bears who wait in their lairs for the sillies who walk unawares. . ." William laughed and said the last line of the poem out loud, "Bears, bears go back to your lairs. Just see how I'm walking only on squares."

He arrived smiling at Professor Schmidt's office at the stroke of ten. They laughed about astrology and how ridiculous it seemed to modern scientists, as William explained the mathematics of his discovery. Professor Schmidt was impressed by the clever way that William manipulated the twelve-square into the zodiac signs. He especially liked the elegant and original way this approach processed data and suggested that there could be different applications, maybe in the field of signal processing, for William's technique.

William smiled, "Maybe someday it'll be known as 'William's Method' for solving a class of problems, but astrology is the only application I can think of for it now."

"Let me know what happens with the patent. I take pride in the original work done by our students. Patents are one indication that we aren't all asleep."

"I'd gladly trade the patent for pyramid funding, but maybe a real patent will at least encourage people to look more kindly next time I ask for money."

William went back to his apartment, started his ancient Honda Civic, and drove to the offices of a patent attorney on Sand Hill Road. As he looked at the rows of new red-tile-roofed stucco buildings, filled with money, lawyers, slick promoters, new inventions, and the occasional commercially-successful product, he knew that he was in the financial heart of Silicon Valley, the home of many rich venture capital firms. These firms raised money from wealthy people, then invested it in new ideas that might show big profits if the investors were lucky. However, friends had told him that the lawyers and promoters who ran the VC firms always made a profit, since they siphoned off a percentage of the money that flowed through their hands, regardless of the investment results. William's car was the only cheap one in the parking lot.

William looked around and thought of all the money represented by these buildings. He realized that if he had come here yesterday, he would have felt out of place, a misfit with nothing to recommend him, but today he began to feel at home. As he scanned the expensively dressed people and cars, he realized that this was where bright inventors came to cash in their discoveries. This is where he would come when he made his big breakthrough. As for today, he knew exactly where to go since every bulletin board on campus contained advertisements for legal firms that wanted to handle, and skim profits from, new ideas. Having the signature of the Head of the School of Mathematics as witness to his invention gave William immediate credibility. He knew that Professor Schmidt had earned several patents through the efforts of one particular law firm, so he headed through their door. The young attorney assigned to his case joked that astrology was an unusual field for a Stanford mathematician to explore, and probably not very profitable. Together, they expanded the scope of the patent to encompass as wide a field as they dared, with much laughter about future applications for 'William's Method' and the licensing fees it might generate. They both knew that this was a minor patent, with almost no financial future, but also that it was a positive mark on the scorecard of life and perhaps an indication of greater things to come.

After lunch, William bicycled to the offices of the Stanford Daily, the student newspaper. He realized that one advantage of a patent was that it would announce to the world that he was more than just a student, that he was a bit special. If a small article about his work were published, it would shed favorable light on the Mathematics Department, and it would perhaps be a step toward building his reputation and eventual pyramid funding. A student reporter put the following article in Sunday's edition, along with a quickly snapped picture of William.

Stanford. William Stowell, a twenty-year old undergraduate in the School of Mathematics, has just applied for a patent on a new mathematical analysis procedure which he invented last night. Although the initial application for this procedure is in the field of astrology, Professor Schmidt hopes that it will be useful in other fields. William's main interest involves the solution of mathematical problems in uncommon fields, fields which are rarely visited by modern scientists. Yesterday he gave an exciting lecture on the ideas encoded in the Great Pyramid. William's is the third patent application this year from the School of Mathematics, and its patent output per student is higher than that of any other School.

As he reviewed the article, William envisaged Professor Schmidt smiling and perhaps clipping the article to show it proudly to colleagues in other departments. Scoring brownie points with Schmidt seemed a smart idea, and perhaps there was a way to take his advice and disguise his pyramid funding request as a practical results-oriented project.

William went back to work, spending the weekend catching up on his non-mathematical classes, which included advanced Japanese, Electronics, and Computer Science. Someday he needed to take a few history and art courses to fulfill graduation requirements, but he didn't have time for that now. He was taking the maximum number of units allowed, nineteen, yet managing to find time to spend half his waking hours on pyramid research.

Monday morning William's telephone rang as he studied in his little apartment. "Are you William Stowell?" an unfamiliar male voice asked. "The guy who just invented some math related to astrology?"

William caught his breath: what a surprise. He hadn't even finished the paperwork on the patent. "Yes, that's me. Did you see my article in the Daily?"

"We work near your patent attorney, and he knows that we're in the astrology business, so he thought he'd do us both a favor."

"The astrology business? Is this a joke? Nobody does that, do they?"

"Hey, it's time for you to smarten up. Can you be at Rozatti's tonight at seven for dinner and a serious talk?"

"Maybe, but will it take long?"

"You can say no in a few minutes and leave, or sit down and listen to our pitch carefully."

"What sort of pitch? Are you some kind of telephone spammer?"

"Be there exactly on time. You're lucky enough to be having dinner with the president of VP Associates, Gloria Von Pappen. You don't know how many guys would give their left nut to be in your position."

"How will I recognize her?"

"You will, and she saw your snap in the paper. Don't be late whatever you do. She'll shred your guts if you make her wait."

After he hung up, William Googled VP Associates and discovered one of the oldest and most respected venture capital (VC) companies in the Bay Area, but unlike most VC firms, he couldn't learn much about its interests or products from either its website or a half hour of searching. A combinatorial search for astrology and VP yielded no hits either. In his gut William knew that there was something fishy about the phone call and the idea that a respected VC company was suddenly interested in his work: what a waste of his time. Then an idea crept into his head. VC companies represented money, so perhaps there was a way to use the situation to obtain funding for pyramid research. From this perspective, the dinner could be interesting.

William found a clean shirt and drove out Page Mill Road wearing a smile, arriving at the expensive Italian restaurant hidden away in the foothills five minutes early. His excitement evaporated as he looked around and realized that he didn't have a clue as to the person he sought.

When the headwaiter approached, he asked, "I'm supposed to meet a Miss Von Pappen at seven, but I don't know what she looks like."

"You must be the only person who doesn't. Her table's over in the corner by the window. She's waiting for you."

William expected to be meeting a severe serious business woman, and was startled as he approached the table, where a beautiful young blond was just finishing a call on her phone while she studied a stack of papers. She motioned him to sit without looking directly at him. He was in shock as he looked at the strong full-figured young woman who appeared to be about his age.

"You must be William. I saw your picture in the paper, but it wasn't half as nice as you look in person." As she said this, William realized that she didn't have many clothes on. He couldn't help but notice her short tight skirt and thin partially unbuttoned blouse: it didn't leave much to his imagination. William stared at her warm nearby body as he became aware of her perfume. She continued to read her papers, only glancing at him sideways occasionally.

"Yes, I'm William, but I don't know, I mean, I'm pleased to meet you, or how can I help you," he stammered with confusion and embarrassment as over-sexed thoughts ran through his mind. He really wanted to comment on her striking body and clothes, but knew that he couldn't.

"I'm Gloria Von Papen. Your work aroused my, ah, curiosity, so I read your initial patent application. You could be quite useful to

19

me."

Gloria moved slightly closer to William. He was startled both by her luscious body, and by the fact that someone was actually interested in his astrology patent.

"You mean you liked the math, I mean you couldn't like astrology, er, what I mean is, I'm curious to know what application you have in mind for the math. I didn't realize that anyone would be able to look at the application so soon."

"Actually, I do like astrology, and I'd like to discuss your ideas on the subject."

William realized that he knew nothing about astrology except the names and shapes of the Zodiac symbols. "Oh. Sorry, I'm a mathematician, er, I don't have a clue about the stars."

"I don't either, but I'm making plenty of money with the little that I do know. Look, you told Jake, the guy you talked with on the phone, that you're busy and that you don't have much time tonight, so I'll come straight to the point. I want your brain for as many hours a week as I can get, and I'll make it worth your while. I need a sharp mathematician on my team, and you fit perfectly. That's the deal, you can run back to your homework now, or stay and talk business. Your choice."

How bewildering. He had completely misjudged the warm-bodied person next to him. He was bowled over by her sexuality but was just beginning to realize that this was a serious meeting, and a very important one for his career. Gloria confidently poured him a glass of the chilled Italian Prosecco she was drinking, then passed it to him: a fruity sparkling wine, pleasant, fun, and not as serious as champagne.

As he recovered his wits and accepted the glass, he wanted to express his surprise, but didn't quite know how to do it. "Miss Von Pappen, please excuse me, I don't know what to say, I mean, of course I'd love to stay and talk with you."

William was troubled by her actions and something about her attitude. He had been raised by elder relatives who took politeness and manners seriously. None of them would ever have buried their heads in a stack of papers, reading constantly while a guest sat at their dinner table. Yet Gloria stayed focused on her papers and never once turned to William: she talked into the pages instead of to him. He wondered what she was reading and why she didn't look up. He wasn't ugly or a monster, or at least he didn't think so.

"Gloria is what my team-mates call me, and I can tell that you're going to become one of them. Prosit!"

William drank a little of the Prosecco, and smiled: he had never tasted anything quite like it. "Gloria, thank you very much.

What exactly do you have in mind? I don't know what you do with astrology, or how you turn it into money, or how a mathematician can help, but it does sound interesting."

"Since we're both busy people, I took the liberty of ordering dinner so that we can concentrate on business. Let's get started. You're a very smart person, but you could spend the rest of your life wandering around schools, writing papers, giving lectures, and maybe someday rising to the rank of full professor, with a salary at age sixty less than that of my secretary, Jake. Or, you could refocus your life, work your ass off for me, make a ton of money by age thirty, then do all the private research you want. Think of Bill Gates and Steve Jobs. They flew out of school and into the world of real money by age twenty, same age as you are right now."

William's idols were men like Fermat and LaPlace, not nouveau riche computer personalities, but he understood her message clearly, and realized that he had reached a major decision point in his life. "My whole life, my relatives, everyone I know almost, has been on the academic side, not the, er, money side, of life. I don't know what to say."

"Someone in your family, a long time ago, made a pile of dough so that his descendants could goof off amidst dusty books and papers forever, and now the funds are running low. I checked up on you. It's time for you to get busy and revitalize the family fortune, and then, and only then, peacefully study whatever your heart desires."

"You make complex decisions seem simple," he replied as he wondered about this strange conversation, carried on by Gloria with her head buried in paperwork: she had yet to look at him.

"That's part of my job. I'll give you twenty-four hours to make a decision, and in the meantime I'll tell you a little about my activities. You probably think that working in business is dull, bean-counting, and worrying about paperwork and personnel records. It's not like that at all, at least not up at the top where we operate. We farm-out all that crap to service firms and focus our efforts on converting new ideas into as much cash in our own pockets as possible."

Silently, an unusual sushi plate had arrived, complete with chopsticks, warm washcloths, and an open bottle of German wine, which the silent waiter poured into small cut-crystal glasses. William had been studying Japanese for six years. He loved the mathematical purity of its grammar, and considered himself well-versed in Japanese customs, but he had never seen sushi like this, especially in an Italian restaurant.

"What's this stuff? Are the Italians trying to learn how to make sushi from spaghetti?"

21

"The Itamae-san would love to hear your comments, considering the hour he just spent preparing his signature plate of sea urchin, conger eel and frogfish for us. Don't touch it, I'll send out for a big mac and a coke, or would you rather have fish and chips, or a peanut butter sandwich?"

With this comment Gloria turned toward a waiter. Before, William had seen only the beautiful and perfect left side of her face. As she turned, he saw that the other side of her face was badly scarred with masses of grotesque red and purple tissue. He knocked over his wine glass, almost fell out of his chair, and could not help but stare. Then he forced himself to avert his eyes, as he scrambled to wipe up the mess, breathing heavily with embarrassment and confusion.

"Please Gloria, I'm sorry, I mean I love sushi, I'm just so surprised, so surprised by everything. There's so much I don't know."

Gloria smiled at him with the left side of her face, "Yes, that's obvious. This is an Italian specialty, 'crudo', which is derived from Japanese sushi, and you will find that the Charles Schleret Gewurztraminer complements it perfectly, once you refill your glass."

As she said this, she calmly washed her hands with a warm cloth, then expertly mixed a touch of wasabi into her little dish of shoyu and began to eat. William worked to recover his composure. He was dying to ask what had happened to the other side of her face but didn't dare say a thing about it. He knew she must have seen him jump because of her face, yet she said nothing about it. As he washed his hands and mixed wasabi, he moved the conversation to a safer topic.

"Where did you learn about Japanese customs?"

"I was raised among Germans and Japanese in Argentina where my grandfather knows quite a few interesting people."

William carefully sampled the different kinds of sushi on the plate, following Gloria's lead as to the sequence in which they should be eaten. "This is wonderful sushi, the flavors are perfect and the fish is so fresh. I had no idea that such a combination existed."

"You're poor and young and haven't had a chance to experience what we might call the more exotic aspects of life. As a member of my team you'll learn something of the real world, the world that exists outside of mathematics, the world based on emotions, on fear, love and greed. Now, let's talk math. That's why we're here."

"How will you use my patent? I mean what kind of data will we be manipulating with it?"

"None, unless you see a way to use it. My team is very small and tight. We have one person for each key job, and I see that we need a very sharp mathematician to advance from the niche where we're operating."

"But I thought we were here to discuss licensing my patent. You mean you want to hire me just as a mathematician, and that my patent is worthless to you?"

"I'll license it if you come to work for us, and you can use it if you want. Let me put you in the picture. I picked-up the assets of a defunct dot-bomb company on the cheap, mainly their astrology website and software, and one of their people. I have five employees keeping this turkey running, and an average of over fifty-thousand paying customers. Now, I want to expand, and to do it, I need serious math. We're pulling in almost five million a year, running the site on rented hardware, and covering most of our promotion by running ads from other sites. I'm netting about two million bucks of clear profit each year. Christmas bonuses for those five employees were very nice last year. You could be number six."

As the dinner progressed, William learned that far from being just an astrology website, Gloria offered customers customized psychological advice, twice-daily predictions, answers to very personal questions, and much warm comfort. It was perfect for lonely people who were unsure of themselves, people who needed a bit of help making daily decisions. And, all of this came from a large clever computer program, with minimal human intervention. As the advice was mostly random, some people were pleased and continued to pay well, while others dropped away, to be replaced by newbies.

The big push right now was to translate the site into French and Spanish as Gloria had concluded that these two markets offered the best chance of gaining additional rich and gullible customers at the lowest cost. Two of the five employees were behind this effort, a linguist and a user-interface expert. One of the others was a computer guru who kept the whole mess running, and there was an astrology expert. The fifth person was Jake, who doubled as the financial manager and Gloria's personal assistant. Although Jake had an MBA from Harvard, he was delighted to be spending part of his time as a PA, earning more than his fancy classmates on Wall Street, and definitely having much more fun.

After a wonderful dinner, William and Gloria walked out the front door, where a valet had brought his old Honda and a bright yellow Ferrari roadster. The Ferrari's V-12 exhaust rumbled deeply, perhaps frightening his quiet little Honda four. Gloria turned to him, "You don't need to choose exclusively between school and work. Why don't you drop your dullest classes, get down to twelve units, and start working at VPA (Von Pappen Associates) at least twenty hours a week and see how you like it?"

"I'll think it over and call you tomorrow. Is this your car?"

"It's one of them. You can take it for a spin sometime if you like. . . and, if you work hard, save your pennies and keep your Honda, you'll be rich in no time at all. Bis Morgen fruh."

As William drove away he realized how careful Gloria had been to position herself so that he was always on her good side. He had only caught one glimpse of the other side of her face during the whole evening. She even avoided mirrors so that a reflection of her other side never showed. He wondered how a person could live with such a handicap. When he had first sat down in the restaurant, he had been intimidated by her superior, worldly, sexy personality, but now he realized that she was far from perfect and had problems that he could only imagine. She was a real person, not someone to fear, and was offering him a rare chance to move up. William went home to a sleepless night, tossing in bed and wondering what to do. Finally he stopped thinking about Gloria and focused on his own situation. He was taking nineteen units, keeping up with all of them, and yet finding time to do many hours of pyramid research each week. Of the 168 hours in the week, he slept forty-nine, and worked, or thought about work, almost all of the remaining 119 hours. Dropping down to his core math courses and maybe Japanese 401, would cut his school load by at least twenty or thirty hours, and he could probably do a bit less in the world of pyramids. From a logical standpoint, part-time work with Gloria was certainly possible. And she had been dead right about his family finances: what had been a fortune in 1724 was now a trickle, bled almost dry by the combination of horrendous British taxes and a lack of financial initiative for many generations.

William's problem was the illogical side. He had been surrounded by British academia and its value system, where knowledge counted for much more than money. It almost seemed that taking a salary, let alone a salary from a company that exploited gullible customers, was far beneath him. Yet Gloria's comment about a distant ancestor making it all possible by earning a fortune, struck a solid chord. He knew that the silver platters used at family meals, the Georgian estate where his uncle lived, and where William had been raised, and many of his family's most valuable possessions, had all been bought by one clever and resourceful solicitor who had invested heavily in the East India Company in the eighteenth century. He had made the family fortune that had supported William and his ancestors for over two hundred years. In some ways, this ancestor had done more for academia by granting dozens of his descendents financial freedom, than any of those who followed. From this perspective, working for Gloria was almost a duty, and he could imagine a lively debate on the subject around the family dinner table.

After a sleepless night, he telephoned VPA and reached Jake on the second ring. Now that he knew a bit about Jake, he felt almost like they were friends. "Hi, I hope I'm not calling too early."

"No trouble. We work flexible hours depending on what's happening. When are you coming over?"

"You already know my decision, don't you?"

"If you're as smart as your papers indicate, you'll be here this morning. Have you had breakfast yet?"

"No, not really. Actually, I didn't have much sleep."

"I didn't either before my first day here. Drive over and we'll have some muffins and coffee around the corner and begin to know each other. You'll be surprised, but you're going to have a blast working here. This is one of the most exciting and challenging business environments on the planet."

William smiled to himself, realizing from the friendly start to the day that he had a new friend, an exciting job, and that he had made the right decision.

Jake turned out to be muscular, athletic, maybe thirty years old, with a completely shaved head and a slightly brusque Teutonic manner. William was surprised that he was dressed in a white tennis shirt, shorts, and sneakers. Jake told him that the tennis courts, owned by VPA, were the envy of all the nearby companies, so Jake never had trouble finding a partner for a quick game during the day, and there was no dress code at work. William had played tennis earlier in life, but hadn't made time for it at Stanford, even though the school had dozens of courts.

After breakfast, Jake gave William a quick tour of their offices. From the street, VPA seemed to be a small office, in a row of similar offices. Behind the modest front door was a receptionist and a lobby. Then the building expanded and William realized that the interior was large and that it encompassed the area behind many of the other offices which fronted the street. The VPA offices were arranged in a square, two stories high, around a central open courtyard dominated by a large multi-tiered fountain. Covered walkways on both levels shaded the windows, yet allowed each room to look out onto the fountain and the peaceful garden that surrounded it. Jake explained that the astrology project occupied the rooms on the south side, in the shade, both upstairs and downstairs, and that William would have a suite to himself. The other rooms held people working on other projects, as well as a few lawyers who were renting space.

Gloria's office was in a corner on the second floor. Jake left him there as she arrived for the day. William looked around and was startled to see a life-size color photo of a muscular male nude, whose head was covered by a black hood. The man held a whip in one hand

and sported a startlingly-large erection. William was embarrassed to look at it, and turned away as Gloria laughed at his reaction. As he turned from the photo, he noticed a large movie poster for *Triumph Of The Will*, the famous Nazi propaganda film from the thirties which he had seen twice in history classes. William noted that her good side was always toward him.

Gloria was laughing, enjoying his embarrassment. "Do you like my German porn? I could get you a life-size leather girlie shot for your office."

"No thank-you, er. . . I prefer math, I mean, I like girls too, but I'm here to work."

"Good answer. We can have your rooms painted or wall-papered or anything you like. Most people like a soft couch where they can catch a nap or a maybe a girl, or perhaps a boy."

"I don't have time for that, but, what exactly am I supposed to do?"

"Most of our customers leave after a few months because the predictions we generate don't prove accurate enough to justify the cost. We keep sucking in prospects, but they're expensive to catch and process. Your job is to find a way to make our predictions appear to be more accurate, so that customers hang around longer and pay more. If you could get them to stay ten percent longer, we'd clear an extra million each year."

"I'm not sure I understand. I mean, I don't think I know how to do that."

"You're an expert in pattern recognition. I'm convinced that semi-repeatable patterns exist in what these people are asking and in the answers they desire. The pattern generating mechanisms may not be stable over time, but the characteristics might be predictable. Maybe the underlying math is related to fractals or chaos theory. We don't need perfection, just slight improvements. Every extra day they hang on is pure profit."

"That's a big subject. There're so many variables and unknowns, and most are impossible to quantify."

"You'll be pleasantly surprised to discover that we have a complete archive of every question, answer, and result, for about half a million customers. We have tons of data just sitting around, so there must be some patterns lurking, just waiting for you to discover them."

"Holy shit. I mean, excuse me, that's an incredible problem, I don't know how I'll find time to do my school work, and make any progress."

"You're very clever, and I can see the wheels already turning in your head. You're the house mathematician. If you don't know the answers, buy some books, or hire some other mathematicians, or consultants, or professors, or computers, or something. You have carte blanche, just make progress. But first, find Jake and fill out the personnel paperwork. Then get on our website and sign up for the deluxe package and use it every day. Charge it to your own credit card. I want you to get the full, daily, experience of being one of our best customers so that you can see the system from their eyes, and wallets."

"When do I start working?"

"You've already started."

William turned to leave, but then his excitement faded as he realized that he had no idea how much he would be earning. "Er, Gloria, this may sound tacky, but I don't have a clue about how much I'll be paid."

"Don't worry about that. After you settle in and show what you can do for us, we'll set a nice figure. Then after a year or so we can talk about equity participation. I want you logged in every day for at least a few minutes to pick up your horoscope and personal predictions so get moving."

"Yes sir, I mean yes Gloria."

Gloria smiled as he turned to leave, "Hey, welcome aboard William. You're going to be damn busy."

As William entered his new office, he wondered what he had walked into. The new job was exciting technically and perhaps financially, but the neo-Nazi aspects of Gloria were un-nerving. He wondered what else was going on here, and realized that his new friend Jake could easily pass for a skin-head storm-trooper, just by changing his clothes.

Chapter 4
Brain Waves

The school Registrar as well as some of William's professors were surprised when he dropped enough classes to get down to twelve units, the bare minimum that would qualify him as a full-time student. Only a week after meeting Gloria his school work had shrunk to two advanced math courses and Japanese, nothing else. He knew that the people who oversaw his scholarship would eventually ask questions, but by then he would be earning a fortune and would be able to afford the school fees himself if they cut his scholarship, or so he hoped.

On the way to his weekly Senior Seminar, William ran into Professor Schmidt and Professor Skilling in the hall. Schmidt smiled. "I saw in the paper that you applied for a patent on your translation technique. Thanks for crediting the Department."

"You won't believe it, but I've already licensed the rights to a VC firm on Sand Hill Road."

Professor Skilling was startled by the news. "What technique? What are you talking about?"

Before William could reply, Professor Schmidt answered. "William has developed a very clever way to manipulate matricies, and automatically plot the results. He applied it to an astrology problem, but the real application is probably in a more serious field."

Skilling looked annoyed, and turned to William. "Is this why you've dropped three classes without consulting me?"

"I've started a part-time job doing topology research. I didn't feel that I could carry a heavy academic load and do justice both to it and to my boss."

Schmidt raised an eyebrow and looked at William carefully, "Do you plan to graduate, and perhaps do advanced studies?"

The excitement of working on a massive practical problem in uncharted mathematical territory, combined with a chance of earning enough for his pyramid research was taking more and more of his attention. "I intend to graduate, but perhaps not in the normal four year time span. My outside task is fascinating mathematically, the work environment is pleasant, and the situation pays well. I'd be a fool not to take this job seriously."

Skilling sneered, "I suppose you're working for some penniless dot-bomb for a ton of worthless equity."

With that remark, Skilling and Schmidt turned into the classroom, followed by William. Schmidt's comment hit William more than he dared show. He was working long hours for Gloria, but not a penny was flowing into his pockets yet. In fact, he was loosing money as the charges from his daily interaction with Gloria's computer program began to mount.

The seminar started with a brief talk by Schmidt, as he reflected on the difficulty of finishing formal education when faced with temptations from the outside world. He summarized the mathematical aspects of William's patent and his current situation, to the surprise of both William and the other students. Schmidt was not critical, but expressed his sadness at perhaps loosing one of the department's brightest students so soon.

Later, William was in his office at VPA and had just logged in to Gloria's website, YFN, "Your Future Now". Soft music came from the computer, as it asked how yesterday's predictions had worked out. As William typed his replies, he could envision the giant database growing with each keystroke. The computer asked a few personal questions, such as what was troubling him now, and in what areas he was experiencing uncertainty. In many ways, it was a pleasant interview with a psychologist, and it only cost five dollars a day instead of hundreds. Jake had delightfully told him that this simple fee added up to $1825 per customer per year, if only they would stay connected that long. After a pleasant question-and-answer session, the computer advised William on the best way to apply his current horoscope to the problems that he had identified. The whole experience was warm, reassuring, and friendly, and if only the answers had validity, this site would be worth a fortune.

As a joke, William asked YFN about Zarlie and why the parting image of her face still drifted through his consciousness. He was shaken by the reply, "*Venus is aligned with Neptune. Deep mysteries are about to be revealed. Within the week you will know more than you ever imagined possible.*" William didn't believe in astrology, or in the forecasting ability of the YFN computers, but what a strange answer to his question.

The first thing William had done in his new office at VPA was to pin a large modern blowup of the Great Pyramid on his wall, to remind him why he was working. Then he ordered copies of the sketches by David Roberts done in the 1840s. These showed the old Egyptian stone monuments partially covered by sand as camels and Bedouins stood nearby. To William, these were artistic impressions of mysteries that were waiting to be uncovered. They represented, visually, the hidden secrets that William hoped to reveal as soon as he had enough money and time to mount an expedition. William had ordered Roberts' *Pyramids of Gizeh* and *The Approach of the Simoom, Desert of Gizah* for his office. Soon they would join his GP picture.

The Great Pyramid amidst ancient ruins

At VPA, William's current task was studying the innards of the computer programs which powered YFN. The guts were deceptively simple, and consisted of three major hunks of software. The first was an astrology program, a canned package that spit out predictions based on the current time of day, the customer's location and date of birth, and the current year, using the same techniques and rules that human astrologers employed to make predictions and forecasts. The second hunk was a very fancy version of the old Doctor Program, which had first been written in the sixties. This program emulated an interview with a psychologist. A clever programmer could write the original version in less than a page of code if he wrote in the programming language LISP, or in three pages of the BASIC or C languages. The doctor program asked pseudo-psychological questions, then massaged the customer's answers into further questions. It could go on forever, as the program sucked-in nouns and verbs from the customer's answers, then turned them into questions. Whenever the program was stumped, or the customer wouldn't answer, the Doctor Program would ask, "*Tell me about your mother.*" The third hunk of code was the only original part of the YFN computer program. It was written as a series of AWK shell-scripts which combined words from the customer's previous conversations, after manipulation by the Doctor code, with the current astrology forecast, to generate "personalized predictions." This section of the software was nothing more than a giant text-processor that cranked out reasonably-believable but totally random sentences. The whole thing was hidden behind a slick user interface, and it ran on computers at an IBM server farm in San Jose. The financial side, collecting credit card numbers and keeping track of the customer's log-in time, was done by off-the-shelf web code written in the language PERL.

William marveled at the cleverness of the whole assemblage: it was nothing more than a bunch of computers running clever software, but to a user on a faraway computer, the effect was just like talking with a friendly personal advisor. He could see why customers liked the experience, at least initially. He hoped that none of them took the advice too seriously.

So far, William's only contribution to the team effort was a brief conversation with Jake late in the week as they sat by the fountain. William had asked, "We have all this personal information on the customers. Do you ever try to merge it with credit reports or financial data, to figure out which customers might be able to afford fancier services?"

Jake was startled by the idea. "No, but we have their credit cards and socials, so we could learn almost anything about them."

"Maybe it would pay to find the richest customers, then put a live human on line with them, to give them real personal service, at a high price."

"They might like that. We could call it ethereal palladium service or something exclusive and personal."

"You could start just by scanning a sample of the existing customers, to see the range of wealth they represent."

"We already know that each has a computer and a credit card, and time to use both, so they aren't poor."

"Right, and there are probably other characteristics. Perhaps we could do market research right in our own database, so that it would be easier to reach new customers."

"Hey watch out, I'm the one with the MBA, you're not supposed to talk about marketing, and the cost of customer acquisition," Jake said, laughing.

"Well, I hope it's a good idea because I haven't done squat this week on improving our prediction accuracy."

"You just did. I'm going to profile our customers, then maybe we can fudge the answer box to give different answers to the richer clients. Maybe we can categorize the customers into financial

31

groups, then run the answer box a bit differently for each batch."

William went home smiling. He had wanted to contribute something, and hoped that next week he would have a more substantial idea. He realized that it might be much easier to analyze the customers than the mountain of data they had left behind.

On Sunday morning, the silly YFN program randomly told William that he must take Sunday night off and relax, for he had an "*exciting week ahead.*" William was caught up with his homework and had already done forty hours for Gloria, so he decided to take a rare break: he would follow YFN's advice and go to the Sunday night flicks even though he knew the program's advice was worthless. On Sunday nights Memorial Auditorium was filled with students goofing off before classes started again on Monday. No one cared what the films were; people laughed at everything, enjoying the break. Some students were carrying milk cartons from dinner, filled with beer or booze. There were many obscene comments in the dark as the movie played.

The film this night was *Casablanca*, and while watching the airport searchlight rotating in the final scenes, William had an exciting idea about mathematical rotations of sets of numbers through arbitrary angles. Rotation, before trying to match the sets to each other, might be a key to finding correlations. He couldn't wait to explore this idea, and rushed from the theater and sat down on the grass against a tree near Frost Amphitheater. He opened his laptop and began to furiously type details of the idea and its implications. Perhaps he could use this to improve the astrology program, and maybe apply it to the pyramid project: a home-run idea.

After awhile he became aware that someone was crouching nearby watching him. He turned and realized that it was a girl, not only a girl, but Zarlie.

"Hello William, I'm a bit surprised to find that it's you here," Zarlie said as she moved closer, but not too close, a bit like a crouching cat stalking prey. She kept to the shadows.

"Yes, er. . . I don't understand but can I help you?"

William was startled and confused as he looked more closely at Zarlie. She wasn't strikingly beautiful, but still very attractive when she moved into the moonlight. There was something exotic about her manner that was hard to put in words. Perhaps it was her accent, or the way that she moved. She was slightly taller than average and had a well-proportioned athletic figure, a classic rather than a modern beauty.

"I don't know how to put this, but please bear with me for

just a few minutes. I've almost never dared talk with anyone about this, and I'm taking quite a chance right now. I'm not quite sure how to put this, but your mental activity is so damn weird that I've just got to talk with you about it."

"My what? My mental activity? What do you mean?"

"Haven't you ever had a premonition, or a feeling that someone was following you, or maybe a warning that something bad was about to happen?"

"Of course. That happens to everyone."

"Have you ever stopped to analyze the phenomenon? Could it be that your brain has detected a kind of energy and processed it into a suggestion?"

"That's silly. I mean, you can't analyze stuff like that: it just happens."

"Is pyramid math more valid? I didn't see many believers at your talk the other day."

"That's different. Pyramids are real."

"And you just said that everyone feels presentiments, or warnings, or perhaps they might be called vibrations."

"So? That doesn't make them real. What I mean is, is oh, I don't know."

"Please listen carefully. You must promise never to reveal what I'm going to tell you," Zarlie said as she sat down in the shadows a few feet from him.

"How can I promise before you tell me. Look, I'm really busy, maybe this can wait?"

"No, I've gone this far, now promise."

"OK, I promise not to tell anyone, now what is it that I'm not supposed to tell?"

"This is not a joke. I'm taking a hell of a chance telling you about this, and I wouldn't dare do it if your vibes weren't so special. I've never felt anything like them before." If anything, Zarlie was more confused than William, but she was on to an interesting discovery and although it didn't make sense, she knew instinctively that she was pursuing an important lead. Her rational brain told her not to talk about her special powers or gifts, but that didn't overcome her curiosity.

"Sorry, but, I mean, I'm a bit startled and I hardly know you, and well, of course I'll keep your secret," William answered in confusion as he realized that he was sitting on a wet patch of grass that was soaking his butt.

"Just let me explain. I feel what I think are brain waves, and sometimes I can actually tell what people are thinking. Don't start smirking, this is real. Everyone can do it a little, and you just admitted that you feel things too. Before someone says something, can't you occasionally tell what they're about to say? I'm a lot better at listening to these things and much more sensitive than most people because I've practiced a great deal. I was sitting in the flick and I felt an unusual kind of brain wave. I've felt thousands of different people's thoughts, but this was very strange, and the only other time I've felt waves like this was during your lecture. I was taking notes on your brainwaves as you talked about pyramids and math. I followed the signals tonight, thinking that maybe I had found another person with the same kind of odd waves. I was concentrating so hard that I almost fell in the fountain by Hoo Tow. I followed the signals right to you, and I'd love to know what you're thinking about."

"You're not fooling, are you? You really believe that you can feel brain waves?" Inside, William was highly skeptical of such an idea and wondered if perhaps Zarlie had some form of mental illness. Maybe she did think that she could receive these waves when in actuality it was a form of auto-suggestion or delusion.

"Yes. I know you're a scientist and think you can prove using math and Maxwell's Equations that the signals are too faint to be picked up, but I can do it quite well, even though the signal-to-noise-ratio must be incredibly low."

"Does anybody believe you?"

"You're almost the only person I've ever told, and remember your promise. My field is like pyramid research in that most people think both are crack-pot subjects."

"What are you majoring in?"

"I hold the Hoffman-LaRoche fellowship in biological sciences, and my main interests are cellular biology and abnormal genetics. I want to find out how cells and people might send and receive signals, and how the ability might be transmitted genetically. Of course, that's not exactly what I tell my professors."

It began to dawn on William that Zarlie was very bright, but if so, how could she believe such a thing, something completely foreign to his technical training. "How far do the signals travel? How clearly can you read people's minds? How accurate are you?"

"I can't actually read minds in detail, but now and then I can feel the general idea of what people are thinking. Like driving in dense fog when shapes loom in the distance, but you don't know exactly what they are. Of course it's easier some times than others, and some people are hard to read. You're impossible. Everyone can do it a little, and I think animals may be quite good at it, especially at sensing danger. People could probably do much better if they believed and practiced a lot. And if you want a concrete example, I'm pretty sure that Professor Skilling cut your lecture short and hurried from the room because he had to take a dump: you can ask him to see if it's true."

"Damn, he could have just excused himself instead of cutting me off." William was half tempted to ask Skilling, but he saw immediately that phrasing the question tactfully would be rather difficult. As Zarlie talked, William could not stop comparing her appearance to Gloria's. While Gloria delighted in showing as much of her body as possible and using it to gain advantage, Zarlie was well-covered from head to foot in clothing that revealed nothing of her undergarments or body. What a different sort of person. She might be the most conservatively dressed girl on campus.

"How do you think it works? I mean, the signals must be really faint, and there're so many people around that their messages would get all jumbled up."

"I don't have a solid theory yet, but think about a cocktail party when everyone is talking at once. If you put a microphone in the room and asked a computer to analyze the sounds it would never be able to understand a specific voice, but yet a person can hold a conversation and filter all the noise to hear what someone is whispering. I think the brain has receiving and filtering capabilities, perhaps in the subconscious, that we haven't begun to appreciate. Maybe the brain is like a really sensitive radio, and it can pick up weak signals and tune out the static, that is, if it's trained well."

"I wish I had more time to talk with you, but I have so much to do, and well. . . "

"I'm fascinated by your brain waves, and if we could just spend a little time together, I could try a few experiments: get you to think different things while I listen to the waves that result. You're really a unique subject."

William's new cell phone, which Gloria had insisted that he carry, beeped. It was Gloria, reminding him that he had agreed to meet her at ten o'clock, and it was now nine forty-five. He squirmed and thought of the damp spot forming on his seat of his light khaki pants, wondering how he would have time to change.

William spoke into the phone, "Yes, well I almost forgot, but I've had a brainstorm, so I'll be a few minutes late. Bye." (to Zarlie) "Sorry, I'm not used to being on a leash."

He stood up, closed his laptop and started walking rapidly up Galvez Street, as Zarlie talked with him.

"William, why don't we meet somewhere quietly next Friday night at seven? How about the bench in front of the Mausoleum? Maybe I can teach you how to receive brain waves."

"What, I mean, OK, I can do that I guess, I mean shouldn't I be asking you out?"

"Don't be so shy, we're not going out on a date, you and I will just have a scientific discussion about unusual fields of research. I'll bring food for a picnic dinner, and you bring something to drink."

"This is so strange, how can you be studying such a subject."

"I have a long way to go. In your field, pyramid math, your only problems are getting money and ideas. In my field I need not only those, but I must also overcome prejudice about how the human body is supposed to work. Lots of people think research on mind-reading is off limits or sacrilegious, and it's not Politically Correct."

"Can you imagine what would happen during an exam if one person could read the minds of the others. You could get in big trouble if people found out."

"So don't talk about this, OK? What are you doing for the person who just called?"

"At first, I figured it was the ends-justifying-the-means, in that it looked like a chance to make a bunch of money on a slime-ball project so that I could fund my pyramid expedition. But now, I'm beginning to realize that the mathematical challenge is immense, as are the rewards for solving it, and that a good solution would make a lot of people happy. I'm so naive about these things, and my boss is a business genius, hidden in a gorgeous body that I can't help starring at whenever I see her. I mean, she hardly wears any clothes, you can see everything when she walks by."

"I'll bet you don't get any work done while she's around."

They were walking in the dark on Alvarado Row, when Zarlie stopped abruptly and held her head. William asked, "Are you OK, is something bothering you?"

"I hear, or feel, a voice inside my head, a man's voice, but it's distorted, like a wrinkled tape, with the words sort of warbling as the pitch varies, and I can't begin to place the accent. It's almost like a computer-generated voice, but I've never heard anything like it. It's been coming to me in dreams, but lately it's started happening in the dark even when I'm awake. I heard the voice briefly during your lecture the other day when the projector died."

"What's the man saying?"

"It's some kind of long story. I try to write down what I can remember, but it doesn't make any sense, but now it's stopped again. The voice fades in and out like a distant radio station at night, very weak, right on the edge of sensibility, with lots of static and noise."

"Is it scary?"

"No. The voice is friendly, informal, like someone telling an old tale to a child, but I have no control over it: I can't start or stop it, or call to it or tell it to go away, and its in pieces that don't fit together, that don't make any sense, like disconnected dreams. My lack of control is the only scary part."

"Sounds like when I'm trying to go to sleep and a math problem won't leave me alone. I roll over and over but no matter what position, I can't stop thinking about it, I can't turn it off and go to sleep."

"At least you can pick the problem. The voice gives me no options."

"I wonder whose brain you're hearing: it must be a wave coming from someone, maybe far away?"

"It's not like brainwaves, it almost like a feeling, an emotion, but with words: it's weird."

They continued across campus and approached William's old Honda. "I'd better run, sorry we can't talk more now, but I'll be at the bench Friday night," he said as he climbed into the car. "I'll try to forget to bring the phone."

As William drove off, he thought about Zarlie and her field of research. She might have mental problems, and hearing mysterious voices wasn't a good sign. Maybe she was going nuts? Suddenly he thought about witchcraft and realized that everything he had ever read or heard said that it didn't really exist: it was a delusion, perhaps caused by chemicals or brain damage, but in some ways it was frighteningly like Zarlie's description of brain waves. But what if Zarlie could actually read minds, then other things might be possible, and maybe witches did exist. Could she be one? What an odd thought, right in the midst of one of the most scientifically-oriented universities in the world. But if she was mentally OK, and if she were even partly right, the biological sciences were about to be totally reworked. She could get a Nobel Prize for a discovery like this. Damn, he had to get busy with his own research projects and stop fooling around. Zarlie might be onto a huge breakthrough, while he was lost in trivia. Of course, she probably didn't know squat about math and computers, so maybe he could help her analyze Brain Waves and share the Nobel Prize with her? And why were his waves so different from any others she had felt? Maybe, just maybe, his brain was extra powerful and he really was going to make a big breakthrough. Wow, so much to think about.

Chapter 5
The Blue Star

Wednesday afternoon William was looking forward to a special treat, a ride in the yellow Ferrari with Gloria. As they walked to the car, Gloria handed the keys to him much to his surprise, then climbed into the passenger seat, firmly attaching her four-point belt.

"Be careful William, this thing can hit 60 in less than five seconds, and pin the speedometer at 180."

"Wow, I've never driven anything like this. Is there a top if it rains?"

"For only three hundred grand, this Ferrari 550 Barchetta came with a little manual top, and the top is only safe to seventy miles an hour. Barchetta is Italian for 'open car', so that's the way it's supposed to be. This car was made to go fast, but not to travel in the rain."

William looked at the controls in wonder, then started the engine. "This clutch takes muscles: it's so different from my Honda."

"This is more like a real race car, with 485 horsepower at seven thousand. Just be careful, do everything slowly at first. You'll get used to it."

William started the car, but stalled while trying to back out of the parking space, as he misjudged the vast acceleration of the V-12 engine. Then he nearly hit another car in the parking lot as the tires squealed inadvertently. Gloria's nearby body and his mathematical thoughts interacted to confuse the driving lesson, and he almost quit in frustration.

"Lighten up William, and take it slowly. We have all afternoon."

"It's a great car, but, ooops, damn, I mean, it isn't as easy to control as I thought." William was becoming embarrassed by his ineptitude and tried to calm himself and move more slowly.

"Let's run down to San Gregorio beach via La Honda Road, then return through Pescadero and Alpine Road. If you can master that loop, you're all set. Turn right on Sand Hill and head west, and watch your speed: this car is a magnet for radar traps," Gloria instructed.

"I've never been to the beach here. What's it like?"

"You're kidding? This is one of the most beautiful drives in the whole state. The foothills are filled with lovely scenery and little roads, and the coast is spectacular."

"Maybe, but I'm too busy to fool around. When I'm not sleeping, I study and work."

"That mode of living has ended. William, you must learn to work smart, instead of so hard. Your brain will be much sharper if you apply it to other things every few hours to shake it up and make new neuronal connections. Now, watch out, there's a sharp left hairpin just ahead, drop down a gear."

The area where they drove was intertwined with narrow curving roads, weaving through canyons, up and over the ridges of the Coast Range, then down to the beach. Often there was a fog bank on the ocean side, so the climate shifted abruptly from one side of the hills to the other. Driving along the mountain spine, a driver could see solid fog on the ocean side and a bright sunny, perhaps smoggy, day on the inland, Silicon Valley, side. Crossing the ridge, the temperature could change twenty degrees in a few minutes. The inland side was covered with houses, and lower San Francisco Bay. The ocean side and the foothills were rural, covered in redwood and Eucalyptus trees, with farms and ranches on the flat places. Wealthy estates were discretely hidden among the trees. The contrast between the crowded life of silicon valley, and the deserted, foggy, ragged coast was extreme, yet they were less than an hour apart. Interstate 280 ran along the ridge, but other than that one big highway, most of the roads were small, their contours dictated by rugged geology and a lack of traffic. The nimble car was perfect for the many sharp turns and steep grades. Although it had six forward gears, William never made it into top gear, and was rarely in fifth, or even fourth.

He thought he had mastered control of the car, and speeded up, delighting in the acceleration, when they reached the left turn onto the Coast Highway at San Gregorio. No sooner had he stepped hard on the gas, when he had to hit the giant brakes even harder to avoid an ancient Winnebago that pulled onto the road in front of him.

"Gloria, this is too much car for me, why don't you drive us back to campus?"

"No way William. You're thinking too much about math and my body, and not enough about driving. Just focus your mind on the road, and drive with precision. Make every move exactly. Use your brain, instead of instinct. Excellent driving is a skill and you can learn it, starting right now."

William began to drive more carefully, ignoring the urge to go fast, and paying as much attention as he could to the business of driving the car on the narrow, twisting, hilly roads. The simple trip to the beach had already taken over two hours. Although William was enjoying the drive, the car, his new skills, the scenery, and Gloria's company, in the back of his mind he was regretting the time spent away from his desk.

As they neared the little town of La Honda, nestled among ancient redwood trees, Gloria started to give detailed instructions.

"Where are we going now?" he asked.

"I want to show you how to get to my house, so you can find it yourself."

They were back on La Honda Road, retracing their path. Gloria asked him to turn into a narrow, inconspicuous, unmarked gravel road which ran between two rows old Eucalyptus trees. They climbed higher for almost half a mile without seeing any signs except 'Private Road' and 'No Trespassing', then a wooden rustic house came into view atop a small hill.

"That's my house, wait 'til you see the view from the deck."

"Holy cow, do you own all this land around here," William asked in astonishment.

"Grandfather bought it in the early fifties, and thought at the time that it was way over-priced, but he loved the view. Of course, now it's worth a fortune, and the taxes are awesome. I'm counting on your clever brain to generate some fat profits to help me out."

At first the large house appeared to be rustic and simple, but on closer inspection William realized that it was fireproof construction, cleverly disguised to look like wood. The roof was actually cement tile that looked like cedar shingles. Steel beams attached the solid roof to a cement foundation. This was the first private home that William had ever seen which had a full fire sprinkler system in every room, as well as a large private water tank.

Gloria led him out onto the deck, which had a priceless view through the treetops of silicon valley with San Francisco Bay in the distance.

"Wait 'til you see the view at night. There are millions of lights out there," Gloria said as she opened a pool-side refrigerator and poured two glasses of Pejou Sauvignon Blanc.

They sat side by side on a bench admiring the view and talked about math. William asked where she had studied, amazed at her extensive knowledge. Although Gloria said that she was a citizen of Argentina, she looked as German and Aryan as anyone he had ever met. Fair skin, blue eyes, short blond hair, strong muscles and bones, and tremendous self confidence. It was almost as though she knew that she belonged to the master race, and what's more, was very proud of it.

Gloria liked talking about her grandfather, who was still alive and working. "He was a really famous scientist, in charge of the development of secret weapons. He had a huge lab underground on the Polish border with thousands of workers inside. I still can't tell you much about his discoveries, but he had a repulsine motor running in 1940. Bet you've never heard of it."

"It's some kind of anti-gravity device isn't it?"

"Right. One day I'll take you down to his lab, and you'll be amazed at the things he knows."

"How did he escape? I thought all the scientists were captured by us and by the Russians at the end of the war?"

"He and a few others, with all their notebooks, flew an experimental aircraft to Argentina in the final days. You can imagine how tricky it was to dodge the Allies as well as the remains of the Luftwaffe."

William knew enough of the history of the war to realize that her grandfather must have been quite special, as well as very resourceful, to make such a trip near the end of the war. William asked how he had managed it, but Gloria said that the details were confidential.

Gloria slowly moved closer to William, and as they sat together on a bench, their bodies touched. Her leg was casually rubbing against his. He could see her bare breasts between the buttons of her shirt, which was stretched tightly over them. William suspected that if she took a big breath, that the buttons would pop, and was tempted to ask her to try. Somehow he had the feeling that she would do it. William had never been so sexually aroused and was afraid of wetting his pants at any moment, as he had a huge erection and suspected that she had noticed it.

Just as he was about to loose control, he turned away, crossing his legs and blushing. William had experienced several particularly dreadful moments when unwanted erections had made obvious projections. Once three intoxicated girls had unmercifully teased him at a party, and had almost pulled his pants off before he could run away.

Gloria ran a hand over his back, and laughed lightly, "Don't worry I won't hurt you, I just love teasing men, and you embarrass so easily. I should let you get back to work."

"I'm sorry, please forget it, you're right, I mean, you're lovely, but I just don't know what to do. I wish I knew more about girls, I mean, what a dumb thing to say, but you're right, I really need to get to work."

"I understand, and I'm sorry that I bothered you. Next time I'll be a little bit more careful, but not too careful. You do like girls, don't you? We could have some fun together."

"Of course, I mean, I can hardly take my eyes off your body, your breasts, oops, I mean, oh damn, you'll have to excuse my stupidity. I know a lot of math, but not much else, as you've already discovered."

"Don't worry, you're just a healthy young man. Thanks for spending a few hours with me. I know you want to go back to work, but please try to insert non-mathematical breaks every hour or so: it will make your brain function much better."

"It is I who should be thanking you, for so much fun and good advice."

Gloria was lightly running a hand over his back, gently massaging it. "Is anything bothering you, I mean other than the bulge in your pants?"

Before William could think about what he was saying, he blurted out, "I don't know how to put this, and don't answer if you don't want to, but what happened to your face?"

Gloria's hand froze, its five sharp nails digging deeply into his back, causing him to wince in pain. "Sorry I scratched you, just a reflex from a bad memory. I was only three when it happened, the pain is my first memory. You should have seen my face before the plastic surgery. The bones were showing."

William turned to face Gloria and placed one of her hands in his, "Don't tell me, I'm so sorry I asked, I didn't mean to hurt you."

"No, you'll find out and I want to be the one to tell you. As I mentioned, my grandfather and his friends were brilliant scientists, and we lived in a pretty-much all-German compound in Argentina, about fifty miles outside of Buenos Aires. Degenerate schweinhunt were trying to kill the few remaining Reich heroes. They attacked our compound with fire bombs. My brother burned to death in the inferno. I can still hear his screams. Lift your eyes, take a careful look at my face, don't turn away, see it clearly, caress it with your hands, and think how it was before the attack."

Gloria was crying as she carefully placed William's hands on her face, forcing them to feel its contours on both sides. She kissed his hands as she moved them over her lips. "How could people do this?"

"The attackers were killed, but that's no consolation for my face, or my brother, is it?"

"No, not at all."

Gloria brightened and stood up, wiping her tears away,

signaling the end of the conversation. "Don't turn away when you see me from the other side, look me straight in the eye, that's all I ask."

"I will, it's the least I can do, and thank you for telling me yourself."

"Now, why don't you run the car back down to the shop. Please drive carefully, and don't think about math when you're behind the wheel of any car, especially mine!"

William drove away carefully, thinking of what he had just heard. He had studied many books on the war, but he began to realize that most of what he had read had been written from the perspective of Germany's enemies. The pro-German view, their side of the story, was not in the history books. He parked the car in its special slot, and returned the keys to Jake, who seemed to know all about the car, and probably much more about Gloria. Someday he needed to talk with Jake about her, but not now.

On the way back to his apartment, William thought more about Gloria and some of the things she had said. He now knew that with her advanced knowledge and her friendly matter-of-fact approach to life, she would be very easy to talk with about sex. William had very little experience with girls, or even with normal dating, and didn't have a clue how to find a girlfriend, or what might happen if he did. And he had never talked with a girl about sex, though he was very curious. He could probably ask Gloria questions and learn a great deal from a woman's perspective. William already had misgivings about meeting Zarlie to talk about brainwaves. What was she doing asking him to meet her at an obscure bench at night? This was exactly the kind of girl-question that he was sure that Gloria could answer in a flash.

As William removed his clothes to take a shower, he saw five small red blood spots on the back of his shirt, and when he looked in the mirror, he saw the clear half-moons that Gloria's fingernails had dug into his skin. He shuddered as he thought of the pain that she must have endured as a child. His back would heal, but her face never would.

He slapped a cup of noodles into the microwave, and buried himself in mathematical studies for hours. It was past ten by the time he felt that he had a bit of time to do something else, to take-a-break as Gloria had suggested. William surfed his favorite Japanese websites, looking for something interesting to read at his comprehension level. By chance he noticed that scientists at a Japanese observatory had posted unusual data about the spectrum of a star that they had discovered. He knew that one of the few ways that stars can be analyzed is by looking carefully at the light they emit. The light from a single star can be passed through a prism, then the rainbow from it can be examined in detail. Different kinds of stars emit different mixtures of colors of light, and this indicates the elements that make up the star as well as the star's speed of movement, relative to the earth. The speed is deduced by observing how much the entire spectrum is shifted lower toward the red end of the rainbow, or blue, toward the upper end of the rainbow. William was hooked by the article, as it combined numbers in a strange pattern, Kanji he could read easily, and the hint of a mathematical mystery.

The scientists described the star as unique, since it was the only star yet discovered with a blue-shifted spectrum. This could only mean that it was headed toward the earth, rather than away, like all the other stars, which have red-shifted spectra. William knew that the universe is supposed to be expanding, so that all the stars are moving away from each other, and away from the earth. The Japanese discovery was odd, and something about their data was vaguely familiar to William, but he couldn't put his finger on it.

William had an inspiration and as a lark, logged into YFN, and asked his personal five-dollar expert what the star data meant. Of course the YFN program didn't have a clue, but William had fun teasing it by giving it the spectrum data from Japan. As he did this, delighting in the silly astrological answers which the program returned, he suddenly remembered what the data reminded him of. Damn, Gloria was right, taking a break had jogged his brain into gear.

It took two hours of digging, but William eventually found a copy of the hydrogen bomb spectrum data that he had seen on the web a few weeks earlier. The light from the bomb blast had been measured just like star light, with a prism and careful analysis. This data was supposed to be a US defense secret, but a disgruntled worker at Sandia Laboratories had posted it on the web. It had already been wiped from most sites, but one in Russia still posted a copy, probably as much to yank Uncle Sam's chain as for any other reason. Doubtless, the Russians knew perfectly well what the spectrum from an H-blast looked like.

William was able to study columns of numbers and envision how they would look if plotted as a graph in different ways. He could see in his mind the shapes that the data could generate. He had already envisioned the Japanese blue star data as a plot on graph paper, and it was the shape of this plot that resonated with the graph he remembered, then found on the Russian site. With a bit of imagination, plots of the star data and the H-bomb data looked about the same.

William spilled his filthy tea cup while furiously copying both sets of data into a Mathematica workspace where he could manipulate them fluidly inside his computer. (Mathematica is a large computer program for analyzing complex mathematical expressions: it is supposed to be as smart as a graduate-level math student.) When the plots were superimposed inside the computer, the two data sets didn't really match as well as he had thought, but then, after hours of work, he realized that the star data had come through the earth's atmosphere, so it needed corrections for the features which had been absorbed by chemicals in the air. William shouted "Kowabunga" and jumped for the ceiling as he saw that the corrected star data was almost a perfect match to the H-bomb data, when the H-bomb data was shifted far up toward the blue end of the spectrum. This could mean that the star was traveling at 80% of the speed of light, right toward the earth. He laughed as he thought that maybe it wasn't a normal star, but an atomic-powered spaceship!

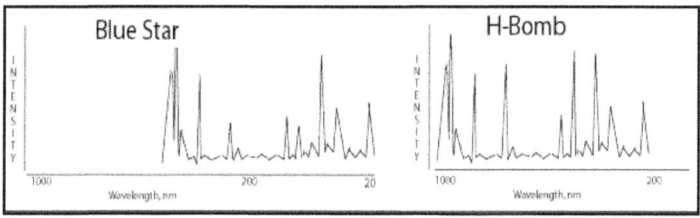

Comparison of Blue Star and H-bomb spectra

The sun was just rising as he composed an exciting email in Japanese and sent it to the observatory that had found the blue star. William wondered what they would think about his news, that they had discovered a spaceship headed to earth that would be here within his lifetime! He collapsed on his bed and was instantly asleep.

子どもたちが、ますます
かわいらしく見えるわ
ね。それに、あたたかそ
うだこと。わたし、前か
ら、青と赤の毛ふがほし
いと思っていたのですよ
と、うさぎのおくさんは言
いました。
ねずみは、とてもうれし
い気もちで、さよならを
言って、家に帰りました。

"Esteemed colleagues at Tsukuba University. Thank you for posting most important blue star spectral data on website. I have corrected it for absorptions that occurred as the star light passed through atmosphere. The data you recorded is almost exact match for the spectrum from a hydrogen bomb explosion, when the bomb data is Doppler-shifted to 80% of the speed of light. What you have discovered is not a blue star, but a hydrogen-powered space ship headed to the earth. My preliminary calculations show that it will be here in several decades. If you would please send me more data, I will refine the arrival time calculation. Congratulations on your first class discovery!"

By the time he awoke, he had missed several classes, and felt wiped out. However, when he went over his notes and re-read his email and analysis, he was as excited as he had been last night. What if the spaceship analysis were true? He would be famous! However, William had made enough bogus discoveries to realize the odds against him: the star was unusual, but not likely to be newsworthy or a spaceship. He smiled then laughed out loud when he thought of the expressions on the faces of the Japanese astronomers when they received his email. What an R.F.! Seeing their orderly world hit by this would be a hoot, like a whipped cream pie in the face!

Almost before William realized, it was Friday night and he was standing nervously next to Leland Junior's cold grey stone tomb among the dusty eucalyptus trees near the Cactus Garden. Nobody came here, especially at night. An evening with Zarlie might be fun, but he was apprehensive about the secrecy concerning their meeting and the pledge he had made never to reveal her discovery. He was also worried about what to say and do: meeting her at night was probably what other people might consider a 'date', and he wasn't quite sure what was expected of him.

Zarlie danced from the shadows of a dark path, smiling, "Hi William, hope I'm not late. I brought some great snacks from a Hungarian Deli in The City."

"No, I was early. . . it's a nice night isn't it?"

"I've been meaning to ask you about the Great Pyramid and what makes it so special. I didn't dare say anything during your lecture, but you were so excited about it."

William could talk for hours about his favorite subject, and began, "It's really different from anything else on the planet. It hasn't been reliably dated by any scrupulous technique, and almost everything about it says advanced mathematics. There are other pyramids, but they're nothing special, just poor copies. The

Egyptologists have dated its construction by jamming the G.P. into some silly royal classification scheme that any Freshman physics student could explode, so no one knows how old it is. The so-called experts think it was built maybe four thousand years ago but they're way off. My calculations, based on modern data for the rate of tectonic plate movements, give an age of about twenty to thirty thousand years, long before the last ice age ended."

"Let me explain. When modern surveyors measure the bearings of the sides of the G.P., that is the direction each side points to, they're all, north-south-east-west, close to exactly right, within about one part in ten thousand, which is extremely accurate even by modern standards. It would be really hard to make a perfectly-square building today where the lines extended from the four sides pointed exactly north, south, east and west. But the exciting thing to me is that the errors are all in the same direction. It's just as though the whole pyramid has been rotated slightly, about two and a half minutes of arc on average, which is about one thirtieth of one degree. Then when you look at the historic tectonic data that geologists are only beginning to measure accurately, you can see that the African Plate is slowly moving northeast, but on a curved path, in collision with the Eurasian plate. I traced the path back until its curve rotated about two minutes of arc. The data's rough, but between twenty to thirty thousand years ago the G.P. would have been perfectly aligned with the cardinal directions, so that's the first scientific way to tell when it was built. It's a major breakthrough, but I haven't told many people yet."

"Most people don't realize that everything on the earth's surface is moving. Right now, under our feet, we're riding on the edge of the North American plate. The Pacific Plate is just on the other side of the hills behind campus and it's moving north-northwest an average of a few centimeters each year. Normally you can't feel the movement or see it. When the Pacific Plate makes a big move all at once, like in 1906 when it moved ten feet, you get a giant earthquake at the joint between the plates."

Zarlie encouraged him to continue, "Why didn't they write something on the Pyramid to tell how great it was?"

"They did, but the Arabs ripped the white limestone casing from the surface: it was perfectly white and covered with mysterious writing, but that's all gone now, lost in the sixteenth century when the Arabs trashed Cairo and the pyramids looking for cheap stone to build harems and palaces. And by the way, the Sphinx is just as old as the G.P. They must have stood alone together on the desert for thousands of years until the Egyptians arrived."

To William's surprise, the evening was off to a good start

before he even realized it. His worries about conversation and what to do or say with Zarlie had evaporated. Somehow the conversation had moved to Watkins' Ley Lines in England, mysterious ancient straight tracks across the countryside from prehistoric times that relate to Stonehenge. They both felt that modern scientists were completely wrong in their interpretations of the lines. William had explored some of the lines and had read all the books he could find. When he told Zarlie about the theory that animals could navigate on these ancient pathways by sensing magnetic anomalies or earth currents, she exploded with excitement and went on for an hour describing how some animals can sense magnetic and electric fields, talking about electric fish and sharks' fantastic sensitivity, and the spiny-nosed mole and how it can sense electrical fields in tunnels and navigate underground. She had studied the physiology of the mole, which is also called the star-nose mole because of the strange shape of its nose. There are little finger-like organs attached to its nose, and some scientists think these are for feeling in the dark, but others have demonstrated that these sensors can detect faint electric signals and help the moles navigate and find food.

They were so busy talking that they ate too much, so a long walk seemed like a good idea. William wanted to tell her about his spaceship theory so he led Zarlie up into the hills for a clear view of the sky.

As they passed a streetlamp, the light caught her eyes and he realized that they were an unusual shade of green: they almost glowed. When he asked about them, she became embarrassed and he realized that he had said something stupid and tried to apologize. As they walked Zarlie told him that she was a Rroma, but that he, being British, would probably call her a 'Gypsy', and that among Rroma such eyes were not uncommon, but people laughed at Rroma and didn't trust them and so she didn't talk much about it.

Her real name was Czardas, which is a form of lively Hungarian Rroma music, but everyone called her Zarlie instead. William told her that he thought being a Gypsy must be cool, but as fast as he said it, he realized that he had done the wrong thing. As soon as he had uttered the word 'Gypsy', he could tell by her look that he was in trouble. "If you want to continue this conversation, please learn to use the correct word, 'Rroma', which begins with two 'Rs'."

William had no idea that the word 'Gypsy' was impolite. She explained that it was a term that rude people used when referring to Rroma. William hoped that she knew that he was trying to say that he thought her background made her more interesting rather than less.

"Are there other Rroma here? Your friends? I mean, I just never noticed, there are so many foreign students around."

"No, at least I haven't met any: I'm all alone."

"I'm sorry, what I mean is that don't you wish there were others here you could talk with in your own language?"

"Thanks, but my English is OK, so don't worry about it."

He could sense that she didn't want to talk further about her background, so maybe it was time to tell her about the blue star as they walked up through the fields to the dish, a large radio-telescope on the hills above campus. There was a warm breeze, clear sky, and the lights of Palo Alto and other cities were spread out beautifully below. They could smell the night blooming jasmine that grew over much of campus and it reminded him of grape chewing gum.

Zarlie didn't know astronomy so he told her that all the stars that can be seen are moving away because the universe is expanding. Astronomers believe this because when they look at the spectrum from each star, the lines are shifted toward the red end of the spectrum. This means that the wavelengths are longer, which is caused by the Doppler shift from stars moving away from the earth. This is the same effect as a car or train approaching and then going away: the pitch of the sound changes from high to low as the motion changes from approaching to receding. The wavelengths of the sound from the approaching train are compressed by its movement toward the listener, so its sounds are higher pitched. Then the pitch drops as the train goes away and the wavelengths expand. He made a sketch to explain it to Zarlie. Now, he told her, for the first time a star had been found with its spectral lines shifted the other way because it was coming toward the earth.

William made a sketch for zarlie on a page in his notebook, showing how starlight is passed through a prism to separate the light into its various colors. Then the strength of each wavelength, each color, can be measured and plotted on a graph. He drew the normal spectrum of a star, then how it appears to observers on earth: to these observers, all the wavelengths are shifted toward the blue end of the graph.

They could just see the star, and with some imagination, it did have a slightly bluish tint compared to the other stars, but it was faint, and it seemed to pulsate.

William asked Zarlie to tell him what his brain waves were like during all of this, but she could only say that she was so interested in hearing about the odd star that she hadn't been trying to read his waves.

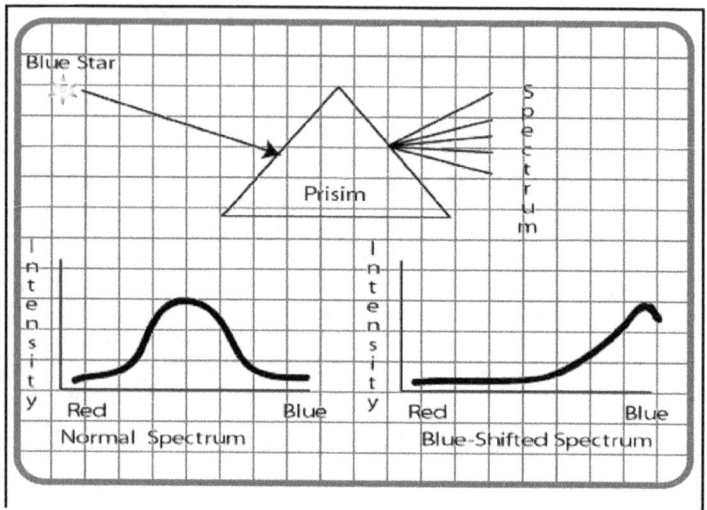

William's notebook sketch for Zarlie

William told her that his calculations showed that what they were actually seeing was a huge spaceship headed for earth, at close to the speed of light. She grabbed his hand and blurted out "We must warn the world about this".

He thought to himself, "Talk about a dumb idea", but when her hand held his it was like an electric shock: he hardly knew what to say. William recovered by suggesting that if she would teach him how to read minds, or even to feel the waves from them, that he would write a paper on the spaceship theory and publish it on the internet.

Later William learned a little bit about brain wave transmission when they went down to the Student Union for coffee. A pretty girl was sitting nearby, wearing a thin, almost transparent, white blouse. There was a sweater on her table that she could have worn if she had been cold. Zarlie told him to glance once at the girl and fix her image clearly in his mind, then look away. Zarlie quietly told him to think the sexiest thoughts that he could imagine about the girl, but not to look at her; he was to particularly try to imagine her cold and without any clothes. William was amazed at the suggestion, but did what he was told. After several minutes the girl nervously put on her sweater and looked around apprehensively. She had unconsciously felt his thoughts, at least that's what Zarlie said had just happened. Zarlie explained that the girl probably felt uncomfortable, but didn't know that it was William undressing her in his mind that made her feel nervous.

From a scientific viewpoint, he couldn't tell if it was baloney, because he didn't dare walk up to the girl and ask questions, and how could she answer if her action had been a reaction to an unconscious feeling. When he considered that Zarlie's ideas about brain waves might be a form of mental illness, he was even less convinced. Still, it was thought-provoking and he wondered how it could be tested: maybe they could devise a controlled experiment and prove or disprove the existence of brain waves. Remembering his earlier thoughts about witchcraft he realized that if he had just done what Zarlie said that he did, in a way he had just put a mild spell or charm on the sweater girl. If a normal person could do this, with essentially no training, what could an expert do after years of study? And, holy cow, what if Zarlie had put a curse on the girl, while he actually did nothing. Devising a scientifically valid experiment was going to be quite hard if they both participated.

As a sudden thought, William asked Zarlie if she had ever looked through a microscope at living cells and identified the mechanisms that sent and received brain waves. In reply, Zarlie invited William to meet her in a bio lab where they could watch living cells early on Sunday morning.

Just as they parted for the night, Zarlie told him to look up articles on panspermia. She joked that all the talk about stars and spaceships had reminded her of another idea that proper scientists avoided. Panspermia is the theory that advanced civilizations on distant planets have scattered DNA throughout the universe. Sometimes the DNA lands on a fertile planet, like Earth, and life based on the DNA develops. The reason that at least a few scientists are interested in this theory is that it is the only clear explanation why the DNA in all Earth's plants, animals, bacteria, and viruses is essentially the same. It's all made with the same four chemical bases, and it's all organized according to the same rules. The official Darwinian view, that life on Earth developed randomly, can't begin to explain why trees, bugs, mice and people all have similar DNA. Until recently scientists had claimed that DNA could never travel through space: it would be destroyed by the vacuum, the cold, and the radiation. But a mathematician had just shown that DNA molecules could easily fit inside carbon Fullerene spheres, where they would be protected until they landed in a good environment. So far nobody has found one of these spheres, but that doesn't stop the speculation. Zarlie said they were having a huge argument about it in her advanced genetics class, with the Prof trying to defend the Darwinian view against the students.

Zarlie ran off, shouting over her shoulder, "Maybe the spaceship people are coming to see how their DNA is growing." William was speechless.

Saturday morning found William at VPA, putting in time on the astrology project, trying to make sense of the massive data collection on almost a thousand CD-ROMs. Gloria wandered into his office for an informal chat. Things were going well, and she was at ease. No one else was around, so he sensed that this might be a good time to ask personal questions.

"Gloria, I know so little about girls, and well, you know so much, that, can I, well, can I ask you how they work and I mean, how they think about things?"

"Should I tell you about the birds and the bees and how babies are made? Want to play doctor? Want to take your pants off? Or mine?" Gloria moved over to him and started to undo his belt, but he turned away blushing.

"No, I mean not now, things happen and I can't figure them out, and I wondered if you could explain them?"

"OK, give me a specific example and I'll try to help. I know where you're coming from. Most guys don't even know enough to ask, so you're already on the right track. What's bothering you?"

"I've met this gypsy, er, Rroma, Zarlie Istvan. She's made a discovery and she's very nervous about it and swore me to secrecy so I can't tell you about her research. But she asked me to meet her last night and we wandered all over the campus and talked about weird science, and now she's asked me to meet her tomorrow morning to look through a microscope. I'm worried that maybe I'm getting too involved with her, I mean, I think about her all the time and it's distracting me from work."

"What's she look like?"

"Look like? Well, she's not beautiful, I mean, nothing like you, er, excuse me, but she's unusual. She wears strange clothes and walks fluidly, like she's gliding around things, like a dancer, and talks, well, she's Hungarian, so her accent is odd."

"But what does she look like? Her eyes, her figure, her breasts, her lips, her smile, her hair?"

"Her eyes are a really strange shade of green, like a cat's: they almost glow. She's trim and athletic, but she wears so many clothes that I can't tell you anything other than that she seems, well, normally-proportioned. Her hair's long and black."

"I asked you because I wanted to see how much you had noticed, to gauge your interest in her, to get a feel for your attachment to her."

"Attachment, I just met her, am I missing something?"

"Yes, you have a pretty clear idea where you and I stand with respect to one another: we have a clean relationship, kind of like teacher and student, or big sister and little brother: no problems either way. But you think you have no connection to this gypsy, yet you can describe her quite well. I'll bet you can't describe our receptionist as well, even though you're seen her a dozen times. You don't even know what color our receptionist's hair is!"

"Maybe, but Zarlie is very exciting intellectually: we have so many weird interests in common, and she's really sharp in the biological sciences. What should I do?"

"Shit, you're so naïve, it's time to bail before you get in trouble."

"It can't be that bad. You're exaggerating."

"Tell you what. You're a scientist, so run a simple experiment. Ignore her for a week and see what happens: see if you forget her, and see if she comes after you."

"But she's just trying to be friends, to talk about scientific stuff."

"She's razor-sharp behind those soft eyes. Those thieving gypsies don't miss anything. Damn, I wish our ancestors had killed more of them, but we'll talk about that later. I'll give you my instant summary. She's poor, she's on scholarship, she's got a criminal background, a forged passport, and a dubious green card. So now she meets an interesting guy whom she would be delighted to spend forever with, so she has a problem. How to clean up her act and hook you. That's the skinny, and watch if it doesn't play out just like that."

"How can you be so mean, you haven't even met her."

"Write those words down this instant, and nail the paper to your wall! You're already defending her like some precious idol, and you don't even realize it. Write! Now! Dammit!"

William, shaking from the verbal attack, grabbed a sheet of paper, and began to write, as Gloria hovered over him correcting errors, and making sure that he had it exactly right. '*How can you be so mean, you haven't even met her.*'

"William, I'm sorry I went off the deep end, but please take my advice and drop her, cold turkey, don't even call to send your excuses. I know this seems extreme, but you asked for advice from someone who knows the score, and you're getting it. Now let's pin that paper on the wall right next to your computer so you don't forget it."

Gloria moved to his side and rubbed his shoulder. He reached up and patted her hand, holding it for a moment.

"You'll find someone else, someone who is even more exciting."

"Thanks, I had no idea of what I was getting into."

"Please come to me with your problems, and I'll try to help." Gloria brightened and ended the conversation with, "Hey, girls are something I know a lot about, but math, that's your department, so it's time to flog those numbers! I'll send out for lunch around the fountain at one?"

"Great, thanks for helping me."

As Gloria walked away William tried to go back to work, but he couldn't stop thinking about the violent conversation they had just had. She could be so nice, but then change in an instant to such a mean person. He had innocently hoped to receive an unbiased answer to a simple question, but now realized that Zarlie's Gypsy background made it impossible for Gloria to discuss her rationally.

Chapter 6
Egyptology & The Lab

William had no intention of following Gloria's advice. He also realized that further talk with Gloria about Zarlie would be a bad idea. He liked being with Zarlie and didn't see what harm a visit to the lab Sunday morning could do.

As they entered the lab building, Zarlie made him put on a long coat, gloves, paper booties, and a disposable face mask, before they passed through an air-lock. William hadn't realized that he was going into a live animal lab, and that precautions had to be taken to prevent cross-infections between the animals and the researchers.

Zarlie led him to a Nikon teaching microscope which had two sets of binocular eyepieces. "You look through that side and don't touch anything, and I'll drive. Is your side in focus?"

William was fascinated by all the equipment, especially the computerized machinery humming away, as well as by the cages of animals, mostly rats and mice from what he could see. He looked through the eyepieces at the specimen Zarlie had prepared.

"What are all those things wiggling around? What are we seeing?"

"It's a piece of living mouse brain, and I've stained it slightly to increase the contrast. You're looking at live brain cells as they move around normally. Your brain cells would look just the same, if we could peek inside your head."

"They're so busy. I thought that brains just sat still and everything that happened was chemical and electronic, like a biological computer."

"The life sciences aren't so neat and tidy. The chemical and electronic levels are way down below what we're seeing, but this is where research starts, at the cellular level. Each of those cells is a complete living organism, eating, growing, reproducing, and maybe thinking."

"Cells don't think, do they, I mean they're mechanical, just copying their DNA, and dividing and all that stuff?"

"That's high school bio. Look for yourself. Where's the dividing line between the nuclear DNA and the mouse's thoughts about the cat he sees sleeping next to the cheese? Do you see any divisions, any place the picture of the cat is stored?"

"No, I mean it's not that simple, is it? Where are the brain wave senders and receivers?"

"When we find that, we'll bag the Nobel for sure!"

"Hey, can you detect brainwaves from animals? I mean, you just said that our brain tissue is just like this mouse's, so if there are sender and receiver features in our brain cells, then other animals must have the same capability that we have."

"I never thought to look, I don't think I've ever heard an animal."

"I saw a cat over by the door, let's go listen to it."

They went to a cage where a cat was snoozing peacefully. Zarlie opened the door, removed the cat and petted its soft fur. A very friendly ginger cat started to purr softly.

"Put it's head next to yours: maybe the cat signals are very faint, or on a different frequency or something, so you normally don't hear them," William suggested.

Zarlie gently pressed her head against the cat's and concentrated hard, with her eyes closed. "Maybe I can feel something, or maybe I'm just telling myself that I can."

"Saint Francis was supposed to be able to talk to animals. People think that's just a Bible story, but maybe he really could, maybe his brain was extra sensitive to animal communication wavelengths?"

"Then George Orwell's story, ANIMAL FARM, could be true, with all the animals talking to each other," Zarlie joked, as she put the cat back in its cage.

"Yes, and then pigs will rule the world and we'll all be slaves, feeding them! So what else is in the mouse's brain besides those cells we were looking at?" William wondered aloud.

"Nothing, except blood that flows around the body, bringing up oxygen and food, and carrying away the waste products, and some liquids between the cells. That's it."

"Then if there are a physical receiver and transmitter, they must be in the cells, because there isn't anywhere else to put them," William exclaimed, "we've just been looking at them, but we haven't seen them."

"You're talking about a basic cellular property that hasn't been uncovered by the thousands of people doing cellular research all over the world. It seems a bit far-fetched," Zarlie muttered to herself.

"Maybe that's because we, and they, don't know what to look for. Maybe it's on another dimension, in a hyperplane that hasn't been explored. That's math talk, but what I'm trying to say is that maybe brainwave communication is not an electromagnetic process like radio and TV but something different and undiscovered. I was just reading an article about gravity fields, how gravity is so weak compared to electromagnetic and nuclear fields, and how maybe gravity is really strong but we have looked in the wrong places to measure it."

"So where should we be looking for it?" Zarlie was puzzled and trying to understand where William was going with his line of thought, and she had no idea what a hyperplane was.

"What the scientist in the article postulated is that when we move to small sizes, much smaller than a millimeter, that maybe other dimensions open up. Normally we sense only three dimensions, but there may be more on extremely small distance scales, and his idea is that gravity is a big player in the other dimensions. He gave an example that from far away a straw looks like a line with just two dimensions, length and width, but when we move up close, we see that it has thickness, a third dimension, that we didn't see from far away. Somehow we need to look at the cells in a new way in order to see the receivers and transmitters. Probably people can't see in this new dimension with their eyes, but we could build equipment that could visualize in this new dimension."

"Then maybe we're talking about a new kind of radiation, signals that only living cells generate and receive?"

"Right, and you were born with a really sensitive receiver in your head, and probably a great transmitter too," William added.

Zarlie became serious and turned away.   "William, just think back a few hundred years, to Ben Franklin's time, when people thought that electricity was something that made sparks in dry weather, and then Ben and his kite showed that lightning was the same stuff. Those guys didn't have a clue what they were messing with. They could have been killed."

"Yet two hundred years later we have computers, telephones, TV, lights, radar, microwaves, satellites and spaceships, all based on a detailed knowledge of electricity."

"Could we have stumbled onto something as important as electricity, but that nobody's ever seen?" Zarlie wondered.

"People have seen it, at least manifestations from it, they just don't realize it! Maybe all the ESP stuff, your brainwaves, the sense of fear, poltergeists, dowsing, remote-viewing, witchcraft, and all those things that people experience but don't understand, are aspects of the same basic natural phenomenon, Living Waves!" William exclaimed with excitement.

"Not so fast, those are different, they're abnormal, they're not, or at least I think they're not, part of this. We have to be very careful." William's sudden insight had caused a sharp reaction inside Zarlie, almost a mild panic attack. She had always been extremely careful to hide her ability to cast spells and detect brainwaves: she knew that most people thought that anyone with these powers was a witch or at least a mental case that belonged in an asylum. Zarlie began to fear that this new line of research, and William's involvement with it, might lead to her unmasking. What if they published results? People would want demonstrations and she would immediately be labeled a nutcase or worse.

William continued, he was too excited to notice the change in Zarlie's demeanor. "It's hard to believe that we're standing here talking about founding an entirely new branch of science, something that we could spend the rest of our lives working on: this is incredibly important. Wait 'til we publish: people will be blown away."

"I don't think publication is in the cards, at least not for a very long time." Zarlie turned to William and took his hands in hers. She was nervous, almost whispering. "William, there's a lot you don't know about me and I'm not going to tell you, so please don't pry. I'm an orphan, from an extremely poor and difficult background. You have no idea what it was like growing up as a Rroma orphan, passed from relative to relative like a bag of trash. If I weren't so damn smart, I never would have escaped, I'd be working as a whore, or a sex-slave, but most likely I'd be dead by now. As for this research, I'm sorry, but I need to move quietly, and alone."

William was almost overcome by the surprising pain and sincerity in her voice. "I gave you my word that I'd keep your secrets and I meant it, especially now. I'd really like to help you in some way. I'd do anything, I just don't know what to do."

"Thanks for the great ideas, and for being a good friend. I'll keep in touch, quietly. I have to be careful." She released his hands and walked away from a very puzzled young man.

As William slowly bicycled back across campus, he wondered about Zarlie, and about the abrupt and emotional ending to their conversation. Something was very wrong with her. He felt drawn to help, but didn't have a clue as to what to do. He thought that she was almost crying for help, but couldn't ask for it. One thing that he knew definitely was that the promise he had lightly made, to keep quiet about Living Waves and her brainwave sensitivity, was far more serious than he had imagined, and he was now more interested in her than ever.

William believed that he could solve the mystery of the pyramids, a straight math problem that would yield to analysis once he had sufficient and accurate data, but developing a whole new branch of science was an undertaking on a completely different scale. It was a life-long commitment to the pursuit of knowledge, with incredible value for mankind. Exactly the kind of challenge that the major scientists in history had surmounted. Zarlie could go down in the record books beside his heroes. She could easily be as important as Madame Curie or Einstein. William felt that he was partially the co-discoverer of Living Waves, and that he could do a tremendous amount to help Zarlie with her research in their new field. He could devise mathematically-correct tests of their theories and perform extensive analyses on the data if he had the chance. As William bicycled slowly he realized that he was on the verge of tears, torn by his confusion over Zarlie and the mysteries of her condition.

Tuesday afternoon Gloria wandered into William's office and casually asked how he was doing and if Zarlie had contacted him yet. He was about to lie, but decided that he would learn more by being truthful. He told Gloria about going to the lab, and that Zarlie hadn't contacted him since. This didn't seem to bother Gloria: perhaps she had known that he wouldn't really take her advice.

"It's time to leave her to her own problems. Hey, when I look around this room, all I see is sand and pyramids and old Egyptian stuff. Are you a closet anthropologist or something?"

William noticed the abrupt change in subject matter. He would have liked to talk about Zarlie, but realized that it wasn't something that Gloria wished to discuss, and of course, he loved to talk about the pyramids. "It seems that I tell you everything, even my deepest secrets. Someday I'm going to solve the mystery of the Great Pyramid, it's that one in the big picture. It's completely different from all the others: it's mathematically perfect, I just know it."

"Where's the secret? It looks like the others. What am I missing?"

"The secret is in the dimensions, and how they relate to math. Lots of the dimensions fall on the numbers of the Fibonacci Series, which can't be an accident, and many are factors in the mystical number 5040. The height is exactly Pi times the circumference of the base. There are loads of unusual math relationships. As soon as I've saved enough money, I'm going there to measure everything with differential GPS equipment. That thing was built as a monument to knowledge by an ancient civilization, long before the Egyptians lived in the area."

"Well, if you'll pardon advice from an outsider, I don't think you're on the right track. If I were some ancient smart-ass, I wouldn't put my secrets on the outside, where the sand and locals could mess them up. I'd hide my secrets deep inside, maybe in the dimensions of interior features. Aren't there some strangely-shaped galleries and shafts deep inside, with lots of odd stones and shapes. That sounds like a better place to hide a secret, if you ask me."

"That's a very good point, and one that I hadn't appreciated. The Grand Gallery is unusual, maybe the strangest ancient room on the planet. And it's more or less intact, I could go there and check it out right now."

"No way, you're going to get my profit level up before anything else. Then you can take a vacation and play with the stones."

"In the meantime, I'll bet I can find some photos on the web or in the library."

"Good, and thanks for goosing Jake with your market research idea. He's already found some interesting correlations among our customers and we've started shifting our advertising to focus more on the best targets. You don't need to make big breakthroughs: lots of little ones add up nicely over time, so keep up the good work."

"Thanks for the encouragement, I haven't really done anything yet."

"Yes you have, and to prove it, I'm going to set your starting salary at fifty dollars an hour and let you invest it all in our private bonds, which pay twelve percent. That'll start your fortune growing, and keep you from being tempted to spend money on silly things like young women."

"Wow, thanks and thanks again, that'll be great. I was going to ask you about money and I don't have a clue about investments."

This simple bit of praise encouraged William to work hard, digging into Gloria's mountain of data with enthusiasm. He laughed to himself as he thought that compared to his interests in Living Waves, pyramid secrets, and blue-stars, it should be trivial to massage this pile of crap into something useful.

As a start he would write a shell-script, which is a kind of computer program that uses other computer programs to do the actual work: this is analogous to a symphony conductor leading his musicians. The conductor doesn't play an instrument or make music himself, but he controls the people who do. This script would direct a big computer to search all the text in the mountain of customer data for key words, those words that appeared the most often. William knew that probably some words would be much more common than others. He would skip all the short ones, and focus on the big and hopefully important words. This is one of the basic techniques used in code-breaking. He would begin with a frequency analysis, to see how often each word was used, and let the programs run all night, scanning through the back-up copy of all the data that lived on the server farm. Then tomorrow, he would look for patterns in the text adjacent to the key words, and so begin to see how the words were used.

Hours later, when the script was debugged and churning through the data, he knew that he had done a good day's work and headed home.

The next afternoon, he visited Professor Mackie, a Scottish lady who had the distinction of being the only professor of Egyptology on campus. Although there were no students of Egyptology, she taught Arabic and Middle Eastern Studies to keep her position. Her office was in the dusty old museum, with giant pictures of desert ruins on her walls and hieroglyphics everywhere. Statues and pieces of rock, as well as maps and aerial photos of Egyptian sites were piled on the floor and tables in her office. As William entered he was very interested in finding detailed pictures of the Grand Gallery and the innards of the Great Pyramid.

She greeted him with curiosity, as few students came to her with Egyptology questions, especially such bizarre theories as William had proposed. "Good Afternoon William, what crazy ideas bring you here today?"

"I need detailed pictures of the innards of the Great Pyramid. I'm sure the ancients encoded mathematical secrets in the interior dimensions."

"The Egyptians didn't seem to do that in any of the other old structures. Perhaps you're on the wrong track, again?"

"The Egyptians didn't build the G.P., it was there long before they arrived."

"That's ridiculous, many scientists have deduced its exact age through carbon dating the relics nearby."

"Carbon dating using nearby artifacts is a joke. It's just like picking up a cigarette butt next to Westminster Abbey, measuring the C-13 ratio in the tobacco, then proclaiming that the ancient structure was built last year." William knew that carbon-dating, which was invented in the forties, is a technique to measure the relative abundance of two forms of carbon in a sample, and that the C-13 isotope is unstable. The idea was that living creatures breathe in air which contains both kinds of carbon. After the living organism dies, the C-13 isotope slowly disintegrates. By measuring how much C-13 remains in the sample, a scientist can calculate how long ago the sample died. This works for animals and plants, anything that used to be alive.

"You don't understand anything about the careful procedures

used in archeological dating," she replied, trying to keep her voice under control.

"But you have to admit that you don't have one shred of scientific evidence dating the actual stones in the G.P., and when my math shows how sophisticated the builders of it were, you'll need to push the construction date back thousands of years."

"Then why didn't your smart builders leave something else for us to study? Why just one monument?"

"They did the Sphinx too. Haven't you read Professor Schoch's analysis of the weathering of the stones that comprise the Sphinx? They prove that it's at least three times older than your official dates. He used well-documented water erosion data to date it scientifically, instead of vague conjectures."

"I have read his paper as a matter of fact, and it's all hogwash: it doesn't fit with anything else in the area."

"It fits perfectly with my pyramid thesis."

"Thesis is the operative word in that statement."

"I'm onto a fact, an incontrovertible fact, that will prove the age of the G.P. exactly, as soon as I get the math working. Last week I told you about tectonic plate data and how twenty to thirty thousand years ago the sides of the G.P. would have been perfectly aligned with the earth's rotational axis. So that's one clear and solid scientific way to date the GP. Now here's another. You know the story that the builders aligned the pyramid, by building the descending passage so that they could watch the star Thuban shine down the tunnel. Well, when you move the construction date way back and rotate the pyramid so that it's correctly aligned with earth's true north, then the Descending Passage inside the G.P. no longer points toward Thuban. That star couldn't have been used during construction to locate true north because Thuban's position in the sky twenty thousand years ago was far away from earth's north rotational pole."

Professor Mackie was exercising great patience as she quietly listened to William's excited voice.

"At first I thought that I'd made a big mistake with the tectonic data, but then I read about the cycles in the precession of the earth's rotational axis. The earth's axis points to loads of different places in the sky, but it moves in a very predictable manner, and you can calculate exactly where it was pointing at any given time. There's a 41,000 year cycle in the axis obliquity, or tilt, with a variation of over two degrees, so the Tropics of Cancer and Capricorn move up and down on the earth, they aren't constants. And there's a 100,000 year cycle in the eccentricity of the earth's orbit around the sun. Some equations also consider Lunar nutation with a period of 18.6 years, solar nutation with a period of half a year, and even Chandler

Wobble which has a period of 428 days. All these cycles are caused by gravitational interactions between the earth's rotation and the sun, moon, and planets. These cycles also drive the occurrence of ice ages on earth. Indeed, ice age research papers are where I found all this information. To my point, all of these cycles have an effect on where the earth's rotational axis points in the sky. The net result is that the axis moves through the sky approximately in a circle, whose radius now is 23 degrees, 27 minutes, and the circle completes every 25,920 years. When we're lucky, the axis points to a star, which makes navigation easy. For example, now it points almost directly at Polaris, which we have called the North Star for the past 500 years. When your Egyptians were active in 2800BC, the axis pointed close to Thuban, which is also called Alpha Draconis. You can verify the precession yourself by going to Paris and looking at the celestial map that the French ripped off the ceiling of the Temple at Dendara. It shows the precession of the equinoxes for thousands of years. You could date that temple just by looking at its celestial map."

"Well, there are certainly more conventional ways to date Dendara, and we know they used a written map for that painting, and that temple was rebuilt many times."

"Right, they had to rebuild it as the axis precessed, just like the various iterations of the Karnak temples. They were trying to align their buildings with the stars, so they must have eventually discovered that the stars appear to move, even though it's really the earth's axis that is changing. The axis only moves one degree every seventy-two years, but in a millennium that's fifteen degrees, so it's a big difference when you're trying to sight the summer solstice shining down a long narrow temple axis. But let me continue with my theory. The descending passage under the G.P. slopes down at 26 degrees, 17 minutes. It's like a long tube, 350 feet long, and if you're at the bottom, the angle of view toward the sky is only thirty-six minutes, about half a degree, wide. And you know the exterior opening of the shaft is accurate within a fiftieth of an inch, incredibly precise stone work. The Latitude of the G.P. is now 29 degrees, 58 minutes, 51 seconds. However, continental drift is changing the latitude since the African plate is going north and east, so we need to correct the latitude to what it was long ago, around twenty-nine degrees depending on the date. So the difference between the angle of the descending passage and the north celestial pole is about three degrees. We need to find a star near the north celestial pole that could have been used for the construction alignment a long time ago."

Professor Mackie tapped her fingers on her desk, "William, where is this going?"

"Please, just a minute more. I found the star, and what's

more important, I found the date. 24,000 years ago Kochab was exactly in position near the north celestial pole. It was the only bright star even close, so building the descending passage while watching Kochab's inferior culmination, where the bottom of the star just grazes the edge of the opening, each night would have been perfect. Right now, I'm using a planetarium program for the star data, but it's only approximate so I don't want to say anything publicly until I have this right. I've sent for a book with the detailed astronomical equations and when it arrives I'll get the exact year when the difference between Kochab and the north celestial pole allowed a match to the adjusted pyramid latitude. That's when the G.P. was built, about 24,000 years ago. Everything fits, the tectonics, the stars, the alignments, and the date!"

"William, there were no civilizations that long ago building anything of consequence."

"Not true. What about the elaborate underwater city off the coast of Yonaguni Island in Japan? Check it out on the web. It must have been built during the ice ages when the sea was a hundred meters lower. It's beautiful, showing the skills of a highly-developed civilization, and it was probably exactly on the Tropic of Cancer back then. And recently the site of Angkor Wat in Cambodia has been dated to 10,500 BC because it's laid out as an exact match to the constellation Draco at that time, even though the temples on the site currently are only a thousand years old. And there's the stuff around Lake Titicaca high in the Andes that could be really ancient too."

Professor Mackie shook her head in amazement. "You've been reading the wrong kind of books and not enough scholarly material."

"How about Heliopolis? Even Egyptologists know it was a big center of astronomical knowledge long before the other pyramids were built, long before 4000 BC. The Pharohs didn't suddenly wake up one day and start building: their ancestors had been studying the stars and developing a sophisticated written language for millennia before them. You can see the inscription in the Temple of Abydos, where it says that the Followers of Horus, the mystery teachers of heaven, lived in Heliopolis."

Professor Mackie smiled with resignation, "Will you let me review your er, scientific paper, describing all this before you publish? I might be able to save you some embarrassment."

"Sure. I know re-dating the G.P. construction will be a big shock to Egyptologists, but wait until I get busy with my math on the inner pyramid details and what they really mean. Oh, I also want to ask you about the Postglacial Climactic Optimum, that's when the climate was ideal with much more rain and warmth, around 5000

B.C., about when your Egyptians started to flourish. I found it in the ice age research papers. No wonder your guys could afford to build all those temples. Plenty of food for the slaves and builders in those days. Do Egyptologists know about that?"

"I've never heard of such a thing. What does it have to do with Egyptians?"

"It caused rain over much of North Africa: the countryside was green and fertile then and the underground aquifers were filling up. Ever since, Egypt has been drying out, turning into desert, and Egyptian civilization has been tanking. It's all math and cycles. Don't Egyptologists read climatological studies?"

"William, some of us actually do understand math, and are quite capable of doing our own research. Email me the climate references. I'll let you know what I think after I've read them. At least your climate ideas may make sense."

"You'll be surprised. Bet you could match the rise and fall of Egypt to long term changes in the weather."

"Now let's calm down and talk about facts instead of guess-work. Did my picture of the side of the Great Pyramid help your presentation?"

"I appreciate your help, but the projector died when I was half-way through my pitch, then the prof cut me off before I could finish. The Math Department doesn't have the money anyway."

"How can I help you today? What's this about interior photographs?"

"My idea is that ancient pre-Egyptian people built the G.P. and that they left their signature in the numbers that we can find by measuring it. Well, the outside is weathered and worn, and no matter how carefully I measure it, we'll never see it as it was originally built. But, the inside is almost like it was when it was new, so I want to focus my efforts on what I can measure inside."

"Have you read SECRETS OF THE GREAT PYRAMID, and Tompkins' descriptions of the interior?"

"Twice, from beginning to end, what a great book."

"Well, I wouldn't go quite that far, but for your purposes, he does have a lot of information as to what's inside."

"I know, but it's all sloppy. I need finely detailed pictures of the stones on the walls, the angles, and the joints, the things that can be measured precisely."

"Unfortunately, most of the detailed measurements were done in the nineteenth century with the equipment current at that time. Researchers seem to have lost interest in measuring the G.P. in the twentieth century."

"It's a shame because we have such accurate equipment now.

I'm working part-time to earn enough money to mount an expedition to Egypt so I can measure everything carefully with differential GPS equipment."

"Have you given any thought as to how you will gain permission from the Egyptian authorities to do that?"

"Er, no, I mean, I intend to buy the measurement equipment and do the work myself."

"When you get closer to planning your trip, you and I need to have a serious talk. Permissions are not easily obtained, even for serious work, and permission to investigate unconventional ideas is nearly impossible to obtain."

"You mean that I need to disguise my true purpose, or something like that."

"Yes, you need to find some other reason to go wandering around with GPS equipment, which won't work inside the G.P. anyway. You'll need laser rangefinders, computerized leveling equipment, and things like that for checking the interior details precisely. Find a current book on how Engineers survey mines and tunnels: your needs are much the same."

"It seems that every way I turn there are difficulties that I hadn't expected."

"That's what happens when you have original and unconventional ideas. You are just beginning to see how knowledge advances, and how major new facts are gathered."

"You're right, and the bigger the problems, the more valuable the solutions will be."

"Precisely. Now, since you are so interested in pyramid mysteries, let me introduce you to a relatively recent discovery. This problem is only about ten years old, so it's almost brand new, in both our time frames."

Professor Mackie then described an expedition by German engineers who sent a small crawling robot up a long ventilation shaft, a shaft which started in the Queen's chamber, deep inside the G.P.

"Of course it wasn't really a ventilation shaft, because the bottom end, in the Queen's Chamber, had been sealed by the builders until Victorian times. In 1872 a British engineer, Waynman Dixon, hired a carpenter to cut through the stone sealing the bottom end of the shaft. Even though the walls are composed of giant stone blocks, the rock was only five inches thick at the bottom of the shaft. He found the right place by tapping on the walls of the Queen's Chamber until he heard a hollow sound. After opening the shaft, he measured the location and cut a hole on the opposite wall and found another shaft entrance, directly across the room from the first. Both shafts were empty except for a few bits of wood and stone, which have been lost, so the shafts can't be dated with modern tools."

The Queen's Chamber, showing corbelled niche in the center and the robot hole on the right-hand wall

She then showed William the videotape of a television program about the expedition: it included footage that the robot's video camera had made. The robot had crawled up the dusty shaft and then come to a door --- a door inside a tunnel that was only ten inches square. The tunnel was cut through huge carefully-placed stones. Someone had gone to incredible trouble to make this shaft.

The film showed one of the German engineers reaching up the shaft to retrieve the little robot, named UPUAUT. It had become stuck and the only way to remove it was to pull on its cable, causing a big crash deep in the shaft. William loved the clever robot; it was like a little tank. It had rubber treads on the top and bottom, so it worked its way along by pulling on the ceiling and the floor. From the sketch shown on the video, much of the shaft went up at about 32 degrees, which was quite steep, especially when dragging a long bundle of wires behind.

The footage from the little camera on the robot showed it creeping along the shaft, which had a sandy floor most of the way. Then it came to a step in the floor, about an inch or two high, which the robot slowly climbed over by lowering its top treads, then the walls changed to smooth stone, a completely different kind of rock, polished and finished. The shaft was accurately square and went straight, diagonally, through huge stones.

William was fascinated by Professor Mackie's description of the stonework surrounding the tunnel. The builders had used sloping stones for the floor of the shaft, then made matching stones with an upside down 'U'-shaped channel in the bottom to form the walls and the ceiling of the shaft. It must have taken amazing skill to do this, and to fit these sloping stones into the overall construction of the GP, which was made from huge blocks. Whoever built the shaft had lots of time and skill. Even today, with air drills and modern equipment, people would have trouble duplicating this, and of course the big question was: why do it?

The most amazing thing about the whole video was at the end, about 200 feet up the shaft, when the robot reached a solid limestone slab across the shaft. It blocked the passage and had two small copper pieces, like handles, or locks. One copper piece had fallen onto the floor. On a lower corner of the slab there was a triangular cutoff, just inviting a fiber-optic probe like an endoscope, a miniature medical camera on a long cable, to poke through and see the other side. What a great adventure, and to think these Engineers were so close to finding the secret purpose of this shaft. From the sketch they showed, it looked like they were 80% of the way from the Queen's Chamber to the surface of the pyramid. Perhaps the slab was a door that could be raised by a better-equipped robot. These Engineers could have built one, but they weren't allowed to investigate further because they showed their video on television, in violation of their agreement with the Egyptian officials.

Professor Mackie explained that the Egyptian government had blocked further exploration because they didn't want foreigners to make discoveries in the G.P., so the video was the only thing scientists had. The Egyptian government didn't have much money and it could barely cope with all the tourists who visited the country. There was zero support from the US government for Egyptology and few students were interested now. She mentioned that the only Professor who made money from Egyptology was Elizabeth Peters: Mrs. Peters wrote mystery stories set in Egypt.

Later, when William reached his computer at home, he searched the internet for "UPUAUT" and found a site with detailed information on the robot and its journey. The Engineers speculated that they saw the back of a door but had no idea what was on the other side.

More than ever William thought that there was something weird about the G.P., and that most people had completely missed the meaning of it. Then he ran into a quote from Professor Carl Sagan, discussing the search for extra-terrestrial radio signals:

"We are again seeking messages from an ancient and exotic civilization, this time hidden from us not only in time, but in space. If we should receive a radio message from an extraterrestrial civilization, how could it possibly be understood? Extraterrestrial intelligence will be elegant, complex, internally consistent, and utterly alien. Extraterrestrials would, of course, wish to make a message sent to us as comprehensible as possible. But how could they? Is there in any sense an interstellar Rosetta Stone? We believe there is a common language that all technical civilizations, no matter how different, must have. That common language is science and mathematics. The laws of Nature are the same everywhere."

William just knew that the secrets of the G.P. must have something to do with math!

Chapter 7
Alienology And The Jar

Next Sunday, William was walking through a parking lot, a block off University Avenue in Palo Alto, headed toward Fry's computer store, when he spotted Zarlie sitting on a quiet bench under a tree. The bench was in a small park next to a modern office building and it was surrounded by roses and camellias. She was drinking coffee and reading a biology book as he approached. "Hi Zarlie, how's the world of Living Waves?"

"Some progress. Actually I was working on it as you approached."

"Does that book describe living waves?"

"No, the book's a prop. Do you know what's in the building behind me?"

"Yes, it's the local outpost of the Alienologists."

"Right. I come here occasionally to listen to brain waves when those creeps pass nearby: they're the easiest people I've found to read. It's good exercise. I try to see how far away I can detect one of them coming."

"I wonder if it's true that they get a twenty-five grand bonus for snaring a new member?"

"They take all your money if you join, so it makes sense, but I don't know why anyone would sign-up."

"Have you learned more about how living waves work?"

"I didn't want to tell you when we were in the lab, but while we were there, I could just begin to understand a few of your thoughts: to feel them, if not to actually read them. Want to try a simple experiment?"

"Sure, is there a girl around who needs a sweater?"

"No, sit here next to me, and think of simple numbers from one to ten, and remember what they are. Think of each very clearly, and I'll try to detect them and write them down. Focus clearly and send me five random numbers to start, then we'll move further apart and try again, and see what the range is."

"And then you send to me, to see if I can detect yours. Maybe you have a great transmitter, as well as receiver, and I'd like to see if I can do it too."

They worked at these basic experiments, trying hard to send numbers to each other, writing answers, calculating percentage correct, and slowly moving apart, oblivious to the rare passer-by for twenty minutes. At first William did no better than pure chance would suggest, receiving only one number in ten correctly: this wasn't working, no matter how hard he tried. Zarlie smiled softly and encouraged him, "William, focus all your thoughts on me, stare at my head. Try to visualize the numbers forming inside my brain."

Slowly his accuracy improved. The more they worked, the better he became, then all of a sudden he froze with his mouth wide open: he couldn't believe it, this was impossible. He had just received four numbers in a row perfectly, and his average accuracy was moving up. There was absolutely no way this could happen: everything he knew about science argued against it. He waved his hands, his arms were in spasm as he tried to speak. Zarlie laughed, "Oh William, I know what you're feeling, it happened to me the first time I clearly read someone else's thoughts."

"This just can't be happening. Either I'm learning how to do it or you've got a fantastic transmitter that is pushing numbers into my head."

"Probably some of both, but it is fun isn't it. Living waves are real and we're going to do some great research."

"Focus carefully and see if you can get this number."

Zarlie focused as he concentrated, then smiled, "Two-point-seven-three. Hey you're supposed to send whole numbers."

"That's the value of the math constant 'e', but instead of sending it I tried to send an expression that equated to it. You're fantastic."

"Maybe your subconscious was thinking about the actual number all the time and you only think you were trying to fool me."

"Did you ever read about those SRI experiments in the sixties where a few subjects sent brainwaves that were so strong they registered on a distant magnetometer. There was a book, I think it was called MIND REACH."

"Shhh, we'll talk about it later."

Three men in suits came out the building and approached them. "We've just detected that you two are very special people: won't you please come inside our offices and let us give you a free test? There's absolutely no obligation."

William was about to refuse their offer when to his surprise, Zarlie laughed and said that they would be delighted to take the tests. He was hesitant, but Zarlie was in such a good mood that he knew something was up. She was far too sharp to let these clowns waste her time.

They entered a modern office with expensive tables, leather chairs, and a soft green carpet, the color of money. The men gave William and Zarlie each a test form to complete. Zarlie elbowed William and whispered to him to concentrate very hard. He was to imagine a blank tick-tack-toe grid, and she would begin by sending him an 'x', a kiss as she called it, to one of the nine squares. As soon as he received it, he was to send an 'o', a hug, and to try to win the game. They would play a round then compare notes as soon as they had an opportunity.

Both started to focus strongly while looking at their test forms. William drew a small grid in a corner of his paper and marked the first 'x' he received. He thought it was a dumb opening move, as she had picked the middle square on the right side. He knew from mathematical game theory that this game could always be won or at least tied by putting the first move in a corner. He quickly replied with an 'o' to the upper left corner. Almost immediately he felt an 'x' arrive just below his mark. William began to realize that as long as he focused on the grid and imagined the brain waves coming and going that the game moved quickly. However, as soon as he started to read the test questions, the distraction ruined the communication: the brainwave connection was so fragile and difficult to maintain.

The suits were watching carefully and noticed that neither William or Zarlie had answered any test questions, though both seemed to be concentrating very hard. One suit asked, "Is the test too hard? Would you like to try a different one?"

Zarlie answered, "Au contraire, this test is perfect, we're just waiting to clear our minds so that we can answer the questions accurately and truthfully."

She knew that 'clear' and 'truth' were magic buzzwords among Alienologists, who were supposedly experts at happy uncluttered thinking, and smiled to herself when she saw their surprise at her choice of words. William randomly marked a few answers on the test and wondered what sort of game Zarlie was playing with these fools and with him on the grid. Suddenly two things happened at once. First he realized that Zarlie had just won the game with a really unique series of moves that he was dying to analyze carefully. But more importantly, a small hidden door in the adjacent wood-paneled wall had just opened. A frightened short man burst into the room through the doorway. He was wearing an orange jumpsuit and headphones and his hair was standing straight-up. The suits started mumbling with him in the far corner of the room and Zarlie could sense that they were afraid of her. When one of them pointed at Zarlie, she turned and made the 'V' hex sign at them with two fingers of her left hand as though she were casting an evil spell: they ran for the exit in fear and confusion. Zarlie couldn't help herself and started laughing as they retreated.

Quickly, she jumped up, grabbed William's hand and ran for the secret doorway. Before the suits knew what was happening the couple was in the hidden room. Immediately William smelled burning electrical equipment, which reminded him of a fire on the London Underground that he had barely survived. He looked around. What a surprise: the small drab room was filled with old vacuum tube electronic gear that looked like it belonged in a World War Two movie. Then he saw the body. A man in an orange jumpsuit was lying on the floor: blood oozing from his head. The man didn't move, his dead eyes were open staring straight up. Zarlie ignored the body as she scurried around the room studying everything, poking in corners, clearly looking for something. Then she found it, an ancient six-foot high black crackle-finish electronic rack labeled "A-meter". She ran her fingers over the control panel, which was covered with knobs, dials, and round Weston milliammeters. Smoke flowed from cracks: maybe it was on fire.   As the suits rushed to the entrance of the secret room, William and Zarlie ran through a different door, passing a coat rack full of orange jumpsuits, labeled 'decontamination gear'.

They ran down the stairs, through a few parking lots, then ducked into a crowded Baskin-Robbins ice cream store. The suits were not following, or had lost the trail.

Zarlie explained to William what they had just discovered. She had read that the Alienologists claimed to have an electronic brainwave detector, which they taught rich suckers to use; suckers who had taken all the other courses, and who still had money to burn. Before this afternoon she had been sure that such a machine couldn't exist, but apparently her waves were strong enough to be detected and to damage, and perhaps ruin, their equipment.   What a find, proof that brain waves existed and that they could be detected by a machine. They had just seen a link between the biological and physical worlds. Maybe she could use the machine to scientifically analyze living waves. The Alienologists claimed that their machine could detect space aliens, whom they believed were on earth, disguised as humans. Supposedly the aliens were going to take-over the planet, unless people paid plenty of money to the Alienologists. Neither William nor Zarlie understood how anyone could believe such nonsense, but unfortunately many people did, and spent their life-savings taking courses. Zarlie longed to examine a working A-meter carefully.

William changed the subject, "You can send brain waves,

and we proved it by sending numbers and playing a game."

"So?"

"You pretended to throw a curse at those jerks, but maybe you really could do it. If you focused very hard, perhaps using your fingers to help your concentration, could you shoot bad thoughts into their heads?"

"That's silly, or I mean, it's not practical, the receiver has to cooperate," Zarlie answered after a bit of hesitation.

"Maybe if the target was mentally weak or hypnotized, you could poke thoughts into his mind."

"That's close to witchcraft and I'd rather not talk about it if you don't mind. By the way, have you heard from Japan? Any news about the blue star or spaceship?"

"Not a word, and it's been over two weeks. I'll bet they were shocked by my analysis. I wish I'd sent it in English, to be sure that I conveyed the information accurately."

"Have you told anyone else?"

"No, and probably the Japanese guys just laughed and threw away the message. Well, I'd better get moving or I won't accomplish anything this afternoon."

"Thanks for your help with my experiments. I'll bet that now you believe in brainwave communication."

"It's weird, but it works, at least with the two of us, and you're the sharpest game-player I've ever met. We need to do a double blind test. Let's get together some time and I'll bring sealed identical envelopes containing slips of paper with purely random numbers printed on them, then we can be sure that we're really onto something."

"See you around quad."

They went their separate ways. William picked up three bright yellow four-pair computer cables at Fry's electronics store, then went back to his apartment to finish an experiment. He was still buried in math when the phone rang just after midnight with a call from Zarlie.

"William, I need a really big favor from you, and I don't know how to present this or what to offer you in return if you'll help me just this once."

"Sure, or maybe before I agree, I should ask exactly what it is that you want me to do?"

"What I need is more information on the A-meter we saw this afternoon. If Living Waves really exist, this box is a link, maybe the only link, between them and the non-biological world. It's incredibly important to my work, but I know those creeps will never willingly show us the thing, let alone let us poke around inside it. It's Sunday night, and no one is downtown at this hour. We could easily slip inside their building and study the thing and find out how it works."

"How will we get inside, I mean, they must have locks and burglar alarms and that kind of stuff."

"I know all about other people's locks and alarms, one of the legacies of growing up where I did. I'm just asking you to come along and provide moral support: I'm too afraid to do it alone, even though there's no danger of us getting caught."

As he dressed his gut felt bad: would they be arrested, thrown in jail, kicked out of school? Why had he agreed? He imagined the look on Gloria's face if he told her about this: she'd do more than make him write a sentence and pin it to the wall. Then he remembered Gloria's analysis of Zarlie, and in particular Gloria's comments about the likelihood that Zarlie had a criminal background. Damn, he wanted to stay home with his computers, not creep around in the dark like a crook. Twenty minutes later he parked downtown in the dark, wearing a black shirt and dark jeans. Zarlie had exerted a strong pull on his emotions, maybe much too strong a pull. Zarlie was also in black, and she even had black track shoes and sox, and a black scarf around her head. Her tight black sweater and slacks revealed a very nice figure, quite an interesting change from her normal appearance. Her catlike body silently glided through the shadows.

Using her master keys, they quietly unlocked the alley door, silenced the alarm, and entered the testing room. They tried to open the secret door leading to the lab, but it had an invisible lock. William could feel the outline of the door, but nothing else. They looked for a switch, and then found a row of buttons under a desk. The buttons weren't labeled and William had a premonition that the wrong one would set off a fire alarm or something bad. Every time he heard a noise he thought goons were about to pop through a door. Finally Zarlie snapped the secret door open with a big screwdriver that she had found in a closet. The body still lay on the floor, and the smell had become worse, sort of like a cross between a Cairo crapper and an electrical fire.

William gently pushed the A-meter but it weighed a ton: they couldn't budge it. He pried open the equipment's back door and they looked inside with their flashlights. A mess of burned wires, vacuum tubes, transformers, steel chassis, and ancient electronics. William kept whispering to Zarlie, asking if she had sensed any danger yet, or if she could feel anyone coming their way. She was poking at the gear and quickly snapping digital photos, when a loud alarm went off, just as she sensed people coming. She yanked hard at something inside the rack and pulled out a weird glass sphere-like thing with wires wrapped around it. William tugged her arm hard and finally dragged her away. They just made it to the door in time.

They ran into a hallway, then jumped into the Women's restroom as they heard people coming and saw the elevator door opening.

They stood together on a toilet seat hoping that if anyone looked, they wouldn't be seen. It seemed like forever and the more they waited, the more he felt that he had to take a leak. Maybe it was the surroundings, or, more likely, fear. Once the door of the restroom had opened, but they weren't discovered, as a flashlight beam quickly scanned the floor and the room. In the distance they could hear thuds and crashes, but had no idea what the sounds meant. Three hours later they slipped out of the building into the early morning light.

Just before they left, William left a false clue, by using Zarle's marking pen to write a Japanese message on a restroom mirror, 'Death to Alienologists'.

ちょうじょうをめざせ

He knew that Alienology was banned in Japan, and thought it would be clever to imply that Japanese had raided their building tonight.

After so much trouble, they hardly knew more about how the machine worked than before. Reviewing their photos, they saw that the inside of the A-meter looked like the innards of a war-surplus radar, with nothing newer than 1950 technology. The only unusual thing that it had contained was a glass sphere filled with amber liquid, with a biological specimen inside. Zarlie still had this sphere, which she had liberated from the A-meter before their hasty exit. As she examined it now, she could see that there were three coils of wire around the little four-inch sphere, and the wires were wrapped in a screwball way. They knew that there must be some connection between Zarlie's brain waves and the technology in the A-meter, and the sphere was the only strange item that they had found. They started calling it 'the jar' because it reminded Zarlie of jars containing biological specimens in her lab. William thought that perhaps the A-meter was based on a secret ancient technology, and that the men they had seen yesterday might not have any idea how it worked. As she continued to study the photographs, Zarlie noticed a sign on the front of the A-meter that identified it as serial number five. Perhaps there were very few of these machines in existence. Maybe the secret of their construction had been lost long ago.

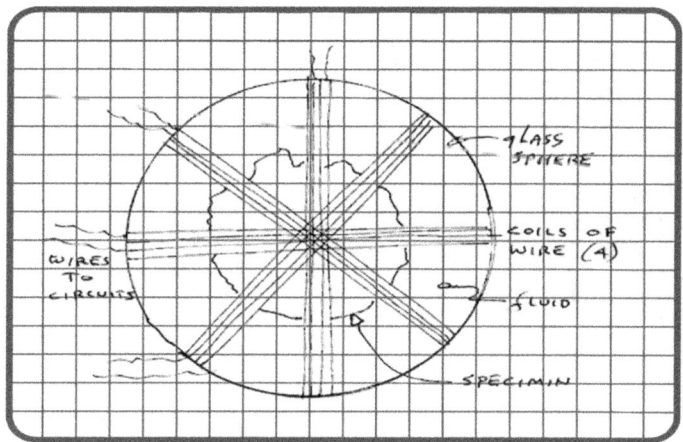

William's notebook sketch of the jar and the coils of wire that surrounded it

Tuesday afternoon found Zarlie in the Advanced Genetics Lab learning how to run the new sequencing equipment. The TA gave the students time to fool around, to analyze their own DNA, before getting down to class work. The gear was complex, and most students had trouble getting it tuned-in and making it run correctly. In the "old days", which might mean a few months ago, geneticists had to do many of the steps by hand, and it took days to make a cytogenetic map of the DNA in a sample. Now, a person could clean a sample, pick it up with sterile tweezers, and place it inside the machine. Then computers and robots chewed away, and in ten minutes the results appeared. Of course, you had to know how to set-up the machinery, and that is what they were studying.

The TA was on the other side of the lab when Zarlie ran a sample of her own hair. As the results printed out, she nearly fainted. Fortunately she had the presence of mind to quickly fold the printout, stick it in her pocket, and leave the lab. Her heart raced, her shallow breaths were coming quickly: fainting seemed like a real possibility. Zarlie had never been more startled or afraid. She sat down in an empty classroom and stared at the paper. She knew that normal people have 23 pairs of chromosomes, numbered by size except for the XY pair. Chromosome-1 is the biggest pair and it has the most genetic information. As she stared, she saw that her DNA had two of the big chromosome-1 pairs, one more than everyone else, and the four strands from her two big pairs were intertwined. She had never

77

seen anything like it in the textbooks or in the literature. Nothing else had DNA like this, no plants, animals, or bacteria. The only other living people with extra chromosomes were Down's Syndrome babies, but they had an extra little, #22, chromosome.

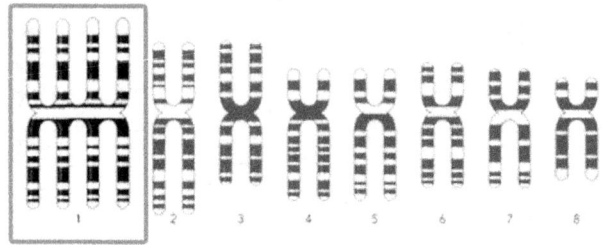

Zarlie's first eight chromosome pairs showing her very odd
#1 chromosome with its four strands

Mutant embryos with other genetic abnormalities always died, or at least that's what the textbooks said. Zarlie knew that a few apparently-normal people were missing large chunks of DNA and that it was possible, in rare cases, for genes to migrate to other chromosomes generating what were called copy number polymorphisms. The scientific side of Zarlie was intrigued by the discovery of such unusual DNA. She could envision many experiments and wanted to do a Representational Oligonucleotide Microarray Analysis comparing her DNA to that of a normal person, to see what other differences her DNA possessed.

But in contrast to her excitement about research possibilities, the emotional side of Zarlie was in turmoil. She pinched her arm. Yes, alive and looking like a normal person: who could ever tell that her DNA was so strange. Yet she already knew that her brainwave abilities were special, and she guessed that probably there were other things about her that most people didn't share. What could all this extra genetic material be coding in her body? She wondered if all Rroma had genes like this, but quickly realized that if that were the case, it would be in the scientific literature.

She started to cry silently as she thought "Damm, how could I ever have children? What would they look like? What happens if I go into a hospital, or apply for insurance and they check my blood? How long can I live with DNA like this? Maybe I'm on borrowed time already?" Slowly she wandered home, lonely and afraid, unsure of her future or what to do next.

Chapter 8
Tubes & Tunnels

William sat in his apartment studying the digital pictures which Zarlie had made of the A-meter. He had downloaded an encrypted copy of them into his computer for safe-keeping and was trying to form some idea of how the thing worked. He knew little about vacuum tube electronics, though he was well-versed in solid-state circuits which were based on transistors and integrated circuits. From 1900 until 1950, all electronic gizmos such as radios, televisions, and radars had been built around glowing vacuum tubes: things that looked like small dim light bulbs. Then in the late forties engineers at Bell labs had developed transistors, which were very small and efficient replacements for tubes. By the time William had been born, tubes were usually found only in history books, or in the hands of hobbyists. The A-meter was the first piece of working tube gear that William had ever seen, except in old movies.

Then he discovered that a Ham, a guy who played with radios for fun, had scanned a complete 1955 copy of THE RADIO AMATEUR'S HANDBOOK onto the internet. William devoured the chapter on 'Elementary Electronics', which described the functioning of vacuum tubes and their associated circuits circa 1955, perhaps the era when the A-meter had been built. He began to realize that in terms of function, tubes were similar to transistors, even though their appearance and size were completely different. A transistor could be the size of the eraser on the end of a pencil, whereas a typical tube was bigger than a lipstick, and the tube glowed when it was running. Both devices allowed a weak electrical signal to control a much stronger flow of electrons. The result was that the weak signal was amplified and made stronger, typically by a factor of ten to one hundred. In the vacuum tube, a heater, originally the filament from an incandescent light bulb, heated a piece of metal called a *cathode*, causing electrons on its surface to boil free. The electrons were negatively charged and so were attracted to a nearby positively-charged piece of metal, called a *plate*. A current could flow from cathode to plate (more correctly called the *anode*). Now, if a third piece of metal, a little screen called a *grid*, were placed in-between the cathode and anode, a faint signal on it could control the current, by helping or interfering with the flow

79

of electrons from cathode to anode.

This relatively simple device, originally built inside a light bulb around 1900, allowed radio, television, radar, computers, sound movies, electronic phonographs, and a myriad of useful equipment to be built and enjoyed all over the world. William realized that transistors were just a refinement of the original idea, that of using a faint signal to control a strong one.

He saw that Field-Effect Transistors (FETs) worked in almost the same way as tubes. In the FET, electrons flow in a very small piece of semiconductor material, called the *substrate*. A *gate*, which is a thin layer of metal deposited on the surface of the substrate, controls the flow of electrons inside the substrate. A faint signal applied to the gate controls a big flow of electrons.

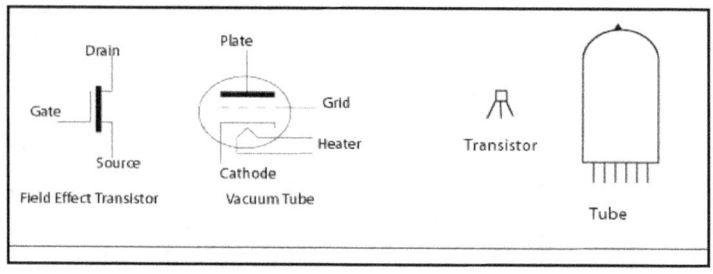

Comparison of Tubes and Transistors

William reasoned that the circuitry inside the A-meter could probably be duplicated, in miniature, using simple transistor circuitry which he understood. The electronic aspects of the thing could be deciphered if he could trace the wires connecting all the pieces inside the A-meter. Everything would be clear, except the jar: its function would still be a mystery, as nothing like it appeared in any electronics textbook. Unfortunately a practical problem, that of obtaining access to innards of an undamaged A-meter, precluded circuit analysis and there were no A-meter drawings on the internet.

The combination of work at VPA, staying on top of classes, and pyramid research (which now focused on examining photos and sketches of everything known to be inside the Great Pyramid), left William little time for wondering about brain waves and Zarlie. He didn't see her for nine days, then met her at a secluded bench in a small garden behind History Corner, just after dinner. They were both supposed to be studying for midterms.

William was surprised at Zarlie's demeanor. Instead of her serious busy energetic self, she seemed quiet and subdued. He asked hesitatingly, "Is something bothering you? Are you still worried about the spaceship?"

"No, much more down to earth problems have come up, but I'm learning to cope. It hurts, but I've survived worse."

"Is it the wrong time of the month?"

"William! Mind your own business dammit. I'm sorry, I know you're trying to help, but don't press me."

William knew he should change the subject, and wondered why she had wanted to talk with him, if she didn't want to talk. "May I ask what you've been doing? Have you learned more about Living Waves?"

"Actually, I've been in the ethnographic library, studying Rroma migrations, trying to figure out who my ancestors might be, and get some idea of where I fit in the human race."

"That's, that's a bit different. Er, do you know anything about your parents, like their names, or where they lived?"

"I thought I did, but now I'm not so sure. I'd rather not talk about them, or my background, if you don't mind."

"Sure. Do you think the Alienologists have any idea who took the jar. I mean, we'd be good suspects, if they had any brains."

"No, and the strangest thing is that I drove by there yesterday and the building is empty. There's a for-rent sign on the front window. They've packed up and disappeared."

"On thinking about them, I've had a vague sort of idea about the jar. It must be the key to how that box works, and I wondered what would happen if we hooked an oscilloscope to the wires wrapped around the jar while you focused strong thoughts on it. A 'scope would amplify the weak signals from the jar, then display them on a small screen, kind of like a little TV set: it would let us see any electric signals that came out of the jar. Maybe the jar is some sort of detector or antenna that can pick-up living waves and convert them into electrical signals."

"That's a very good idea. Can you borrow an oscilloscope from a lab?"

"Sure."

"You're going to be surprised when you see where I've hidden the jar. Meet me back here around eleven with the 'scope, and wear old clothes and bring a flashlight and thick winter gloves. And I hope you've destroyed or hidden your copy of my photos."

"I encrypted them in a very clever way, then hid the files on a CD with an old music label, so don't worry."

At eleven, William and Zarlie were back at the same secluded garden, with a small battery-powered Tektronix 'scope. He wondered what would happen if a fellow math student saw them together, and had no idea what to do with the heavy gloves. He felt much odder than he looked.

Zarlie checked to be sure they were alone, led him behind the nearby oleander bushes, lifted a two foot diameter conical metal vent cover, and climbed down a metal ladder into the steam tunnels. William, mystified, followed carefully, quickly putting on the heavy gloves after feeling the top step of the ladder and nearly burning his hand.

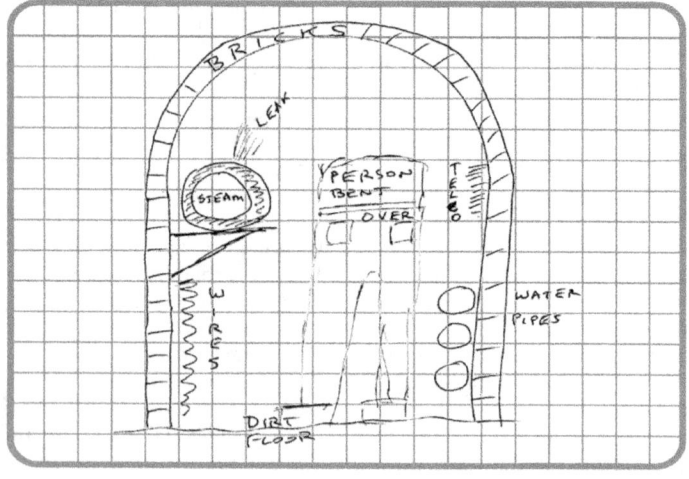

William's sketch of his bent-over body creeping down the tunnels

The tunnels ran all over campus, carrying steam, water, and wires everywhere: he had never been in them before, though he had heard scary stories about burns and large rats. The hissing steam leaks, and the rumble of huge pipes clanking as they expanded and contracted, reminded William of an old haunted house horror movie with Abbot and Costello that he had seen on TV. In the flick, Costello is frightened by a huge steam furnace in the basement of a dark scary house. The fire inside the furnace flickers, shadows wiggle everywhere, and Costello thinks the furnace is alive. To Costello, the furnace and its long white insulated pipes looks like a huge scary ghost with many arms. William wasn't quite as frightened as Costello had been, but he was very apprehensive: once again Zarlie had taken them into places where they didn't belong. The steam tunnels were brick, with arched ceilings about five feet high, and much of the cross-section of the tunnels was taken up with dangerously hot pipes and a tangle of wires. The floor was dusty red clay. Here and there he could see a bit of steam shooting out of a leak, but the really bad leaks were invisible, where the live steam was so hot it couldn't be seen because it hadn't condensed into visible water vapor. They were very careful at the flanged pipe joints, and he was glad to be wearing thick gloves and a heavy jacket.

After a very careful trip with much dusty crawling through holes and around leaks, they reached a sealed-up ancient chem lab that Zarlie had found under the modern earthquake supports for the old Quad buildings. Nobody had been down here for decades. They could almost see the ghosts of students working at the benches amidst the dust and Bunsen burners. The original entrance to the lab and one wall had been bricked-over, so the room was sealed, except for a hole where the steam pipes entered: they had just carefully crawled through this opening. Zarlie's flashlight revealed the jar resting on an old chemistry bench and insisted that they remove any finger prints and always wear gloves. She didn't want any way for the creeps to trace this thing to them if it were ever found.

William connected the oscilloscope and watched for signals in the various coils as Zarlie bombarded the jar with brain waves. Nothing happened at first, but then he connected all the coils together in series so their signals added together and adjusted the 'scope to its most sensitive setting. As she closed her eyes and focused all her energy on the jar, a few faint wiggles appeared on the screen.

"Holy shit Zarlie, look, open your eyes, your thoughts are on the screen."

The wiggles vanished as she looked, "Where, I don't see anything."

"Focus again, but keep your eyes open. This is fantastic, I've just seen signals from inside your head."

"What did they look like?"

"Static, or random noise, damn, we should have brought a better scope so that we could record this stuff."

Zarlie moved closer to the jar and stared at it and at the 'scope screen behind it. Random, wiggly lines appeared. She breathed deeper, and then started to smile as stronger signals appeared.

"Don't speak or move or do anything for a few minutes, just watch with me."

The signals grew in strength, then she leaned away and the signals were weaker. Zarlie moved back and forth, seeing how far away she could move from the jar and still activate it.

"William, this is just like bio-feedback. As long as I watch the screen, I can see what works and what doesn't. I can almost begin to control what happens. What a breakthrough, I don't know how to, I mean, I can't put it in words."

"I'll bet this is the first time anyone's seen and controlled living waves."

As William marveled at the 'scope traces, Zarlie looked at him strangely. "What are you thinking about, while you stare at the 'scope?"

"Nothing, well actually I'm envisioning the Fourier Transform of the trace and wondering how I could get these signals into my computer so that I could manipulate them mathematically. I'd love to analyze the way the electrical currents vary, and get you to think specific things and do repeatable experiments."

"Are you envisioning something like a graph or a series of numbers?"

"Yes, sort of, actually I was thinking about the math used to make the plot, but the end result is a graph or list of numbers."

"Think about it some more: I can sort of see vague graphs and numbers coming from your brain as you think. The visualizations aren't clear enough to draw or even talk about, but let me practice."

"I'll think about something easier to envision, like equations that generate simple geometric shapes and you tell me what the shape is."

"It's not that clear, but go ahead and try. Focus really hard, like when you are worrying over a real problem."

As they worked in the dark dusty old lab by flashlight, with Zarlie trying to sketch her visions and William thinking about different aspects of math, they heard traffic sounds and occasional rumbles from the pavement above. To Zarlie, her visions were like looking through haze and seeing moving three-dimensional shapes that didn't make sense. When she started to talk about the images, he stopped thinking so that he could listen, which stopped the visions.

"What I am seeing is just like a dream, and just as hard to remember as soon as it stops. The image fades so quickly, but it is so tantalizingly close."

"We've stumbled onto a new way to analyze mathematical problems by activating our brains simultaneously! It's Brain-to-Brain processing. Maybe if I envision equations that have no known solution, you could see the answer, or some part of it."

"I see things, but I don't know enough math to describe them to you."

"I wish I could climb inside your head and watch for

myself."

After half an hour of this, Zarlie suddenly squeezed William's hand and put her index finger to her lips signifying silence, then whispered in his ear, "I feel something bad, listen, feel, maybe you will sense it too. Be quiet. We have to get out of here."

They retraced their path in the tunnels, but didn't use the ladder up into the vent behind History Corner. Instead they continued until they were in the basement under Engineering Corner. Zarlie led in the dark, shielding her flashlight so that it's beam illuminated only a small area in front of them. She whispered, "We're going to come out in a closet near the TA offices. All the doors open outward for fire safety so don't worry about them. There won't be anybody around at this hour, so the lights will be off. When we get outside, we need to walk normally, like two tired students who have been studying all night."

As they emerged into the darkness, William wanted to head as far away from Quad as possible, but Zarlie had other ideas. "Let's sneak back and see if we can tell what was bothering me. Come on, we look perfectly normal." Reluctantly, William followed.

As they peeked around a corner and looked out onto Quad, they saw a strange sight. A small truck filled with surveying equipment had parked on the quad and two surveyors with yellow hard hats were working in the dark with flashlights, transits and storey-poles measuring distances and angles. To anyone else the only odd thing was that they working at night, perhaps so as to not bother tourists and students during the day. But William and Zarlie had other ideas since the workers were directly over their secret lab measuring and examining the pavement. William gasped suddenly, as he saw the air conditioning unit on top of the truck rotate then stop. He whispered to Zarlie, "That truck, look, that thing on top of it is moving, like a radar antenna, and I'll bet it's looking for the jar. Maybe there's some kind of homing device in the jar that we didn't see."

"Maybe we activated it by blasting waves into it while we were experimenting. Just try to feel what they're thinking: don't focus any energy on them. Maybe they're tracking signals from the jar instead of from us."

"I wonder how we could get inside that truck and analyze their electronic gear: it must be related to Living Waves somehow."

"Damn, we've got to move the jar to a safe place before they find it. It's the only physical link between our Waves and the scientific world. We can't let it go: our research is just beginning."

"Don't you dare suggest that we go back down there now and get it."

"You stay here and watch them while I go back and get the

jar and move it to a temporary home."

"You're crazy. Where will you put it?"

"In the genetics lab for now, then somewhere safe after that. Just watch them for half an hour, then fade away. I'll call your cell when I get to the lab and hide the jar. Don't think about them, or send any waves their way."

"Don't go, it's not worth the chance."

"Bye."

Zarlie slipped away toward the nearest steam tunnel vent, then disappeared underground. William sat behind a bush, carefully watching the surveyors as the radar-like gizmo on the truck slowly rotated. He worried that they might somehow catch Zarlie. What sort of trouble had he ventured into. If only he had taken Gloria's advice and abandoned Zarlie weeks ago, he would be home studying the G.P. and planning an expedition, not hiding behind a bush like a crook. As the minutes slipped away he watched and waited, unsure of what to do if the creeps started digging. Suddenly the radar started spinning rapidly and the surveyors ran to the truck. They started arguing. Something had changed: they were packing their gear. His cell phone vibrated as Zarlie called to tell him she was safe, and that the jar was in a high-security part of the lab where contaminated material was stored: hopefully the creeps could never get permission to enter, even if they detected the jar's new location.

The next day William did an elaborate computer search trying to learn about the Alienologists and perhaps about the A-meter. To his surprise he found that his mountain of archival data at Gloria's contained records of Alienologists asking questions about the A-meter. How strange, they were members, perhaps high-ranking members, but he knew much more about the A-meter than they did. It must be a secret that only the top Alienologists understood. However the most important thing he learned was that there was an Alienology group called Alien Death Squads, ADS. These people were supposed to hunt down space aliens that had been found with the A-meter and kill them, to save the planet. What a pile of crap, but he had a strong suspicion that the ADS went around disguised as a survey crew.

Chapter 9
Data Mining

After weeks of processing Gloria's voluminous data, William had several ideas about the YFN predictions and how to improve them. He invited Gloria and Jake to come to his office for a presentation on Monday morning, to start the week with a bit of excitement. He used the weekend to prepare graphics and to solidify his understanding of the results of his work.

William began his talk, "What I have is not momentous, but I think we can take a few small steps which should increase profits."

Gloria replied, "Hey, any improvement is money in our pockets."

"At first, I didn't know what to do with all this data. I identified one hundred and thirty seven variables we could analyze, but when I tried to fit curves to the data and solve for the coefficients of all the equations, the solution went nowhere. I tried all sorts of math stuff, but finally I had a simple idea. I decided to focus my effort on the customers who were the most satisfied with our predictions. I hoped to learn why they liked us, and if possible to then expand these characteristics to the wider customer set. We do have some happy customers who pay for months at a time, so I wondered why they're special. I sorted the customers by length of service. I figured that the ones who liked us best would stay the longest, in general terms. Let me show you a graph showing the length of service for the entire customer set. As you can see, the top ten percent stayed with us for over three months, while at the bottom are all those creeps who left after a few days."

"But each of those customers cost us the same amount to catch and sign-up," Gloria interjected.

"Right, I'm coming to that, but let's look at some other things first. I decided to focus a detailed study on the top ten percent, the happiest customers. I wondered what sort of questions they were asking, thinking that maybe they asked easy questions, so we were just lucky to please them. I searched for key words in their questions, and went down many, many blind alleys. Along the way I looked at the answers we gave them and at the results. We have lots of triplets of data, each comprising a customer's question, the answer we gave to the customer, and the true answer, which we usually discovered the next day. Incidentally, we need to tweak the code a bit to force the customers to always tell us if our predictions are right or wrong. About a third never give us any idea if we scored or not. Perhaps we can phrase it nicely, to indicate that we're not perfect but trying to improve, so we need their help. I organized the data that I did have, that is the answers with clear replies. That's when I made an interesting discovery."

William shuffled his notes, then continued. "Many of the questions this group asked were questions with a positive or negative outcome, but no middle ground. Things like, 'will I be happy with my new girlfriend', or 'does Mary love me?' When I looked at the results, I made a huge discovery. In about seventy-four percent of the cases, a positive answer was the correct one. That is, although I expected the results of these questions to be about fifty-percent positive and negative, in reality positive results are much more likely to be correct."

Jake interrupted, "We should get a shrink in here. I'll bet these people already feel that things are going to be OK, and they're just looking for confirmation from us."

"Exactly. We gave those people random answers, yet the results show that the correct answers are not random. We can make a big improvement if we make a few subtle changes. The first thing is to change the doctor program so that it coerces people into presenting clean positive-negative questions to us. We get terrible results when they ask vague questions, like what is the weather going to be tomorrow. I couldn't even begin to find any patterns in the results or answers to vague questions, so let's minimize their occurrence."

Gloria smiled and said, "Then we give roughly three positive answers for every four clear-cut questions, and everyone will be happy much more of the time."

"Right, but that's not all that I discovered. As you two probably know, paying five dollars a day adds up. I was shocked to get my first credit card bill for a hundred and fifty dollars for thirty days of service. So I wondered if the people who pay five-a-day for the deluxe package drop us much more quickly than the people on the el cheapo dollar-a-day scheme. Was I surprised. The suckers who pay five dollars a day are the most likely to hang on for long runs, while most of the churn is at the low-end. We can really boost net profit by dumping these cheapskates. Let's limit the cheap package to at most a thirty-day trial period, after which they must upgrade or quit. And for that matter, I have a feeling that we could easily boost the bottom end to a dollar-ninety-nine a day without loosing many people. This change will give us fewer, but more valuable customers."

Jake laughed, "If they pay more, they'll think that our advice is more valuable. Jewelers, art galleries, and all sorts of hypesters have known that for ages: when in doubt, raise prices."

Jake rapidly fumbled with his papers, found a copy of THE ECONOMIST, quickly turned to a page he had marked, and exclaimed, "Listen to this article, it's exactly on your point. 'His policy was to make the firm's goods ever more alluring by increasing prices, not reducing them. He was in the business of selling luxury items, and his customers expected to pay very high prices: otherwise they would be worried that they were not being offered products of the finest quality.' This is from Henry Racamier, who rescued Louis Vuitton luggage from obscurity, by jacking up its image, and its prices."

"William, can you outline the changes to the software that we need to make, then get Denny to implement them quickly," Gloria asked.

"I've already written them up, but I was waiting to hear your views before sending him my notes. I also wondered if we should give high-end customers the chance to sign-up for discounted annual subscriptions, like magazines offer. We could try to lock them in for a whole year, and to pay in advance, with no refunds. It's rare that anyone stays over four months, so maybe we could make the annual rate something like six or seven months of fees and see if we can boost length of service, or at least the length of payments, that way."

Gloria was smiling as the financial wheels in her brain turned rapidly. Jake was working with his HP-17 financial calculator quickly running numbers as he spoke, "If tweaking the doctor program boosts retention rates by maybe ten percent, and if maybe half of the cheapskates jump to deluxe payments, and if we charge the cheapskates two bucks a day, then our annual profit will go up by almost two point three million, and that's not counting the frogs and Spaniards we'll snare by year-end. They'll get the same profitable treatment."

Gloria left quietly with a big smile and returned in a few minutes holding a folded piece of paper, which she presented to William. "Great job William. I know how much you like computers, and how you chase the pyramids all night on an ancient Dell box. Here's a purchase order to IBM. Lease yourself a personal super-computer, something that'll really suck the secrets out of those old pyramids. You've earned it."

William smiled with excitement. In almost no time he was in his car headed for the IBM marketing center in Santa Clara. One advantage of his scholarship from IBM was that he was thoroughly familiar with their lines of multi-processor High Performance computers, even though he had never imagined that he could actually have one of his own. Maybe his status as an IBM Scholar would get him a hefty discount so that he could afford a really giant machine and still stay within Gloria's purchase order. While other boys dreamed of girls at night, William sometimes fell asleep thinking of the options available on powerful computers, and how he might apply such a machine to pyramid research.

The IBM Marketing Reps had trouble believing that a student, and one who looked a bit shabby, was holding a purchase order to lease an sixteen-way p5 computer and that he wanted immediate delivery to his garage apartment. They normally sold these machines to mid-sized corporations and wondered how William could fully employ a machine capable of sixty-four bit processing at many gigaflops, especially a model with 50 gigabytes of chipkill memory and a terabyte of fast disk. To William this machine was perfect. It would run reliably without hassles so he could devote full time to research instead of computer-repair, it was probably 200 times faster on math problems than his old computer, and it ran Linux, his favorite operating system. Best of all, the low-level AIX code automatically handled all the details of dividing the workload across the processors: no hand coding of complex parallel algorithms would be required. He could plug it in and start work immediately.

If they had been surprised at the order, they were even more astonished when William began to tell them about pyramid research and the elaborate mathematical tools he wanted to apply to the shapes and dimensions in the pyramid. When they verified that William was indeed one of their most distinguished scholarship students, they offered him an extra discount. He thought Gloria would be pleased if he used some of the money for his VPA work, so he ordered a comparatively small P-630 Intellistation for his office at VPA as well as a maxed-out T-series laptop for himself. He left holding a thick stack of manuals and the laptop, almost dancing across the parking lot with excitement as he thought of new problems to attack.

By the next weekend, William's machine was up and running, twelve cubic feet, 400 pounds, of raw computational power sitting in his little apartment. It was about the size of a deep two-drawer filing cabinet with a few blinking lights on the front, but it gave William a tremendous capability. The university had much bigger computers, but they were shared among many students and professors. The new machine ran his normal problems so fast that he had almost no resting time before it was finished and waiting for the next task.

Learning to use the fancy computer was not William's only

adventure this week. On Thursday night, Gloria had invited him to her house for dinner. A chance to get to know each other a bit better, was how she had presented the invitation.

They talked about many things and William began to realize that she knew almost as much about him as he did himself. "If you don't mind me asking, I'm a little startled at how much you know about me."

"Oh it's simple really, the world of private detectives and lawyers. I knew we needed a mathematician, so I looked into the most promising students in the math department. People whom I thought could really help me make money. But, when you applied for an astrology patent, I knew that you were the one I wanted, so I did a bit more research, and here you are."

"I wish I knew more about you. You're so different from other girls, I mean, women. It's as though you have outgrown them by leaps and bounds, and every time we talk, you learn more about me, but I don't learn much about you."

"I'm not a mystery William, just a young woman having fun, doing what she likes to do. There isn't much more to learn, really, but I'm fascinated by you."

They had been drinking wine in the warm dark evening beside the pool, and admiring the view of all the lights in the distance. Gloria put her glass down, stepped in front of William and very slowly, one button at a time, opened her blouse, then tossed it into his lap. Then she carefully unzipped her skirt and placed it on top of the blouse. She smiled, slipped her panties off, and dropped them in his lap. He couldn't believe his eyes. She slowly walked to the pool and smoothly dove into the water with hardly a ripple.

William wanted to follow her, and began to take his shirt off, but then stopped and turned away. Gloria swam back to the near end of the pool, and peered over the edge at him. "What's wrong, I bet you don't know how to swim. Come in and I'll give you lessons."

"It's not that. I was on the school swimming team. It's just that, well, I'd rather not."

"Are you afraid of me, or what I might do to you?"

"No, I mean, you're fantastic, it just that...."

"No one can see us up here unless they're in an airplane or a drone or something."

"It's not that at all. Maybe I should be going."

"Shit. Don't tell me, you're not stuck on that gyppo scientist are you? I'll bet she's worthless in bed."

"Gloria, remember, you said you were big sister, not well, something else. I'm sorry, but Zarlie and her problems have really gotten to me and I'm so confused. Part of me knows I should have

91

taken your advice to drop her ages ago, but the other part of me is hooked and I'm in pretty deep, so I don't want to become entangled with another woman: I can barely cope with one!"

"It won't last and you're going to get hurt, but there's nothing we can do about that until it happens, so peel off and come for a swim, the water's fine and I'll bet I can swim faster than you can."

William stripped, dove into the pool and began swimming beside Gloria. He couldn't help but stare at her naked body gliding through the water next to him in the eerie underwater pool lighting. After a few laps, Gloria asked, "Ever seen this much of a girl's body?"

"Good grief no, I mean not in person and so close, I could reach out and touch you."

"Why don't you?"

"I know you're teasing me, but I'm enjoying it immensely."

"I can see that. Would you like to come inside and spend the night in my bed?"

"Gloria, please don't, well, yes and no, some other time, but not tonight, OK?"

"William, you're so foolish, but let me know when you're ready to play."

"I will, and please, if I say anything stupid about you or about girls, will you tell me right away. I don't want to offend you, and I worry that I shouldn't be talking with you about Zarlie."

"You can tell me anything you want, and I like having your body near me, so don't worry about it."

As they swam laps slowly, William noticed a dark spot on the front of Gloria's right thigh, near her pubic hair. The underwater lighting didn't show it clearly, but it looked like a Japanese character of some sort. "It almost looks like you have Kanji on the front of your leg."

"It's a Japanese tattoo, I'll let you see it more clearly."

Gloria rolled over and firmly grabbed William's head, burying his face in the tattoo, then wrapped her legs tightly around him, squeezing his head with her legs and hands, holding him underwater. William struggled for air, totally surprised at his predicament, thrashing his arms and legs to no avail, as she rode up and down on his face in the deep end of the pool. Her strong fingers held his long hair tightly, with her legs under his arm pits, locking his face against her firm body. Finally he did the only thing that he could, he bit her and shoved against her body with all his strength. As he escaped and gasped for air, spitting out hair and blood, Gloria swam away in pain, heading for the bathroom and a medicine cabinet. "Shit

William, you didn't have to bite me. I wasn't going to drown you, I was just giving you a big surprise."

"Remind me not to ask anymore about your body."

In a few minutes Gloria returned wearing a robe, holding a bandage over her bite. "Sorry I became a bit rough back there, I just couldn't resist the temptation to shock you."

"I'm OK if you are. So what's the tattoo that caused all the trouble?"

"It was part of an initiation ceremony into a secret group that friends of my family belong to. I don't know why I joined as it's mostly Japanese and German businessmen in South America, and the tattoo, applied in front of all the members, is part of the deal. I wore a G-string Bikini, and the electric needle hurt like hell. It was a mistake, but I wanted to prove that I could do it. I'll bet you've done a few things that you wouldn't do again if you had the chance?"

"Like biting you just now."

"I shouldn't have held your head so tightly."

"Are all girls like this, I mean, do they all like to surprise guys in totally unexpected ways?"

"I don't know. You give me much too much credit for worldly knowledge: I'm not all that smart."

"But you're so beautiful and powerful and clever and seem to have been everywhere and done everything."

"If that were really the case, would I be swimming nude with an undergraduate math geek who doesn't even want to climb into my bed?"

"I mean, you must have lots of men in your life, I'm just an employee, not someone you'd be interested in socially."

"There isn't as big a gap between us as you imagine. You think I'm so confident and strong, but maybe it's just a front, just a protective shell that I present to the world when inside I'm worried about what people think when they see my face. You dropped your wine glass when you first saw my ugly side. Total strangers point at me and gawk when they see both sides of my face, like I'm a freak or something from the circus. What I'm trying to say is that I don't have many boyfriends, and you accept me the way I am. Can you see why I might like you a bit?"

"I never looked at it that way. I guess that I never thought of what it would be like to be you, to live with that for the rest of my life."

They talked quietly for hours, then as William was about to leave, he turned to Gloria, "I don't quite know how to ask you, but can, or may, I kiss you goodnight?"

Gloria melted into his arms and gave him a long wet full-body kiss that he would remember for months.

Chapter 10
Shield Room & Lunch In
The City

As he worked toward his pyramid expedition, William had mixed feelings about his relationship with Zarlie. On one hand, he wanted to help a friend who was in a difficult situation and doing exciting research, but on the other, he realized the danger and trouble such a course would have for his future. If he stayed involved, he could be caught in a crossfire among the Alienologists, Zarlie, and Gloria. Logically, it was best to focus on the pyramids and forget Living Waves and Zarlie, but inside his breast his heart was pulling him slowly toward her.

William stayed glued to his new computer and schoolwork until Zarlie called him late Friday night. "William, you'll never guess what I found this afternoon."

"Er, what?"

"I found the old shielded room that the guys at SRI built for their remote viewing experiments in the seventies. It's way back in a corner of what used to be electronics labs. It's just a storeroom now, but we could fit inside, then close the door."

"I don't understand what you're saying."

"Look, we don't want to get caught by the creeps and their detectors when we work with brainwaves, so let's go inside this room and try our experiments again. We can find out if the shielding will block living waves. The room was built to block parapsychology signals, so it has every form of shielding engineers could think of, like copper, lead, steel and concrete and god knows what else. We can do it tonight if we're careful. I want to see if you and I can send numbers back and forth through the shielding, then if the shielding is good, we could move the jar inside and work safely there."

William had worked hard to suppress his thoughts about Zarlie, but as she talked, he saw her smile, her soft green eyes, and remembered how much he enjoyed being with her. However, he could also see that another night of experiments might lead him deeper into a dangerous situation.

"I'm hesitant, I mean, I'd love to help you, and the shielded room is a great find, but I'm a bit, er, afraid is maybe too strong a word."

"Afraid of what? The surveyors won't detect us over there. It's perfectly safe."

"It's hard to describe, I can't talk about it, it's just a feeling."

"Let's mull it over tonight. Meet me at eleven behind the old women's gym. The shielded room is only five minutes from there, and there's something else we've got to talk about, something very strange."

Acting against his logical brain, William followed his heart and walked to the gym on Panama Street, then watched apprehensively as Zarlie used her keys to slip into a warehouse area perhaps built in the fifties for lab space. All of a sudden, she turned to him with an odd expression, and he realized that she had sensed something of his fears. He focused quickly on what he could remember of the SRI experiments, trying to redirect his brain. Zarlie didn't say anything, but he felt that she had briefly sensed his true feelings.

William remembered that the SRI work comprised carefully-conducted double blind scientific experiments concerning remote viewing, a fringe area of parapsychology. In each experiment, the investigator asked the subject to imagine the place where a third person was standing. The subject was to describe the location, the buildings around it, the colors, anything that he could see inside his mind about the third person's location. All the answers were recorded carefully. Then the subject and the investigator opened a sealed envelope and read the true location of the remote third person. Some of the experiments were done inside this very shielded room to see if it made a difference. Normal people would find such experiments laughable, but the investigators were well-educated scientists who were serious. They found that most subjects could do slightly better than random and that practice and training could improve a subject's performance. However, a few subjects were naturals who could almost always see details of the location where the third person was standing.

An odd aspect of this whole business was that after Targ and Putoff published a book in 1977 detailing their experiments, both seemed to disappear: there were no further publications from the pair, even though their work looked promising. Then in 2002 Putoff was interviewed about his career. He had been employed for twenty years on secret government projects where his most capable subjects tried to view activities inside the Soviet Union, a 'remote spying' effort, which apparently had some measure of success. The projects stopped when the Soviet Union imploded and the Cold War ended.

When last seen, Putoff was involved in anti-gravity research, trying to learn if any of the stories and theories circulating on the web were credible.

There was nothing especially interesting in the warehouse except the odd little ten-foot square room, with walls two feet thick and a heavy door like those on walk-in refrigerators. Cardboard boxes of old papers and inactive electronic gear were piled to the ceiling. A musty dry smell pervaded the room. They could both fit inside the room and close the door, using their flashlights to see.

"First, let's repeat the experiments we did in the parking lot, where we sent numbers to each other. Let's be sure we can repeat those results in here," Zarlie whispered.

"I feel odd, like maybe I can't do it now."

"You're waves are strange. I can't tell what you're thinking, but you're disturbed, you're afraid of something aren't you?"

"Yes, but maybe it's that I'm afraid of being caught. I'm not used to creeping around in the dark and opening locked doors."

"Calm down and think of math, think of numbers. Let me worry about the rest."

They started sending numbers back and forth, with both inside the room, then taking turns with one outside and the other inside. Zarlie took copious notes and William became involved in the data collection and analysis of their experiment, though he was on his guard emotionally.

After two hours of experiments, they had determined that the shielding was quite effective, but that Zarlie's transmitter was strong enough to send signals through it, at least to William. His accuracy level, receiving these numbers through the wall, was only around 30%, but that was still better than pure chance, which would have been 10%, since she used the ten digits, zero through nine, when sending to him.

Zarlie opened her backpack and produced the jar, in a lead-lined bag designed to hold radioactive waste. They hid it deep in the shielded room underneath a pile of old papers, then left.

As they walked across campus in the dark, William saw a dog sleeping by a street light a block away. "Can you send a signal to that dog way over there? Your waves seem to be growing much stronger the more we practice."

Zarlie smiled, then looked hard at the dog. All of a sudden it jumped in the air, then ran off howling in fear. "Wow, I hope I didn't hurt it, I hardly know my own strength."

Zarlie stopped walking. They were standing in the shadow of a Eucalyptus tree, as the warm night breeze gently rustled the thin leaves above. William stood on acorns and strips of bark as he noticed the aroma of eucalyptus oil from the nearby trees. Zarlie turned to William and took his hands in hers. The moonlight filtering through the tree cast flickering shadows on her face.

"There's something I must tell you. I haven't told anyone else, and maybe never will."

"Maybe you shouldn't tell me either."

"You're almost my only friend. I've got to talk with someone about this: it's driving me nuts. I tested my DNA in the lab and it's so strange: there's nothing else like it in the books. I'm unique, or at least my DNA is. Maybe I shouldn't even be alive."

"And now you're worried that you're some kind of space alien that the surveyors want to kill?"

"Don't be silly, this is serious. I mean, what if I want to have kids, or medical treatments, or I don't know what. I'm some kind of freak, not a normal human being."

Zarlie started to cry as William wrapped his arms around her trembling body and tried to think of a way that he could comfort her, a way to ease her pain and fear.

"Tell me how you tested your DNA, how it works, I mean I don't have a clue how it's done."

"We have a new experimental machine in the lab. It's full of robots and computers and it can do in half an hour what used to take a person all day."

"Computers! That's your problem. I'll bet those computers are loaded with software written late at night by student hackers. Buggy software strikes again! Have you tested your DNA the old way, using reliable old-fashioned equipment?"

"No, dammit, why didn't I think of that. You're a genius!"

"I bet your lab has all the gear, you could do it tomorrow."

"No, I'm going to do it right now, you don't know how much time I've wasted worrying about this, when maybe there isn't even a problem." Zarlie laughed and ran off into the night.

A few days later Zarlie called William, begging him to meet her. "William, let me drive you up to The City and buy you a bowl of goulash. I need to get away from here. My life's falling apart, and I don't know where to turn."

What could he say. He was falling deeper and deeper into Zarlie's orbit and had no control over the situation. They drove up I-280 and 19th to San Francisco, then started walking down Geary Boulevard, out in the Avenues, among the Hungarian, Russian, and Central European restaurants, shops, and delicatessens.

William didn't know this part of the city, but saw that Zarlie knew it well. She was on a first name basis with Hungarian shop-keepers who gave William sausage and cheese to eat with black-crust over-baked sourdough bread. Zarlie and the clerks talked in Hungarian, with many laughs. She was happier than he had seen her in ages. He had no idea why they were here or what her new problems were, but the excursion was fun and she was happy.

They were sitting at a little table in front of Café Beroska drinking coffee, when William asked her about a book he had read, THE MYSTIC AND OCCULT ARTS (Gibson and Gibson 1969). He explained that the book divided the psychic arts into Clairvoyance, Precognition, Telephathy, Radiesthesia, and Astral Projection. He wondered if Zarlie could do all or any of these things.

"William, it's not like that at all. Those books are written by people who can't do anything except talk."

"Where do they get all those ideas? There must be some truth to it?"

"Much of that is just old stories and legends. I just feel things, sometimes before they happen."

"Rroma are supposed to be fortune tellers. Is that part of the same thing?"

"Want me to read your palm? Do you have a crystal ball handy?"

"I know you're putting me on, but can some Rroma really do it?"

"I'll put it this way, I've never seen other people do anything that couldn't be explained by a good magician. Read some of Houdini's books. He debunked scores of mediums and fortune tellers and told how each one performed his or her tricks." Zarlie laughed, then continued, "And, by the way, Houdini was Hungarian so he was very smart!"

Zarlie stood up and smiled at William, "Let's walk a bit. I'll tell you something that I haven't told many people."

As they walked, Zarlie described an experience from her childhood in Hungary. As far as she could remember, this was the first time that she had used her brain's sensitivity to escape trouble. A vivid memory from age six.

She had been staying at an uncle's, in an ancient gray stone house near the town of Kovagoors, on the north shore of Lake Balaton, in the middle of Hungary. Only Zarlie and the Uncle and Aunt were in the house. There was a terrific thunder and lightning storm rumbling outside, and in the middle of the flashes and noise, Zarlie had a strong premonition that something bad was about to happen to the three of them. She warned the others, but they said it was just the storm and tried to calm her.

Zarlie, frantic with fear, broke away from them, and ran

out into the storm, oblivious of the rain and wind even though she was only a little girl. She was so afraid that she ran blindly down to the town dock and jumped on the ferry boat that crossed the lake to the village of Balatonboglar. She stayed on the other side of the lake, cold and shivering, until the storm passed. Then she went back across the lake and walked slowly to the house. She knew something had happened.

Police cars were parked in the drive and a few men wandered about. Zarlie shivered with apprehension and asked a neighbor what had happened. The neighbor told her that bad people had taken her aunt and uncle away because they were Rroma. The police were investigating, but not very seriously. The bodies were never found. Rroma, especially ones with nice houses, were not popular.

Zarlie was quiet and pensive as they walked. William asked softly, "Did you know, or understand then, that you were special, that you could do things that other people couldn't?"

"Yes, that's when I started trying to learn more about it."

"Did you tell anyone, or ask for help? I mean, you were pretty young to study something so complex."

"If you and I didn't have so many shared secrets, I would never be telling you this, but yes, I did talk to someone, a wrinkled old lady, all in black. She did fortune telling and magic spells, love potions, and that sort of stuff."

"Did people think she was a witch?"

"Yes, but I didn't know it, or what it implied about my skills. I just found her warm and easy to be with, so I told her about my abilities and she helped me develop. Sometimes I hid under the table and told her what the customers might be thinking. It was a kick being her secret informer and we never told anyone. You see, I really had the gift, the power, even then, and she didn't, but she could fake it, and she taught me a lot about magic and fooling people."

William replied, "I found an old book about witchcraft in England. Even without the Catholic Church and the Inquisition, there were people who claimed to be able to find witches. When one was found they would torture her until she confessed, even young girls. The old woodcuts are gruesome. Henry VIII made it a crime to use enchantment to harm a person's body or find treasures back in the fifteen hundreds."

"That's enough William. For you, it's a curiosity, but for me it's serious. I don't talk about witchcraft because that old lady put so much fear into my subconscious with her tales of burnings and torture. I shiver and shake all over when I think about it. To hear her talk, witches were just as likely to be burned tomorrow, as in the past. Late at night as the last firelight flickered she would tell me in excruciating detail what it would feel like as they tied you to the stake, ripping your flesh with the ropes, then smashing wood and tinder against your body. Your clothes were torn away and everyone laughed at your naked body. People spit on your breasts, slapped your face, poked your guts with pointed sticks. Then they danced around singing as the fire started. They would tease, and burn just a little bit, then more and more. First, you would smell the fire, then feel the heat, then your feet would start to burn, and if you were really lucky you fainted before the rest happened."

"And she would tell you this as you both looked into a fire, watching the wood disintegrate?"

"So you see, I have always been afraid, afraid that I really am a witch, and that people will find out. That's why you are the only one I've ever dared tell."

"You're not a witch, you're an exceptionally talented beautiful person with a wonderful gift."

"Don't be so sure. I know you're dying to ask, but too polite to push me, so I'll tell you. I ran my DNA through the old gear, twice, using two different techniques, and the results were all pretty much the same. My DNA's unique, though the different methods gave slightly different answers, and, you won't believe it, but even the mitochondrial DNA in my cells is screwed-up: that's never supposed to happen. It's from ancient bacteria."

"Could you send your DNA or some cells to another lab for confirmation?"

"No way, so far you're the only other person who knows and I'd like to keep it like that."

"If you told the professors you'd be famous: they'd all want to study you and your DNA."

"Just like a freak show. No thanks, not me, not yet anyway."

"Aside from your brain waves do you have any other abnormalities, I mean, any other features that might be special?"

"Not that I'm willing to talk about."

"Maybe I could search the internet for other people with the same DNA?"

"Don't bother, I've already done a huge search and emailed labs all over: no luck."

"Can you use your waves to sort of analyze yourself, I mean, can you see inside, or meditate, or get an idea of what's going on?"

"My only thought so far is that I'm so odd that I might not have long to live."

William suddenly had an insight. "Maybe you'll live to be a thousand like Methuselah and Bible-story people long ago. Could be they had the same special DNA that you do? Maybe it's a blessing, not a curse. You're going to do great things, I just feel it, so stop worrying about your DNA."

Zarlie smiled and squeezed his hand.

Chapter 11
Japanese Characters

After a day of trying to work on his studies, while wondering about the star, the Alienologists, Gloria, Zarlie, and Living Waves, William was totally confused. He decided to take a piece of advice from Gloria and turn his brain off, to take a break from thinking and confusion. He switched on TV, randomly flipped the channels, then decided to watch an old Sherlock Holmes movie called *The Musgrave Ritual*, the 1940's black & white version with Basil Rathbone as Sherlock creeping around an old English house. William loved puzzles and tried to figure out the *ritual* before Holmes understood it. The puzzle was related to chess, but with real people as the chess pieces.

Just as the film became interesting there was a commercial for **Gasaway** that knocked William to the floor in hysterical laughter. In the commercial a girl was headed for the toilet, when the doorbell rang. She looked surprised, straightened her skirt, and then her date entered. She was looking pained as they left and she was holding her butt. The voice-over said something about "Wish you could let one go, but can't find the opportunity?" She looked worse and worse in the elevator which was filled with people. They reached his car and he opened the door for her. She entered the car and he closed the door. There was a big closeup of the relief on her face as she let a tremendous fart escape. Her date came around and opened his door, then to the girl's horror, he introduced the couple sitting in the back seat. They were asphyxiated! What a great close-up of their expressions. Then the announcer came on with the pitch for Gasaway, which the boyfriend sprayed into the car to clear the air. William was laughing so hard, that he missed part of the movie.

Near the end of the film, Holmes made the other characters in the old house stand on particular squares on a huge stone checkerboard floor in a giant dark room. Each person represented a chess piece. Candles cast flickering shadows around the room as the people were positioned. A scary dark old country house on a stormy night. Their positions were dictated by Sherlock's chess interpretation of the old ritual's words. After they were in position,

Holmes walked down the staircase and stepped onto a specific square and with a big rumble, a secret passage opened in the back of the fireplace! Everyone rushed to see where the hidden passage led.

William jumped up and exclaimed to the TV that the key to the Great Pyramid was that he had to push on the stones in one of the interior passages in just the right places, all at once, with just the right number of people, and then a secret door would open. What a great idea! He was lost in visions of the interior passages of the Great Pyramid, wondering how many stones were involved, how hard to push, and most of all, what would he find when the secret door opened? He hugged himself with excitement and ran around his small apartment.

William had read stories of lost secret passages and subterranean rooms that some people thought were beneath the Great Pyramid and the Sphinx. The authors talked about lost secret entrances and hollow places below the ground. There was much conjecture about an entrance below the Sphinx's left front paw, but only a few ruins had actually been found below that area. The Giza Plateau was covered with old stones, holes in the ground, and parts of structures so nobody really knew what was in the layers underneath. There had been a little scientific research, but not recently since the Egyptian government frowned on 'quackery' as they called it. William suspected that a properly-equipped seismic crew from a modern oil company could locate the lost rooms and tunnels easily, if any existed. Recently he had read intriguing tales of a possible underground city in the ruins on the shore of Lake Titicaca, high in the mountains of South America. Dreaming of discovering sealed rooms filled with ancient mathematical knowledge kept William awake much of the night.

The next morning he received a complex email in Japanese. It had been four weeks since he had written to the blue star astronomers, and he had almost stopped hoping for a reply. In order to translate it correctly, William visited his Japanese Professor, taking him a single perfect carnation as a goodwill present.

Professor Saitei-Saiaku was formal and properly Japanese with a black suit and white shirt. His office had only a few visible work papers, and his Spartan decorations were carefully positioned. There was a small Ikebana flower arrangement with one blossom and a few twigs on his desk and he thanked William profusely for the carnation. William greeted him in Japanese and they talked green-tea for awhile, making obligatory small talk with many apologies from William for interrupting the professor. William first showed him the Japanese email that he had sent to the scientists investigating the blue star. The professor corrected the grammar and punctuation in the original email and was startled by the message it contained. He couldn't believe that William had dared to send such a poorly-written and nonsensical message to the Director of a famous Japanese observatory. Then he looked at the reply in astonishment.

The reply had so many unusual characters that it was far beyond William's abilities. Professor Saitei-Saiaku almost lost his aloof composure. As he read, he had to look in several dictionaries, so this wasn't an ordinary message. One of the characters was so unusual that the professor drew it carefully and explained it to William, stroke by stroke. (Oriental characters are described in terms of the sequence of strokes with which they are composed).

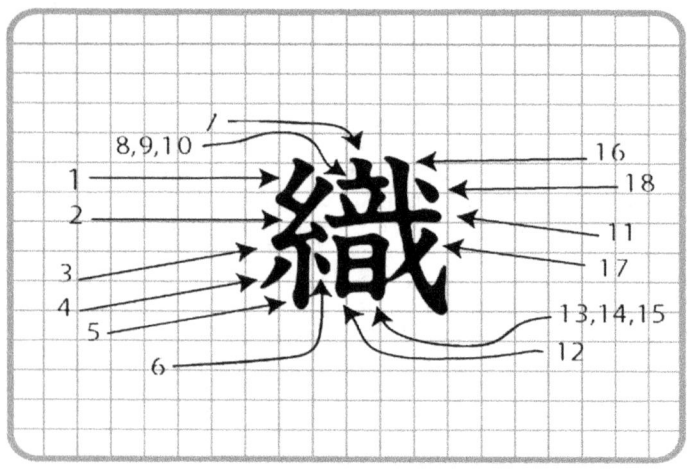

18-stroke Japanese character

"Look carefully William, for the very wise Director has created a complex new eighteen-stroke character in response to your message. This character is in no dictionary, but we can understand it as follows. The first six strokes are a very old symbol for the sky, and it is only used by scholars today. The next four strokes mean far-beyond, so these strokes together imply something far beyond the sky. Of course you recognize the next three strokes, which mean the color light-blue, as in the shade of a robin's egg. Now most of the rest is very peculiar, but it probably means a person with a defect, or a stranger. And the seventeenth stroke you have seen at least once in class, a dagger implying danger or fear. So the whole character is an original symbol representing your faraway 'spacemen', from beyond the blue sky, who may be coming to visit us, perhaps on a dangerous mission."

Finally Professor Saitei-Saiaku wrote out the entire email in English and they talked. He was both surprised and proud that one of his students was communicating personally with the Director of a major Japanese observatory, a person with very high status. He said that the most amazing thing to him was that the message was written in the style that would be used between equals, and not that of a superior person talking down to an inferior one. William was much more interested in the content, but this was Japanese, and social nuances between sender and receiver were very important. Part of the Professor's consternation was the contrast between what he saw with his eyes (a scruffy student), and what he imagined in his head (a proper Japanese Director in elegant surroundings). How could these two socially-disparate beings be communicating on the same level?

The message said that while William's analysis of their published data was unorthodox, and not anticipated by current science, it bolstered their argument that the star was very special, so they were interested in his approach. Their team wished to collaborate and were sending their unpublished raw data, in hopes that William could refine his analysis and reformat it into more conventional terms, so that the rest of the team could do further experiments.

Professor Saitei-Saiaku said that William should take care to do a prompt and careful analysis of their additional data, and then let the Professor help compose the reply, so that it would have the correct social nuances. He commented that if this went well, William might apply for an obscure Japanese math scholarship for graduate school. William mused to himself: "What a lark that would be, studying in Japan, wearing a black suit and green socks!"

William left the professor's office and walked along the east side of Quad, inside an arched passage, a passage lined and built with thousands of regularly-cut stones. He glanced at the stones which he had seen many times as he thought about the Japanese message and the meaning of several rarely-used Kanji characters. Suddenly, William stopped walking and stared at the nearby stone wall. In a flash he realized that the oddly-shaped stones which comprise the walls of the Pyramid's passages might also be characters in an ancient language. Each stone might represent a word or thought, just like the Japanese characters. The angles at the corners of the stones, the number and lengths of the sides, and the inter-relationships among the stones could all be parts of a long-forgotten system of writing, a system that created messages which could survive thousands of years, and that could only be understood by a Mathematician. The idea of oddly-shaped stones being part of a language, and the need to press on some of them to open the secret passages, were a perfect fit. What an insight! How well the different aspects of the stones complemented each other!   William's confusion evaporated: time to drop everything and focus on his big breakthrough, solving the language of the stones. He started for home, his mind buzzing with ideas.

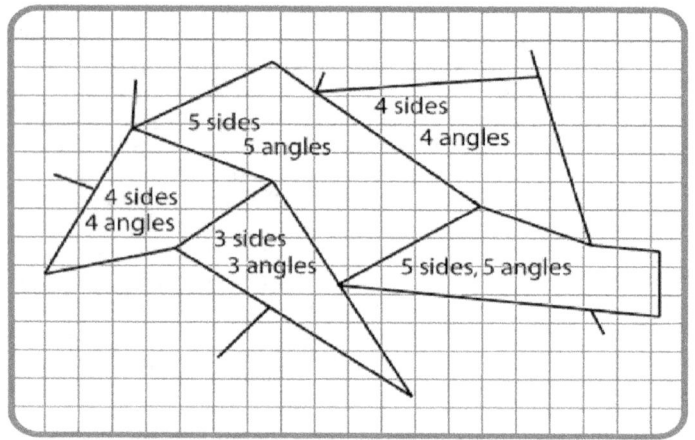

Stone-Language: Part of a wall inside the Pyramid

As William hurried along Lomita Mall, he looked more carefully at the rectangular yellow sandstone blocks which had been used to construct the original Quad buildings. These big machine-cut stones were all in straight lines, and clearly had no hidden meaning, but seeing them stretching out in long rows reminded him of something much more important. William had seen photographs of ancient megalithic stone structures in remote parts of the world. The stones in the ancient walls and ruined buildings were always odd shapes which fitted together perfectly, showing the great skill of their builders. Although normal historians disagreed, Astro-archeologists had dated the construction of many of these ancient structures to at least ten thousand years ago, maybe even much older times. In each instance, local legends referred to smart people who had built them in the distant past. William now realized that these structures could also be writing in the lost language of the stones. An ancient forgotten race may have left messages all over the world and the Great Pyramid was only one of their writings.

One of the walls that William passed

What an idea, what a discovery if he could decode the old writing. He remembered a photograph of 'the stone of twelve corners' which is in a wall in Cuzco, and the amazing stonework in the nearby fortress of Sacsayhuaman Hill. These stones weigh hundreds of tons and would be in position forever, perfectly joined together. Some of the blocks in the three zig-zag walls on the Hill weigh 355 tons and at least one stone is over eight meters high. What a wonderful way to write a permanent message for posterity, if only he could read it.

Damn, his cell phone rang in the midst of these complex thoughts. He listened impatiently as Gloria reminded him that he had only put in twelve hours this week. He promised to make up the time, then realized that he had to extract more money for his labor. So far he hadn't actually seen a single penny from all of his work, and in the back of his mind he vividly remembered Professor Skilling's remark about "working for a pile of worthless equity." He didn't even have enough money to buy a plane ticket, let alone organize a real expedition, and at the rate things were going, Gloria might hang onto all of his money forever. Whenever they talked about money, she had a reason to keep it. Now the time had come to assert himself, to act more like his ancient ancestor who had amassed the family fortune and less like a weak academic. William knew that now he was on to an incredibly fertile area of research. The results would be revolutionary if he could decode the stone writings all over the world. Time to stop playing, collect the money owed and as much more as possible, and mount the initial expedition. Egypt was just the first step in a lifetime of decoding ancient megalithic writings.

Tuesday night William was in his office at VPA carefully analyzing the results of the changes that they had made to the YFN software. People had already started signing up for his discounted full-year subscriptions. And to William's pleasant surprise, the volume of low-end business remained about the same as before, except that now VPA collected a dollar-ninety-nine a day from each person instead of just one dollar. William calculated the effect this would have on their bottom line.

Gloria entered his office. "Hey, long time no see. How's it going," Gloria casually asked as she walked over to him and laid a hand on his shoulder.

"We're making money all over the place: this is going to be a very profitable year. I need to ask you about something."

"Trouble in the girl world again?"

"No, not this time. I'd like to collect all my pay in cash from now on. I want to see it growing, maybe as a stack of hundred dollar bills."

"Why would you want to leave a twelve-percent investment? Found something more profitable?"

"No, it's just that I'd like to actually see the cash building up toward my pyramid expedition. I'd like the visual and tactile reward instead of numbers on a piece of paper, that's all."

"Not thinking of leaving me, are you?"

"Not at all, but I've calculated that my work this year will net you over a million dollars, so I was wondering about an advance on my bonus. Do you think you could advance me maybe a hundred thousand toward it, in cash? That's less than ten percent of your profits from my work."

"William, where'd you get such an idea: do you think I'm made of money?"

"I've watched the transactions from the suckers' credit cards. You own this place free and clear, and we pay IBM peanuts in rent for computing services, so you're raking thousands every day into your accounts at CSFB."

"But that money's being invested, it isn't just lying around."

"You could invest some of it in me, couldn't you? I'm onto an incredible math discovery and I need to work it very hard. I need lots of capital to finance a big expedition, actually a series of expeditions all over the planet."

"Have you changed? You're not acting like your old self?"

"I'm exploding inside because I've had such a great math idea, a breakthrough that will take the rest of my life to analyze. The pyramid business is part of a larger puzzle and there's work to be done on at least a dozen sites around the world. I need to make as much money as I can by helping you, then use it to finance a long series of expeditions. I want to work for you, then explore, and go back and forth between your world of money and the world of math forever. We can be a great team, but I want to be your partner, for a share of the profits, not just a salaryman working beneath you."

Gloria kissed William lightly then turned away and began pacing the room. "That's possible. You're quickly developing quite a head for business."

"Hey, I'm studying with an expert. I'd love to pull more from our customers' wallets, but a bigger share needs to fall into my pocket. How can we arrange that?"

"I could cash you out at the end of the year. That'll give you some accumulated interest to add to your pile. Is that soon enough?"

"No. Let's do it Monday week instead, and I'll forego the interest. Now what about the advance on my bonus: can you swing a hundred large by then also?"

"Shit William, let me think this over, you're coming on awfully strong for an innocent mathematician."

"Innocent, well maybe about sex and girls, but money's all about math and we're both experts there. I know you can manage the cash."

"My god, you're overflowing with strange ideas."

"It's so exciting: I'm bursting with ideas of how to analyze the math. We have a deal don't we? Let me take you out to lunch Monday in my old Honda: we can fill the back seat with bags of cash worth a hundred times as much as the car."

William put his arms around Gloria and kissed both sides of her face lightly. Gloria's feelings were in turmoil. She was shocked at the change in William and didn't know how to react. He made no sense at all and she felt that there might be much that he wasn't telling. She relaxed in his arms and returned his embrace, pressing her body warmly against his. However, there was no reaction from his pelvis down below. There was something missing: his upper body and his mouth were saying one thing, but his pants were saying another.

"William, there's something going on, you're not telling me everything. Have you fallen in love, perhaps in a girl's bed, maybe for the first time? Are you thinking of her while your arms are around me?"

William gently pushed Gloria away, suddenly realizing that he might have fallen in love, but with Zarlie rather than a bed partner. "I'll never tell, but I can't wait for Monday."

They separated as Gloria nodded her head in resignation. William asked, "In the meantime can I use the company credit card to buy a little camera gear wholesale? You can deduct it from my bonus. The company gets a much better discount that I ever could and I want to start making stone measurements and begin my analytical work."

"Not too much gear I hope."

"Just a camera and a few lenses."

Gloria gave him her card and walked away with a puzzled expression.

In the morning he used the card to buy the most capable portable digital camera available, a high megapixel Canon SLR with a full-frame digital sensor that yielded extreme high resolution. This camera could take nearly-perfect pictures of the stones, then feed the pictures straight into a laptop for analysis. He added a Canon 14mm f/2.8L and a 16-35mm zoom, both with low dispersion glass, the best and most expensive short lenses available for the digital body. He had already realized that the passages inside the Pyramid were narrow, so he would need the widest and sharpest lenses that he could find to take accurate pictures of the wall stones while pressing his back against the opposite side of each passage. The Grand gallery was less than four feet wide at the top, and about seven feet wide at the base. The fourteen millimeter lens had an incredibly wide angle of view, one hundred and fourteen degrees with a flat field, and its sharpness was legendary due to its aspheric lens elements and low dispersion glass. He also bought a 60mm macro lens for close-up detail, two flash units, a carbon fiber tripod with a leveling head, and another heavily-loaded IBM laptop. By the end of the day, William had managed to extract almost fifteen thousand dollars from Gloria's clutches.

People on campus saw William with his camera rigidly mounted on a tripod, making very careful photographs of small sections of the stone walls around Quad. He knew that there were no secret messages in these walls, but the stones provided an excellent way to develop and practice his data-gathering and analytic skills. Much like training wheels preparing him for the complex work ahead. Each photo contained a meter stick and a bright yellow vertical plumb line. He took these photos home and fed them into the computer program he was developing. The first programming task was to write code that could find and read the meter stick and the plumb line against the background of rough stones and their joints. Then he would develop a program that could find the edges where the stones joined. Once this was done, serious math would analyze the stone shapes and, hopefully, decode the secret wall writing. William had just begun to realize the difficulty of the task he had set himself. Even at this simple level, he had to re-shoot compositions to remove glare from the ruler, and to be very careful about the angle of sunlight that raked across the stones. William believed that eventually he would be able to automatically analyze the messages encoded in the inner walls of the pyramid as well as the megalithic structures all over the world. But although the camera equipment and the computer worked perfectly, his home-grown software had a long way to go before it could do anything more than occasionally extract the length of the meter stick from the images.

William was so wrapped up in his stone measurements that he forgot about the Japanese and the blue star for days. Then a pile of raw data arrived from Japan and he realized that he had better make at least a perfunctory investigation. The analysis went quickly, using his fancy supercomputer to crunch the math, but the results were very different from last time. After considerable confusion and revision, William realized that he had made a simple mistake in his initial analysis. A few quick calculations revealed that the star's arrival was only a year or two away, not decades into the future. When he told Zarlie, she prevailed on him to warn the world, so they posted an article on several internet news sites: a good way to pass the problem to someone else and clear the matter from his overloaded brain. William had doubts about the accuracy of this analysis and didn't dare sign the warning or mention his name. His whole body focused on decoding the stone writing, not on making an accurate astronomical analysis of obscure Japanese data.

"Stanford University. Scientists have discovered that a bluish-tinted star, near the center of the dagger in the Orion Constellation, which was recently discovered by Japanese astronomers, is actually a huge spaceship headed toward the Earth. The scientists analyzed the peculiar unique blue-shifted spectrum from the craft and realized that it could only be generated by an advanced form of atomic hydrogen propulsion. The spaceship should arrive near earth in a few years,

but there is uncertainty about the arrival time and the course that the ship will take. Pulsations in the spectra of the light from the spaceship may be a message, but it has not been decoded. Astronomers and scientists throughout the world are urged to analyze the light from the spaceship so as to determine if this is a friendly or dangerous mission to our planet."

A few days later as William worked busily Gloria asked, "How's that gypsy? Seen her lately?"

William tensed slightly, "Oh, I ran into her and we did a few scientific experiments, nothing that anyone could see. We were very careful, per your instructions."

"She's bad news, so watch yourself."

Jake rushed into William's office, panting and out of breath. "Hey you two, have you seen the news?"

William began to feel apprehensive as Gloria asked, "What's wrong Jake. You look like you've seen a ghost."

"It's worse, the aliens have sent for the mothership and it's on the way. Be here next year or maybe sooner."

Gloria was startled but not as startled as William: what a totally strange interpretation of his blue star article. Gloria asked, "What aliens? What's this about a mothership?"

"There're aliens disguised as humans scattered all over earth. Everybody knows it. Now some scientists have discovered a huge ship on the way here. We've got to get busy and kill all the aliens before they take over the planet in preparation for the arrival."

William's guts churned as he wondered what else Jake knew about aliens. Gloria asked, "Where do we find the aliens? What do they look like?"

"Just like you and me. They're well-disguised, but some people can tell the difference by using special equipment. Gloria, I'm sorry but I need to work on this, so I'll be running around for awhile. Can you get by without me?"

"Sure Jake, do what you have to do, and let me know when you find out more: I'd love to see an alien when you discover one."

William wanted to appear much more innocent than he felt. Suddenly he smiled with an idea, "Hey maybe some of them are our customers! I'll scan the database for suspicious entries about aliens and space ships."

Jake shook his head, "They're really smart so they wouldn't give themselves away, but give it a shot. It would be great if you could find a few. We earthlings are going to need all the help we can get."

After Jake left, William couldn't resist asking Gloria, "How can people believe stuff like that, I mean, that there are aliens wandering around trying to take over the planet?"

"He's a good worker, so let him work his own thing. Now do me a favor and scan the database. I know you were being facetious when you suggested doing it, but it's not a bad idea and can you imagine Jake's excitement if you find one!"

As soon as Gloria left his office, William jumped onto the net and started reading the peculiar stories his announcement had engendered. He noticed immediately that Stanford had disavowed all knowledge of the *discovery* and that astronomy experts had debunked it. However a few groups were already treating it as a potential religious experience and one faction was certain that a modern god drove a spaceship and that he was coming down to clean house!

Chapter 12
Star Math

In an early autumn rain William wandered home, his mind churning with problems, but also with mathematical curiosity, oblivious to his soaking feet and squeaky shoes. After reading scattered scientific critiques of his blue star theory, he knew that he was on to an interesting problem, but that he had handled it badly. One of the more serious rebuttals to his analysis pointed out major factors that he hadn't considered. William felt embarrassed, but thankful that he hadn't signed the article. He realized that he didn't know nearly enough astronomical math to correctly calculate the arrival date of the star, or perhaps, spaceship. He also knew that he probably should focus on solving the mystery of stone writing, but the idea that he had made a big math mistake, then published prematurely, bugged him: he would like to correct the star analysis, or at least learn how to come a bit closer to the truth.

He figured that the spaceship's, or star's, *speed* was easy to calculate based on traditional Doppler shift math, but the *distance* was nearly impossible to determine. The star might be so far away that it wouldn't arrive for millennia, or it might be coming next week, and it might miss the earth and our solar system completely. The problem was just like knowing a car's speed, but not its location. Even if the car were going a hundred miles an hour, it wouldn't arrive for a long time if it were coming from Siberia, but if it were in Berkeley, it could be here in a few hours, assuming it was coming to campus and not to a strip club near the airport. He had to find out how far away the star was located, then his knowledge of its speed would yield an approximate arrival date. Thinking this way gave him an idea.

As soon as his wet feet carried him home he phoned the headquarters of SETI, the Search for Extra-Terrestrial Intelligence organization, based in Berkeley, on the other side of the Bay. These people would know all about distances to stars and how to calculate them, and they would be especially interested in his spaceship. As William dialed, he realized that he would need to identify himself as the discover of the ship if he wanted any serious information. Damn, why not forget the star and get back to pyramid math and the ancient stone writing? In the event, his natural curiosity prevailed over common sense as he revealed his work on the star and his calculations to the faceless person at the other end of the line. William was used to dealing with students and professors, where open discussion of all subjects was the rule so he told everything. His associates never held back due to worries about political correctness or sensitivity. However in the back of his mind, his adventures with Zarlie and her extra-legal exploits were beginning to make him feel uneasy: paranoid would be too strong a word to describe his feelings, but he knew that he probably should be more cautious when talking about the star since it had already generated a lot of weird publicity.

In the end, he discovered that the people at SETI didn't actually know much about astronomical math, but they were able to send him to a Russian astrophysics professor who lived outside Santa Cruz, up above the coastal fog near Ben Lomond. William arranged a visit with the professor for the next afternoon after emailing him all his calculations.

After an hour on wet narrow mountain roads between huge moss-covered redwood trees that squeezed the foggy road into one lane at places, he arrived at a little house near the top of a hill. How could this place be so remote, yet only a bit more than an hour from San Jose or San Francisco: what a location! Professor Blinikof was playing an old worn and scratched piano when William arrived, and he continued to play Chopin quietly during their conversation.

"Thank you for taking time to see me. What did you think about my analysis of the blue star?"

"Your email was quite clear, as far as it went, and I myself have had similar ideas, though I wouldn't have thought them, how would you say, well-founded enough, to announce them to the world."

"You're telling me! I never should have mentioned this to the press before I talked with people who actually know something about astrophysics."

"Yes. But now people are starting to ask questions, perhaps the wrong questions, and they are going to make life interesting for experts in the field. You can fade away as you actually know nothing of the subject, but I will need to be careful of what I say, and the SETI people are so excited: they also may make premature announcements."

"So, how far away is the spaceship, that is if it is a spaceship, and if my analysis of hydrogen-powered propulsion is correct?"

"You analyzed the speed of the ship, and you deduced the speed based on very simple math. But, consider that the speed may not be constant, and that the direction of travel is also unknown.

You based your simplistic analysis on one data point. We need to gather information for months, more likely years, to determine the direction in which it is traveling, and then perhaps we can begin to estimate the distance and the arrival time."

"Can't you tell the distance now? I mean, there's all this stuff in textbooks about how far away the different stars are from earth: can't you just calculate it?"

"Those calculations are for specific types of stars, types for which we have extensive measurements of brightness and composition from spectral analysis and many observations: we can determine the distance for normal stars with some confidence because we have lots of data from different observatories and satellites. Your new star is a different type: it is unique, so we have little information on its characteristics or history. No one can tell you how far away it really is, and for that matter, no one, or at least no scientific person, can tell you if it is even coming toward us. Maybe it's composed of strange blue material and is actually going away from us."

"Bummer. I mean what if it is coming next year, wouldn't you be able to tell that?"

"Please. Don't start talking like those fools on television. Your star is very far away, and it is being monitored closely at many observatories, but the scientists following your star are carefully analyzing its movement, not making pronouncements."

"But what about the star NGC-5011-C in Centaurus? The official astronomers were off by thirteen million light years: the stuff in the text books about it is completely wrong."

"Yes a big error, however now the distance has been corrected based on new observations. That's how science works. Your star will be intensely studied and there will be many estimates of its location and movements. However, there will be no more half-cocked arrival time calculations on the web, that is, as long as you resist the temptation to become a celebrity."

"Don't worry, I don't want to be a fifteen-minute hero, at least not over this. I'm working on more important things, so I'm glad to leave the star in your hands."

"You don't need to be so self-effacing, so modest. Step back for a moment and consider the bigger picture. Your actions have brought the world's attention to a major discovery, and although you don't have the background to follow it through, you have opened many eyes to perhaps the biggest event in the history of our civilization. Although no proper scientist would have made such an announcement on such thin evidence, I say bravo! You have awakened people all over the earth to the possibility that we have friends in the universe, and that a few of them may be coming to visit. Think of the fun we astrophysicists will have arguing and calculating the probability of arrival and the likely date. Will you live to see it? Will I? Who knows, but what a subject for study! And, if the variation in the brightness of the star contains an encoded message, major excitement for the earth's cryptographers! Again I say, bravo! Good job William! Give yourself a pat on the back for making a horrendous blunder that will activate many scientists for years to come." With that Blinikof played a loud series of chord progressions and signaled the end of their talk.

William could see why the SETI people had recommended that he visit Professor Blinikof. SETI, Blinikof, and many other scientists would take over the blue star project and he could watch from a safe distance while working on the ancient stone writing, which was far more important for his career. For fun, he stopped in Pescadero to grab a piece of Olalaberry pie and a few cups of coffee. Olalaberries only grow wild in areas immersed in northern California coastal fog, and the little restaurant in Pescadero was one of the few places where you could enjoy them year-round.

On the way in to campus, down Alpine Road from the mountains, he noticed one of the surveyor trucks parked by the side of the road in the middle of nowhere, slowly rotating its antenna, probably still looking for the jar. As he drove past, he felt like a criminal. He and Zarlie were holding a valuable piece of stolen property, even if the goons might never find it with their peculiar technology. Seeing the truck sent a shiver of apprehension through his body, sort of like passing a police car going the other way when you know you are speeding. He checked his rear view mirror to make sure that the truck didn't start to follow him. But then he started to worry, what if the truck had detected him and radioed a description of his car!

When he entered his office at YFN, he found a note and a small paper sandwich bag from Gloria. He opened the bag, saw that it contained a bit of cash then read the note. The rest of his money would be doled out weekly, along with a performance review. What a pain, the cash would come as slowly as possible, with much emphasis on what he could do for her, not the other way around. At least the bag contained five grand in crisp bills, enough to buy a plane ticket to Cairo and a few weeks in a cheap hotel. A small start on his first big expedition.

He also found an email from Zarlie, asking him to meet her at the secluded bench near history corner, at the spot near the steam tunnel entrance that they had used to visit the underground lab ages ago. He marveled at her phraseology: no one other than

William could have made sense of her message: *Meet me at the place where you stupidly asked me if it was the wrong time of the month, at six hours before the last time we met there.* She was being very careful not to give any useful information to creeps who might be monitoring his email.

William realized that he had better start moving as he had less than half an hour to reach her. He walked across campus, then across Quad, heading for their bench among the Oleanders next to the steam vent. As he walked diagonally across the open space of Inner Quad, a group of breathless people ran up to him. One shouted, "William Stowell, stop, stop just for a minute."

William paused in confusion. Until this instant, his thoughts had been completely focused on Zarlie and what their meeting might involve, what she might say, what he would tell her about Blinikof and SETI, and the cash GLoria had given him. Who were these guys with their camera, lights, and microphones?

The small news team caught up with William and surrounded him. The cameraman aimed his lens, complete with blinking red light, at William while a soundman held a microphone overhead. A breathless reporter in blazer and white tennis shirt began, "William, you are William Stowell, aren't you?"

"Of course, I mean, get lost, who are you, what do you want with me?" The cameraman framed a perfect picture of the reporter and a haggard young student in front of the golden murals on the front of Memorial Church at sunset.

"SETI sent us your picture and told us how you discovered the spaceship that's coming next year, or even sooner."

"Oh shit, you have it all wrong, those people don't have a clue, it isn't coming for centuries, even if it is coming, no one really knows about this stuff."

He tried to evade them, but didn't want to get too close to where he knew Zarlie to be waiting: the last thing he wanted was to involve her in this publicity.

"Please, watch your language, we're live on the five o'clock news."

"Holy shit."

"Careful! Now please won't you tell us about the ship and who is coming, and when they will arrive?"

"If I mess up your sound track will you leave me alone? You don't have a clue, the ship isn't coming for centuries, I made a simple arithmetic mistake, the story is dead, none of us will live long enough to see its arrival. Go home."

"Wait, we heard that it's coming much sooner, what's wrong?"

"The math, don't you see? I made a mistake, like two plus two equals five, not four: the story's over, the ship's not coming for ages, and maybe it's not even coming here." Suddenly William had a bad thought. What if the alienologists saw this TV news program, recognized his face, and started following him. He had to stop this immediately.

"How do you know? Maybe you've made another mistake, and it'll be here next week?"

Meanwhile Zarlie watched all this from her hiding place nearby. She had not gone all the way to their rendezvous because she had seen a pair of campus policemen. Normally she ignored the innocent young cops, but not now. Zarlie worried about the jar, about her strange DNA, and about the illogical waves that kept her awake at night: she feared everything. Life was almost unbearable, and she longed to escape. And William, those TV people were asking too many questions!

"Look, the star is far away. Astrophysicists will figure it all out in the years to come. Maybe it's just an unusual body like a pulsar or quasar and no big deal."

"But what if God is coming to visit us? This could be the end of the world! Judgment Day! The Rapture! Maybe He's coming next month, we've got to be ready."

"And maybe it's the Easter Bunny, or Saint Nick, or Captain Kirk: no one has a clue, so leave me alone. I don't have the answers."

With this comment, William turned, shoved his hand into the camera lens, and ran away in the direction opposite that which would have led him to Zarlie. He rounded a corner and ducked into the old bathroom behind Geology Corner then waited in a stall for ten anxious minutes, hoping the TV people had gone somewhere else.

Eventually he circled around and met Zarlie near their favorite bench. They huddled close together, whispering, keenly on the lookout for others who might be listening or watching. Soon they crept away to Zalie's car and drove north to a cheap restaurant on Vallejo in the North Beach section of San Francisco. Zarlie shook with fear and confusion and William trembled with unease.

The Roman Spaghetti House was a small Italian restaurant with red checkered tablecloths, candle-wax encrusted Chianti bottles that provided dim light, and low student-level prices. An x-rated club was next door: drunks slept on the filthy sidewalk. There wasn't a tourist in sight. William tried to comfort Zarlie, who seemed reluctant to talk: she was very worried about something.

"I'll bet that TV crew has smeared my picture all over the

country by now. At least they don't know about you."

"The TV isn't your only problem, you've got much more serious issues to worry about."

"What, what are you talking about?"

"I don't know how to tell you about this, and well, maybe I shouldn't, but shit, I'm just going to lay it all out and see what you think."

"Is your news worse than this cheap red wine?"

"Drink up, you're in for a big surprise. While you've been chasing pyramids, old languages, and spaceships, I've been busy researching my odd DNA, looking for other places it might occur. In thinking about it I wondered who do I know who is rather strange but smart? Who might be a candidate for similar DNA? And, who has weird brain waves? So when we were in the old shielded room playing games and testing our brains, I managed to gather a sample of your DNA, a few of your hairs. I ran your sample, twice, and surprise, you have almost the same strange DNA that I have. We're both off the charts. And the best thing about this is that you have relatives we can test while I'm an orphan, so maybe by studying your relatives we can get a handle on how we came to be so unusual."

"Wait a minute, holy shit, maybe you've got the wrong interpretation: maybe we're both aliens, and the alienologist whackos are out to exterminate us!"

"William, get a grip, that's all baloney. Do you think we arrived by spaceship like E.T.?"

"Listen, I'm serious. Just suspend your logical mind for a minute, OK? Zarlie, the A-meter is supposed to be able to find aliens, and we thought it was a piece of junk, but what if all that crap is true and it really works? We did interact with it, and the creeps were very surprised: they seemed to think they had detected us by using it."

"Well, if that were true, then we could take the jar and build a complete A-meter and maybe find other aliens with DNA like ours before the fools killed them. It would be an interesting piece of research."

"Let me see if I've got this DNA stuff straight. You and I have odd DNA, and it's different from the DNA in plants and animals and most other people, right?"

"Right, so far it's just in people, and just in you and me as far as I know."

"So if you and your friends are right, the earth's original DNA came from outer space, via panspermia, billions of years ago. But we, and maybe other people, have slightly different DNA."

"Yes, I realized that immediately, and thought of at least one scenario that could explain the difference. Supposing we say that you and I and some others have an improved, or upgraded, form of DNA, like a new version of software. It could have come from advanced people visiting earth a long time ago: people who mated with proto-humans and now we're the direct descendants, or throwbacks, from that interaction."

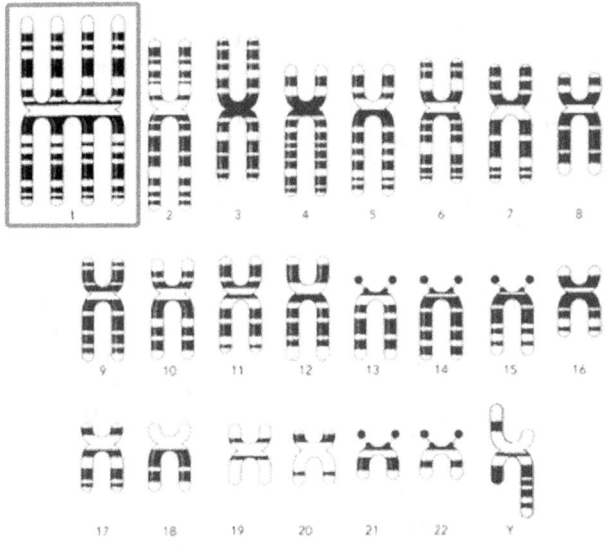

William's very strange male DNA, with extra material in the #1
chromosome

"Hey maybe lots of interesting people in history are our ancestors. DNA testing's only been around for a few years, so who knows, all sorts of neat people down through the ages might have had the same DNA as we have. There're loads of old legends about people with odd characteristics and we think it's all fiction, but maybe some of the stories are about real people, people with advanced characteristics and abilities?"

"Well, I hope that someday we get the chance to do historical DNA work on old graves and mummies, but we have a much more immediate problem, and it doesn't have to do with the Alienologists or historical characters. We've been caught, and we have to make a big decision."

"Caught? What do you mean?"

"I had a premonition that my days on campus were about to end, so I wanted to analyze your DNA while I had access to the equipment. It was easy to slip into the genetics lab late at night. If I could have just run the analysis quickly, I would have had the answer. I was bent over the sequencer, watching the computer slowly print a cytogenetic map of your chromosomes, when the TA startled me, saying 'What are you doing here so late Zarlie?' Damn, I had been so focused on my work that I hadn't paid attention to the danger signals that my brain detected as the TA approached. I tried to cover the printout, and told him I was just trying a personal experiment. I didn't want to bother anyone. Then he hit keys on the computer and your DNA popped to life in bright color on the screen before I could do anything. It looked just like my DNA, two big number-one pairs scrambled on the left, but with a male XY at the end. What a discovery. The TA jumped out of his skin, he'd never seen anything like it. I yanked the power cord from the wall, killing the computer memory and clearing the screen instantly. He was furious as the computer went dark. He screamed, 'What the hell have you done! You've screwed my computer.' I tore off the print, grabbed the sample of your hair, and ran for the door. I knew I was in big trouble with the bio department. Here's a printout of your DNA."

"So what did the TA do? Why are we in trouble? You didn't wreck the computer did you?'

"It's much worse than that. Professor Weiskopf was on my case first thing the next morning. He wants the male body that generated that sample. So I played cool and asked him what it would be worth if I produced it. He thought the sample came from a mal-formed corpse or embryo, some sort of illegal genetic experiment that had gone wrong, and he was hot to study it on the sly. I toyed with him and he finally offered me ten grand for the body, no questions asked. So then I asked him what he would pay for a living, potent, sperm sample from the body, that is if the body were alive."

"You're talking about me, my body?"

"Of course. You do have sperm don't you?"

William blushed deep red and turned away as Zarlie continued. "Sorry I didn't mean to embarrass you. For me sex and bodily functions are everyday subjects. You should have seen him light up as he thought about mating the sperm with a normal human egg. So he raised the offer to fifty grand, which would put us far away in Egypt for a long time if we could do it. Then he asked about the possibility of other samples, so I asked him what a matched DNA pair, sperm and egg, would be worth on the private market. Turns out we could get maybe three hundred thou in cash, then disappear, far from the alienologists. We would be free. We could research forever in peace and quiet."

"Did you agree to do this, I mean, it's just beginning to sink in, I had no idea our bodies were so valuable."

"He could make huge scientific breakthroughs, and he wouldn't even need to know too much about the source, at least about you, but I'd have to go into a discreet IVF (In Vitro Fertilization) clinic for a few weeks to collect the eggs. There's lots of quiet money floating around to sponsor off-the-books bio research. He's making a serious offer, but I didn't accept, but I didn't turn him down either."

"It would be like you and I were selling one of our children, a baby who would have all of our genes, all of our characteristics, but none of our love. Would we ever see him, or her?"

"Or it. There's no guarantee that our DNA's compatible, and test-tube babies often don't make it, but you're right, it's not an easy choice."

"Our DNA must be compatible, I mean how did we get here? Our parents had genes like this and made babies, you and me, so it could work, an offspring could be viable."

"Let's go for a walk and talk about it a bit more. I'm nearly wiped out. Those damn voices keep popping into my head, my research and school work are falling behind, and I just want to get away for awhile. I don't care as much as you do about pyramid research, but I'd love to hang out in Egypt, soak up some rays, and have lots of quiet time for serious thinking. The cash would be useful. I'm tempted even if you aren't, and what's to stop us making more babies some day if we wanted them?"

As they left William had completely different thoughts, far from the scientific world in which he normally lived. He stopped and held Zarlie's hands in his. "What're your brain waves telling you about me, about our future? Will we be together for a long time?"

"I don't know, but I wish I did. Right now I'm afraid, scared stiff, and I want to run away. That's all I know."

They huddled close together and wandered past the shuttered Chinese grocery stores on Stockton as the fog rolled in with a light drizzle. The deep-pitched fog horn on the south pillar of the Golden gate Bridge began to bellow every ten seconds, and soon it was joined by others. A damp wet night in the fog, with visibility down to maybe fifty feet as they walked alone from streetlight to streetlight wondering what to do.

Suddenly Zarlie grabbed William and dragged him down a dark alley. They huddled behind a smelly grocery store dumpster loaded with rotted fish scraps and old vegetables as a surveyor truck slowly cruised down the street, but it didn't stop. As soon as it passed, they ran down random streets, then up the Vallejo Steps, pausing at the half-way point, away from places where the truck could drive. They panted from fear and their running, as they huddled together in the cold and damp night air.

"William, I can't take any more of this, I'm going to call Weisskopf and ask him to check me into an IVF clinic far away. Please come with me. Let's take the money and go. I'll ovulate in two weeks then we can leave for Egypt. You can make detailed research plans after we get there."

Chapter 13
Fight & Run

Later that night Zarlie drove to a remote clinic far up the coast north of San Francisco, while William went to his office at Gloria's to gather computer files before joining her.

He worked quietly in the late night darkness, confused and worried: so many changes in his life in just a few hours. He hadn't bothered to turn on his room lights since his three glowing computer screens were all that he needed to watch. William worked methodically, the only person in the building as far as he knew. Suddenly, he heard voices downstairs near the fountain. He stopped typing, listened hard, and recognized both of them, Gloria and Jake, but could only catch part of their conversation due to the fountain's noisy splashing, and the fact that they were moving around.

Soon he heard them coming up the stairs and into Gloria's office, oblivious to his presence. Old music started quietly flowing from Gloria's office and William recognized it as 'Die Fahne Hoch', one of Hitler's marching songs. He could hear much of their conversation since all the doors were open and they were nearby. Gloria and Jake were discussing the TV news program and how surprised they were that their friend and co-worker William had discovered the spaceship. But Jake had just heard much more startling news.

"Gloria, this may seem really odd to you, as it sure did to me, but I just heard that William is the prime suspect in a big robbery that happened to friends of mine. They recognized his picture on TV."

"Get real, he's as honest and simple as the day is long."

"No, this is true. He and some girl were taking a test when very special equipment detected that at least one of them is an alien, and then the equipment exploded."

"He's no alien, your friends are nuts."

"After the explosion, he and the girl ran into the laboratory where the equipment was installed, then they escaped. Later that night criminals broke into the building, right into the lab, and stole the heart of our most secret apparatus. It's got to be the same two people, or at least one of them."

"Girl? Wait a minute! A girl who broke into a building and stole something? I know who the hell that is, she's Zarlie Istvan, a thieving gypsy who's messing with William."

William strained his ears to hear every word and thought that he could detect. How he wished that he could read people's minds and hear the conversation more clearly. He nearly fainted as he heard them continuing to talk about Zarlie, then realized that he was sweating, not from heat, but from fear. Time to get away before they discovered his nearby presence and grabbed him. He quietly shutdown the computers and slipped into the bathroom his office shared with the next. As he moved, he heard Gloria exclaim to Jake, "Hey, you look a lot better without your pants."

William crept away, going quietly down the back staircase, sweating with fear as he walked into the cool clear night. He shoved a few things into a suitcase at his apartment and was on the road to meet Zarlie in less than ten minutes, still shaking with apprehension.

William drove north on 280, onto 101 through San Francisco, over the Golden Gate Bridge, and continued north to Cloverdale, carefully following the directions Zarlie had written. He turned onto 128, a smaller highway, and then onto 253, a little narrow dark road, at Boonville. He had been traveling over two hours and it was pitch dark as he wove through the mountains toward the coast on the deserted road. Just before he reached the Coast Highway near Point Arenas, he turned onto a dirt road, then through a locked gate that opened with a number key from the instructions. He realized that he had entered a huge ranch just inland from the ocean. He drove several more miles on private roads, to a large ranch-house complex on a plateau at the top of the Coast Range. Oak trees and grassy fields surrounded the buildings. In the dim light he saw a few rich cars, poor cars, old pickups, as well as a helicopter and a small plane parked on the grass. He spotted Zarlie's car, parked next to it, then curled up on his back seat to sleep until dawn.

A friendly nurse awakened William, and she already knew who he was, and why he was here. After breakfast, William and Zarlie sat on a hilltop talking quietly looking at the distant ocean. William told her about his experience at Gloria's and about his fear that they could be caught at any minute. Although Zarlie shared his worry, she felt that they were safe as long as they were careful. Then she changed the subject. She was curious about his parents and relatives, as they might hold clues about their odd DNA. "What's your first memory? What do you remember of your parents and relatives?"

"Nothing really. I don't talk much about my parents,

because, well, I almost never see them."

"At least you have parents, that's something."

"Like you, I was raised by relatives, but in comfort instead of fear. My parents are weird. They both had tons of money at an early age and so they've always done whatever they wanted."

"Like spoiled brats?"

"Worse. In 1994 when mother was in Paris with her girl friends, father, who is a terrible artist, painted the walls of their private rooms with huge nude pictures of every girl he'd ever screwed, in sequence, with dates, many of which were after their marriage."

"What happened when she came back?"

"She laughed and laughed and told him that they didn't have enough wall space for her to paint all the boys and girls she'd been with. I don't know if she was kidding or not, but father stormed out the door into the night. I haven't seen him since. I've heard that he's at a monastery in Tibet."

"Why don't you go visit, it might be fun, and maybe he's a lot smarter now?"

"I'm not sure I want to see him, and mother spends most of her time abroad. I saw her at Christmas last year but it was awkward. We don't have much in common and she's got a mean temper if things don't go the right way. However, my uncle, who's close to ninety, is still sharp and fun to be with. Uncle John and his wife Martha raised me pretty much on their own."

"What happened to the paintings?"

"They're still in the old family home in Dorset and uncle John charges trippers ten pounds to see them. We both think father made up most of his exploits and I've talked with some of the women involved. They deny everything."

"Your parents sound healthy, just messed up. Are there any sick relatives, I mean, any in insane asylums or with rare diseases?"

"Not that I know of. They're pretty normal and at least two are in their nineties, so the genes must be pretty good."

"I'd love to get a DNA sample from as many as possible. If they could just mail us strands of hair or fingernail clippings, we could run the analysis, or get Weisskopf to do it without telling anyone."

"Let's call my aunt and ask her to collect samples and put them in separate envelopes so that we know who's who."

As the conversation with Aunt Martha began they realized that they should have thought much more about how to make the call before starting. Calling his aunt and asking for a sample of her DNA seemed to put her on her guard. Aunt Martha acted puzzled, and became evasive in her answers, as William explained why he wanted the samples. Zarlie put her ear next to the phone and could hear Martha dodging around William's request. Maybe they were about to learn something about other people who had odd DNA and she didn't want to tell. Finally Aunt Martha asked William if he really wanted to know the truth right now, or if he would rather wait until their next meeting. Clearly she didn't want to talk about this on the phone. William paused, then replied that he wanted, that he needed, to know immediately. Zarlie and William waited with anticipation through the silence, then Martha said reluctantly that William had been adopted as a new-born infant because his mother didn't want to deal with the pain and hassle of childbirth. Aunt Martha didn't know anything about his biological parents, and was deeply sorry that she had to be the one to tell him, and especially sorry that she was eight thousand miles away instead of talking with him in person.

Zarlie didn't know what to say. She hugged William tightly and tried to ease the deep pain that she could feel burning in his heart. An important part of his world, of his conception of himself and his place in the universe, had just been ripped away. William dropped the phone as hot tears ran down his face. Moments ago he had been part of a family, not a wonderful family, but his very own world of relatives and their history. He had been anticipating the pride and excitement they would share when he published his big pyramid discovery. Now that dream evaporated, he was nobody, cast out into the world alone. He wandered around the ranch all day, crying a bit, and thinking about his past and the future.

William skipped dinner, but afterwards Zarlie found him and gave him an ice cream cone. They sat in the shade, outside the clinic next to a cyan-colored fountain, it's happy burbling water contrasting against his sad feelings.

"Here William, you've got to eat something and start thinking about the fun we're going to have decoding the pyramid secrets. Bet nobody thinks you can do it."

"They don't have a clue. I'm so close to decoding the wall writing. All I need are accurate pictures of the tunnels inside the Great Pyramid."

"Right, we'll be there in a few weeks, and hey, guess what?"

"What?"

"I used to know a little Arabic, don't ask me why, but I found an Arabic phrase book in the library here and I'm going to be your translator: it's starting to come back and there's a nurse who speaks it. We're already talking."

"Great. So, er, what exactly is happening, I mean with your eggs, not the Arabic?"

"They're giving me medicine to make the collection process

easier and a daily examination. It's no big deal for me: the doctors and nurses do all the work. The drugs stimulate egg production, then they'll carefully collect the eggs from my ovaries with a hollow needle, just as the eggs are ripening inside their follicles. The eggs will be put in nutrient fluid with live sperm, and after a few days, the embryo or embryos will be placed into a birth mother's uterus. It's a complex procedure, and even with experts doing the work, the success rate is only 50%. By the way, it's time for you to start collecting sperm samples and freezing them in the lab. Want me to help or show you how to do it?"

"Good grief, I mean no, just tell me what to do."

"That's the spirit. Let's see how many milliliters you can leave behind."

"Well, at least we're getting something useful from our unknown biological parents."

In contrast to the egg collection process, a large quantity of sperm would be easy to collect then freeze in sterile containers. Zarlie thoroughly embarrassed William as she discussed the details and led him into a lab. She picked up a box of sterile test tubes and a smoking Dewar flask of liquid nitrogen. (The vapor from the thermos-like bottle wasn't smoke but a cloud of frozen water vapor. The extreme cold in the flask caused moisture in the nearby air to condense into a heavy fog that looked like smoke.) William overcame his embarrassment as he began to realize that this was much more serious, emotionally, than he had imagined it would be. They could almost feel each other's thoughts as she handed him the equipment.

He turned to Zarlie and looked into her deep green eyes. "I never thought about having children with you. I mean, not now, not while we're so young, while there's so much to do."

"If something happens to us, if we die soon, if we're killed, at least we're leaving our genes behind. A child, even if from a Petri dish, it might carry on. There is a positive side, and we'll be using the money wisely. It's the start of our Living Waves project."

As the days passed quickly she talked about their collection efforts calmly, while William was uneasy whenever the subject came up. He turned bright red when she asked how many sperm samples he had made, how many milliliters were in each sample, and if he had frozen them correctly,. Zarlie laughed gently at his embarrassment as she encouraged him to collect as often as possible. Meanwhile, William stayed very busy gathering information and contacting friends in Japan, getting ready for the trip. He planned an evasive round-about route to Egypt, hoping to elude anyone who might try to follow them. They feared the all-prying media people who wanted to talk about the spaceship, and the Alienologists who might somehow discover their whereabouts.

As he organized the trip, William realized that he did not have everything that he needed for the pyramid project: he would need to make one quick trip back to his apartment, but dreaded the idea of going anywhere near campus. Surely Gloria and Jake would be on the lookout, and have spies posted near their office and his apartment. At the moment he and Zarlie were safe and with some luck they would leave the country without anyone knowing their plans. But he needed several notebooks which contained his preliminary analyses and a few disks of custom software which he had forgotten in his hasty departure. Cameras and computers could be bought anywhere, but his notes and software, those were irreplaceable.

Zarlie and William discussed different ways to get to his apartment without being caught or followed. They knew that he would need to go himself, as no one else could be able to find the correct books and computer programs. There didn't appear to be any way to send a surrogate or a messenger to gather the material. Once they made this decision, it was a question of planning the safest way to make the trip. Zarlie felt that perhaps their fear of being caught might be excessive: most likely nobody would see them, especially if they came in a different car and moved quickly. They would both go. Zarlie's ability to sense danger and detect the creeps before they were spotted seemed a sure guarantee of success. They could easily borrow an innocuous car from the clinic, drive down in the middle of the night, and be back before dawn.

Time went by quickly as they prepared to leave. The critical day arrived and Zarlie's eggs were collected without problems. The doctors didn't know if the eggs would mate successfully, but at least Zarlie could relax: she had kept her part of the bargain. In the evening Professor Weiskopf arrived to take possession of their genetic material and deliver the cash. In his suit and tie, he looked the perfect senior professor, but he walked like a bank robber, looking over his shoulder warily. As he approached the couple, Zarlie could tell that he felt as awkward as she did.

"Did you follow my instructions? Any problems?" Weiskopf asked quietly.

"No, the sperm samples should be perfect, but the eggs are any one's guess," Zarlie answered.

"Please call me from time to time, and I'll let you know the results of our experiments."

Zarlie was almost crying, "If the embryo is alive, you'll put it in a loving birth mother, won't you."

"Of course Zarlie, we care as much as you do. This is a very special experiment."

"We have to repack the cash into the lining of our suitcases. Is there very much," William asked hesitantly.

"Somewhere just under half a million I think. My partners are ecstatic about the research possibilities. When you come back, we'll do a lot more work, and we'll have much to share."

"I, we, hope that day comes, but it's hard to tell right now. Thanks for everything," William answered softly.

"The three of us are taking amazing risks tonight, but the scientific payoff may be incredible. You two are doing the right thing. I hope I am too."

"We have a big research project of our own, involving brainwave communication. We can both do it reliably, and believe that it's not electromagnetic radiation, but something else. We want to spend the rest of our lives developing the science behind it," Zarlie quietly added.

"I could help in that effort when you come back."

"Let's say goodbye. We have a journey to make, and you need to get these samples into a proper lab quickly," William said.

As they began to part, Weisskopf looked at them carefully and shook their hands and tightly hugged each in turn. William hadn't realized how old and frail the professor was until that moment, until William held him in his arms. They wished each other luck. So much remained unsaid but deeply felt. Just below the surface they were very, very sad, almost crying.

As soon as Weiskopf left, they headed for campus in an old gray car. The trip turned out to be easier than they had feared. After much trepidation, they arrived on campus in the dead of night, slipped into William's apartment by flashlight, collected the software and notebooks, and were back on the road in less than five minutes. Zarlie had strained very hard but had not felt any signs of danger or trouble. What they didn't know was that a hidden infra-red camera near the apartment driveway had been triggered by the car and their movements. Before they left the apartment photos from the camera had been transmitted to a team of surveyors who would now follow at a discrete distance, well out of Zarlie's detection range.

Zarlie and William drove back toward the clinic. After a long ride, they passed through sleeping Booneville and onto narrow winding highway 253 to the coast. They were close to home and very tired. Suddenly William noticed bright quad headlights from a truck behind them. The truck accelerated, going much too fast for the small road late at night. William hadn't seen another vehicle for half an hour.

"Look behind us, there's someone coming awfully fast: wonder what's their hurry."

Zarlie turned around and looked, then had a bad feeling. "It's not a truck, it's the surveyors: they must have followed us somehow."

William sped up, but the tension, the late night activity, and the darkness caused him to misjudge the road and miss a hairpin turn. The car slid off the road and now two wheels were stuck in the roadside drainage ditch. Before he could get the car moving again, the truck rammed into the hillside and blocked them. William and Zarlie jumped out and started to run as the truck doors opened.

Zarlie instinctively moved to a defensive position in a dark shadow behind a tree, then turned to watch the attackers. Fortunately she had prepared for the possibility of trouble at William's apartment. Her belt concealed a sharp-edged Kevlar whip, and her black shoes had aluminum shanks, steel toes and sharp short metallic heels. Zarlie wore black from head to toe, as she carefully unsheathed a very sharp fighting knife from where it had been hidden inside her clothes. William wasn't a street fighter, hadn't seen where she had gone, and was easy prey for the two attackers. One of them grabbed him and shouted into the darkness, "Gypsy girl, if you don't want to watch me stick this knife in his neck, come out and tell us where you hid our detector."

"Run Zarlie, get help, don't worry about me."

Zarlie watched an owl, a sign of impending death in many cultures, as it hooted in the trees above and circled slowly, its eerie moonlit shadow passing over the group. She knew she wouldn't be the first to die.

The other goon kicked William, then slapped his face loudly, yelling, "We'll kill him slowly, maybe with a hundred cuts instead of a thousand. You can watch the fun or come out and talk."

The goon cut William's hand causing him to scream in pain, then yelled, "We don't want your bodies, we just want the detector, so why don't you play it smart."

Zarlie had been watching, looking for the best way to attack. She saw this as a life and death struggle, but knew that the goons would keep them alive until they found where the detector was hidden. She moved silently from shadow to shadow, until she was in position to strike, then with one fluid well-practiced move jumped from hiding and sliced her razor-sharp knife through the first goon's neck, killing him instantly and freeing William. The other goon spun around to attack Zarlie. She pulled the whip from her waist and ripped flesh from the goon's face as he slashed at her with his knife. After a brief struggle she finished him off with a quick stab. As he fell to the ground she delivered a deadly karate kick to his neck with a steel-toed shoe.

Zarlie just had time to realize that she had a serious cut on her arm when William yelled, "Look out behind you." A third goon had emerged from the truck and moved into position. Before Zarlie could do anything he had grabbed William and was holding a gun to William's head.

"O.K. people, this has gone far enough. I'm going to shoot both of you now unless you start talking."

Zarlie was flushed with adrenaline from her two kills and instinctively focused all her energy on the third goon as she stared at his ugly face. Later she realized that she had not even stopped to consider her actions. As the goon cocked his pistol and aimed it at her crouching form, she whispered a violent curse that flowed from every cell in her body. She could almost see her energy field enveloping the goon.

He screamed, grabbed his head and fell to the ground in excruciating pain. He was dead before Zarlie reached the body. She grabbed his gun and headed for the truck but found it empty.

William was panting, adrenaline camouflaging his pain and cuts. "What happened?"

"I nuked his fucking brain with everything I've got. Let's get out of here."

"You're so different, so violent, so strong, you could have killed them easily even in a fair fight."

"Nothing's fair when it's time to kill. If that guy had been a little smarter we'd be dead, but he forgot for a moment, and that's all I needed. We're damn lucky to be running away from this mess, and my head hurts like hell."

As they drove off, Zarlie used the car's first aid kit to patch their cuts then asked, "Do you hear anything inside your head, like a child crying or calling, or something faint, but almost musical?"

"No, but your head must be badly messed-up after the blast of energy you shot into that guy, and your adrenaline level must be astronomic."

"It's so strange. Stop for a minute and help me try to locate this thing."

William was bewildered and in pain as they stood beside the car on the dark road. Zarlie slowly pivoted her painful body with her eyes closed. "When I turn one way, it gets fainter, but when I turn the other way, it's stronger."

She opened her eyes, then pointed. "Which way is that?"

William looked at the stars overhead and recognized the north star, even though the moon obscured part of the sky. "You're pointing almost due south."

"Let's drive south down along the coast and see if it gets

stronger."

"Maybe when you maxed-out the power on your transmitter to blast him, you inadvertently turned up the sensitivity on your receiver. They could be tied together somehow, so you're hearing new things, things that were too faint for you to detect before."

"Damn my head hurts."

As they drove William began to consider their situation. "Do you realize that we just murdered three people? I mean, it was self-defense, but we've got a lot of explaining to do."

"Who's going to ask questions? Dead bodies don't make good witnesses, and I didn't see anyone else, did you?"

"No, but I mean, shouldn't we call the cops and report those guys?"

"This isn't a T.V. show William. We're in the clear as far as cops are concerned: our problem is other surveyors and what they'll do when they find the bodies."

"Have you killed other people? I mean, you were so fast and efficient back there?"

"I'm alive and they aren't: let's leave it at that for now, O.K.? Fate was with us this time and we were lucky, that's all it was."

William would have liked to ask Zarlie much more about her past but realized that he had better wait for a more peaceful time. And what were they doing driving on a deserted road at night instead of packing for Egypt? Life with Zarlie was becoming ever more complicated. They stopped several times on the dark deserted road above the surf and Zarlie quietly oriented herself to the odd voice she heard inside her head. She could feel it growing stronger.

They navigated following the voice to the small town of Point Reyes Station, but then almost became lost on the small farm roads near it. The roads became smaller and rougher, as they passed the old dairy farms with letter names, like "G Ranch". They were in dairy farming country, on the Point Reyes Peninsula, north of San Francisco. There were no other cars on the road, and it was late, almost three in the morning. The only signs of people were a few distant dark farm houses.

The dark bumpy road ended near abandoned whitewashed farm buildings under a line of old Eucalyptus trees blowing in the wind, their long leaves rattling noisily. Zarlie felt terrible: inside her head the voice grew louder as she led them along the Point Reyes Ridge Trail, going north along the spine of the narrowing peninsula. The full moon illuminated their path, but wisps of fog blew over the ocean-side cliff, driven by a bitter cold wind. A hundred feet below, surf crashed on the rocks sending blasts of salty wet air up to the trail. They heard weird squeaking noises, but realized that they were made by male elks: signs said that they were in an elk preserve.

It seemed to take forever, but they had actually walked less than half an hour when Zarlie picked up unusual vibrations somehow different from those she had been following. They stopped walking as she turned to William, "Don't you hear it too? It's changed. It's a noise that I've never heard before: not good or bad, just new."

"I don't hear anything, but maybe it's something to do with that odd mound of rocks over there?"

William saw a little hill, distinctly shaped, an outcropping of old lichen-covered gray rocks, right on the edge of the cliff. A narrow path had been trampled over to it through the brush, but he had no idea if the footprints in the dirt were new or old.

"Let's go look. The vibrations are growing stronger, but I don't see anything." If anyone were here, he or she could easily see the couple, because William had turned on a flashlight to avoid stickers in the brush. Of course, if the thing could send strange waves a hundred miles, it wouldn't need to see them coming to know they were near.

"Do you think it's coming from a person, or something alive, or maybe a machine?"

"I don't know. Did you feel the ground shake when the breakers hit the shore down below?" As they climbed among the jagged rocks, they realized that there were many places among them where anything could be hidden. William and Zarlie were very near the edge of the steep ocean cliffs. William began looking with his flashlight, thinking that maybe a hidden transmitter was sending the message.

"Watch out, what's that?"

Suddenly they heard a crackling sparky electric sound and a bluish glow appeared, like a thin luminous blue fog materializing from nowhere. What seemed to be a very old but large and exceptionally strong wrinkled man materialized in front of them. He had tattered unusual clothes. Strength and confidence flowed from his body. William couldn't tell if the image in front of his eyes was tangible, or a mirage, or a kind of hologram. Maybe a delusion, or a kind of thing never seen before. William froze. He didn't dare try to reach out and touch the man who towered over them. The vision was inches away and William would have jumped back, except that they were trapped in a narrow cleft in the rocks. The man just looked at them quietly. William could feel an emotional message coming through into his brain. A beautiful warm wave seemed to wash over his body. He felt enormous strength and confidence. Even his toes tingled. The old man seemed to be glowing and shimmering, and maybe smiling as he stared into William's eyes without blinking or moving. The vision didn't move or breathe. William didn't know how long this lasted, then it faded, vanishing as easily as it had come.

They heard an elk squeaking nearby, and broke out of the trance and looked around. One of the herds was blocking the path, but it parted, indifferent to William and Zarlie, as they quietly walked back on the trail. William shivered in the cold wind, his body soaked in sweat. Tears had been flowing down his face.

Zarlie broke the silence, "What do you think that was?"

"I don't know but maybe we just experienced the playback of some sort of recorded Living Wave. Do you think such things exist, or that maybe we just imagined it? It could have been an illusion, or a feeling that was just inside our heads, not something external or real. We haven't had any drugs, but what a night. Maybe our emotions or our brains are all messed up."

"Did You see a shimmering strange old man in a blue fog, and feel energy flowing into your body?"

"Exactly, like a miracle, or vision or I don't know what."

"I saw him too, so either it really existed, or whatever happened affected us both the same way. I felt emotions, not a string of words. It wasn't explicit like math or letters on a page. I was crying with joy and sadness at the same time. I think maybe he was saying 'don't worry, you're on the right path, but be careful'. There was some form of warning, but not specific enough to enunciate. Just an undercurrent of concern."

William added softly, "Maybe we just met our guardian angel and he was watching over us tonight. Perhaps it was a once in a lifetime experience. So beautiful."

"I think I know what the vision's message means, in practical terms. We'd better leave for Egypt, as fast as possible."

As they walked, William took Zarlie's hand in his and asked, "I hope that even though our DNA's similar that we aren't related. I'd like to spend the rest of my life with you, but not just as one of your relatives."

Zarlie smiled and looked into his eyes. "Please William, don't get romantic ideas. I'm badly messed up, and I know that I owe you big time for sticking with me and everything, but I can't fall in love, not now. You can have my body if you want, but my heart's been shattered for a long time, so take it easy, OK?"

"Sure. . . Zarlie, at least we'll be together as we work in Egypt, and well, I won't mess with your body, if your heart's not in it. I care too much for you to do that."

Zarlie squeezed his hand in reply. The sun was rising on a beautiful day as they turned around and headed for the clinic and the long journey to come.

Chapter 14
The Long Journey

William and Zarlie boarded a Japan Airlines flight for Tokyo, wearing casual drab student clothes, blending into the crowd as much as possible. Bright clothes and distinctive appearances were a thing of the past. They were going to Egypt by the most indirect path possible to prevent anyone following them. Hopefully, the last thing that a detective would find of their paper trail was that they had bought tickets to Tokyo. William hoped that followers would think they were going to continue investigations into the blue star, at Tsukuba Observatory.

When they arrived at Narita, Tokyo's airport, they were met by William's Japanese friend Takeda, with whom William had made extensive plans for their escape. Soon they were riding quietly in a black Nissan 'President', through a tangle of traffic jams, headed out of the city to meet Takeda's contact with the underworld Yakuza. After four hours of driving, they met two silent men at a remote farmhouse. Each man wore a short-sleeve black shirt that revealed a small portion of his intricate full-body tattoos, and each had lost a finger during an initiation ceremony. Later, William had a chance to quietly ask Takeda about these men, but learned little. Takeda said that questions were not encouraged, but that after he left Japan, William might buy a copy of 'Yakuza: Japan's Criminal Underworld' (by Kaplan & Dubro); the book had been blocked inside Japan.

The men died William's hair black, cut it in the Japanese manner and put proper Japanese clothes on him. Then they cut Zarlie's hair, gave her formal expensive clothes with a few 'Hello Kitty' items for decoration, and fudged their make-up, especially the eyes. William and Zarlie didn't really look Japanese if examined closely, but from a distance, or in a foreign country, they might easily pass for a pair of VIPs from Japan. Zarlie's demure, but fashionably-correct Japanese clothes, her short jet-black hair, her few frivolous child-like accessories, set against an expensive French purse, gave just the right sense of upper-crust VIP smart-person, worthy of much respect.

The men took pictures, faked them into Japanese passports, and were done. These were special passports, ones reserved for associates of the Emperor on important missions. Almost nobody outside Japan had ever seen one, so they were sure that as long as they acted their parts, the passports' veracity would never be questioned. The passports had elegant ribbons and seals. Their slightly-faded-but-expensive luggage was sprinkled with Japanese stickers. William's new socks were a perfect shade of puke-green. William and Zarlie left in an obscure Toyota, headed for the west coast, and a research ship which routinely smuggled cargo to and from Shanghai.

After the transformations, they made a single phone call, from a rural payphone that would never be traced. Professor Weisskopf had isolated an egg and thought it might be viable. He had moved everything to a secluded lab in Mexico where he wouldn't be bothered or discovered. William and Zarlie couldn't talk long, but hesitated to say goodbye. In a strange way chatting with Weiskopf seemed like talking to a father that they didn't know they had until now. He had become their surrogate parent.

When they reached Shanghai in the rusty old ship, they had no trouble making a discrete entry into the city from the Hwangpu River. The ship had docked briefly next to the faded green Russian Embassy next to Soochow Creek. The river, part of the Yangtze delta, held ships from every corner of the world, along with small local boats powered by thumping one-cylinder engines. Theirs was just another wrinkled rust-streaked ship in the darkening haze. Soon they were ensconced in the time-worn but still beautiful old Peace Hotel, built as Cathay House in 1925 by the Sassoon family from India. An art deco palace, a landmark on The Bund along the river's edge, where Victor Sassoon had lived on the top floor in the twenties. The hotel interior glowed with dark wood, etched glass doors, Lalique light fixtures and chandeliers. All the guest rooms had twelve-foot ceilings, marble bathrooms, and beautiful furnishings. Elegant fittings from another era, with a glittering ballroom on the roof. The Peace had been closed for decades as Chinese sentiment wavered between 'tearing down capitalist elegance' and 'earning tourist dollars'. In the end, the hotel had been renamed and restored to a semblance of its former glory. William noticed a strong smell of sewage as they boarded the walnut-paneled elevator: he was glad they were going up, rather than down.

William and Zarlie were still dressed as Japanese, and rich Japanese at that. Whenever they encountered the Chinese staff persons, Zarlie sensed unfriendly thoughts. The staff was always correct and polite, but Zarlie could tell that the Chinese feelings toward the couple were hateful. The Chinese still resented the Japanese, who had killed over twenty million of their citizens in the 1930's and 1940's. They had even bombed the Peace hotel in

1937. Zarlie had read about Japanese germ warfare experiments in China, in the book "PLAGUE WARS", (Mangold and Goldberg) which described the grisly events in detail, for a bio-ethics class. The Japanese had dropped different kinds of bio-bombs on little villages to determine the correct germ-load, then rushed-in dressed as doctors to conduct autopsies, sometimes on living survivors. Zarlie, in spite of her Rroma views on Hitler, thought he looked like a saint by comparison.

The cuts on William's hand and Zarlie's arm were red and painful: Zarlie realized that they were becoming infected and that they needed stitches and professional care. After a night of intermittent sleep, they ventured out of the hotel, worried but determined. William asked questions in English with what he imagined to be a Japanese accent, while Zarlie stood aloof by his side. The doorman found a taxi which took them inland from the river on Nanjing Road to the Ritz Portman hotel, a modern Mecca for foreign businessmen in a hurry, complete with a small but excellent medical clinic. Now, how to obtain medical attention without giving up their disguises. While William hesitated and worried over this problem, Zarlie bared her infected arm and walked directly to the nurse-receptionist. "Hi, I've got a bad cut and he does too. Please help us, we're in a hurry, and we heard that you have the best nurses and doctors in town."

Her direct approach, without any explanation of her nationality or costume, worked wonders. Soon Zarlie and a nurse were discussing different antibiotics and treatment options while William stood by quietly. But later, as the nurse finished bandaging William, she asked, "You two talk like Americans or Europeans, but why are you wearing Japanese clothes and makeup?"

"It's a long story, involving a fancy costume party", William replied cautiously.

"But the day before yesterday we had an accident and the locals didn't have any decent medicine, so we waited until we hit Shanghai figuring that here we would find people who knew what to do," Zarlie added.

William, anxious to leave before more questions were asked, took three hundred dollar bills from his wallet. "Can we pay you with American money? We haven't had a chance to buy any Yuan."

Fortunately the nurse accepted their cash and they escaped without serious questioning. William had realized that changing money would involve a bank as well as identification and passports, and he didn't want to take any extra chances or leave a paper trail.

They stayed inside the Peace hotel for most of the day to minimize further risk of discovery. They were especially careful to avoid the third floor of the hotel which was reserved for rich Japanese

139

visitors, with its own restaurants, in case real Japanese visitors or staff asked embarrassing questions. In the late afternoon William discovered a door which led onto the roof, upstairs past the Dragon-Phoenix restaurant with its ornate red-dragon ceiling, and they spent an hour outside admiring the view, the swarms of people, and the pollution. The people on the Bund down below were playing old waltzes on boom boxes while they exercised in the park, all doing exactly the same movements. William and Zarlie didn't dare stay outside when the rooftop cocktail bar opened at dusk and returned to their room. They ate room-service dinner while watching B-Sky-B TV, the only English language channel in the hotel, and waited for their plane in the morning.

William and Zarlie were staying in the same room because their fake passports said that they were married. He vividly remembered Zarlie's statement about the availability of her body but not her heart, and realized that situations like the one they were in were almost a test of the seriousness of his interest in her. Without thinking about it consciously, he had became more polite and concerned about her feelings. He tried to avoid even casually touching her as they moved about together. Zarlie could read his true feelings, especially when he saw her climbing into bed in her thin silk pajamas, but she took care to avoid teasing him.

The next day they were on Air China, headed for Cairo via New Dehli, two Japanese VIPs making a proper first class trip, extremely careful to preserve their makeup, their diplomatic baggage, and their identities.

While they were on the plane, William almost rolled into the aisle with laughter as he read a Japanese comic book, 'HOT METAL BETWEEN MY THIGHS'. As Zarlie looked at the wildly-colored Manja drawings, he explained that the theme of the book was that motorcycles should have special love seats, with the girl in front, and that the girl's clothing should have a back-to-front zipper to facilitate intercourse when the couple was stuck in traffic jams. The story told of a lawsuit where a couple's zippers interlocked when a light turned green unexpectedly. The couple in the comic hired parodied American lawyers to sue everyone concerned, from the motorcycle company, the clothing company, and the zipper company, all the way through the various bureaucracies and contractors responsible for traffic lights. William was so busy explaining this to Zarlie that he didn't see a nearby stewardess approaching with a full tray of drinks: most of the liquid landed in his lap. Zarlie had a great laugh at his discomfort as he tried to towel himself dry: she couldn't believe that anyone would print, let alone read, such trash.

140

They landed in Cairo at dusk. When they looked out the airplane windows, they saw endless light brown sand coming right up to the edge of the runway: they were on just a little bit of civilization in the midst of a huge desert. Inside the airport, hallways and rooms were dark and dilapidated and young machine-gun carrying soldiers seemed to be stationed everywhere, but they were in Cairo, the home of the pyramids, and ready to explore. However, they were Japanese VIPs with diplomatic passports. How would immigration handle them? Why weren't they met by officials from their local embassy? William worried over their disguises as he saw the guns and the police. In the back of his mind he knew that he and Zarlie had murdered three men only a few days before and that somewhere police were looking for the killers. In addition he hadn't realized how volatile Egypt had become and the militaristic measures that the government used to protect visitors and tourists from surprise attacks.

Desert near the Cairo airport

"Zarlie, if they ask, let's act like we're annoyed that no officials are here to meet us, that there's been yet another screw-up, so we'll just take a taxi by ourselves."

"Relax, just pretend we've been here before and that this is no big deal."

"I can't with all these cops around."

"They're not looking for you, unless you do something stupid, so calm down and let me go first."

"You can speak some Arabic with a Japanese accent."

141

"Don't be a jerk: the officials and ruling class here speak English."

Perhaps Zarlie's inviting smile distracted the customs men, but in the end no one took any notice of the rich Japanese visitors as they were waved through without even a question about their luggage. At the exit they emerged into a sea of shouting porters and drivers. Zarlie had never been in a taxi with a worse driver, but William pointed out that all the other cars were running red lights and weaving from one side of the road to the other as spaces opened up. There were trucks, cars, donkeys, camels, and people all over the streets but nobody seemed to get hurt. Cars parked wherever they stopped, on either side of the road, oblivious to on-coming traffic. Half the population of Egypt lived in Cairo and it seemed to William that most of them were out for a drive tonight.

The rich Japanese couple needed to act their parts so they headed for the Nile Hilton, one of the fanciest hotels for international visitors. It didn't look like much from the outside, but they found it very comfortable inside and the hotel had a great location on the Nile next to the Egyptian Antiquities Museum. While they were checking-in a wedding procession passed through the marble-floored lobby. The bride and groom threw imitation gold and silver coins while laughing children ran to collect them. William handed Zarlie a few of the coins, which are said to bring good luck to a couple. Zarlie thought it an especially good omen for their first night in Egypt. Ever since they had arrived she had felt only friendly and relaxing thoughts.

They ate dinner outdoors on the hotel patio, where there was a smoking area for people with hookahs. Waiters brought lumps of tobacco soaked in perfume and honey. They put the tobacco on top of the hookah's pipe, in a perforated dish. Then they brought a glowing piece of charcoal and placed it on top of the tobacco. Much smoke, which then went down through the pipe, through the water, and out the hoses to the smokers. The smell was quite different from cigarette smoke, and William and Zarlie both liked it, from a distance. She noticed that people brought their own mouthpieces, but that the hotel supplied the hoses and the rest of the gear. She began to wonder how many germs were milling around inside each water pipe.

She also noticed the alabaster light fixtures, and realized that they were cut from real stone, with soft illumination coming through. In the States, these would have been plastic copies, but here they had the real thing, and the grain in the alabaster was beautiful. Zarlie felt relaxed and at home as they moved into their room with a beautiful view of the river, the city lights reflecting on its rippled surface. With imagination, the pyramids were just visible in the distant haze.

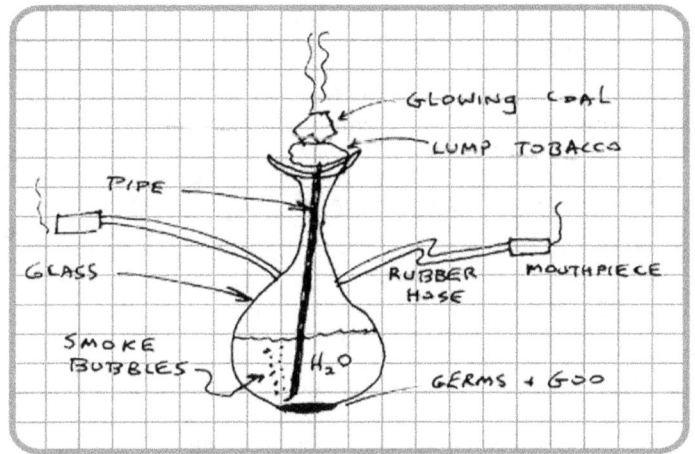

William's sketch of a hooka in action

They wanted to ditch the Japanese outfits and change to clothing that blended into the local scene as soon as possible. In addition, they needed to move somewhere less visible, and somewhere that wouldn't be easy to trace. In sum, they wanted to disappear, to fade into the city, just to be sure they had made a complete escape from the Alienologists, the police, and the media.

Zarlie had read about a section of the city where Rroma lived, and hoped that they could move to this neighborhood and use her knowledge to blend into the community. First thing the next morning they hired a driver for the day and asked him to take them to various sights, based on pages from a guidebook. This allowed them to cruise through the Rroma area several times, and Zarlie mentioned quietly that she could read the Romani writing on the local signs. William made careful note of the locations of the various Rroma buildings on their map.

As a start toward new identities, they explored the Khan El Khalili bazaar, built in 1292 by Sultan El-Ashraf, the conqueror of Acre. Among the narrow streets and walkways overhead awnings almost reached from one side to the other blotting out the sun but not the heat. Many strange sounds and aromas from the crammed together little shops greeted them as they explored the area looking for new clothes. They saw Fellahs in scanty blue kaftans, green-turbaned Shereefs, Bedouins from the desert in flowing bernouses, as well as tourists from all over the world. Zarlie was surprised to

143

see a Sakkah, a water-carrier, selling Nile water from a goatskin bag, something that hadn't changed for hundreds of years.

They bought Galabeyas (long robes), dark eye Kohl makeup and head scarves, normal tourist behavior arousing no suspicions. William even bought a fake beard and flexible pricing made every purchase an adventure. Zarli's Arabic speech elicited much surprise, coming as it did from apparently-Japanese tourists with unusual accents. At a perfume shop William bought Zarlie a bottle of "Secret of the Desert", which smelled like jasmine. He hadn't realized that Egyptian men wore perfume too, and was prevailed upon by Zarlie and the young lady running the shop to buy himself a bottle of "Omar Khayam", which they all liked: many laughs.

After their exploratory drive and shopping expedition, they went back to the hotel to visit the museum next door, to marvel at King Tut's gold treasures and the mummies and bits of ancient ruins. They were standing next to a dusty mummy case when Zarlie had an odd feeling. "William, think of a few numbers but don't tell me what they are."

"Sure, what's up?"

"All of a sudden I just realized that for awhile, I don't know how long, I haven't been able to understand your thoughts in detail."

"Maybe something in your head got messed up when you nuked that goon?"

"I still hear the old story-telling voice now and then, and my head hurts sometimes for no reason at all, like now, as we walked over to this case I just got a terrible migraine."

"Let's go back to the hotel and rest. We can get some aspirin in the shop."

"OK."

"Can you still detect bad feelings, like if some creep is coming after us?"

"I don't know. I didn't feel anything like that at the airport or in the bazaar, but maybe everyone here is friendly."

"You could tell that the Chinese don't like Japs: some of your sensitivity is still OK."

"Yes, and I know what you're feeling when you see me getting ready for bed, but this is different."

As they walked out the door into the hot sun, William asked, "Is your head better now?"

"Yes, actually it is, what made you ask?"

"I thought of that old movie, THE MUMMY'S CURSE, and figured that maybe the mummies don't like us staring at them so they give people headaches when they get too close."

"Idiot!"

"Anyway, I'm glad you feel better."

That night Zarlie decided that the best way to meet Rroma would be to have dinner in a restaurant that advertised Rroma specialities. Once they met a few Rroma they could ask about places to stay in the neighborhood. She knew Romani, but hadn't spoken it outside of San Francisco in years.

William and Zarlie put on their new tourist-Egyptian clothes, then taxied to a popular restaurant. After the taxi had disappeared, they walked a few blocks to restaurant Esbekiyeh a Rroma place that they had spotted earlier. William was still worried about being followed or discovered and hoped to break all links with the Hilton and their Japanese personas once they found a safe home. They were in the Thewfikieh Quarter fronting the Ismalia canal, on Sharia-el-Manakh street. As Zarlie entered the little restaurant, the intense aroma of paprika and Rroma cooking from Eastern Europe brought her back to Hungary and her childhood.

The head waiter stared open-mouthed at Zarlie when she addressed him in casual Romani. He was so startled that she thought that he couldn't understand her accent. Then he threw his arms around her with a big hug and started talking so fast that she had difficulty keeping up. They were taken to a corner table as the waiter yelled at the kitchen for a special dinner. Zarlie knew that she belonged here. The violin and guitar Czardas music were perfect and the friendly feelings in the environment were warm and strong. Zarlie laughed and told William, "These are great people, my people. We probably have relatives in common if you go back far enough. And it's so much fun to speak Romani again and sing the old songs. I don't know how we're going to deal with the pyramid, but I could stay right here forever."

When the waiter returned with the start of a complex meal Zarlie asked if he knew of a nearby apartment they might rent. She told him that the food and music were so wonderful that they wanted to stay close-by, perhaps in a secluded romantic place away from the crowds and the tourists. To her pleasant surprise he offered to rent them an apartment over the restaurant, so that they could enjoy the good music and food, as well as the secure comfort of living among friends. The apartment had a rooftop view of the city. They made arrangements to move the next morning.

William thought that perhaps this was the best time they had spent together since they had met. When Zarlie spoke Romani with the waiters he noticed that she became a different, happier and more care-free, person. The staff laughed about their clothes, and thought it hilarious that they were in disguise and probably up to no good. Suddenly they had many new and very discrete friends. Zarlie was radiant, that was the only word for it, radiant.

Before tonight William had been vaguely aware of Rroma culture and traditions, as Zarlie had mentioned aspects of them from time to time. Now as he looked around the room he saw Rroma culture everywhere. The rear wall had a huge Rroma flag, green and blue with a red chakra in the center. The sixteen-spoke chakra, a wagon wheel, seemed to be on every menu and plate in the restaurant.

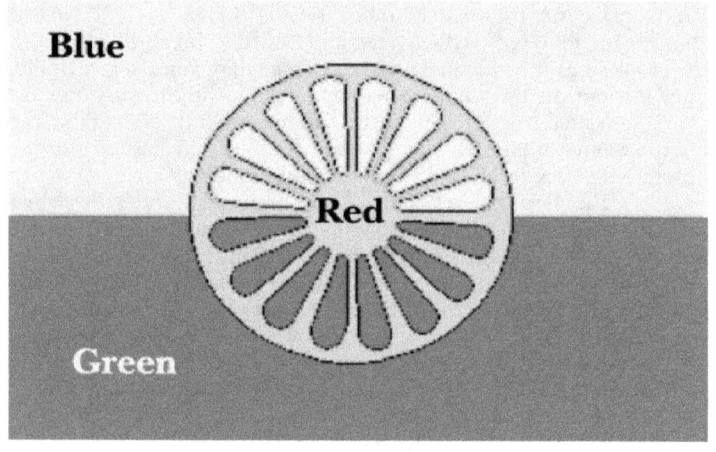

Rroma flag and chakra

Zarlie explained that the heavily spiced food they were eating blended Hungarian folk dishes and Rroma specialties. Both used garlic extensively, and the Hungarian love of paprika seemed to creep into every dish. When the head waiter apologized that there was no hedgehog available William panicked briefly: hedgehog a special delicacy? He couldn't imagine eating one.

Most of the women wore floor-length brightly-colored skirts and when he asked why, the others told him about 'marime', which means polluted, or dirty and the belief that women and girls who had passed puberty should cover the lower half of their bodies because these were unclean. William didn't ask for details. Zarlie had already changed into a multi-colored floor-length skirt that she had borrowed. Many of the women had a cloth covering for their hair, called a 'diklo', and traditional married women were not supposed to ever be seen in public without it. He was glad that Zarlie was more modern, as she had beautiful long hair (before cutting it to become Japanese) and it would he a shame to cover it.

The next day William and Zarlie, as two Japanese big-shots, checked out of the Hilton and took a cab to the airport. A perfectly normal thing for rich visitors to do. They went into the airport restaurant to have coffee and kill an hour or two. While there they saw a TV running CNN for tourists. The program showed a group of crazy Americans on the desert outside Palm Springs: they were chanting and praying to the sky. The reporter said that they were praying to a distant spaceship because they believed that God traveled in it. They had heard a TV preacher state that "God was coming in a chariot of fire to separate the good from the bad". William fliched involuntarily when they showed a picture of him from his brief TV interview, and referred to him as their prophet. How fortunate that he now wore makeup, dark hair, and a beard.

After an hour, the young formal Japanese couple went to the bathrooms and emerged wearing conservative middle-class Egyptian clothes. Zarlie even had a veil which covered much of her face. There were people from all over the world in Cairo, and so many different native costumes that the couple merged into crowds without trouble. They hired a different taxi and went to the Rroma apartment with their baggage, then unpacked for a long, peaceful, and productive research visit.

Chapter 15
Secret Research

William's first impressions of the Pyramids were colored by the intense heat, the dust which covered everything, and a general sense of disorganization. Huge stones were scattered randomly in the sand, and rude camel-drivers pestered him while ragamuffin kids begged for coins. Somehow he had thought that the Great Pyramid would be off in a remote place, clean and mathematically-pure, not a mess, almost in a slum, with hordes of people wandering around.

However, the scale and size of the Great Pyramid truly impressed William. No amount of reading and math prepared him for how it felt to actually stand beside the ancient structure.

Tourists sitting on the Great Pyramid

He had read about the weights of the stones and their sizes, but he felt so different, almost overpowered, as he stood in the baking hot sun, and touched the first row of the pyramid's huge stones. Then as he looked upward, he saw that each row above him was just as large, and the rows of stone seemed to go up forever. In photographs, the pyramid looked orderly, but now he could see the erosion and disarray that the centuries had wrought. Originally the Pyramid had been covered in perfect white limestone, but that layer had been stripped and used for building palaces and mosques in Cairo. The stones that he saw now were just the supporting structure, rows of huge rough blocks, each almost as tall as William. William smiled to himself in spite of the mess: inside this gigantic pile lived a mystery that had been hidden for thousands of years, and he was about to decode it.

Like the bus-loads of tourists, William and Zarlie bought tickets to go inside the GP. The tourists had cameras, smelly clothes, and guides. The couple joined the line that snaked inside. In the press of humanity, William could begin to sense that his idea of carefully-examining and measuring the stones without interruption was unrealistic, perhaps impossible, and the stink from the unwashed visitors crammed together in the heat made him nauseous.

Tourists fill the Grand Gallery

William wanted first to see the Grand Gallery, a long sloping passageway inside the Great Pyramid. There is nothing like it in other Egyptian structures. The sides consist of rows of stones, with the stones cut at odd angles and shapes: all fit together perfectly: a razor blade cannot be inserted between the stones. The stones are of very high quality and some are extremely large. The most striking thing is the shape of the walls. The Gallery is narrower at the ceiling than at floor level, and the width changes in narrow steps, like an upside-down staircase. The floor slopes and was steep to walk originally. A wooden walkway with hand railings and garish orange sodium-vapor lighting had been installed so that tourists could go up through the gallery to the King's chamber.

William wanted to stop and examine the walls carefully, but the people behind him were pushing, talking incessantly, and flashing their cameras, so he just caught glimpses of the things he wanted to study. The edges of the stones were much more rounded than in the photos he had studied. Stains ran down the walls, obscuring details. How to make accurate measurements? And the narrow passageway was so high. How to measure the stones up in the dark corners, if they could even be seen in the dim uneven light? How to see everything clearly, while sweat ran down his face? And the creaky wooden walkways for the tourists covered some of the most interesting stones. The old photos he had studied were so much better than the actual site. William began to fear that all of his plans and hopes were for naught.

Horde inside the King's Chamber

When they went back outside, Zarlie led him to a shady spot where they could talk, sitting on the sandy stones. "Cheer up William, you're just experiencing culture shock. Now that we know what to expect, we can come back tomorrow and do things properly.

Your project's going to be great."

"I can't believe the mess here, the beggars and camel-coolies, pushing and shoving, camels crapping and people grabbing, begging for anything. The Egyptians in the hotel and our Rroma friends are so polite and friendly, but I guess they don't come to the tourist places."

"Hey, have you ever been to European beaches on a hot summer day? It's almost as bad, with dogs crapping instead of camels. Tomorrow morning I'm going to take you on a proper tour of this pyramid, and we'll have some fun. Let's get ready for action," Zarlie said as she jumped up with energy and enthusiasm.

She led William on a shopping expedition to buy light cotton pants and shirts, flashlights, water bottles, and light backpacks. They returned to their apartment at dusk, ready for an exploratory adventure in the morning. In the early evening light William looked around their rooms and realized how beautiful the apartment appeared at this time of day. Light came through the stone latticed windows casting shadows which almost perfectly matched the geometric designs carved in the woodwork. Such mathematical precision blended perfectly with beauty. There were old paintings on the walls and ancient carpets. The brown leather couches that had once been elegant were covered with more rugs. He lifted several of the rugs onto the heavy old table to protect its intricate inlaid surface from his two computers. William hoped that they could stay here a long time, such a perfect place for their research efforts.

After dinner they sat on the roof of their apartment watching the city lights and the evening sky. Zarlie turned to William, "You know how well I can read your emotions, your inner feelings. You're being so careful not to touch me or to even bump into me, because of what I said about my shattered heart."

"I can wait a long time for your heart to recover, and it's nice just being near you. I have no right to ask for more."

"You've put me on a pedestal William, but I'm a living, breathing, warm human being. I'm your girlfriend. You can hold my hand when we're walking together, and kiss me good night and good morning. My heart's recovering. I have a lot to get over, but being here among my people, with a man who deeply cares for me, helps, it helps a lot."

He reached out with his bandaged hand and held Zarlie's hand tightly. "I've never been this happy, never in my whole life."

The next morning they wore light modern clothes, and packed their robes, cameras, notebooks, and water bottles into backpacks. They arrived at the gate to the pyramid area just as it opened and were near the front of the line as they entered the Great Pyramid quickly. Zarlie had cash ready as she approached a guard who stood in front of the iron gate which blocked the Descending Corridor. A discretely-passed fifty-dollar bill, a month's wages for the guard, and a few words of Arabic opened the gate for a private visit down a normally closed tunnel.

Starting down the Descending Corridor

They had decided to begin their exploration at the bottom of the pyramid and work up, so they started with this Corridor, which cuts gradually down through the pyramid's stones and into the bedrock of the Giza Plateau. There are a few electric lights, but non-tourist passages like this are dim if you don't have a flashlight.

The Descending Corridor is 350 feet long, and straight as an arrow. It is almost perfectly cut, and it's original opening points directly toward the circumpolar north stars, as William had calculated. It was hot, dusty, and with a strange musty smell. Walking was difficult since the passageway is only forty-seven inches high and forty-two inches wide, with a precise downward slope. It was far too long for crawling on hands and knees, so they stooped over and scooted on bent legs. William wondered how anybody could have dug this tunnel so perfectly, especially without electric lights or modern equipment. And why was it exactly this size? He was sure that there was a mathematical reason. There is a long section of this passage, about 150' near the entrance, where the accuracy of the construction is within 1/50th of an inch of being perfectly straight, according to Flinders Petrie's measurements made over a hundred years ago. As they moved down the passage, William stopped to examine the perfectly-cut lines in the wall at irregularly-spaced intervals. He thought that perhaps these marked important astronomical alignments, but then again, the critical aspect could be the distances between the lines: perhaps these measurements could be part of an ancient message.

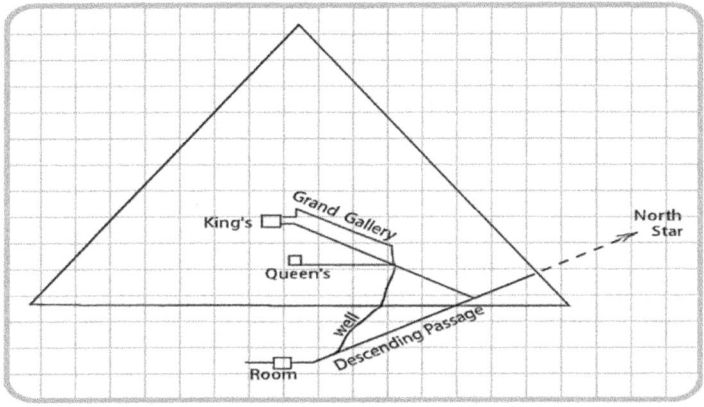

William's sketch of the Descending Passage

The shaft slopes down at exactly twenty-six degrees seventeen minutes, and seems to go on forever. As they neared the bottom, they passed the entrance to the 'Well', which is an irregular shaft that leads up to the lower end of the Grand Gallery. It isn't actually a well since there is no water here, but its sloppy construction perhaps looks like an old well shaft. Then the sloping section of the corridor ends and they crawled for twenty-nine feet through a low horizontal section. Finally they were in the Subterranean Chamber and could stand up, right under the apex of the pyramid far above. They were in a big room, with many odd holes and excavations. Egyptologists don't know why it's here, so they say that it is an incomplete tomb. Again William wondered at the peculiar dimensions and the math behind them, as well as at the incredible craftsmanship.

William felt apprehensive as he thought of the weight of the pyramid above them. He saw math everywhere, in the precisely cut angles and craftsmanship, but the feeling that they were so far below such a huge pile of stones overpowered his logical thoughts. He couldn't help but wonder how the builders had dug this huge room and carried out the rock chips, all the way up the narrow shaft, and what did they breathe, and how did they see. There was no trace of smoke from torches. During the cutting, no matter what tools they had used, there would have been endless dust, yet they did it somehow. If they could have done this, and the perfectly-cut passage leading down to it, then all manner of secrets could be hidden in the rock, and in the stone structure far above. More and more he realized that the official explanation, that this was built with primitive copper and bronze tools 4500 years ago, was totally unrealistic. He knew that this must have been built by a very smart advanced civilization much further in the past, and with much better equipment than experts would admit.

One of the books that he had read described this underground Chamber perfectly:

"Were it not for a single low-wattage electric bulb installed in modern times, the visitor would be in complete darkness. The light that the bulb casts has a greenish, sepulchral hue, and what it reveals is a most peculiar room, considerably larger than the King's Chamber, measuring 46 feet along its east-west axis, and 27 feet one inch from north to south, but with a maximum height of just 11 feet six inches. In the approximate center of the floor, on the east side, is a railing surrounding a square pit reaching a depth of about ten feet, and beyond that, penetrating the south wall, is a second horizontal shaft, 28 inches square, running due south in the bedrock for a further 53 feet and terminating in a blank wall. Looking to the right, one notes that the floor on the western side of the Chamber rises up into a kind of chest-high platform. This has been irregularly trenched, creating four parallel fins of limestone running east to west, almost touching the relatively flat roof at some points, but with a clearance of up to six feet in others." (Hancock and Bauval 1996, p 49)

The same book said that scientists with radar and seismic equipment had been in this room and that they detected hollow areas below the floor and in the walls. However, nothing has been done to explore these potentially secret rooms. From a math viewpoint William thought that the two most interesting areas were: (1) under the floor of the shallow horizontal passage that provides the only entrance: perhaps the descending corridor continues further down into the rock to a secret chamber below, and the horizontal floor covers it, and (2) the location directly under the apex of the pyramid: it seemed logical to him that the axis and the descending passage would meet at an extremely important place, but that location is deep under the floor, near the entrance of the big subterranean room, and no one has tried to dig for it. The level of the Nile is about ninety feet beneath this floor, and he wondered if a secret passage went down to a source of water.

While they were exploring and making casual photographs, Zarlie stopped and turned to William. "When we came here yesterday as tourists, I could feel something odd, but in the press of all those people and the confusion, I couldn't be sure. But now that we're in a quiet place, I can feel, or hear it clearly. If I sit very still and concentrate, I can feel a faint, faraway sound. It's a bit like hearing a child in the distance faintly calling my name. It's so puzzling. I want to move closer, to hear it better, but I can't tell which way to move to make it stronger."

"Maybe it's another ancient recording of Living Waves. Does it sound like the voice that led us to meet our sparking blue angel? It doesn't make sense, but perhaps that's the explanation."

"It's similar, but different, I can't explain, but it's only inside here, not outside on the desert. Do you feel anything?"

"Before I met you and learned of your world, I would have just said that this place gives me the creeps. I'm frightened, and more than a bit claustrophobic, but I don't hear anything or feel any unusual communication. When my scientific side thinks about where we are, under tons of rock, waves of goose bumps ripple over my skin and I want to run for the door. But when I think of the math, the carefully-formed shafts and excavations, my curiosity takes control and I can't wait to explore further. I want to go down every passage, slither into every corner, and measure anything I can find. It's so exciting to be here, especially with you."

In the afternoon, they bribed their way into the two other large pyramids. Each had a simple tunnel underneath, leading to an old burial chamber under the apex. The construction and workmanship were poor compared to the Great Pyramid. No fancy alignments or long pure shafts or any evidence of mathematics. It confirmed to William that the Great Pyramid was built by much smarter people, a very, very long time ago. Perhaps other people came along much later and built the other two big pyramids as copies, and then maybe eons later, rulers tunneled under the two copies and installed burial chambers for themselves. It could be that the Egyptologists were correct in their dates for the burial chambers in the other pyramids, but completely off on the construction dates for the actual stones. The Great Pyramid was in a class by itself. Much better workmanship, much more intricate design, much more math. It stood alone in the drifting sands, perhaps with the old Sphinx, for millennia before anything else appeared nearby.

In the other pyramids, Zarlie didn't hear faint distant voices like the one that she had heard under the GP. Those pyramids were silent, another proof that they were different from the GP. William had read eighteen Great Pyramid books with a wide range of theories as to how, when, and why it was built, from scholars, crackpots, mystics and engineers. He was now fascinated to see the actual stones and passageways that they had described and measured.

They went back inside the GP as sweat-drenched tourists, and entered the Queen's chamber, through a perfectly horizontal shaft 127 feet long, and only forty-seven inches high.

Shaft leading to Queen's Chamber

William wondered if perhaps the builders had used really short people, or monkeys, as construction workers. No 'queen' was ever found in the Queen's Chamber. The name is a relic from imaginative explanations for the purpose of the room, since it is below the King's Chamber, another misnomer. This chamber is twenty feet high, and about eighteen feet square, with an unusual corbelled niche in one wall. William looked for signs of the little German robot that had been here ten years earlier, but saw nothing. The authorities weren't advertising its findings. He stood right on the spot where the robot had entered the wall on its adventure. There were no photographs or plaques to indicate the mystery that still lay, unsolved, just up the little shaft.

As they were about to leave the Pyramid, Zarlie suddenly hesitated then pushed William into a corner just inside the doorway whispering, "I feel something bad, someone's outside looking for us."

"Can you see them or tell who it is," William whispered back.

"Not yet. Quick, let's put our robes on." Fortunately they were carrying their galabias in their backpacks and covered their bodies with the light robes and head scarves, hiding their backpacks inside their robes. From a distance, they looked like Arabs instead of tourists.

"Let's rent camels and ride out into the desert, then come back a different way."

Standing behind the entrance guards, they looked around and guessed that the bad signals might be coming from a group of people near a small private bus. They spotted three empty camels with a driver and walked to him quickly. A handful of cash rented the camels, as Zarlie told the owner, "Please take us out into the desert so we can watch the sunset on the pyramids."

The camels bent their legs so that the three could mount, then rose and trotted off into the distance. The bad waves faded as William and Zarlie bounced in the unfamiliar saddles. From a distance they looked like locals riding across the sand.

Late that night, as a special treat, William and Zarlie's Rroma friends brought them to a Moroccan restaurant. Hundreds of candles with multi-colored geometric shades decorated the low-ceilinged room. People sat on large pillows around a huge table. As soon as they were seated, waiters brought silver water urns and washed everyone's hands. As was customary, they were to eat everything with their right hands, there being no knives or forks, except those used by waiters. William examined the menu, written in both English and Arabic, and learned some of the words which described their feast.

First, the harira arrived, a tomato soup with lemon, basil, and cardamom flavoring. Then a salad, with cumin scented carrots, chioga beets, and peppers. There was also baked goat cheese, more tomato soup of a different kind, grilled Merguez sausage, and a chicken bastilla, which was a big pie filled with chicken and saffron and unusual spices. Too late William realized that these were just the initial appetizers and that they hadn't even started the main meal.

Fortunately there was a break and they walked outside to recover their appetites and stretch. While resting in a walled garden they talked about the alienologists and how they had managed to land in Egypt, "I never should have told Gloria about my pyramid project. She must have told Jake, so they knew where we were headed the moment we left the country."

"Egypt is a big place, so as long as we're careful, they'll never find us."

"But they'll hang around the GP waiting. Maybe they'll bribe the guards or stick someone inside to watch for us?"

"Don't worry so much William. The Rroma will protect us, and the goons won't know the local territory. There're lots of ways to get around them."

Back inside, William's worries evaporated when he saw a gorgeous belly dancer wearing a revealing red mesh top and almost transparent thin bright red harem pants. Zarlie laughed and squeezed his hand. He couldn't believe the ways the dancer moved her body, especially her pelvis, gliding around the room, almost rubbing against each customer as money was stuffed into the waist of her low-hanging trousers. Zarlie smiled as the belly dancer rubbed against William, causing him to glow bright red with embarrassment as he gingerly tucked money into the belt which brushed his face. He felt the soft texture of her costume and wondered at the mixture of aromas wafting from the hot undulating body: he hoped she would come back to him soon.

The main courses appeared, lamb shanks with couscous, honey-kumquat sauce, charred eggplant, lamb Kadra, prawn tagine, rabbit tagine, charmoula sauce, and assorted shish-kebabs. The others kept eating, and William realized that they had not eaten nearly as much of the first courses as he had. His stomach was full, and yet food was still coming.

When everyone had finished eating, the waiters returned for more hand washing and another belly-dancer appeared, a tall thin girl in a blue costume, who moved even more anatomy. She could hold the top half of her body perfectly still, while rhythmically rotating her mid-section, much to the amazement of all the men in the room. The music went faster and faster as she moved around the room.

William tried to describe the dessert to himself but found that he could say little except that it was even better than the other courses, with subtle flavors of anise and almonds and spices he couldn't pronounce, as well as deep dark chocolate concoctions, all washed down with mint tea.

After desert a third belly-dancer, in a flowing, transparent white costume, seemed to float around the room, gyrating and smiling at each customer in turn. Out of nowhere, a Whirling Dervish appeared, spinning to the same music that the belly dancer used. He went so fast that his huge round skirt flew out horizontally. He rotated his head unevenly, while his body spun smoothly. The Dervish would look in a fixed direction with his head still, while keeping his body turning. Then he would snap his head all the way around in one motion, catching up with and passing his body. The Dervish and the Belly-dancer flew around each other as the audience cheered wildly. The Rroma were ecstatic, and William realized that he was lucky to be watching a most unusual performance. He didn't see another Westerner in the room. When the performance and clapping finished William could hardly move his well-stuffed body.

He rose from the cushions and looked for Zarlie, but she had slipped away. As the crowd thinned he asked the others if they had seen her leave, or if they knew where she might have gone. As his worries started to build, they checked the rest rooms, the dancers' dressing rooms, the space outside the restaurant, but no Zarlie. William thought immediately of the goons, the killings, the bad vibrations, and all the evil things that might have happened to her. Where could she have gone? What had happened? One of the waiters seemed to remember Zarlie walking out the back door during the third dance, but apparently she hadn't said anything about her destination.

The Rroma made William return to his apartment while they searched for her discreetly. He desperately wanted to help in the search, to run down every street, to look in every doorway that they passed on the way back, but that was not allowed. He realized that asking the police to search for her would be a very bad idea since he and Zarlie were not in the country legally. Alone in the apartment, William paced the floor as he imagined one bad possibility after another. His worries and fears knew no limits, and the idea of an innocuous explanation for her actions never occurred to him. At three in the morning Zarlie returned and found William curled up in a chair wrapped in an old rug, sound asleep.

She gently woke him, running her fingers through his hair then shaking his shoulder slightly, "Wake up William, everything's OK now."

"What, who, what happened? Where have you been?"

"I don't know really. Something about the Dervish spinning triggered a funny feeling in my head, and I guess I just wandered off. It was sort of like I heard a voice, and it took control of me, or maybe that's just what it seems like in retrospect. Maybe a trance or a spell or a form of sleep-walking or auto-hypnosis."

"Holy cow. How did you get back here?"

"I remember the Dervish, and I remember walking out from the feast, then, somehow, I was outside knocking on the door of the restaurant downstairs. I know there's a gap of several hours but I don't have a clue where it went. When I told our Rroma friends about it they said that I had been mesmerized by the Dervish and that sometimes Dervishes cast evil spells. You and I know that's not a good explanation, but I don't have a better one just now."

William wrapped his arms around Zarlie, but said nothing for a long time, his mystification at the events overcoming his thoughts. Eventually he quietly asked, "Please sleep close beside me, let me hold onto you through the night, I can't bear to loose you again."

The next morning, William and Zarlie had a lazy start. They didn't dare go near the pyramids in daylight, but felt safe in their apartment, hidden in their robes among the Rroma. Zarlie went to talk quietly with them about gaining private access to the Pyramid at night.

William went across the street to an internet café and read American newspapers on the net. What a shock: on the front page of yesterday's Petaluma Chronicle was an article about a vicious criminal attack on innocent construction workers near Booneville, along with pictures of William and Zarlie. A generous reward was offered for information on their whereabouts, since the couple were reported to be the last persons known to have talked with the workers. The Alienologists had turned out to be a whole lot smarter and more resourceful than he had imagined.

William also went to the VPA website, where he had inserted a secret trap-door into the VPA computer code. This was a way for him to remotely enter the computer systems at VPA and make surreptitious adjustments from far away. All he had to do was to log on to the VPA site, navigate to the right section, then type a password and he would be deep inside. When he had written this code, he hadn't had a specific purpose in mind, but knew that eventually he would devise a way to either collect the money owed to him, or at least to block further profit from his efforts. Sitting in the internet café, he entered the trap door ten thousand miles away and felt very pleased that it worked. Once inside the huge computers that ran the VPA code he altered subtle control parameters in the prediction program so that it would produce mostly wrong answers, thereby driving customers away and eliminating Gloria's profits.

After lunch William and Zarlie rested in the afternoon heat trying to nap before a long night inside the pyramid. William had an idea. "Zarlie, I'm wondering about the goons and our fears, and how fear works. What if there aren't any goons here, what if the alienologists have no actual power in Egypt, and if the only power they have is the fear inside our own heads: the fear we generate ourselves. I think that's how Stalin and Hitler controlled millions of people: everyone felt so much fear that they always did what the leaders wanted, even when the secret police weren't looking."

"But I felt the presence of goons outside the pyramid, I'm sure of it."

"I know you think you felt it, but maybe it's just your guilt over killing the surveyors."

"That was self-defense, no guilt involved. The goons are here, looking for us, so don't let down your guard."

"I saw a picture of our faces on the internet, with a ten grand reward for information."

Zarlie flinched, then reached over and held William's hand tightly as she curled up next to him and tried to sleep. William gently ran the fingers of his other hand through her hair, trying in some way to be a comfort. He couldn't sleep, caught between his emotional desire to protect Zarlie and his scientific excitement over the coming night's research.

In the evening twilight, after the Gizzah Plateau had been cleared of tourists and camels for the night, William, Zarlie, and a Rroma friend carefully approached the guard office. The head guard, a Rroma, had been pleasantly surprised to learn that the couple wanted to pay a thousand dollars to spend a few nights studying inside, and further that they wanted to rent ladders for an additional fee. Zarlie had told William earlier that they were offering the head guard twice the average Egyptian's annual income for just a few nights of looking the other way. She knew that the he would pocket most of the cash himself, but some would filter down, and she planned to heavily tip the men who actually helped with the ladders.

William and Zarlie had a simple plan. Bribe the guards, get inside, and spend the whole night photographing and measuring every stone they could reach. Just like an all-night cram for finals. It didn't seem like a big deal. William couldn't wait to start work. They had come so far, and he knew that if he could gather the data for each stone that he could translate the message written on the walls.

Once they were inside, William realized that there were many more stones than he had originally calculated, and that obtaining accurate data on just a hundred might take all night. He had originally planned to measure each stone, its sides and angles and location, and carefully record all the data, but there just wasn't time. The stones were so rough that measuring one of them accurately took half an hour. Therefore, William and Zarlie measured some of the stones directly, and photographed as many as possible of the rest. William thought himself quite clever to include a bright red laser-generated plumb line and a ruler in every photo, so that he could compute the exact angles and sizes later.

The Grand Gallery late at night

William was near the top of a rickety narrow wooden ladder. The trembling of his tired and tense muscles caused the ladder to vibrate and shake, frustrating his photography. Suddenly a bat flew in front of the lens as he focused on several oddly-shaped stones. He almost dropped the five pound camera and flash unit. "Dammit!

Zarlie, isn't there some kind of bat repellant that we could wear?"

"Don't you just wish! Their olfactory organs are small, but their sonar is fantastic. Watch out if you they mistake you for a mosquito!"

"They leave a terrible stink when they fly by."

"Hey, next time you're down here, checkout the size of the rats munching the tourist trash under the wooden walkway."

"So that's why you're sitting up on the side wall. How's your faint voice doing? Hear anything?"

"I think it's stronger in here, compared to down below, but it's hard to tell. It's not really a voice, just a feeling, there aren't words, but sometimes it feels like it might be a child's voice. What's that odd tinkling sound?"

"Probably just the surface stones cooling, as they shrink a little in the night air."

"I hope you're right. This place feels strange, especially at night when we're all alone."

"Do you happen to have a Bandaid in your pack? The cut on my hand's just opened up again."

They worked quickly, first taking as wide a shot as possible of a section of wall, then moving in for medium shots, then close-ups that showed each stone at full resolution. Zarlie wrote furiously describing the shots and their reference numbers as William shouted out the details. Some of the stones were big and hard to photograph clearly. Often it was difficult for William to position the camera as far from the stones as he would have liked, even with his back against the opposite wall. In these cases, he was grateful for the fourteen millimeter lens's wide coverage. It allowed a nine-foot wide stone to be shot from only three feet away, albeit with considerable perspective distortion. Each of his precision wide angle lenses weighed almost two pounds, the magnesium camera body added another two, the battery at least a pound more and then there was the flash unit. His arms grew tired as the night progressed. In addition to carrying the camera gear, they often had to move the laser-level, which generated a vertical red reference line, as well as the awkward and primitive ladder.

Near midnight, a cold breeze began to disturb the still warm air of the Grand Gallery, and dozens of bats left the relieving chambers above the Kings Chamber, heading for the Pyramid entrance.

"William, I feel someone coming, someone we don't know."

"Damn, I haven't finished half these stones."

"Quick where can we hide?"

William scampered down the ladder and put his arm around

Zarlie's trembling shoulders. "Take it easy, we don't need to run away. It's all right. And anyhow, we've got too much stuff to hide."

"I don't like being cooped up in here with no way to escape."

A guard appeared in the distance, climbing up the Ascending passage and into the Gallery. As he approached they realized that he carried a straw basket filled with fruit, chocolate, freshly-baked rolls, and water bottles. A friend, not an enemy. They chatted for a few moments, then the guard left as silently as he had arrived. As they ate a little, William smiled at Zarlie, "Isn't this great, we're getting so much data in spite of everything."

"It'll take more than a bit of chocolate to make me feel happy about being in here. I still don't like it, but I know how much this means to you."

"I know you're afraid, and that I can't make your fear go away, but I'll keep trying."

"Thanks, now let's get busy so I that I don't have time to think about it."

William changed camera and flash batteries and inserted fresh memory cards into the camera. Each full-resolution picture used 15MB, and he was making many exposures.

The Pyramid interior had actually been very quiet, with the only noises being the stones cooling and the occasional scampering of rats and bats. William, high up the ladder, began to hear rumbling and almost musical noises as the night progressed. It made no sense to his logical mind and he worried that physical exertion was causing him to imagine sounds that weren't real.

"Zarlie, do you hear anything, sort of musical, sort of rumbling?"

"Yes. I thought I was going nuts, but if you can hear it too, then it's real."

"I think it's getting louder, whatever it is."

"It's coming from the King's Chamber, but nobody's in there."

"Let's take a quick look, and see what it is."

William put his gear aside and helped Zarlie up the steep walkway. As they walked the noises became stronger.

"William, if you're right, and there are secret passages hidden in the walls, then it could be almost anything."

"Well, I know it's not some goons who have come to carry us away."

They heard a change in the strange sounds. A somewhat higher moaning musical note had started. The noises were uneven, and ranged in pitch from low rumblings to higher frequencies and whistles. As they climbed under the heavy portcullis stones and entered the Kings Chamber the noises became louder, seeming to come from all directions. They walked around mystified. There could see nothing in the room, no person, no musical instruments, no equipment. William walked to one of the ventilation shafts and placed a hand over it. He could feel a vibration as air pulsed in and out of the shaft. Suddenly he exploded with an idea.

"Zarlie, do you know what's happening? We're inside a giant organ."

"What do you mean?"

"There're passages running through the walls, and they're different lengths. The wind must have come up, and as it blows across the ends of the passages, or pipes, it makes musical notes, just like organ pipes."

"Like when you blow across the top of an empty beer bottle."

"Exactly, and there must be lots of short and long passages to make all the notes we're hearing."

"And when the wind changes direction, the notes change, depending on which passageways are at the right angle to the wind."

"The biggest open-ended organ pipes in churches are thirty-two feet long, and they make those really low rumbling notes, around sixteen Hertz. There could be passages a hundred feet or more in length here, like this vent shaft, which make notes so low that we feel the shaking from the vibrations instead of hearing them. Sound travels about eleven hundred feet per second, so an open ended pipe three hundred feet long, wound generate sound with a wavelength of six hundred feet, around two Hertz, sort of like a watch ticking or a fast heart beat."

"Hey, low frequencies, below the range of normal hearing, have psycho-acoustic properties: they can do strange things to your mind if they resonate with normal bodily rhythms. That's part of hypnosis, and doctors can see low frequency patterns inside our brains on an electroencephlegram. People are especially sensitive to sounds in the range of three to five Hertz."

"Maybe the builders of this pyramid knew that, and liked to freak-out visitors who didn't know what was happening?"

"This shows that there're lots of undiscovered features in the Pyramid, so we're on the right track."

"And it also shows how smart the guys who built this place were. Damn, I wish I had a spectrum analyzer and a microphone: we could measure the frequencies of the notes then calculate the lengths of all the passageways that are making the sounds that we're hearing."

"Let's get back to the ladder and finish what we started: this can wait, it's not going anywhere."

"You're right, and we can listen to the wind music while we work."

"What a strange idea, to think that maybe the builders designed groups of notes, or chords, to tell which way the wind was blowing."

"Or to scare people who came in here illegally."

When the guard arrived in the morning to help put the ladders away, they knew they were going to be successful when he suggested that they lay them down alongside the wooden floor so that they could use the ladders again, on another night, perhaps with a direct payment to this particular guard and his friends. Zarlie thanked him profusely in Arabic and in cash, as they dragged themselves to the entrance. The reason for the wind-generated noises became apparent when they neared the door. A sandstorm had come up during the night, and the air was filled with dust, sand, and wind from the southwest desert, the Khamseen. Finding a taxi in the storm took an hour, but they did have over five hundred digital pictures and tons of data to study.

Exhausted, they slept most of the day, then started to analyze their findings. As they drank magenta-colored hibiscus tea, Zarlie turned on the TV. She wanted to see if there was news about the people on the desert who believed that William was a prophet, or perhaps about the search for the killers of the surveyors. She caught the end of a news program, where a commentator babbled about the star and how it couldn't possibly be a spaceship, and about William who had disappeared, as pictures of him were shown: his followers were offering a reward for his return. The amount would be a fortune for anyone in Egypt. Zarlie realized that leisurely secret research had ended and it was now time to work quickly, before someone recognized them and claimed a reward.

It had been difficult dragging two laptop computers and all of his notebooks and camera equipment through the airports, but as soon as William started analyzing the data from the Grand Gallery's stones, he knew they were on track. He had the right tools and great data. Decoding the wall message was close as long as the power didn't quit and they didn't get caught. The dust storm blew outside the heavily draped windows as he and Zarlie puzzled over the data long into the night.

A sensible person would have said that they were crazy to assume that each stone in the Grand Gallery walls was a character in an ancient language, and that the angles and sizes of the stones were the strokes of each character, but no one else had anything like this idea, and the mathematics were elegant.

William first set out to categorize the stones. There were over four hundred on the west wall, which they had managed to photograph completely. There were at least that many on the opposite wall, but they weren't photographed yet. He would be ecstatic if there were exactly 666 stones, a mystical number, but wasn't worried about that now. When he had first looked at the photographs, he had realized that the stones which were perfectly rectangular, that is with all four corners of each stone forming a ninety-degree angle, were special. These stones were grouped in straight lines which divided areas of irregular shaped stones, perhaps like punctuation marks, or lines on a sheet of paper. The rectangular stones might be divisions between sentences or ideas.

The computer worked hard on the photographs, looking first for the boundaries and edges, the lines between the stones in the photographs. This allowed the computer to generate an image for each stone by itself. Then the computer would analyze each stone, to determine its dimensions and the angles at each stone's corners.

The next step was to search for identical stones, stones that were the same size and shape, but in different locations on the wall. Finally the computer compared all the stones to each other and printed a list of the unique shapes and sizes.

William jumped with excitement when he saw that there were exactly thirty-six different stone shapes, since thirty-six is mathematically a very interesting number. He theorized that these thirty-six different stone shapes must be the alphabet in which the wall message was written. When he looked at the properties of the thirty-six stones, he saw that all the angles were exact multiples of thirty degrees. No matter what the shape of the stone, the corner angles were in the set [30,60,90,120. . . 330]. Although the walls looked as though they were comprised of randomly-selected stones, they were actually made from well-engineered interlocking shapes.

They puzzled over the stone shapes and what they might mean, then Zarlie had a brainstorm and asked him to printout the unique shapes on paper, all to the same scale. As the printer worked, she danced around the apartment in excited anticipation. Furiously she cut each shape from the printout with her pocketknife and began to move the shapes around on the floor, looking for ones that fit together. She remembered William's first lecture and his conviction that the magic squares and pyramid were related, but thought that perhaps he had been right, but in a different way than he had suspected. Perhaps these unique shapes could be arranged in a perfectly-meshed six-by-six square, just like a jigsaw puzzle.

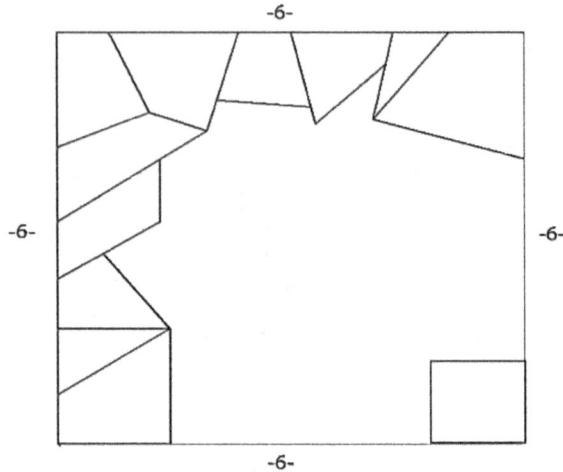

Zarlie Starts to Assemble The Alphabet Square

William saw in an instant what she was trying to do and leapt to the floor to help. The puzzle didn't quite fit together and he had to make additional passes with the computer and the software before they had shapes that were truly in scale with each other. Finally they had the square, thirty-six unique stone shapes that meshed perfectly in an exactly square pattern, and with six stones on each side. Suddenly he remembered that thirty-six was a key number in the six-by-six square of the sun, which contained all integers in the set [1,2,3,4. . .36]. Maybe each alphabet stone could be assigned a number between one and thirty-six, based on the arrangement of numbers in the six-by-six magic square, where every row, column, and diagonal totaled 111.

6	32	3	34	35	1
7	11	27	28	8	30
19	14	16	15	23	24
18	20	22	21	17	13
25	29	10	9	26	12
36	5	33	4	2	31

He grabbed a printout of the six-by-six square of the sun, thirty-six numbers in total, and was about to lay it over the jigsaw puzzle when he stopped. Sadly he realized that they had no idea how to orient the numbers from the magic square onto the shapes in the stone alphabet square. The magic six-by-six square of numbers could be rotated, flopped, inverted, and mirror-imaged, without changing its properties: there was no way to tell which side was up on either the stone square or the number square. There were twelve different ways he could lay the numbers from the magic square onto Zarlie's jigsaw puzzle. All were equally valid. There was no true top or bottom, left or right to either square.

He tried a few arrangements, but nothing made sense. Both of them stared at the jigsaw puzzle wondering what to do next. Finally Zarlie had an idea. "William, let's do all twelve overlays, all twelve matches between the numbers and the stone shapes. It's not an impossible task. Then after we make each overlay we'll use it to assign a number to every stone on the wall, using that particular match of the square to the stone jigsaw. We can make your computer put the numbers for every stone onto the wall. When we're done, we'll have drawings of twelve different walls covered with numbers, numbers that match the stone shapes. Then we'll use our brains to see if any of the twelve arrangements seems to have a meaning."

"I'll generate the twelve orientations and you write them on the shapes. Great idea."

They worked furiously for hours at the project, and sometimes the numbers seemed to overlay the shapes on the wall more nicely than others. They dogmatically worked at all twelve arrangements, one at a time in no particular order. When they finished a match-up they instructed the computer to printout the entire wall, with each stone translated into its number.

As the seventh pattern printed, William screamed in delight. "Look, look at the upper left hand corner of the wall, at the numbers there. This is it! The numbers are 3, 14, 15, 9, 27. It's the value of pi to seven decimal places. Then look, next to it, that's the value of 'e', a critical transcendental number in the world of math, 2, 7, 18, 28, 18. We've solved the puzzle."

"Hey, down here, lower on the wall, that's, my god, that looks like part of the Periodic Table of the elements. Whoever did this was incredibly advanced."

"I don't recognize most of the other numbers, wow, maybe they're things that we haven't discovered yet, and hey, here's 25, 5, 9, 2, which is the number of years in a precessional cycle, the number of years it takes the earth's axis to move through the heavens. These guys knew everything. All over this wall, they're showing off, telling us how smart they were."

Then in a sad flash, Zarlie realized, "William, there isn't squat about secret passages or magic stones to press to get into them."

"Who cares, we've got to write a paper and publish this. What a breakthrough. I can't wait to see the look on Professor Mackie's face when she hears about this."

"Er, William, you're forgetting a few minor details, like we don't dare publish and give our location away."

"But this is so fantastic. To think this has been lying here for millennia, just waiting for us to decode."

"And once you know the secret, it's not so complex. Wonder what's on the other wall. As I recall it's completely different."

"Damn, we've got to get back in there fast. Now that we know the key, it won't take long to categorize the stones. Hey, look at the printout down there, it's a Fibonacci Sequence running the whole width of the wall."

They couldn't wait to go back and photograph the rest of the stones. One more night would do it. They were dead tired and so close to reading the message inside the Pyramid. Sleep was instantaneous.

After resting most of the next day, they were back inside the pyramid at night. This time William and Zarlie knew exactly which stones to analyze, and in contrast to last time, they knew that they were going to be able to read a message in the stones.

Once inside, they looked with new knowledge at the west wall. Given the secret of the code, they could look at the wall and almost read it visually, seeing the stones as numbers that made sense. Then they looked at the east wall and tried to read it, but life was not that easy. The rectangular dividing stones ran at odd angles across the wall, instead of separating orderly groups of angular stones into messages. It was undecipherable, though the component stones seemed to be part of the same alphabet.

Again, the night was spent making careful photographs of the entire wall from top to bottom.

The night went so fast that they mapped all of the remaining stones, and were finished when the guard came to let them out. They emerged into a brilliant sunrise. The storm had blown itself out during the night and the weather was perfect.

After a quick sleep, they began to analyze the pattern of the stones on the east wall. They assumed that the rectangular blocks were parts of lines, dividing ideas and thoughts, so they ignored these. The rest of the stones didn't make sense, they were just scattered small groups of meaningless numbers.

"I guess it was a bit crazy of me to think that there was a secret entrance to the hidden passages here, and that we could push on stones to enter it." William was sorely disappointed.

"Don't quit, we've come too far for that. Let's look at this from a new direction, like in your article about that scientist who searched for gravity waves in new dimensions. Close your eyes and envision the east wall and us standing next to it. If there are stones to push, they must be about five feet off the floor, so that the priests could easily give each a good shove. Let's see what's unique in that area. Forget the computer and let's just look at the photos."

"It's all so confusing, but you're right."

"Where's your frequency analysis of the west wall showing how many times each letter in the stone alphabet occurs. Are there any stones that don't appear often on the west side?"

"Now that you mention it, the number 25 only appears once on the west side, and it's a special shape, a small perfect equilateral triangle."

"Right, and over on the other side, look, the 25 triangle stone appears only about five or six feet off the floor, and there are twelve of them. Those must be the push stones, and they probably somehow relate to the 5x5 magic square!"

"Maybe all the confusing lines made with rectangular blocks aren't writing at all, but a map. The few non-rectangular shapes are names of things at intersections. It's just like a map we would make."

"We've got it. The west wall is the smarties showing off their knowledge, and the other side is a map of what's underground and how to get there."

William and Zarlie ran around their apartment with so much excitement thinking about the twelve triangular push stones and imagining that they were actually movable. These stones looked just like the others, covered with the stains and dust of millennia, but William couldn't help but mentally push hard on each one, just hoping for a slight hint that it would move. And where would the secret door be? What would open when a group pushed on all the stones at once?

Chapter 16
Trouble In Paradise

William and Zarlie had made an incredible scientific breakthrough, but it was only in their heads. In order to preserve their work in case they were injured or killed in the ancient tunnels, William summarized the key discoveries and their data, burned it all onto three sets of CD-ROMs, then shipped one set to Professor Mackie and another to Professor Weisskopf. The last set was given to the Rroma for safe-keeping. Whatever happened, their discovery would be preserved. William felt a great sense of relief when the runner returned from the Fed-X office and announced that the air freight packages to Stanford were on their way.

The wall-writing didn't tell how hard to push, or how long, but since the wall hadn't been opened for thousands of years, they suspected that it would take very strong pushing, maybe even machines, to open the secret door. While they were decoding the map on the east wall and looking at the push stones, Zarlie had thought of their Rroma friends. Twelve of the strongest could slip into the Pyramid at night and together they could try the stones and see what happened.

Over glasses of mint tea Zarlie began to explain the idea to Zandar, the Head Waiter who seemed to be in charge of the local Rroma. "We need your help in a great adventure, one that may bring fame to the Rroma community, and perhaps a bit of treasure as well. Can I trust you?"

Zandar had been studying his two young visitors with great curiosity. Although their pile of cash was tempting, he was more interested in them as uncommonly smart people who were working furiously on a secret quest, and one that was obviously outside the law. He knew it involved the Great Pyramid since he had arranged their nocturnal visits through a distant cousin. "I give you my oath, to keep your secret in any way you desire. What is the adventure? What can I do?"

"We've been studying the interior walls of the Great Pyramid and think that perhaps we have found a way into tunnels and passages that have been hidden for thousands of years."

William interrupted, "Please understand that we're not sure, this is just an experiment, a big experiment, there's no sign saying 'here's the door' or anything obvious, but you can help us try to open what we think is a door."

Slowly a large smile formed on Zandar's face, a grin almost stretching to his ears. "My kind of adventure! Can we try it tonight? I'm sure we can get back in."

"Yes, we need twelve or maybe thirteen or fourteen very strong people. Each will push hard on a particular stone, all at once. At least I think the key is that we push all twelve stones together, but maybe we need to do them in sequence, but once we're all in there pushing we can try different approaches."

"We have no idea how hard to push on these stones since they haven't moved for thousands of years," Zarlie added.

Their conversation was interrupted by a shouting Rroma, Alkazar, who ran up the stairs into their apartment. He had been watching television in the kitchen and had just realized that William could be the prophet sought by the spaceship worshipers on the desert. Alkazar walked to William, "Please sir, when I look into your eyes and think of your face without its beard and your hair without its black dye, I think I see the desert prophet who discovered the spaceship. Is it you?"

"Damn. Yes, but I'm not a prophet, I'm just a mathematician playing with numbers. Those people on TV are nuts, but please don't tell anyone about me, at least not for a few days."

Zandar couldn't believe what he was hearing. Not only was he about to participate in a potentially very profitable adventure, he was also hosting one of the most sought-after men on earth. "Alkazar won't tell a soul about it, and he will come tonight on our adventure. You two must stay up here in your apartment until night. Stay out of sight. No one else will interrupt you."

Zandar and Alkazar left the building to gather men and supplies for the coming adventure. Zarlie turned to William, "We don't need to worry about those two, but others downstairs could have figured out who we are, and maybe applied for the reward. I've got a bad feeling about this."

"Let's take the professional approach."

"What's that?"

"It means having confidence in our ideas and expecting success, while planning ways to handle trouble if it comes. That's how Gloria operates, at least when she's thinking of business."

"O.K. Let's stuff our backpacks on the assumption that we might not be coming back here after tonight: that's a sensible precaution and one that's easy to take. We could be down in the secret passages for days. In some ways, this is sort of like that old Elvis song, 'It's Now or Never': we won't get a second chance at this."

"I'll make maps and reload the flashlights, you bring money and passports so we can leave the country if we have to."

At dusk they were lying on the bed, resting before their next trip into the pyramid at night. Zarlie was asleep, while William was lost in thought about the triangular 25-stone, trying to relate it to the 5x5 magic square. In addition, he had a suspicion that the 9-stone, a parallelogram shape, was related to the 3x3 magic square and that somehow these two stones were very special, and perhaps both were part of the key to the old passageways. They could have complex additional meanings that he hadn't decoded. In particular, the 9-stone appeared often among the map's lines on the east wall, but he had no idea what it meant.

Suddenly Zarlie woke and leapt to her feet, crouched in a defensive posture, quickly scanning the room, whispering, "Goons are coming. Get ready."

"It's OK Zarlie, you just had a bad dream. Take it easy. Relax."

"Dammit this is real. Shhhhh, be quiet and hide until we see what happens. Take this stick, you may need it."

She handed William a short broomstick, pushed him behind a curtain, then grabbed the butcher knife they had used at lunch to carve a few melons. Zarlie positioned herself behind the low wall that surrounded the staircase that came up into the room, knife gripped hard, ready to attack. William was confused, thinking that Zarlie was reacting to her fears instead of reality, but he did as he was told: better to wait for awhile until her fears subsided. Then much to William's surprise, a man in a blue European suit crept up the stairs, carrying a pistol loosely at his side as he started to look around the dark room. Before the visitor knew what had happened Zarlie chopped her heavy sharp blade across his gun hand nearly amputating it. The gun fell to the floor as the man started to scream in pain. But before he had time to make a noise, Zarlie grabbed his head and sliced his throat, killing him instantly and silently in a sea of blood. William didn't dare move as the goon slumped to the floor. Zarlie turned to him with a finger on her lips: he must remain silent.

Quickly she picked up the gun, pleased to see that it was a familiar Beretta 9mm compact pistol, a model favored as a carry weapon by many crooks and people who travel in undesirable neighborhoods. Reflexively, she checked the twelve-shot magazine, verified the chamber loaded indicator, turned off the safety and placed her finger on the trigger. At the same time she moved to a perfect defensive position, high above the bottom of the stairway, looking down onto the back of anybody who climbed it.

It seemed like forever, but it was only a minute or two when she heard a voice below softly calling to the first goon. Then she saw a shape starting up the stairs. Zarlie waited until she could see clearly that it wasn't one of the Rroma, but rather another foreigner, and like the first he was moving stealthily, creeping in the shadows against the wall. Zarlie knew the first rule of gun-handling, 'don't point a gun at someone unless you intend to use it.' As the man walked under her position she carefully fired a staccato pair of perfectly-aimed two-hand shots, straight down into the top of his bald head, killing him before his knees hit the floor.

By the time the smell of gunpowder reached her nostrils, Zarlie had scooted back to the bloody corpse at the top of the stairs. She searched his pockets until she found a spare magazine for the pistol. "William put on your robe. It's time to run."

"Are there more downstairs?"

"I don't think so, but these guys were just the advance party. See if that body on the stairs has spare ammo, and grab his gun while I write a note to Zandar."

"Remind me to thank you for saving my life again."

"Later, hurry up."

William had never touched a corpse, let alone a warm fresh one with blood pouring from what was left of its face. However, this was not the time to be squeamish or ask questions. He found extra bullets in one of the pockets and brought them and the gun to Zarlie, who de-cocked it and set the safety. "I'll show you how to use this later, for now just stuff it in your bag."

"While you were asleep I removed the hard drives from the computers and packed them also: there's nothing here we can't replace easily."

Zarlie put on her robe, grabbed her backpack, and headed for the roof, "Let's go, I know a way across the rooftops to another building and a quiet exit."

When they had first entered the Rroma restaurant, they had been excited and happy at finding new friends and a safe place to work for a long time. Now they were running away into an uncertain future as their research plans, dreams, and perhaps their lives collapsed. After riding in three different taxi cabs they arrived in the early evening darkness on the desert sand, within sight of the distant Pyramids.

Along the way, they had called Professor Weisskopf and chatted with him while they could. In contrast to their dangerous situation in Egypt, Weisskopf was warm and friendly, and filled with

175

good news as he worked in his lab. He had fertilized Zarlie's egg and the embryo appeared strong, in spite of their unconventional procedures. He theorized that perhaps some of their extra genetic material helped to make the reproductive process robust. The embryo was now growing inside a birth mother, developing normally.

William told him about the Pyramid and their excitement at decoding the ancient messages as well as the Fed-X packages. They laughed briefly at the surprise they could all imagine on Professor Mackie's face when she received their data: she would have new students of Egyptology, perhaps transfers from the Math Department. It was sad to say goodbye, but they didn't dare stay on the line more than a few minutes out of fear that the call might be traced.

Now, as stars replaced the twilight William and Zarlie sat alone, out on the desert, within a mile of the Pyramid, huddled on a few old rugs that they had bought for warmth. Zarlie shivered as her adrenaline rush faded and her fear returned. Her excitement at victory was tempered by the knowledge that the relatively-inept goons that she had killed were probably the first of many who would seek their bodies. Somewhere deep inside, she knew that she needed to shake-off her fear and take the offensive, to find a way to avoid sitting still and being attacked again.

William's emotions were in turmoil. He had just made an incredible math breakthrough, but the pleasure he had anticipated from the discovery had evaporated. Instead of writing scientific papers and exploring secret passages, he was running for his life like a crook. His comfortable academic and student life had drifted away, leaving a cold bitter reality in its place. As they sat quietly, Zarlie explained the nuances of the second pistol to William. He had shot a twenty-two at targets, but had never fired a heavy weapon at a person in a life-or-death situation: a world of difference.

"Damn it Zarlie, we were so close to opening the old passageways, and now we're out here arming ourselves. What a letdown."

Zarlie reached over and rubbed his shoulder. "We need to do something to salvage the situation, something positive that will turn things around. It's not as though we don't have options. For instance, in the morning we could surrender to the US Embassy and ask for protection. It would be a smart move, and give us a chance to regroup then find another way to continue research here."

"They would be pissed about our passports, and hey, we're not even American citizens. Suppose they turned us away?"

"Wouldn't happen if we told them the whole story, and we could get Weisskopf on the line as a character reference. Maybe the worst that would happen is that they would put us on the first flight out, but we'd still be together."

"I hope we have a better idea in the morning," said William as he stared at the distant pyramid in frustration. He still wanted to go inside and press the triangular stones to see if they moved.

They stared at the Pyramid as a gentle night breeze rustled their clothing. Zarlie had a far-away look in her eyes as she turned to William and took his hand, "What about our future, our hopes and dreams? What if we defeat the goons and open the pyramid? What then? What of Living Waves and all our other adventures? If you could do anything you wanted to, anything in the world, what would it be?"

William thought silently for a long time, considering all that had happened, the changes in his professional and emotional lives. He had lost his family, but made the first of what he hoped to be many huge math discoveries. Their DNA was mysterious and years could be spent in genetic experiments. Professor Weisskopf and the Math Department could be allies in fascinating research projects. But far more important than all this was the beautiful young woman at his side. Anything could be possible with her, while nothing would be worth doing without her. He knew instinctively the answer to Zarlie's question. "I love you Zarlie. I want to give you my life, everything that I am or ever will be. Will you accept it? Will you spend forever with me, will you marry me?"

Zarlie wrapped her arms tightly around him in a long embrace, then pushed away slowly, tears welling in her eyes. "William, you don't know anything of my background, of my past.

I'm not good wife material, especially not for a soon-to-be-famous mathematician."

"What do you mean? You're perfect, you're wonderful, how can you say such things?"

"I'm also a murderer, a criminal, a thief, and I'm wanted by the police in at least two countries."

"You killed the goons to protect us, that's not a crime, and stealing the jar, what of it? They don't have any real proof of who took it?"

"That's recent history. I've been on the run a long time. How do you think I made the transition from a filthy kid on a Hungarian fortune teller's floor to a scholarship student at Stanford?"

"I don't know. You must have won science contests or earned a pile of money or something?"

"No, there were no prize contests for Rroma children, and not much schooling either."

"So what happened, what did you do?"

Zarlie was silent, then she looked away and began softly, almost whispering with pain, as she remembered. "This isn't going to be a lovely story, or even a nice one William, but it's what happened. I didn't have many choices, and you know I was smart but different from other people. Starting at an early age, I learned how to steal, mostly for food and just to stay warm, to stay alive. Then I graduated and learned how to kill, and then finally, I learned how to use my body to snare men into bad situations. The last guy, a fat rich businessman, smuggled me into Switzerland, where he expected to play with my body forever, or until he tired of it. I killed him and took all his money: his family is still looking for me. That money bought me a new identity and a flight to San Francisco."

William was speechless, but not entirely surprised. He had long suspected that there were unsavory aspects to her background, ever since Gloria had given her estimation of Zarlie's situation. He wrapped his arms around Zarlie, hugging her crying body to his as he looked up at the stars. Finally he made up his mind.

"Zarlie, we're not so different from each other. We both have messed up DNA, we both stole the jar and we both are being chased by fools. Maybe we don't have long to live, so let's face our problems together and enjoy each minute of the time we have left, together as one."

Zarlie smiled. They had a little bread left from a cold supper. She broke it in half and told William of an ancient Rroma wedding ceremony, an 'abiav', a wedding under the stars, a ceremony that involves only the two persons who wish to marry and two pieces of bread. She opened her knife, "William, may I take your hand, now and forever?"

He was surprised, but trusted her completely as she held the knife next to his left hand. Zarlie gently pricked one of his fingers, then squeezed it so that his blood fell onto one piece of bread. "Now take my hand in yours and put my blood on the other piece."

William took the knife, as Zarlie held out her hand. He wasn't sure how hard to press and didn't want to hurt the soft gentle hand which rested in his. Zarlie was offering her life to him. The knife was very sharp and her finger started to bleed before he realized that he was cutting. Her blood dripped onto the other piece of bread as she smiled into his eyes. They exchanged the two pieces of bread, softly promised their lives to each other, then carefully swallowed each other's bread. Symbolically they were now part of each other, their blood was united. By Rroma law, they were married. They were joined for eternity. They wrapped themselves in each other's arms and embraced under the rugs. Who knew what tomorrow would bring, but they would face it together, united as one.

Chapter 17
Breaking Through

As dawn broke across the desert, they decided to celebrate their marriage with a fancy breakfast while thinking over their new life together and planning a way to escape from the goons. William realized that his world had grown much larger overnight. He was now responsible for his wife, Zarlie's, life as well as his own. His steps were filled with purpose, confidence and pride: he felt somehow taller and stronger as he assumed a new mantle of responsibility. They walked hand-in-hand across the desert to The Mena House, a beautiful old British hotel, built in the days when the ruling class traveled by ship between India and England. This was the only first class hotel anywhere near the pyramids and had once been a major stop for travelers. William and Zarlie couldn't help glancing at each other, smiling and sharing their good luck at being happy and in love, even though they knew that their future was precarious.

The huge windows of the elegant high-ceilinged dining room looked out over the nearby pyramids as the sun rose on a lovely day. A great spot for a perfect wedding breakfast. After they were seated, William watched with curiosity as a party of Sumo wrestlers entered with their Japanese tour guide. Huge men, incredibly strong, and all talking loudly in Japanese as they headed for the best tables in the room. "Zarlie, let me have my Japanese passport and lots of cash: I've just had an idea."

He took the passport and Zarlie's backpack then approached the Japanese tour leader with a strange request. William figured that it would be impossible to be in more trouble than they already were, so a few lies wouldn't make any difference to their future. William hoped that the Sumos would recognize him as a confederate when he discretely showed his Japanese Emperor passport with its flashy gold stamps and colorful ribbons. He greeted the leader with a formal bow in Japanese, showing much deference to the group's status. The passport, with a painting of the Emperor on the front, caused great excitement. They started to become friends with William as he told them that a Japanese research team had sent him to solve a mystery at the pyramids, and that although his original plans had been compromised, he might still accomplish his mission if the world's strongest men would help. After explaining that the locals knew nothing of the Japanese plans, and that these plans were the result of superior Japanese teamwork, the wrestlers became most interested. Many eyes lit up as William started to remove bills from the bag of money. He offered $2,000 in cash for each of the men who would help and $10,000 for the leader personally, to compensate for his trouble in arranging matters.

Although the Sumo had doubts about the project, the cash, the strange passport, and the fact that they were going to the Pyramids anyway, combined to bring them onto William's team. This was going to be their lucky day. William drew a rough sketch of the Grand Gallery on a placemat then described the triangular push stones with additional sketches.

When William returned to his breakfast, Zarlie teased him about his plan saying that the Sumo were so big that they might not even fit inside the Gallery, let alone push on the right stones. But if any group of people were strong enough to move the ancient rocks, these men could do it. William and Zarlie knew that they would have only one chance to try to open the secret door. Once they all went into the pyramid and started pushing and shoving, it either worked, or they were toast in the eyes of the authorities and ripe for attack by the goons.

Zarlie saw William's picture on the early morning TV news at a set near the lobby. Things were becoming tight, but they were in fantastic spirits. Today was the day that they would see if all their pyramid work was right or wrong: they were almost bouncing with excitement and anticipation. William had to pinch himself to realize that they were married and facing this together. Neither could stop smiling, almost laughing at what the day might bring.

The Sumo bus was the first vehicle at the gate to the Great Pyramid before it opened, but when the gate was finally clear, there was a long line behind their bus, honking and yelling at the guards. From the singing and noise in the bus to their rear they could tell that it held a load of Russians, reeling from too much early morning vodka and sausage. It appeared that their bus driver, perhaps already drunk, wanted to race the Sumo bus to the pyramid entrance for the honor of being first. He was gunning his engine and rocking his bus back and forth, like a panther getting ready to spring. Perhaps he and his passengers were agitated by the sign staring at them from the rear of the Sumo bus, 'You Are Behind The First Class #1 Team', accompanied by a large Japanese flag.

As soon as William's fellow Japanese realized the Russians' intent, they yelled at their driver to get to the Pyramid first. The

Sumo team was used to winning! They started chanting Japanese cheer-leading songs, their loud voices and rhythmically-moving bulk rocking their bus with excitement. When the gate opened, the race down the long access road was on. The busses blasted toward the pyramid in a cloud of diesel smoke and flying sand, scattering camels and baksheesh bandits. The Russian bus tried to pass, but the Sumo bus blocked the narrow road. The busses were well matched in capability, but not sobriety. Near the Great Pyramid, the Russians tried to pass by driving in the sand, narrowly missing a group of camels. As the Sumo bus raced to the finish, the Russian bus rolled onto its side in the sand and slid to a stop. The Russians tumbled out an access hatch on their overturned bus, furious at the Japanese.

Far back in the line waiting for admission was a police car. When the policemen saw the lead bus running down the road at top speed, pursued by another giant tour bus, camels, beggars, and guards scattering to get out of the way, they were furious. The police turned on their siren and tried to move closer to the action, but were blocked by mass confusion in the vehicles in front of them.

As the Sumo raced to the pyramid, guards and guides yelled to no avail. What a sight the four hundred pound Sumo wrestlers made as they leapt from the bus and rushed the entrance. They moved through guards and obstacles like a dose of salts through plugged bowels. The Sumo as well as William and Zarlie were still cheering and yelling. What high spirits, what fun they were having.

William had given each wrestler a map and a position to stand in as well as instructions on which stone he was to push, but hadn't figured on the Russians, who now were trying to elbow their way in. The rude comments and gestures in Russian and Japanese would have been hilarious to a disinterested observer, but the activity looked like a disaster to William. The narrow fragile wooden walkway in the Grand Gallery was no place for a fight among so many big people.

Zarlie and William barely had control over the wrestlers, as the Russian hooligans surged about waving sausages and three liter vodka bottles. Zarlie saw more than one Sumo lift a Russian and smash him over another like a wet noodle: the yelling and screaming were echoing in the passageways, combined with bottles smashing and sausage flying. William and Zarlie were trying to position their team so that it pushed on the correct stones, but they were continually distracted by the Russians and other tourists and guards who had no idea of what they were doing. In the distance there were police whistles and sirens, as William and Zarlie screamed at their teammates to push harder.

The Russians were pushing on the wrong stones: they saw

the Sumos pushing so they started pushing too, but they had no idea of what to do and were confusing the pressure pattern. Some Russians looked at his maps, but the maps were in Japanese. The guards were yelling and William had no idea what was happening outside in the long line of tourists who were pressing for admission.

Just as the police entered, frantically blowing their whistles, there was a deep rumbling groan from the stones and a huge cloud of dust engulfed the corridor. An entrance swung open near the floor. William grabbed Zarlie and they leapt toward it. They were quickly over the railing and through the doorway, disappearing into the darkness below. The lights in the pyramid flickered, flashed, then went out with a rain of sparks, crackles and confusion. Yelling and screaming came from all directions. The police just barely saw the open doorway as the lights failed.

Several Sumos may have followed them into the passage, and maybe a Russian or two, but William and Zarlie were far ahead. They not only had the only interior map and flashlights, but they knew what had happened and why. The others were completely bewildered. When the wrestlers had stopped pushing, the door had closed. Simultaneously everyone in the Grand gallery tried to escape through the narrow Gallery doorway, from the darkness and choking dust, out into the sun and fresh air.

Underground, William and Zarlie could hear voices in the distance yelling and swearing, as the others banged on the closed door, trying to re-open it. There was no way for William and Zarlie to tell what was happening up above. They could hear sirens far away and low rumbles in the distance as they walked through the long and empty tunnels.

Zarlie knew that their luck was a bit too good to be true as they slowly became lost. They had been walking steadily downwards for a long time. At each intersection, William looked at his computer printout and tried to decide how it related to the marks on the walls and the passages running at odd angles deep into the darkness. Navigation was far trickier than he had imagined, as most intersections had a variety of stones, and some had new symbols they hadn't seen in the gallery. The tunnels were larger than the others that they had explored. These passages were for people, tall people, walking upright. The walls were solid rock, beautifully cut, straight with sharp angles, beautiful craftsmanship. The floor was deep in dust and there were no footprints: nobody had been here for thousands of years. The atmosphere was damp and he suspected that they were close to the level of the river, which would put them hundreds of feet below ground level.

For some reason Zarlie started thinking about the old Flash Gordon films from the 1930's and the Claymen, who blended into the walls of underground passages on the planet Ming, then crept away after Flash and his people passed. She was almost expecting to see the Claymen emerge at any moment.

Finally at a particularly unintelligible intersection, Zarlie stopped and turned to William. "Put the paper away and save your flashlight. Just hold onto my belt and let me lead."

Zarlie was afraid, but she could feel the distant voice: it poured into her head in a way much stronger than before. It seemed to be calling, beckoning her to come toward it. She focused her whole being on the voice and started walking carefully forward in total darkness. At each corner she stopped and listened, then went in the direction of the strongest signal. They moved slowly, feeling the walls for intersections. They were afraid but they were moving and they believed that they were on the right path. Zarlie was tightly controlled, moving with strength and tense confidence, every ounce of her body attuned to the distant voice, every step purposeful and carefully directed toward the voice.

Their attitude changed subtly from fear to hope: now they knew they were doing the right thing. Earlier they had been talking nervously about what they would find and what was happening up above, but now they were silent, walking slowly, deep in concentration, feeling their way forward.

Up in the Grand Gallery, the police had brought flashlights, and were repairing the wiring. Everyone looked at the doorway, which was closed. However, its outline could be seen plainly, now that centuries of dust had fallen away. Tapping noises came from the other side of the doorway as the police and guards tried to understand the Japanese pressure maps that William had made.

Slowly the pressure pattern was re-established with help from the Sumo. The door creaked open, and the trapped people were rescued and taken outside. The police entered the door, switched on flashlights, and started to follow the footsteps in the dust. They moved much faster than William and Zarlie since the trail in the dust was clear.

At several places they needed to backtrack, retracing errors that William and Zarlie had made, before they had started to follow the voice.

Up ahead, William and Zarlie came to a small river. Fortunately they heard its running water before they stepped in it. They switched on their lights and looked in wonder. The stones around the river were elaborately worked: it was perhaps a shrine or sacred place. They both wished that they had time to explore, but the voice led them down a little, almost invisible, side passage on a narrow ledge beside the river. William remarked that down here the floor was washed clean by spray from the river, no dust and no footprints. They would not be able to retrace their path by following their footprints, but nobody could follow them either. They were really on their own, putting all their trust in the distant voice. William started to make small scratches on the floor at each corner in case they had to find their way back.

William and Zarlie had been walking for miles and now the voice grew stronger and stronger as they moved. They both wished that they could come back and map the other passages and see where they went, but they were just moving toward whatever was sending the strong signal. Eventually it was strong enough for William to feel it and to be able to navigate by himself.

All at once, the voice stopped. The silence was eerie. They had walked into a huge room without realizing it. They turned on their lights. Zarlie don't know what they had expected to find, but there wasn't much treasure here at first glance. Small piles of black sand were everywhere. Then William noticed a corbelled niche in the far wall. It was a miniature version of the one in the Queen's Chamber. But to their surprise, this niche was decorated with a large gold six-by-six square engraving, containing the thirty-six oddly-shaped characters used in wall-writing, perfectly arranged and enmeshed, with a bit of unknown writing on each stone symbol. William stared at it in fascination: whomever had built the pyramid and this room knew math, perhaps much more math than William. He couldn't wait to study the unusual writing in each of the shapes in the square.

As Zarlie looked around, she discovered a machine-like device in the niche made from unfamiliar materials. They opened the device and found a stack of very thin gold plates, much like sheets of paper. The golden pages were covered with math and writing. Neither William nor Zarlie could understand the writing, but they reasoned that it must be very special to be here. They looked through the pages and saw that some sheets were in wall-writing, similar to the stones in the walls of the Grand Gallery but most was unintelligible. They had found a very special treasure, probably from the people who built the pyramid. After they carefully packed the gold sheets into William's backpack, they noticed a small box near the machine. The box was very curious. Inside was something like an electronic device, and there were other gadgets that they couldn't comprehend, so they put them into Zarlie's backpack.

Zarlie noticed an interesting pattern or decoration on the walls. It was not regular, but varied as it wrapped around the room.

It might be a form of writing that must be very important to be here. When they looked carefully, they realized that the symbols were made from gold, pressed into slight depressions in the stone. William noticed that the symbols were a form of numeric writing, and that the symbols could be seen as numbers, somewhat like a cross between Hieroglyphics and Japanese numerals. He started reeling off the numbers as he walked around the room. The digits didn't make any sense to him, but he enjoyed the curious numbers, which he started to write down for further study. All at once Zarlie had an inspirational flash, and dragged William to the corbelled niche. "Start reading the numbers here, this must be the beginning of the series. I know what they mean. Read slowly!"

William carefully read the numbers and Zarlie pointed out that the numbers were in groups, delineated by other symbols, and her inspiration was that the first group was big and that the last group, all the way at the other end of the string, was small, and that there were twenty-three groups. That meant only one thing to her, this was a genetic sequence for a human chromosome, and it was probably the sequence for the people or person who had built the pyramid. She ran to the last group and exclaimed, "Look, this is the XY chromosome and it's male. And the first chromosome is gigantic, just like ours. Our ancestors built this pyramid!"

They danced around the room in excitement, then made careful flash photographs and notes on the writing.

Looking at the maps they had made earlier, William now could tell where they were. Although they hadn't really understand the maps when they had entered the tunnels, now the directions made sense because they could see the treasure room, where they were standing, on the map quite clearly. It appeared that there was a way up to the surface from this room, and that it didn't go through the pyramid.

William hadn't given any thought as to how they would escape, especially as they were now carrying extremely valuable treasures and information, but an exit away from the pyramid seemed like a very good start.

After looking around the room a little more, they wrote a message on a piece of paper and left it on the machine with one of the gold plates for anyone who came afterwards. Zarlie smiled, then signed the note, "Mr. and Mrs. William Stowell". William kissed her as she wrote.

Further back in the tunnels, the guards were having trouble following the trail. Some were becoming afraid and wanted to quit. They reached the water, after hearing it in the distance, but then did not know which way to turn: no more dusty footprints. The leader wanted them to separate and explore the various paths simultaneously, which would be efficient, but the others were afraid of becoming lost. The leader, frustrated at their unwillingness to take risks, yelled at them to follow directions. They struggled. The leader tried to push them in the right directions, but instead, he tripped and fell into the stream. They helped him out of the water, then all headed quietly back toward the surface.

Zarlie felt as though there was a different voice leading her now. Perhaps the devices in her backpack modified the signals, but they were in the right passages according to the map, as well as according to her feelings, but they were walking in such a long straight tunnel.

They struggled up many steps and observed that whoever had built them had had long legs. Each step was an effort and their energy was near zero after all their activity. Up on the surface day had passed into night, yet they were still walking slowly. Zarlie's knees were killing her but they kept moving. They were running only on adrenaline and just hoping it would last until they came to a safe resting place.

They heard distant rumbling noises, but couldn't tell if the sounds were in the passages, or in the pyramid, or maybe on the ground above. The map was so old that they had no idea what they would find when they emerged onto the surface above. They might appear right in the middle of town, or far out in the desert, or behind a blocked doorway in a cellar. Neither could relate the map to the modern buildings near the pyramid.

Around five in the morning William and Zarlie felt the first faint tingle of cool air in the tunnel, and the steps they were climbing became sandy and difficult to locate. After many falls, crawling through sand ever upwards, they emerged onto the desert in the midst of a dark rock outcrop. They collapsed onto the ground, breathing fresh air deeply, so glad to be out of the tunnels.

"Look way over there Zarlie, I know where we are. We went by here on our camel ride."

"Right, we're miles from the pyramid, out on the desert in the middle of nowhere."

William wrapped his arms around Zarlie hugging her tired body tightly with his last bit of strength. "I still can't believe all that's happened; our love, our happiness together, our discoveries, and the future. We'll be reading stone writing all over the planet: we've got the secret. I can't wait to try it everywhere."

"And the genetics. I'm just beginning to realize how important that part of our discovery is, and what it's going to do for biological research. Wait until we decipher the writing on the genetic code around the treasure room"

"And can you imaging Professor Mackie's face when we take her down there: she'll go ballistic. Egyptology is about to have a whole new meaning."

"She'll have to join your Russian professor and the SETI Institute!"

"The sun's just coming up. Let's look at the gold plates again and see if we can get some idea of what they mean."

They started carefully leafing through the plates, looking at the engravings in the dim pre-dawn light as a cool breeze rustled their clothes.

"William, stop, just hold this plate at an angle to the sun, tilt it so that the engraving shows clearly. I can read it. I can't tell you how, or why, but it's like the voice that I've been hearing over and over. The same guy wrote these plates."

"Maybe he's the guy who appeared to us on the coast, the blue sparking vision?"

"Want to hear what he wrote?"

"Let me kiss you first, this looks like a long story."

They embraced again, smiled into each other's eyes and kissed as the sun touched the distant horizon on the first day of the rest of their lives. Then Zarlie began to read.

Chapter 18
Ra's Story

Plate-1:   Blasting Off Toward The Green Planet

*F*antastic: you found my plates at last! Greetings from Ra! If you can read this, you must be from my home planet.   I wish you'd been here when I was all alone. That is, I was alone, but there were cats and humans and some other creatures wandering around.   I have so much to tell.   It's a bit disorganized because as you can see I have cut this into some metal and can't erase, so I'll just tell my story as I think of it and you can fit the pieces into the right order.

Where to begin? You found this inside the monument that I had the locals build. I figured that the monument would last at least a million revolutions of their planet about its star, and if these plates weren't found by then, that perhaps my planet would have disintegrated. I had so much trouble finding enough metal to write this. You and I are used to just having things, and it was so strange being in a place that had nothing! I had to figure out how to make everything, and then teach the locals to do it. Some of them were so good to me, and the generations of my children have grown strong and wise.   Perhaps you are one of my children's children. What a happy thought that one of them would one day find my story.

In my time scale, I should try to start at the beginning, when I arrived, or when I realized that I had arrived here, for I didn't know I was here at first.   I was so stupid. I volunteered for a secret mission, with much prestige and all my friends said what a trip, wish they could go too. Of course, I did have some misgivings, especially about the kind of tests they gave me, but once I arrived, it all began to make sense. But that is beside the point. I think on reflecting that I was tricked into being sent here by the national population control center. They had ended my parents' lives prematurely and I had always mistrusted them. But then before I understood anything, I found myself in resplendent uniform, boarding the ship, and being treated with ceremony. I thought I was some kind of hero, *something wonderful. We blasted off into the unknown (to me anyway).*

Plate-2:   Abandoned By The Ship

When I looked around and began to realize that they had left without me, how I burned and ached inside.   It was as though a knife cut through my heart and I cried (which I had seen others do, but never had actually done myself), but let me back-up a moment, as I'm out of step with my story.

We slept most of the way (I have no idea how long we traveled) in the big talanium-powered ship, but when we arrived at the green planet, on which you are standing, we circled for several revolutions and ran computer models of the climate and geology. This place has so much variation. The locals have yet to learn to control the weather, so it changes constantly. They let storms rage, ravishing the land, electricity still sparks from the clouds, and uncontrolled oscillations in the climatic system cause major changes. The surface plates are still moving here, so land is being formed and consumed constantly. I don't know how they will ever get anything permanent built.

There was vague talk about a previous trip. This was one of the planets that my ancestors visited long ago, but there was no sign of them, or their home. There had been no news from here for many lifetimes, so we were going to land and check-out the situation. At least that's what they told me. From what we could tell, there had been major geological changes since the last visit. Big meteors had bombarded the planet, making huge holes and a mess of the ecology. Looking at some old computer maps, we figured that the surface of the planet had rotated about 90 degrees from the core since the last visit. The polar areas were now at the equator. There was also talk about the new planet that was between us and the local star. It had arrived since the last visit, and probably caused major gravitational changes locally. It appeared to be a comet that had been captured by the star, and was still undergoing transition. Our ship would visit it next.

We circled the local moon and saw that a relay station which our ancestors had left, to send pictures regularly, had been partly smashed by a meteor. You could see the ruins of the equipment and it was obvious why it no longer made transmissions.

Well, we looked around for the most stable place on the planet, that is the place least likely to be subducted for a long time, (although I could see that major climate changes were about to happen, even here) and prepared for a landing. We leaked in some of the atmosphere and it had a peculiar, but pleasant aroma, quite different as we cruised over different areas, and unlike what we have at home, though quite functional for biological conversion. I was pleased and was excited that we would land and walk around a bit. (I now am almost sure that this idea had been implanted during my sleep). In the midst of the most stable area we set down, making the usual mess of the area with our engines. I was even the first one out the door. Like a fool, I wanted to be the first to set foot on the green planet. I jumped to the surface, ran around a bit, then looked back to see the door closing and the engines fire! Crap, did I screw-up! I knew there must be a mistake ..... they didn't realize I was outside ... I had jumped out too fast .... I grabbed my communicator, I called ... just static ..... then it came through ..... just these words "your instructions are implanted: good luck".

What a mess. Here I was in the middle of nowhere, without food, computers, robots, clothes, purifiers (although the local air seemed ok), or anything useful, and it was getting dark, and I already knew enough about the climate to suspect that precipitation was imminent. As you realize, the green planet rotates much faster that our planet, so practically before you get going in the morning, it's dark again, and I didn't have any chemicals to adjust my body.

Implanted instructions: what a lot of crap. They knew it's only experimental and that most of the time the victim does the wrong thing anyway. Last time I read about it, the likelihood of the victim acting instinctively on the basis of the implanted instructions was about the same as if nothing had been done at all. Some set of instructions, and almost no tools. How could I do anything, even if I knew what to do. (I forgot to mention that just as the spaceship departed, it dumped a small survival toolkit. Of course it didn't contain food, or anything useful. When I saw it fall to the ground, I really knew that they were leaving me here, and that it was no accident.)

That first night was not my best. I was awake, but couldn't see anything interesting, hungry but there was no food, and wet because the rain was out of control. I remember that I sat in the same place all night, feeling sorry for myself instead of doing anything: I had had quite a shock, so perhaps I could be forgiven for inaction, but still, what a pain, and to *think that solutions to my problems were nearby, if only I had opened my eyes.*

Plate-3: Ra Meets Some Primitives

When the planet rotated so that light from the star illuminated the surface near me, I looked around and felt better, just having bright starlight made me feel more at home. The rain had stopped, and the air was pleasant. Everything was so clean and clear. I started walking around and pretty soon I tuned-in a couple of what the locals call cats: rather small ones, only came up to my knees, but at least I could communicate with them. I asked about food and other creatures like myself and if they knew of any, and what they ate. They said that they knew of nothing like me, but that there were some primitives about my size living not too far away, but that these primitives were not only stupid, but mean: they sometimes killed cats just for fun. However, the primitives usually had lots of food lying around, so it was often convenient to take some of it in spite of the danger.

These little cats went a different way than I would have chosen, picking trails that were optimal for creatures of their size and capabilities, but after about half a day we looked down into a small valley which had a fair amount of vegetation and signs of crude construction. I noticed the primitives and realized that they were generally of the same conformation as myself, but un-advanced technologically and a bit small. I tuned into the brains of the nearest ones and realized why the cats called them primitives. They didn't even know how to communicate among themselves except by making noises and gestures.

I walked up to a small primitive who was alone and communicated with her, (which proved to be a rather startling experience for her!). After she calmed down, I decided that I had better learn how to talk with her via gesture and noise, and so observed her abilities in this area. It was rather easy to learn how to do it, and the noises were vaguely reminiscent of some old languages which I had studied a long time ago. I realized immediately that the problem with this primitive's abilities was that she was using only 10% of her brain: no wonder she was living in such circumstances. Almost immediately it occurred to me that I could probably teach these primitives how to use their in-built biological capabilities much more efficiently. I did not see this, at the time, as an implanted instruction: it just seemed a natural

192

thing to do, so I started to smarten-up this particular primitive.

It wasn't long before I could converse with her on her own terms, but it was almost dark and I remembered my hunger and so asked her what she ate and how I could find some food.

Although a simple request, it turned out that it posed a problem because I was an outsider and food was not given to strangers or visitors because of a perception that they were all enemies. The young primitive, who I now realize should be called a girl, trusted me and of course was somewhat disoriented by the day's activities. I asked to be taken to her parents, discretely, so as to not cause too much disorder.

You can imagine the situation as we quietly approached her hovel built of mud and grass. The parents had been looking for her all day and now she returns with this rather tall creature, wearing unusual garments, trailed by two cats.

I communicated to them immediately that they should have no fear, and as a stroke of genius on my part, I told them that I was a god and that they should bow down and honor me. Of course what I really wanted was food, as well as to calm them down, but this ruse had a good effect. The cats started teasing me and implied that I was taking advantage of the situation, but I told the cats to stick close to me and that we would all have fun. Time to start making a success of this expedition.

<u>Plate-4: Ra Builds A Small Laboratory</u>

If you're smart enough to read this description, you can fill in the activities of the first few weeks after my arrival from a simple knowledge of human nature. Soon I was living in the best house, being treated like a god, and the local felines were in pleasant circumstances. This could have continued indefinitely except that we were not the only civilization in the area. As I quickly realized, there were enemies and the battles among competing groups were brutal. I saw that a good part of the reason the locals were being so nice to me was that they expected me to protect them from their enemies. They didn't know that I was not a god, and that I was unarmed, at least in terms of their weaponry. Therefore, I asked them for all available information about the enemies and weapons usually used.

One of the things I had noticed about the locals was that they had almost no knowledge of biology and chemistry. It seemed reasonable to assume that their enemies shared this lack, so I decided that this was an area where we could have a good advantage, but not in a traditional battle.

The idea of a bit of harmless biological warfare against the enemy meshed with my well-known (on our home planet) skill at practical jokes and pranks, which almost put me in deep trouble a few times, but I'll tell you about that later. I talked with the cats and ascertained where the nearest band of enemies was living, then sent a feline recognizance mission to scout the territory with particular emphasis on food and water habits.

I wanted to modify the enemy's water supply: I didn't want to kill them, only convert them, so I rounded-up simple ingredients and began to build a small laboratory. I needed a few helpers, but mostly peace and quiet, so I told everyone that it was a very dangerous area where they would die if they entered without the secret knowledge. The girl who I had taught first, and the two cats I initially contacted became my first assistants. I gave them fancy clothes and colored rocks to mark them as special.

Plate-5: Poop Attack On Local Enemies

Two locals rushed to my lab and reported that the enemy was coming our way: drat, my plan was to peacefully enslave them via their water supply while they were sedentary. I thought hard about what I knew from chemistry that would be effective against a few hundred primitives, without actually killing them, and which of course would also be fun to do....then it occurred to me, so I called for new ingredients and worked frantically: after all, my status as a god was at stake.

The locals had become accustomed to my requests for the strangest ingredients, in the simple belief that whatever I did was going to be bad for their enemies, but dung-collection had not been one of their tasks before, (I did need all the nitrogen compounds that I could amass, and dried dung was the only local chemistry store.)

The enemy was within an hour (green planet time, 1/24th of a revolution about its axis) of our camp when I finished. Girl and I, with a few strong helpers, moved upwind of the enemy as the locals watched from a safe distance: I told them all to get upwind of me and stay there.

We released a bit of stink into the wind, which eventually caused the traveling enemy to stop and consider what was this mysterious odor they could begin to detect. Now that they were stopped, we could have more fun.

I touched-off a simple chemically-powered rocket which flew up in the air trailing a shower of sparks, and which then descended upon the enemy and laid a big cloud of smoke. The key item here was the smoke, which they had to breathe as much as possible to get the desired effect.

By now the enemy was somewhat panicked, having never seen a rocket, nor breathed this strange mixture. Soon the smoke started to have the desired effect, mainly that of causing total incontinence among the breathers. As they pooped and peed and tried to run away, they slipped and slid in the mess and eventually fell down, not in pain, but in great discomfort, embarrassment, and confusion.

A watchman from my tribe reported back to the others all that he had seen, boosting my status as a god considerably. We waited a few hours, so that the smoke could clear, and then, staying upwind of the stench, approached visibly: myself, the girl, and the two cats. The enemy looked in wonder at us (we were adorned in our finest god-like clothing and paraphernalia). I touched off a small rocket to add impact to our arrival, and from their viewpoint we seemed to appear from nowhere, arriving with a flash of light and puff of smoke. They were impressed.

I communicated to all of them, telling them to bow down and worship, for I was a god. I was getting good at this sort of stuff and now knew the right feelings to impart. In essence I told them to stop fighting, obey me, and live in peace with each other. Seems simple, but it was a new message, and by now I had a the beginnings of a long-range plan for my activity on the green planet: if I was stuck here, I was going to make the most of it, and try to improve the place a bit.

Plate-6: Extinction Genes

Perhaps things have changed on our home planet by the time you read this, but maybe you haven't been there for a long time, or ever. You probably wonder why I seem to be in a hurry and make mistakes that I could avoid through a bit more thinking and planning. The reason is simple: I don't know how much more time I will be alive.

A long time ago my ancestors conquered disease and as they did, we lived longer and longer. Of course the first thing they did was take control of reproduction, terminating any un-planned embryos. But things were getting rather difficult in terms of resource-depletion, so the doctors started implanting randomly-selected extinction genes during the fertilization process, to ensure that there weren't too many warm bodies wandering around. The end is quite painless: while walking along, people just drop dead in an instant: no pain, no problems. At home, you can have your genes analyzed and, if you want, find the exact moment when you'll terminate: most people don't want to know, and I never asked.

Here, I have a huge task, that of educating and repopulating an entire planet. There is so much to do, that I often don't get it done as I would like: much too frantic at times, but I can't wait for all the answers.

Plate-7: Ra Nukes a Mean Primitive

Over the next few years (a 'year' is one revolution of the green planet about its star) I continued my conquests, and soon it was relatively easy to annex tribes as they heard so much about my exploits that they didn't struggle. However, on a few occasions I had to demonstrate extra god-like powers, usually when I was really mad at someone.

At first I wasn't aware that I had unusual powers mainly because they would be impossible to use among communicating creatures, like cats, or residents of our home planet, but I found them to be quite effective here.

The first case was quite by accident. A cat came to me with a tale of woe: one of the recently conquered enemy people had been particularly mean to cats, burning them alive and such cruelty that the cats appealed to me to do something uncommonly bad to this person. I was much more mad that I would admit, as I usually tried to maintain an appearance of control and superiority. The cats could sense that they had me excited and demanded that we attack this person immediately.

I didn't know what I was going to do, perhaps have him eaten alive by a thousand cats, or some such, but we ran off to confront this evil person. The person looked evil, and when I communicated to his brain (what little of it existed) I could see a real stinker.

I was so mad that I focused all of my energy on his brain, deluging it with radiation tightly focused on the frequencies of its operation. Maybe I instinctively thought that I would erase his brain. Before I realized what effect this might have, at a very high and focused energy level, he burst into flames, starting with his head. I had never seen anything like it before and was as surprised as the onlookers. The big difference was that I quickly realized what had happened, but they thought it was yet another god power and ran to tell their friends what they had seen. I did make a special point of telling everyone that the reason that I had done this was because the

196

person had mistreated cats: naturally this pleased the entire feline world no end and led eventually to a surplus in their numbers.

Plate-8: Moving And Impregnating The Primitives

By this time I had learned to ride a camel which allowed me to cover a large geographic area and to start operating on a bigger scale. I knew the geography of the entire planet, which the locals did not, and I also knew how the climate was shifting from the computer models we had run in the ship. Early-on I had decided to withhold such information and to use it as part of a larger plan. I realized that the less I told them, the more mysterious I would appear, and that was in my favor.

To the surprise of the locals, I began herding them to the valley of a large river. I knew that this river would flow for a long time, as its source was well-placed to collect water from a wide area regardless of climatic change. I then encouraged them to plant crops which I selected to be appropriate. I also taught them the little that I knew of plant genetics and developed a class of agricultural experts to whom I entrusted the operation of the food supply.

This was no trivial accomplishment, and part of my wider plan, because I wanted to develop a stable civilization that would endure in spite of the coming climate changes. These primitives had been living on land that was rapidly transforming to desert, but they could not see the global factors driving the change. The decline in rainfall on, and hence the productivity of, their area was one of the forces driving them to fight each other because of the scarcity of the dwindling food supply.

The herding of the people and the establishment of river-based agriculture required many years, and during this time I mated with a wide range of females so as to generate as many strong offspring as possible. The locals at first didn't understand my method of selection for these highly-honored positions, but they began eventually to realize that I was after particularly smart mates, especially ones with appropriate biological features to enable them to bear rather large babies. I suppose from their viewpoint, I wasn't always selecting wisely, and you can imagine the funny-business that occurred as various locals tried to gain my favor by pushing their daughters at me.

For my part, I have always been a fairly compassionate and gentle person, so I treated these mates fairly, giving them all the same status and

197

costume, and causing as little emotional turmoil as possible. I viewed them simply as a means to re-populate the planet with brighter creatures, and felt it my duty to impregnate as many as possible. Of course I liked some better than others and remained especially attached to the very first one, whom I had met as a little girl, my first human friend. In spite of my efforts at prolonging her life, she died at barely 25 years, which was quite long considering her genetic background.

I also had realized during this transitional time that I lived on a different time scale than the locals. It was unusual for them to live for more than fifty revolutions about their star, while at home the average lifetime was probably a thousand or more of these cycles. Relatively long lives were normal on my home planet, and was the main reason for very strict and unpleasant birth-control activities.

<u>*Plate-9: Tragic Birth of Ra's First Child*</u>

Actually, I wasn't planning to tell you about this, as I wanted to present the appearance of a successful adventure on the green planet, but I realize that it is critical background to the understanding of other things that happened. Initially I wanted to portray myself as very wise, calm, and unemotional: ideals that would be cherished on our home planet. However, that is not how my experiences here actually developed. I now wonder a bit about socialization effects on behavior: I was the superior being, who, I thought, would not be molded by the local situation, but who would instead change the local situation to fit his desires. I was quite wrong, and now realize that I have been very much changed by my experiences here, and it is definitely for the better. More and more I want to find a way to share my knowledge with my home people, who are so backward in some ways.

After exactly ten revolutions of the green planet about its star, exact to the day, I commemorated the event of my arrival by impregnating the girl who was my first friend and student. She was apparently delighted, and had grown quite fond of me. We were together every day, and communicated easily. I had no emotional attachment, but realized that it was time to start improving the genetic situation. I gave the whole process scant forethought, regarding it mainly as the first of a series of experiments in genetic engineering.

As you can see I did not consider the girl's feelings, or biological capabilities. I did not pay the slightest attention to her suitability for the task, nor did I examine other candidates, for what I thought was to be a great honor. All that I observed was that our sexual parts were relatively compatible in size and operation.

In retrospect, I realize now that I had never had anything to do with childbirth on our home planet, probably because it was such a rare event and my mother didn't live long enough to tell me about it. I had no female friends who had ever experienced it, and many probably would never be given the chance: it just wasn't something anyone I knew ever discussed.

The girl, who's name was Mariah, grew large as the child developed inside her. The women who were experienced in such matters visited daily, ministering to her and commenting on how big and healthy the child inside must be. Eventually its vigorous kicks and wiggles could be seen and felt with my hands. I also observed how much pain the childbirth process was causing Mariah, and began to have misgivings about what I had done to her, my first friend. Looking back, I realize that her cries of pain caused in me my first true feelings toward a green planet person. Before this, they were, to me, just biological specimens. Now, one was actually touching me inside and I had not experienced these feelings before. I didn't know what to do either, as the situation was outside my skills. To make matters far worse, the locals thought that I knew everything and could certainly emotionally handle pregnancy and childbirth, which were routine occurrences here.

I found that when Mariah cried in pain, I could feel it too: I discovered that strong pain was something she could communicate to me mentally, even when we were not close physically. I could not block this transmission and realized also that it was special, as the pain of other locals did not affect me. Somehow there was now a bond between us, and I realized that even if I could stop receiving her pain, I would not do it, for I felt full responsibility for her condition.

As the date of birth approached, the comments of the women began to bother me: they were not just being polite by saying that the baby appeared to be large, but they were worried as they had never seen a mother holding such a large baby inside, and they were concerned for Mariah's success in releasing it. It dawned on my feeble brain that Mariah was relatively small physically, and that a larger woman might have more easily held the child inside. Also, though I did not realize it then, the women detected my unusual concerns and deduced that I was also worried. Since *they thought of me as a god, the impression that I was worried instead of confident, caused them much grave muttering, they wondered why I didn't help Mariah. Why didn't I do something to ease her condition? Surely I must have known what I was doing. If only they had realized my ignorance and pain.*

The pain became intense, and I was torn between staying to see the situation through and running as far away as possible. I made simple compounds for Mariah which eased the physical pain, giving a little comfort, and as I administered them, I vowed to become much better at chemistry before ever trying this again. I had made a big mistake and was now just beginning to realize how smart I wasn't in many areas.

The night of the birth was very bad for me, as I felt all the pain, but had no physical struggle to compensate. I wish that you who come after me never experience such a night.......In the end, I ran out into the darkness as the baby was born....and as Mariah died. I ran until morning. I ran until I dropped to the ground. I rose and ran again and again, trying to run away from myself and my grief.......

Plate-10: Making a Tombstone

After wandering in the desert a long time I returned to the village, emotionally far older than I had been a year earlier. I had now known failure and the loss of the person most dear to me. I treasured the memory of the time we had had together, but of course had squandered it, thinking that we would go on being together for many more years.

My return was curious. I felt foreboding. I had really goofed, and I knew I could do nothing to atone for my stupidity. As I arrived, looking somewhat messy and hungry, with many scratches and bruises, the locals came out to greet me as some kind of hero. I was completely unprepared, and in no mood to assume the mantle of perfection I had carefully crafted.

Gradually I realized that the baby, a girl, was doing very well and that she was the finest baby (in size, coloring, and voice) that any of them had ever seen. People were coming from other villages to see her, and I became curious too. I was asked to name the child, and was startled: the thought had not occurred to me. On my planet, everyone already had a name. I felt that this was perhaps the highest honor I had ever been accorded and considered carefully. Finally I settled on Marlan, a contraction of Mariah and LaLan, my mother's name. I made many vows to myself on that day, but the most important was that I would raise this child to the best of my ability in honor of both of the wonderful women in her past.

As a small step toward atonement for my errors, I helped dig Mariah's grave and carved a marker for it in a style which I had seen on old graves on the home planet. The inscription I wrote in both the local dialect us well as in our normal language, so that anyone who came after could read it. This activity sparked my first interest in stone construction. The existing tools and skills were dreadful. As I started on Mariah's monument I immediately became aware of the need for strong tools and my first, temporary, effort was limited to a poor structure in soft stone. I wanted something better and started seeking the appropriate minerals with which to make decent tools. There was plenty of hard stone about, but nothing with which to work it.

Plate-11: Early Explorations of The Green Planet

I should back up and tell about the start of the explorations. Every time that I saw the river, or went north to see the larger body of saline water, or wandered toward our distant borders, I remembered that far away, somewhere, was the place where the breeding couple had lived. As I could not hope to build a space ship, or even an air ship, with the primitive materials at hand, I knew that the only way to find their home was by exploration of the planet on water and on ground. How I longed to send a message home: to communicate with one of my own kind and ask for a return flight. I felt certain that if I could reach the remains of the breeding couple's original civilization, that I could find the parts for a long-range communicator and send a message. Therefore I had a strong interest in boats and encouraged all manner of nautical activity.

I figured that since the Breeding Couple had been here for a long time, that they must have taught the locals writing and that therefore, some fragments of the writing might survive, perhaps telling how to get to their home-site. So as I sent out each exploration team, I carefully instructed them to bring back any writing or weird symbols, or metals that they encountered. As these started to trickle in, I put them all into a stone building, that slowly expanded as new discoveries were made.

Plate-13: Developing Carbanno Glass Implements

You of course know all about metallurgy and have already asked

201

why I didn't get some iron ore and make steel, using just a simple process with charcoal and ceramic blow-pipes. I had read about this in school, but in my normal existence, metal of any quality was readily available: you didn't go to the store and buy ore, and smelt it in your kitchen.

Looking at the countryside, which was mostly rock with some vegetation, it was not apparent to me where I would find ore of any kind. I realized that I would need to enlist the help of the locals. Perhaps they knew where to find suitable ore. I was becoming much more respectful of their abilities and less confident in my own.

The elders had heard of a variety of rocks to the south, but the general tribal warfare situation away from my immediate area was a barrier to any of them venturing far. I would need to subdue many people, even to explore for rock, which might not even be any good.

So I considered the possibility of making hybrid materials, perhaps types of very hard glass, as I had much silicon dioxide in the form of sand and advanced knowledge in this area. As you know, the only problem with the carbon-modified silicon glasses is that they spontaneously disintegrate, usually just when you need them most. Still, I could probably make tools with this material, and even though the material would only hold together for a few years, I could teach the locals to make more, and a good supply of raw materials was at hand. The glass would make great weapons for them to use against outsiders as we expanded the realm. Of course, it was also very useful for day to day activities, such as quickly chiseling rock and stone. You wouldn't believe the so-called tools that they used before my arrival. I once saw a bunch of primitives cutting a line through hard rock just by beating on it with other rocks. They were lucky to cut a centimeter or two with a whole day of hard work. They had nothing that was sharp, hard, and durable.

I organized a team, my first serious industrial effort. Some members were responsible for gathering material for fires and carbon, some for gathering the best sand and some for running the smelter. As we began to succeed, I added a casting department, which molded the carbanno glass into standard shapes. This took longer than you might think, since I was intent on training the people to do it themselves, and to develop the process as their own.

They were amazed at how wonderful these new pieces were: they could cut rock in a day that used to take weeks. The knives were so sharp they opened up all sorts of possibilities, not just industrially, but in food and agriculture as well. And the military aspects proved fantastic in battle. Our swords, knives, spears and arrows cut through anything the enemy used for protection.

However, I remember the first time that a piece disintegrated spontaneously. I had warned them of this, but the carbanno was so wonderful compared to their existing materials, that they didn't really believe that it wouldn't last forever. A mason was chiseling a rock when, as he hit the tool, it collapsed into a pile of black sand. He just stared at it for a long time, then told the others. Much discussion about going into battle with weapons which might turn to sand during the fight. I told them to lighten-up. They had excellent material, and it would last at least a year, and they could make more as long as they wanted. Further, they were the only tribe on the planet with such excellent sharp-edged hard tools. Life for them was just beginning to be fun.

Plate-15: Helwan: Biological History of The Green Planet

I am Helwan, formally known as Ra-5-31-155, and am in the fifth generation of Ra's descendents (born 155 years after his arrival). Based on genetics, I have almost the same chromosomes as Ra, as my lineage directly through his various offspring shows. I am about the same size and strength, though of course as I am a woman, I have some differences from him (I am much better looking).

Ra has begun to teach some of us to write in an old script that he studied as a child, as his writing is too complex for us to master, yet. As a writing exercise, and as an honor to my status, he has set me the task of writing down all that he has told us of our planet's history (which has many gaps, as he isn't as smart as he pretends to be).

A long time ago (he doesn't know how many years it would be: actually, he isn't all that good with numbers) people from his home sent genetic material into space, scattering it in all directions. They sent many different varieties and hoped that some of it would land in suitable environments. The launching was not well organized, with competing groups and other screw-ups, but over the years they kept sending stuff, slowly getting a bit smarter about how to do it. Some of the stuff must have landed here, starting plants and animals on their way. From what he has said, the things that we see here are a very small sample from the total that might have developed from the genetic material. He says that much more interesting creatures developed on other planets, but I am glad that it didn't happen here: we have enough to contend with as it is.

As near as I can tell, after repeatedly questioning him, is that the initial genetic dispersals happened at least a billion of our years ago, and perhaps even further back in time. When they started sending the genetic stuff out from their home, they didn't have the means to go after it and watch what happened. They just sent it off, hoping that some day they would have ships good enough to enable them to go out and see the results.

The people on Ra's planet had lots of problems, struggles, famines, wars, and other misfortunes, but they finally calmed down and started living more sensibly. They learned to live in peace, and to match the size of their population to the available resources. Perhaps a key factor that led to their survival was that they also learned a lot about genetics, and were able to breed out most of their undesirable characteristics, so that citizens were able to live without what we call crime, war, and disease.

As their era of struggles ended, they could think about building spaceships to visit nearby, and eventually far-away, planets to see what was growing. I wish that he knew more about these voyages, but he seems to have skipped those lessons. However, he has the impression that as voyagers returned there was much discussion about helping and correcting the life forms that appeared on the more promising planets. This led to a whole range of experiments. My planet is one of the corrected sites.

An expedition was sent here about a million years ago (very uncertain date) to establish a colony of updated people. They weren't quite sure what would survive in our environment, so they sent a variety of kinds of people as frozen embryos. I have actually seen some of these other kinds of people, as strangers from far away have returned with exploration parties. They also sent a specially-trained male and female to supervise the developments. The couple had a ship that could travel through the air, so that they could plant people in the most promising parts of the planet. They also created many generations of people on their own.

The couple (which Ra always calls the Breeding Couple), built a city with all the comforts from their own planet. Unlike Ra, they arrived well-equipped with lots of fancy stuff so that they could have a long and comfortable life and set a good example for their many offspring and eggs. They sent pictures back to their own planet showing how nice my planet is.

Ra thinks that he can find this city, but he is worried that as the climate of my planet has changed, the city may have been buried. No one has found it or even heard of it, as far as a I can tell.

As Ra has told you in his writing, he was not told where he was going or what he was supposed to do, so about all that he really knows about my planet is what he glimpsed as the spaceship circled a few times looking for a landing spot. He can describe the size of the planet, and the extent of the waters and lands, and he was very impressed by the climate-modeling that the ship's computer (whatever that is) did.

Plate-95: Ship Captain Farewell

I'm Captain Negroni, the best sailor in the world as near as I can tell. (I was told to write down the truth, and so I am). Each of us was given a plate to write a few notes to posterity (whoever that is) just before leaving, so here's mine. Tomorrow we set sail, probably never to return, so I won't see this tablet again. It's pouring rain, and it has been for a long time: the river is high, our ship is dry inside and we're afloat. We've stocked it with everything useful we could think of, and a bunch of extra junk Ra insists on bringing. You can read about it elsewhere: it's a pile of useless crap, taking up space in the hold where we could put some more food or water or sails or at least some more booze.

My only problem is that I don't know where we're going as Ra has kept the destination and some of the maps in his head instead of sharing them with me. What a fool. Supposing he croaks, or falls overboard. How'll we ever get there? About all that I can tell is that he expects it to be plenty cold when we arrive judging by the stuff he has packed, and it is very far away judging by the amount of provisions on board.

If only he didn't want to bring along so many of his wives and children. They've no place on a serious ship which may be in trouble tomorrow and need every able hand to work the lines and sails. None of them has been at sea more than a day or two. They'll all puke their guts out as soon as we hit the real ocean. I've been in seas where even the largest ship was tossed about like a leaf in the gutter, and where fish bigger than a ship cruise by spouting water, then disappear forever. These people haven't a clue: good thing they have me and my crew. Now, if the rain would stop, the sails would be a hell of a lot easier to handle. If you find this plate, look for our remains in some cold place on the other side of the planet, or (more *likely) at the bottom of the ocean.*

Plate-96: Daughter's Goodbye

I'm one of the pure daughters, and so must stay here, carrying a pure baby inside, but I want so much to be on the ship with him: it's like a magnet pulling at my heart. Ra told me once about what it was like when he left his home and came here and the long space voyage: so sad, so lonely, so uncertain. Yet I wish that I could go with him now, even if it's dangerous and there's no coming back. I would go anywhere with him. I don't think that many others know about his voyage here and how difficult it was for him to leave all his people and join us. In a way, I cry and feel that in some way I am leaving him, and that he is my home. Maybe there'll be another voyage some day and I will live to go on it and follow him west into the sunset.

Plate-97: Weatherman

Like the others, I'm writing a plate to leave for future generations to read before setting sail tomorrow. I'm old and won't be back. I'm on board because I can read the weather, or at least people think I can, and that's almost as good. I'm only eighty-three percent Ra: all the pure ones are staying behind. They think they're smarter, but it's all in what you learn during your lifetime.

I've been studying math, weather, and maps my whole life: my mother was 100%, and a great mathematician. She even worked on some of the inner parts of the great pile, as we call it. My biggest concern is that the weather is making a major change. This storm is no short-term thing. I've been studying old records, old rocks and trees and mountains and valleys. You can learn a lot from these things if you open your eyes. The fact is inescapable that the planet is getting colder, and that ice-covered regions are moving closer to us every year. Areas that once were fertile are dry, and becoming covered with ice more of the year. You can see it in the dead trees if you travel widely, or read the reports of those who do. Tribes from the North are moving south, and our outlying commanders are seeing strange people and animals that have never reached our northern borders before.

Something's wrong with the weather, and frankly, I don't like the idea of setting out on a sea voyage with so much uncertainty. Of course, it wasn't my choice. I have the honor of being part of the crew: so much hype and B.S. Sometimes it doesn't pay to be so smart that you stand above the others. Well, one thing is certain, and that is that I'll be seeing parts of the planet which are rarely visited, so it's an opportunity to learn new things for my maps. Hope I can figure out a way to send them home afterwards. Look for a message in a year or two. Keep your eyes open and scan for friendly sails from a distant land (and buy some warm clothing before the prices go up.)

Plate-98: The Ship's Destination

To those who find these plates, a bit of information. As near as I can tell, the Breeding Couple's home base was near the current southern polar axis and in the eons that they lived there, it was a warm fertile land. When we flew over in the spaceship, this land was covered in snow. I don't know how deep this snow is, but I hope it is shallow, and perhaps melted at this time of year. From what I have been able to calculate, when I arrived on this planet, the polar axis was such that the southern pole was receiving little sun. When we arrive there in a few months the southern polar region should be as warm as it ever gets, so perhaps the sun will have melted the snow and we will easily find their old base and enough equipment to send a message. Time to say a few more good-byes and finish packing.

Plate-99: Goodbye

My final plate. I wish that all my children could come on board, but there's no room, and we can't make it any bigger, and of course I must leave the best behind or all my genetic work would have been in vain. Such emotions. When I think about my arrival centuries ago, and how little I cared for these primitives compared to now, when they are my whole life, my whole reason for being. I burn so strongly toward them. I cry when I think of leaving them on the shore. I feel that my time is coming soon, yet I still cherish the thought of reaching the old base and sending a message. Just one message, to tell the others how wonderful life can be when you love so many people.....

--the end--

End Notes

Chapter Notes
The number 666
The Magic Squares
The Great Pyramid as an observatory
Technical Glossary
References

CHAPTER NOTES

All illustrations and photos are by the author.

Chapter 1:
Stanford University's motto, "Die Luft Der Freiheit Weht" means "Let the winds of freedom blow"

Topology, the mathematical study of patterns and shapes. William was very good at detecting patterns and relating them to other patterns.

A Magic Square is a grid of numbers, where all the rows, columns, and the two major diagonals add to the same sum. The most interesting squares start with the integer '1' and contain unbroken sequences of integers.

In an article (Hoffman, 2003) Rutan stated that he was convinced that aliens have visited the earth, perhaps before the last ice age, and that one proof of their visit is the Great Pyramid.

Chapter 2:
(Forbes. 2002) contains a description of turtle navigation, suggesting that they use the vertical component of the earth's magnetic field.

(Velikovsky, Immanuel. 1950 and 1955) was a respected scientist, perhaps even a Nobel Laureate. He wrote two major books on the thesis that the planet Venus was a comet or meteor captured by the sun, and that this happened within human memory. One book supported this thesis with geological and scientific data. The other book supported his thesis by analyzing the oldest legends and folk tales from all over the earth. Both books told how the comet passed close to the earth, caused "the flood" referred to in the Bible, and that the comet rained petroleum onto the earth. He was very controversial and filled with unorthodox ideas, many of which turned out to be valid. However the Venus-was-a-comet thesis appears to be false.

Stanford University has outstanding biology, chemistry, and genetics departments with Nobel laureates and many famous professors.

"Birds may Get bearings From Beak Sensors" is an article describing the discovery that some birds have clusters of iron oxide crystals in their beaks. These sensors may be used to detect the earth's magnetic fields and aid bird navigation. An article on Yahoo news by Gerta Fleissner at the University of Frankfurt, 3/14/2007.

Chapter 3:

Magic Squares have existed for thousands of years of recorded human history. Many references and resources related to them exist on the internet. Later in this Appendix are drawings of the squares from 3x3 through 12x12. Note that any one of these squares can be rotated and flipped without changing its properties.

Genetic Programming, a branch of Evolutionary Computing popularized by Professor Koza at Stanford (Koza 1992), is a way to teach a computer to grow a solution to a problem. This is used when the person writing the program does not know the exact solution. In many practical cases, the computer can 'grow' a useful solution by cross-breeding many randomly-generated candidate solutions until a useful answer appears. The most difficult part of this approach is developing criteria which enable the computer to recognize good solutions, and to discard the bad ones. Genetic programming has been used in the real world to develop 'good-enough' solutions to problems which defy formal analysis.

Linear Algebra is a branch of mathematics concerning techniques and rules for manipulating columns and arrays of numbers. The arrays can have any dimension, but two-dimensional arrays are the easiest for most people to visualize.

The offices on Sand Hill Road, which is the northern boundary of the Stanford campus, are indeed the heart of Venture Capital activity in the San Francisco area.

Italian Sushi, called 'crudo', exists and is quite popular in Italy: references and recipes are on the internet.

Bill Gates, perhaps America's richest person, dropped out of Harvard during his Freshman year so that he could found a software company and write the BASIC computer language. He never went back to school.

Chapter 4:

The 'Doctor Program' is exactly as described in the text and has been around since perhaps the sixties. The LISP implementation is the most elegant. LISP is a list-processing language loved by Artificial Intelligence investigators. It is particularly good at picking apart lists of words, such as sentences.

AWK, C, Shell-scripts, PERL, and other technical terms are described in the glossary later in this Appendix. The material in the text is accurate: the author was a Computer Engineer for many years.

Years ago, and perhaps even today, old movies were shown every Sunday night in an auditorium on campus for ten cents. There was always a bad cartoon: few if any took the movie or the cartoon seriously.

Stanford Mausoleum: an obscure part of campus, where Governor & Mrs Stanford's only son is buried: the university is named for him, Leland Stanford Junior University.

Chapter 5:
Ferrari information is correct, as is the description of the roads between campus and the coast.

Spectrum: a continuous distribution of colored light produced when a beam of white light is dispersed into its components. When the spectrum from a star is spread out and examined carefully, small black lines can be observed among the colors. The number and position of these lines can be used to deduce which elements exist in the star, or in any compound that is burning and emitting light.

Red-shifted: All the colors of the star's spectrum are shifted toward the red (long wavelength) end of the color range, because the wavelengths appear, to an observer, to be longer when an object is moving away from the observer.

Speed of Light: 300,000 Km per second, 186,000 miles per second. Light takes about eight minutes to travel from the sun to the earth.

The Japanese message is bogus.

Alfred Watkins (Watkins 1925) discovered Ley Lines ca 1900: he was a traveling salesman covering rural England on horseback. While looking at the view from a hilltop he realized that there were ancient straight lines running across the landscape for miles. These lines were composed of roads, hedges, changes in vegetation, mark stones, and other ancient landscape artifacts. He spent the rest of his life exploring these lines, writing about them, and visiting them with friends. The advent of aerial photography greatly expanded the number of lines that were found all over the British Isles. These lines pre-date the Romans and are perhaps contemporaneous with Stonehenge: they are not "convenient" paths, but go straight through and over obstacles, as though they were made by sighting or from the air, rather than by people or animals trying to find the easiest way to get somewhere. At many of the intersections there are ancient mark stones, some of which have been incorporated into very old churches. The lines exist, but there are no official explanations for them except vague conjectures about ancient artistic or ceremonial significance. There are many legends however, some concerning giants who moved huge stones along these magic pathways....

There is an excellent introduction to Rroma culture at www. Patrin.com.

The "dish" is a large radio telescope on a hill in the fields behind the Stanford campus. The nighttime view of distant city lights from near the dish is spectacular.

Panspermia: In 1998, a scientist proved, mathematically, that it would be possible to send DNA molecules, encased inside spherical carbon Fullerene molecules, throughout space. The carbon spheres would offer sufficient protection to the DNA so that it could safely travel through the universe for eons.

Panspermia: In 2000, scientists (THE ECONOMIST, page 94, 10-21-2000) found salts in caves in New Mexico containing ancient bacteria, perfectly preserved from the Permian era. These bacteria form spores which lie dormant perhaps forever, wait until climatic conditions are correct for growth: these particular spores are at least 250 million years old, and are being grown now. It is quite possible that bacteria like this could survive inter-stellar journeys. "This theory, known as 'panspermia' (literally 'seeds everywhere'), turns on the existence of organisms tenacious enough to survive long and difficult journeys across the vast distances of interstellar space. The work of Dr Vreeland's group provides the most convincing evidence to date that such creatures do indeed exist. Crossing the galaxy in their crystal ships, these spores could then flourish on any planet where they found a hospitable environment."

Panspermia: Rainer Glaser and scientists at the University of Missouri-Columbia showed that clouds of adenine molecules may exist in space. Adenine is one of the four chemicals that make up DNA, so it is possible that DNA can travel through space. Adenine has been found in meteorites. An article on Yahoo news, from the journal "Astrobiology", 9-11-2007.

Eugenics: the science of breeding humans, to encourage desirable characteristics and eliminate undesirable characteristics, in the same way that animals are bred to improve their features. The goal is to grow better humans. To do this, defective humans are forcibly killed or sterilized, and desirable humans are encouraged to have as many children as possible. This was an active topic of discussion around 1900 and the Nazis tried to accomplish it during WWII by . exterminating many Central Europeans.

Chapter 6:

Electromagnetic radiation includes light, heat, radio waves, microwaves, radar, television signals, x-rays. The radiation can be analyzed as fields of energy (like the field surrounding a magnet), or as particles of energy, such as photons of light. The movement of electrons inside the neurons of animal brains generates extremely weak electromagnetic fields. To analyze these neuronal signals, doctors place electrodes on a patient's skin and record ECG's, electroencephalographs.

(Arkani-Hamed, 2003) describes gravity waves and the possibility of looking for them in other dimensions. String Theory, which is a mathematical description of the physical laws governing the universe, postulates that there are thirteen dimensions to the universe: humans only perceive three of these dimensions.

Remote Viewing: some people can envision distant scenes which they have never visited and describe them accurately. (Targ 1977) gives a full description of the phenomenon. There is evidence (Cook 2001) that the US Defense Department used this capability during the cold war.

Ca 1990, Professor Schoch of Boston University and a group of Scientists went to Egypt and studied the erosion in the rocks surrounding the Sphinx. This team contained experts in rock weathering. They concluded that the rocks had been eroded by heavy rainfalls, which had occurred at least 7000 to 9000 years ago, and possibly much further back in time. This dates the Sphinx, by actual measurements of the erosion rate of the stones. The official date, from Egyptologists studying nearby pottery etc, is around 4500 years ago. Egyptologists were furious at Schoch's discovery. A paper on his work was read by the Geological Society of America, and many other scientists agreed that the science was technically correct. To add even more controversy, an independent scientist, John West, has found support for even older dates in ancient writings: he thinks that the Sphinx is a remnant of a much older civilization, perhaps from before 12000 years ago. In response to this scientific data, the Egyptian government has not allowed any more geologists to study erosion around the Sphinx.

(Imbrie, 1979) describes the astronomical math behind the Ice Ages and long term cycles in the earth's weather.

The ceiling of the Temple mentioned in the text is a star map, and analysis shows that it was redrawn several times, so as to match changes in the apparent positions of the stars as the earth's axis precessed through the sky. The long rows of columns at the Temple of Karnak are not in straight lines either: there are jogs as additions were built at much later dates, to match the change in the position of the solstices.

The Reference section of this Appendix contains information on some of the Egyptology books that William studied.

(www.cheops.org) has information about the robot-crawling-up-the-shaft videotape, which was shown in the USA on The Discovery Channel near the end of the Twentieth Century: the lead engineer was Herr Gantenbrink. The documentary also showed the German Engineers working with the little robot and then sending it up the shaft, trailing a long cable. In September 2002, the

Egyptian government sent a new robot, made in Boston and funded by The National Geographic Society, up the shaft. It drilled a hole in the 'door' at the far end and poked a fiber-optic camera through. There is another door behind the first one. This team also explored another shaft and found another little door. A television program was shown about this work, and the Egyptian government obtained funds through its release.

(Sagan 1980) made this statement as part of a discussion of the search for extra-terrestrial intelligence.

Chapter 7:

Alienology is a parody of the many pseudo-religious scams that try to separate the gullible from their money. According to an article that appeared in "The Los Angeles Times" in the 1980's, when the archives of one of these organizations became public for a few days due to a tax scam detected by the IRS, the 'A-meter' is supposed to tell which people are aliens. Learning to operate the meter is the highest skill level taught, and the classes cost thousands of dollars. Also, according to the article, most members of the organization never hear about the alien threat but they learn that there are 'secret truths' that the only the top people understand.

The Japanese is bogus.

Magnetometer: device that can detect and measure changes in very weak magnetic fields. Used in geological explorations to detect slight changes in the earth's magnetic field, which help indicate the presence of ore deposits.

Double-blind: in such a test, none of the people involved know what the answers are until after the test is over. This precludes any chance of cheating.

Cairo crapper: never cleaned over the millennia and said to be used by camels and donkeys, as well as humans: each one has a unique aroma, and supposedly the Cairenes can navigate the dark streets at night by the different smells.

TA is a Teaching Assistant, usually a graduate student.

Zarlie made the sketch of her DNA from a normal person's map, as shown on page 307 of "DNA Technology", by Alcamo, Harcourt/Academic Press, 2001.

Computerized DNA analysis: Harvard Magazine, March 2007, page 11, in an article entitled "A Personal Genome Machine", describes a technique being developed which can analyze an entire human genome in less than twenty-four hours.

Chapter 8:

The information in the text on vacuum tubes, transistors,

and oscilloscopes is correct, as is the description of what it is like to explore the steam tunnels.

Chapter 9:

Data Mining, refers to the process of searching large data bases looking for interesting, and heretofore unknown, relationships among data. It is usually done with the aid of computers.

(Economist 2003) contains the article about Henry Racamier's rescue of Louis Vuitton.

Chapter 10:

(Targ and Puthoff 1977) is a book written while they were working at SRI (Stanford Research Institute) on remote viewing. Putoff was interviewed years later, and this interview is described in (Cook, 2001).

(Cannell, 1931) and (Gibson and Young, 1953) are two excellent books about Houdini and his work debunking false psychics.

Chapter 11:

Japanese character and its analysis are bogus.

The megalithic stone structures, both above ground and under water, are as described in the text, and they can be researched on the web. John Mitchell's book, *The New View Over Atlantis*, is an excellent introduction to all sorts of mysteries such as these. (Hancock, 1998) also has much interesting information on the subject of megalithic structures.

Chapter 12:

SETI exists, but it's main project is radio astronomy, listening to signals from the stars for messages from intelligent beings. Ollalaberries are great and taste a bit like blackberries: drive to Pescadero!

The location of the star NGN 5011C in Centaurus was in error until data from the 3.6m ESO telescope corrected it. More information is available at Space.com, in an article posted 3/12/2007 by Sara Goudarzi, entitled "Ooops! Huge Distant Galaxy Actually Small And Close."

Chapter 13:

www.ivf.com contains much information about IVF methodology. The trail on the Point Reyes Peninsula does indeed go through an Elk reserve.

Chapter 14:

The Yakusa, Japanese gangsters, are reputed to have full-body tattoos and to each loose a finger during initiation ceremonies. The Peace Hotel on The Bund is as described, though in the spring of 2007 it was closed for renovation by The Fairmont Group. The info on Japanese bio-weapons is factual: read Plague Wars for more detail.

The Nile Hilton, the Khan El Khalili bazaar, and Cairo driving is factual, as of the late 1990's. An internet search for 'Rroma' will bring up much information on their history and customs.

Chapter 15:

The description of the GP, its environs, and its innards are factual. Photographs are by the author. (Hancock and Bauval, 1996) has much interesting information on the GP.

Chapter 17:

The Mena House Hotel is lovely, and is as described in the text.

666, *"The Number of the Beast"*

This following information and quotations are based on (Mitchell, 1988, 185-191).

"...666 is related to the Sun and the principle of reason, will, and authority. (it) is the generative power of the male, the call to action, the electrical impulse which regulates the molecular field and gives form and order to chaos. It is the active, inventive, fertilizing current in nature, the material as opposed to the spiritual, side of things"

In addition, "666 is the ... area in square megalithic yards of the circle corresponding to the bluestone circle at Stonehenge with diameter 79.20 feet".

666 is the number that St John ascribed to the Beast in the last verse of Revelation 13. "Here is wisdom, let him that hath understanding count the number of the beast: for it is the number of a man; and his number is six hundred threescore and six".

Originally the Gnostic numbers were not good or bad: they just stood for ideas. However one of the early Greek translations of the Bible translated "beast" as "wild animal", beginning the bad reputation for this number.

"The elemental symbol of 666 is the fiery flying dragon, the opposite of the earth-bound serpent. In China dragons are not slain; rather their electrical power is kept in the realm, in which it can be made useful."

"... the link between Rome and 666 is that this number is the sum of the first six Roman Numerals, I,V,X,L,C,D (1 + 5 + 10 + 50 + 100 + 500). Nineteenth-century Protestant writers were pleased to observe that the Pope's triple crown bore the legend 'Vicarius Filii Dei', Vicar of the Son of God. Taking from that phrase the letters which also serve as Roman Numerals, they pointed out that the sum was 666". Various writers "proved" with numerology that the Pope was indeed the Antichrist, and that his true number was 666.

An interesting modern interpretation is that if our alphabet's letters are assigned numbers in the order A=100, B=101, C=102, etc, then the name 'Hitler' totals 666.

The Magic Squares

Each of the following is based on a consecutive series of integers, starting with '1' (except for the 12x12 square). In each 'magic' square, the rows, the columns, and the two major diagonals all add to the same sum. For example, in the 3x3 square the columns are (4+3+8=15), (9+5+1=15), (2+7+6=15), and the diagonals are: (4+5+6=15), (8+5+2=15).

4	9	2
3	5	7
8	1	6

SATURN 3x3 Square, 15 total

4	14	15	1
9	7	6	12
5	11	10	8
16	2	3	13

JUPITER 4x4 Square, 34 total

11	24	7	20	3
4	12	25	8	16
17	5	13	21	9
10	18	1	14	22
23	6	19	2	15

MARS 5x5 Square, 65 total

6	32	3	34	35	1
7	11	27	28	8	30
19	14	16	15	23	24
18	20	22	21	17	13
25	29	10	9	26	12
36	5	33	4	2	31

SUN 6x6 Square, 111 total

218

22	47	16	41	10	35	4
5	23	48	17	42	11	29
30	6	24	49	18	36	12
13	31	7	25	43	19	37
38	14	32	1	26	44	20
21	39	8	33	2	27	45
46	15	40	9	34	3	28

VENUS 7x7 Square, 175 total

8	58	59	5	4	62	63	1
49	15	14	52	53	11	10	56
41	23	22	44	45	19	18	48
32	34	35	29	28	38	39	25
40	26	27	37	36	30	31	33
17	47	46	20	21	43	42	24
9	55	54	12	13	51	50	16
64	2	3	61	60	6	7	57

MERCURY 8x8 Square, 260 total

37	78	29	70	21	62	13	54	5
6	38	79	30	71	22	63	14	46
47	7	39	80	31	72	23	35	15
16	48	8	40	81	32	64	24	56
57	17	49	9	41	73	33	65	25
26	58	18	50	1	42	74	34	66
67	27	59	10	51	2	43	75	35
36	68	19	60	11	52	3	44	76
77	28	69	20	61	12	53	4	45

MOON 9x9 Square, 369 total

142	318	424	533	575	213	339	119	275	658	220	552
316	412	156	591	209	521	113	285	335	228	550	652
426	154	304	197	537	587	281	329	123	544	660	226
663	227	545	334	112	282	520	588	208	155	305	429
221	555	659	120	280	328	586	196	534	321	425	143
551	653	231	274	336	118	210	532	574	413	159	317
523	571	201	150	308	410	668	224	564	331	129	289
579	199	517	302	420	146	240	560	656	127	277	345
193	525	577	416	140	312	548	672	236	291	343	115
344	116	294	655	237	559	145	301	417	528	578	194
132	290	332	235	547	669	309	415	139	572	204	524
278	348	128	561	667	223	409	147	307	200	518	582

Zodiac 12x12 Square, 4368 total

The Great Pyramid as Astronomical Observatory

The following is based on information contained in (Tompkins, 1971) pages 147-158.

There are many shafts and peculiar structures inside the Great Pyramid. Most of these can be explained by considering the GP, partly completed, as a very precise astronomical observatory. This was first realized by the British Astronomer Anthony Proctor, who was inspired by his work translating Plato's "Timeaus", which references such an observatory in ancient times.

The observatory would consist of the first 50 stone layers of the GP. At this height, the area of the square top surface would be exactly half the area of the base, and the Grand Gallery would arise up through the structure, exiting onto the square platform. This very accurate observatory would be used for mapping the stars, planets, and comets, as well as for telling accurate time and for building an accurate calendar. The Giza Plateau has an almost unlimited view of the horizon in all directions, so it would be a perfect spot for an observatory. The accuracy of the GP's position and shafts is so perfect that the precession of the earth's axis could have been measured. The axis moves only one degree every 72 years, so precise and long-term (centuries, not years) observations would be required to discover this motion.

The first task in building an observatory is determining the exact direction of true north (the direction which is parallel to the earth's axis of rotation), so that the transits of all celestial objects can be precisely measured. Scientists today are still amazed at the accuracy of the GP's alignment with the cardinal directions. It's almost as close as the best that can be obtained today with telescopes, GPS, computers, etc. Proctor points out that the Descending passage, which slopes down at 26 degrees, 17 minutes, and which is almost perfectly straight, would be a wonderful sighting tube pointing exactly true north.

Instead of pointing at the exact north celestial pole (where there is no star) the descending Passage points at the closest bright circumpolar star, Alpha Draconis, at its lower culmination (at various eras long ago: each orientation repeats every 25,920 years). The long narrow tunnel gives a precise timing as this star crosses the aperture. An observer seated at the bottom of the shaft would see darkness, and a very small distant hole, which would be dark until the star passed by. The tube would have been tunneled into the rock before any construction was started, so that the GP, with sides aligned parallel with the tube would be exactly oriented.

Proctor also points out how hard this accuracy would be

221

to achieve above ground, requiring a massive structure and a great deal of work, compared to digging it down through the rock, and checking the alignment each night as work progressed.

In short, the Descending Passage is a perfectly practical way to obtain an exact north-south alignment in an era before telescopes. He also notes that the most critical section of the tunnel is the area near its opening. When inspecting the shaft, explorers have often marveled at how fine the workmanship in this area was done. For 350 feet the error in height is less than 1/10 inch and the error in width is less than 1/50th inch. Such accuracy could only be obtained (before laser sighting equipment) by using a star as a guide as the work progressed.

The bottom of the Descending Passage is under the center of the GP, so this explains its length, in addition to its angle and high quality construction.

As the GP rose above, the Descending Passage was extended outward through the stones (through the first 20 layers). After awhile, it could have been temporarily plugged near ground level. At the plug, a pool of water would have been placed. The reflection of Alpha Draconis, coming down the Descending passage, then off the water's surface, would allow the construction of another very accurate shaft, at the same angle, but headed up inside the GP. This is exactly what is found, in the construction of the Ascending Passage.

It is interesting to note that even today, the reflection of various stars in a pool of mercury is used for very precise transit observations. This is a simple, yet effective, way of measuring angles precisely. Reflections of stars are also used today by land surveyors, in conjunction with sextants, where the exact horizon is not visible due to trees, mountains, etc.

The ascending passage is the floor of the Grand Gallery (GG), ensuring its exact alignment as construction progressed. The GG was the main observatory for viewing the stars and recording their positions. The GG provides a view of the stars through narrow slots (in its ceiling, or its open mouth at the top), exactly aligned north-south. These narrow views scan the heavens as the earth rotates. The GG has some unusual features which make it ideal for this purpose.

One is that the roof stones can be removed one at a time, since no roof, or ceiling, stone sits on the adjacent roof stones. This peculiar construction allows a window into a particular portion of the sky to be temporarily opened, while maintaining darkness in the rest of the Gallery.

Another feature are various holes in the sides of the GG. These are perfectly placed for movable benches that could be temporarily positioned for particular observations.

Another suggestion is that the 24 holes in the sides of the GG could have held star charts, to help the observers determine the exact stars which were in view.

The opening of the GG onto the square observation surface is slightly off-center. This feature would allow a pole to be placed dead center. Its shadow on the square surface would provide more observational opportunities.

The top surface could have been completely level (this is easy to construct by using shallow trenches filled with water as a leveling guide). Various observations could be inscribed in its surface, and sighting devices could have been permanently mounted, oriented to the true N-S and E-W sides.

Another interesting feature of such an observatory relates to astrology. Astrologers in the past, such as Kepler in 1608, used square diagrams to relate the different "houses" and fortune predictions. The square was divided into the twelve signs of the zodiac, with a smaller square in the center. The arrangement of this "standard" form of zodiac is exactly like an overhead view of the GP observatory, with the central square being the observatory platform and the outer square being the base of the GP. This form of astrological zodiac may be the oldest form currently known.

Once the various observations of the stars were completed and recorded, perhaps over hundreds or thousands of years, the top half of the GP was constructed. Ancients record that the outer surface of the complete pyramid was covered with obscure writing, perhaps describing the knowledge gained from the observations. The completed GP would have been visible at great distances, providing the only exact surveying benchmark in the land.

TECHNICAL GLOSSARY

ASCII. This is a standard way to represent letters, numbers, and punctuation inside a computer. Inside computers, everything is either a zero or a one, so a group of eight ones and zeros (called bits) together can represent 256 different things (each is called a byte). For example, the 'space' punctuation character, is 0010 0000, which computer people commonly write in 'hex' (using the sixteen characters 0..9 and A...F), as '20'.

AWK, is a small, dense, computer language which is used for analyzing large databases of text and numbers. Like shell-scripts, the various characters in the language are very important to the program's meaning. The language is named after the initials of the three men who invented it at Bell labs.

BASIC. A computer language originally used for teaching and for writing simple programs. It had low status among cogniscenti, but in recent years its ease of use has been built-upon to generate a very powerful language that can be written quickly. It's a favorite of programmers who want to write practical code with little work.

C. A computer language with tremendous flexibility and power. Most of the computers running telephone systems world-wide are controlled by code written in C, which was invented at Bell labs. Code written in C executes very fast, but the power of the language also allows small goofs to lead to big problems. It contains no 'training wheels' for the unwary, but experts write blazing code with it. The lowest-level guts of most computers are written in a mixture of C and Assembly Language (the absolute lowest level, just above the hardware).

CYTOGENETIC MAP. "The visual appearance of a chromosome when stained and examined under a microscope. Particularly important are visually distinct regions, called light and dark bands, which give each chromosome a unique appearance. This feature allows a person's chromosomes to be studied in a clinical test known as a karyotype, which allows scientists to look for chromosomal alterations." (Karyotype: "The chromosomal complement of an individual, including the number of chromosomes and any abnormalities. This term is also used to refer to a photograph of an individual's chromosomes.") (from www.genome.gov/glossary)

FOURIER TRANSFORM. An oscilloscope shows how the

strength of a signal varies with respect to time. This same information can be manipulated, by Fourier Transform Analysis, to show which frequencies are contained in the varying signal. This information is quite useful when designing music synthesizers and when analyzing signals. Normally FT results are plotted as a graph, showing signal-strength verses frequency.

FREQUENCY ANALYSIS. One of the tools used by mathematicians who are trying to understand secretly-encoded messages. In this technique, mathematicians analyze an encrypted message to see which characters are the most common, and how often they repeat, then try to deduce the meanings of the most common characters.

GENETIC PROGRAMMING. Is a branch of Evolutionary Computing popularized by Professor Koza at Stanford. It is a way to teach a computer to write its own computer program to solve a problem. This is used when the person writing the program does not know the correct solution. In many practical cases, the computer can 'grow' a useful solution by cross-breeding many candidate solutions until a useful answer appears.

LINEAR ALGEBRA. The branch of mathematics concerned with manipulating lists and arrays of numbers, such as matricies.

LISP. A computer language which looks like long multi-line lists of strange words, usually with many carefully-matched parentheses inside. The language is ideally-suited to logical processing of the items in a list. It is rarely used outside of academic circles.

MATHEMATICA. A computer program used for solving complex mathematical problems in calculus and other specialties. It is expensive, and its skill level is comparable to that of a math graduate student.

OSCILLOSCOPE. An electronic instrument that allows electric signals, even faint ones, to be examined visually on a small screen. There are many different kinds of 'scopes and they are found in almost every electronics lab and electronics factory.

PERL. A computer language which is often used to process short strings of words, such as a customer's answers to a fill-in form on a web page. PERL is very common on the servers which interact over the internet with clients.

SHELL-SCRIPT. Very short computer programs which are usually used to invoke a series of more complex computer programs. Like a commander ordering the officers under him to do different parts of a task. The language, at least in Unix implementations, is very obscure but very powerful. Single characters, such as '|' (called a pipe) can mean quite a lot, and just one typo can cause havoc.

TELNET. A computer protocol that allows one computer to control another, by using commands over a network.

TRAP-DOOR. Part of a computer program that allows a knowledgeable user to enter the program and make changes. Such features are often installed to allow administrators to repair programs while they are operating. Usually these doors are obscure and heavily pass-worded to restrict access. A malicious user can easily ruin a program or make it do unplanned things if he can enter such a door.

REFERENCES

NOTE: Many of the older books are available in paperback reprints and multiple editions.

Arkani-Hamed, Nima. 2003. *Gravity.* Harvard Magazine, May 2003, page 10.

Bauval, Robert and Adrian Gilbert. 1994. *The Orion Mystery,* New York: Three Rivers Press.

Cannell, J.C. 1931. *The Secrets Of Houdini.* New York: Dover.

Cayce, Edgar. 1968. *On Atlantis.* New York: Warner Books.

Cook, Nick, 2001. *The Hunt For Zero Point.* New York: Broadway Books.

Economist. 2000. *Panspermia.* October 21, 2000. page 94.

Economist. 2003. *Obituary for Henry Racamier.* THE ECONOMIST, April 12, 2003, page 77.

Forbes. 2002. *Loggerhead Turtles navigation.* FORBES ASAP Magazine. October 2, 2002. page 26.

Gibson, Litzka R. and Walter B. Gibson. 1969. *The Mystic And Occult Arts: A Guide To Their Use In Daily Living.* New York: Parker Publishing.

Gibson, Walter B. and Morris N. Young. 1953. *Houdini On Magic.* New York: Dover Publications.

Hancock, Graham and Santha Faiia, 1998. *Heaven's Mirror,* New York: Three Rivers Press.

Hancock, Graham, 1995. *Fingerprints Of The Gods.* New York: Three Rivers Press.

Hancock, Graham and Robert Bauval. 1996. *The Message Of The Sphinx,* New York: Three Rivers Press.

Hoffman, Carl. 2003. *The Right Stuff.* New York: Wired magazine, July 2003, page 136.

Imbrie, John & Katherine, 1979. *Ice Ages*. Cambridge. Harvard University Press. Seventh Printing, 1998. Page 169-181.

Koza, John R. 1992. *Genetic Programming: On The Programming Of Computers By Means Of Natural Selection*. 3 Volumes. Boston: MIT Press.

Luxton, Leonora. 1978. *Astrology: Key To Self Understanding*. St Paul, Minnesota: Llewellyn Publications.

McDowell, Bart, 1970. *Gypsies: Wanderers Of The World*. Washington DC: National Geographic Special Publications.

Milne, A.A. *Now We Are Six*. poem "Whenever I walk On A London Street,

Mitchell, John. 1988. *The Dimensions Of Paradise*. London: Thames & Hudson.

------. 1977. *Secrets Of The Stones: The story Of Astro-Archaeology*. New York: Penguin.

------. 1972. *City Of Revelation*. New York: Ballantine Books.

------. 1969. *The New View Over Atlantis*. London: Thames & Hudson. [This book is an excellent introduction to the entire field of 'weird science']

Sagan, Carl. 1980. *COSMOS*. London: Book Club Associates, p296

Smyth, Piazzi. 1880. *The Great Pyramid*. New Jersey: Gramercy Books.

Targ, Russell and Harold Puthoff. 1977. *Mind-Reach: Scientists Look At Psychic Ability*. New York: Dell Publishing.

Tompkins, Peter. 1971. *Secrets Of The Great Pyramid*. New York: Harper & Row.

Valentine, Tom. 1975. *The Great Pyramid: Man's Monument To Men*. New York: Pinnacle Books.

Velikovsky, Immanuel. 1950. *Worlds In Collision*, New York: Doubleday.

-------. 1955. *Earth In Upheaval*, New York: Doubleday.

Vercoutter, Jean. 1986. *The Search For Ancient Egypt*, New York: Harry N. Abrams.

Von Daniken, Erich. 1994. *The Gold Of The Gods*. New York: Bantam Books.

Watkins, Alfred. 1925. *The Old Straight Track*. London: Abacus Books.

Be sure to also read:

HAUNTED STEEL ADVENTURES

by E. SCOTT SPENCER

A bright young man, Matthew, and a posh young woman, Azur, struggle to understand strange psychic phenomena. Matt, a practical Engineer, cannot believe what he sees and feels, while Azur, a snooty English parapsychology expert, thinks she knows all about it. A difficult romance develops as they interact with undead creatures who were Matt's ancestors. These entities are playful one moment and deadly the next, powerful in some ways, surprisingly weak in others, with strong interests in practical jokes and sex. Matt is fascinated by their invisibility, but Azur is afraid they will kill her.

The setting for these adventures is a dilapidated English country house that is falling into the sea. Matt is torn between heartaches over Azur and his fight to install steel beams under the large house before it washes away. He is determined to stop the erosion and restore the house to its former glory, even though bureaucrats are trying to demolish it and build a power plant on the site. Perhaps his weird grandparents can help . . . .perhaps he can somehow win Azur . . . . perhaps the rock under the house won't crush him before he installs enough steel . . . .

Details from both the psychic and the engineering worlds are extensive, and somewhat authentic. A complete but not-overly-technical description of the structural engineering is in an Appendix for those who wish to learn more.

please see

WWW.ESCOTTSPENCER.COM

for more information

and read this too, for a great series of laughs:

SENIORS HAVE IT TOUGH

by E. SCOTT SPENCER

Death & Taxes: How Senator Savage almost escaped both

A bizarre story, from the crew's perspective behind the camera, of the making of a hilarious film about crazy old people who grow their own replacement parts on a secret clone farm. Pandemonium erupts when the young virgin clones escape. The book's central character Keith, a twenty-something Soundman-Writer, struggles to forget a mysterious death while falling in love with a cold-bodied psychic Wardrobe girl, Jessica. To their horror, fiction becomes reality as real doctors snatch real parts for a bloody transplant. Although the medical activity in this book is satirical, interesting nuances of actual Hollywood film production are described clearly. The writing style is irreverent, un-sanitized, and far from political-correctness: nothing has been dumbed-down.

"Laughed so hard I wet my pants, then I cried."
"Romantic, crazy, hilarious: can't wait for the sequel"
"I want a new pelvic section, and some fresh parts from those hot young clones"
"Holy SHIT: what an exciting view of medical transplants"
"You cannot print this medical travesty: people may believe it"
"Help: the quacks did a walletectomy, then stole my parts"
"When does this hit the big screen? Where's the DVD?"

<u>Gypsy Waves</u>